The Incident

Inferno Rising

Part 1

Prologue

"I died?" Special Agent Samantha Jameson's question was barely audible above beeping hospital equipment. Her fire-red hair framed her pinup-model face, and her brilliant green eyes blazed despite the grogginess.

"Very much. Twice, they said." Air Force Colonel Brock James shook his head. "Such a bitch move. Did you even think about how I might feel about that? Who would pay our mortgage?"

She smiled weakly. "It blew. No angels or out-of-body experiences. I want my money back."

Brock's reply was interrupted by the doctor's arrival, with nurses and orderlies in tow.

"Visiting hours are over, I'm afraid." The gray-haired doctor was borderline obese and reeked of cigarette smoke, but was friendly enough. "Sadly, there's more poking and prodding in your immediate future, young lady."

"I'm a big fan of being poked, but I prefer this strapping fellow," Sam said, reaching a bandaged arm up to Brock's face.

The old doctor blushed.

Brock smiled. "I don't mind an audience."

The doctor blushed more.

An orderly unlocked the wheels on Sam's bed. "I'm happy to watch, but we have a date with the fMRI first. Cognition over reproduction, I'm afraid. Given that you've been a little bit dead, we thought we'd check for brain damage."

"I'll tag along, given the circumstances." Brock helped wheel Sam out into the hallway, turning right toward radiology.

She gazed up at his unshaven face, swollen eye, and split lip. "Nice shiner. Looks good on you though," she said. He chuckled.

Suddenly Brock's smile died, and all the color drained from his face. "Oh, no. The guard is gone."

Sam understood instantly what that meant. "Run!"

She felt Brock accelerate to a lopsided sprint, her bed jerking in time with each clump of the cast on his broken foot.

"Sir! You can't run with her! No sudden mo–" The orderly's chest erupted in crimson as a silenced slug tore into his back, through his heart, and out between two ribs. Gore splattered Sam's bed sheets.

A second shot punctured her intravenous bag, and saline solution spilled everywhere.

Brock rammed Sam's bed through the heavy hallway doors, not slowing to look behind them at the shooter. He knew without looking who it had to be. Though he didn't know the man's name, the visage of pure evil was forever etched in his memory.

Sam's exploding IV bag slicked the floor, and Brock slipped and fell as Sam's bed sailed through the doors. She heard the snap of another bullet flying through the space Brock had occupied fractions of a second before. The bullet shattered a picture on the wall in front of her bed, calling to her attention the fact that the hallway made an abrupt right-hand turn five feet ahead of her.

Her bed crashed hard into the wall.

Sam felt her body rocket forward, twist in mid-air, and slam against the shattered glass of the picture. The wall knocked all the wind out of her, which was just as well. She would have screamed otherwise, as dozens of glass shards embedded themselves in her back.

Dazed, bleeding, and unable to inhale, she came to rest with her left leg trapped between the side rail and mattress of her bed. Her torso dangled from the side of her bed, hospital gown up around her ears. Her bare ass pointed toward the ceiling. Blood rushed to her throbbing head, which had cracked against the floor.

Before she could even draw a breath, she felt a pair of strong arms clamp around her torso and hoist her up. Two long, hard, painful tugs pulled her leg free of the bed. Brock threw her over his shoulder and began to run. "Hold that elevator!" Brock's shout was clear and strong above the screaming in the hallway behind her. Her breath returned in gasps, but each jerk of Brock's awkward steps made a full inhalation impossible.

As the long hallway disappeared around the corner, Sam saw the doorway burst open again.

Him.

A silenced pistol rose to point at her, but Brock clump-sprinted around the corner and into the waiting elevator too quickly to permit another shot from the attacker.

An eternity later, as if to mock Brock's frantic mashing of the "close" button, the doors began to meander together. Through the narrowing gap, the shooter's snarling face came into view. Sam felt ice cold fear pound through her veins.

The man lunged, his arm extended to catch the elevator doors.

Two of the shooter's fingers curled around the outer door.

But it wasn't enough. The doors closed. Muzak filled her ears. And Brock's panting. And the sobs of the frightened nurse who had held the elevator for them.

The elevator descended two floors before Brock pulled the emergency stop lever.

"Whatever you do," Sam gasped over the clanging emergency bell, "don't call the goddamned cops."

Chapter 1

Nine days earlier

Sam felt his teeth lightly on her back, then his tongue running up her spine, then his lips on her ear. Their bedroom exertions had left them both breathless. "Woman, I can't believe you exist," he whispered.

"Likewise. You were a bitch to find. And catch." She rolled over and smiled at him. He kissed her long and hard.

Her phone rang. *That* ringtone. They both groaned together.

She answered. "Hi, Francis," she said. She listened for a second, looked at Brock, rolled her eyes, and sighed audibly. "You're a shitty boss, you know that?" She knew that Frank Ekman knew he was a shitty boss, because she had told him so on many occasions. But it still gave her a satisfying sense of control to lash out at the man who made it a practice to systematically destroy any semblance of normalcy in her life.

She browbeat the poor guy almost daily, but he was still smitten with her. If Sam wasn't the best counterintelligence agent on the DHS roster, Ekman often claimed, he didn't know who was. But in a cliché midlife crisis kind of way, Ekman also badly wanted to sleep with her, Sam knew, and she used that knowledge to beat him up even more mercilessly.

At the end of the day, though, Ekman *was* her boss, and he could make her come in to work whenever an investigation demanded her talents.

Even at eleven p.m. on a Saturday night.

"Dude. Why doesn't this stuff ever happen during office hours?" Air Force Colonel Brock James had a couple of Master's degrees and a reputation as a fantastic fighter pilot, but he often spoke like a teenage surfer. His protest was lighthearted, but she knew he wasn't happy about another lost weekend.

Sam dressed, feeling a dark anger descend over her mood. Brock was a good sport about it, knew what he was signing up for, and only complained seriously when her ridiculous hours destroyed holidays and rendered Redskins and Senators tickets useless, but she knew something would eventually have to give.

Hell, she knew that *she* would eventually have to give. It really was rough work, and it took its toll. She had a hunch she would return sometime after dawn with more grisly images burned into her brain, the kind of gore and tragedy she used to drink away but now just tried to breathe through.

"Another double got rolled up," she told Brock. "Not pretty, apparently."

"Being a spy sounds like an even worse job than yours," Brock said. "Who smoked him? Good guys or bad guys?"

She answered his jaded, sarcastic question with her customary in-kind answer: "Yes." She didn't bother speaking the second half of her answer any more. *They're all the same. Only the accents change.*

She kissed him softly on the way out. "I'm sorry baby. I love you."

"Be careful. And don't be alarmed if I have one of my bitches come over to keep me company."

"Send pictures." She blew him a kiss.

* * *

There was blood everywhere. And a note, sorry to my wife and kids, and so forth, which clashed sharply with the ligature marks on John Abrams' wrists and ankles. It was obvious to Sam that Abrams hadn't wanted to die, hadn't slit both of his own arms from elbow to wrist, and certainly hadn't scrawled the suicide note, written in child-like script.

He probably also hadn't left his front door unlocked, given that Abrams had spent over two decades in the business of espionage. "They rang the doorbell, I presume?" Sam asked, more as a conversation starter than a real question. She already knew the answer.

"Looks that way. Security system download will tell us in a sec," said Detective Philip Quartermain, formerly an FBI special agent but lately a homicide investigator at DC Metro.

Sam had heard the rumors about Quartermain—kicked out of the Bureau for being gay, though his superiors disguised it as an administrative thing—but she knew Phil knew his stuff. Phil had Dan Gable's trust, and that was meaningful. Gable had been her deputy for three years, and was the only male alive, aside from Brock, whom Sam let herself trust. Father issues, she joked when asked, not really joking.

Sam snapped a photo. "The spy who bled himself cold?"

"Or so the evildoers would have us believe." Quartermain's flamboyant deadpan and unapologetic lisp surprised her. *He probably takes endless shit at the station,* she thought to herself. Cops were a lot like counterintelligence people: ritualistically homophobic.

"You mean he wasn't sufficiently committed to slice his own arms to the bone? Maybe you underestimate the power of a bad day," she said.

"It would have to be a really nasty break-up, combined with both sides of a Smiths record," Phil said.

"Sounds like the voice of experience." Sam watched Phil smile.

"Thankfully not this week. But yes, I've learned to stay away from The Smiths," Phil said. "Give me a hand? I think he's sitting on something."

Sam helped Phil move the dead spy, pausing beforehand to put on a pair of latex gloves. They shifted John Abrams' considerable weight far enough to the right to reveal a cheap chain looped through the eyehole of a small silver key, the kind that might open a music box or young girl's treasure chest. "Sure enough. Impeccable instincts, Phil."

"Well, it's a matter of public record that I know my way around a man's ass," Phil said.

Sam laughed. "I knew I liked you. Any ideas on the key? Abrams doesn't strike me as the hope chest type."

Phil dusted both sides of the key for prints. "Easy enough to find out the lock type, but there are probably several thousand locks that would open for this key. It's not exactly a unique pattern."

"Guess that's why we get the big bucks." Sam examined the

nearby windows for any signs of recent entry or exit. Nothing.

"Don't forget the glamour," Phil said, flat and taciturn. "Lots of people would kill to be sitting in a pool of a stranger's blood at midnight on a Saturday. I know I'd hate to be at home watching boy porn right now."

"Well, at least the nightmares will help keep the experience fresh," Sam said with a chortle. "I'll wander around and admire John's interior decorating."

She did. Nothing to write home about. She was pretty sure Abrams didn't spend much time in this place. Sex pad, maybe, but probably not for the classy girls. The furniture was sparse, and two of the upstairs bedrooms were completely empty. The kitchen cabinets held few dishes, and a layer of dust on the pots and pans told Sam the decedent didn't spend his free time trying out new recipes. At least not here.

Time for the juicy stuff. The black light revealed plenty of biologicals on the sheets in the master suite, located just off the kitchen downstairs. "Phil, it's your lucky night," she called out. "Lots of love-leftovers on the bed."

"The crowd goes wild," she heard him say in the next room.

Then she stumbled upon something that made her catch her breath. Her own name, written on a pad of paper on the dead man's nightstand. And her address. "Sweet Jesus."

"Just call me Phil," Quartermain quipped, walking into the bedroom.

She ignored him, dialing. The phone rang four thousand times before Brock answered, groggy and uncharitable.

"Hi baby," she said. "Don't say anything. Go downstairs and lock yourself in the vault. Call me as soon as you get there and I'll explain." She'd installed the highly secure basement room—steel door, video surveillance, weapons, rations, the whole nine—after a particularly nasty case left her with exit wounds and demons. To Phil: "you'll have to scrape up the dried goo yourself, I'm afraid."

Hustling out of the room with car keys in hand, she only heard part of Phil's reply. She paused on the dead spy's doorstep long enough to snap eight multi-spectral photos covering the entire area in front of the house. They were handy for finding all sorts of hidden things. She'd wake Dan Gable up to analyze them.

But first, she had to get the hell away from the house. She'd been in the crosshairs before, but that didn't mean it didn't scare the bejeezus out of her. *My name and address on a dead spy's nightstand.* She had no idea what it might have meant, but it struck her as decidedly unhealthy. Counterespionage was always personal. That was lesson one at spook school.

She walked to her car as calmly as she could manage, starting the engine remotely with the fob. She heard rustling in the bushes behind her as she reached the door handle, and suddenly her heart was in her throat and a tsunami of adrenaline zinged through her veins.

She leapt into her car and slammed the door shut, crushing the lock with her fist while she threw the car into reverse to screech down the dead man's driveway.

She was a strong girl, five-ten in flats with a wicked left hook and a ball-kick that had sent more than one thug to the ground in a heap. But she knew that she was still human, susceptible to being scared to death. None of that stopped her from feeling rookie-like and embarrassed when she saw the source of the rustling in the bushes that had scared her witless just a second ago: a uniformed policeman.

She rolled down the window. "Sorry ma'am," the officer said. "Didn't mean to give you a heart attack."

"No worries. I could stand to be a little more calm and collected, but that's probably obvious by now." Then something struck her as odd. "What were you doing in the bushes without your flashlight on?"

The policeman didn't answer right away. That was weird.

He kept walking toward her car, smiling. Also weird.

Movement caught her eye: his hand moving toward his Taser.

That was all the prompting she needed. Sam mashed the accelerator and popped the clutch. The Porsche's engine roared as she rocketed away. She saw the cop in her side mirror, putting the stun gun back in its holster and talking into the squawk box clipped to his shoulder.

This is messed up, she decided.

She rounded the corner, alert for any cars giving chase. None appeared.

Her mind raced. Who to call first? Brock? He should have called from the panic room by now. Dan Gable? She knew she would need her deputy's help sorting this thing out. It was suddenly a colossal turd pie.

Oh shit! Phil Quartermain. He was still in the victim's house, with someone in a cop's uniform prowling around outside.

Not wanting blood on her hands, she found Phil's number first, then hesitated before pushing the call button. The cop wore a DC Metro uniform. Phil was DC Metro. Was Metro compromised? Was Phil really in danger, or was he in on it, whatever *it* was? Was the guy in the bushes even a real cop?

The clock was ticking, she realized, and she cursed herself for hesitating. She called. It rang, then voicemail. *Too late? Phil, I hope I didn't just get you whacked!*

She left an urgent message for Phil, then called Dan Gable. His customary response to Sam's all-too-frequent midnight awakenings: "I hate you."

"Likewise. Who's on the response team shift right now?"

"Lemme check." Dan's voice was groggy, and she heard Sara's voice in the background, admonishing her husband not to wake the baby and maybe consider getting a better damn job or at least negotiate some decent overtime pay and don't bother coming back to bed if that baby so much as peeps. Poor Dan. No wonder he spent so much time at work.

More shuffling, then her deputy's voice again. "Ainsworth, Curry, and Meyer."

"Great. Larry, Curly, and Moe. Anybody we can call who doesn't suck? There's a situation."

"Really? I thought you woke me up at midnight to talk about your feelings."

"You know me so well," Sam said. "So let's talk about my feelings. I feel largely indifferent but more than a little inconvenienced that John Abrams got smoked a few hours ago, and I feel confused about why a Metro guy just jumped out of the bushes and tried to Taser me. And despite my tough-girl exterior, I do feel apprehensive that my name and address were on Abrams' nightstand."

"Wow, boss. That *is* a situation." Dan thought for a second. "How about Williams? He's just back from admin leave but I could probably send him out."

"Yes please. To Abrams' house. Say nothing about my name and address on the notepad, and keep everyone away from my home."

"Why don't you ever trust the good guys?" Dan no longer sounded sleepy.

"Just because they're on the payroll doesn't mean they're good guys." Sam knew Dan was probably rolling his eyes at her. She'd foisted her dim view of her fellow Feds on him more than once.

She changed the subject. "I've got some multi-specs for you to analyze."

"Can it wait? Or do you want to be responsible for my divorce?"

"Sorry, but I'm on Sara's side. You work way too much. But it definitely can't wait."

Something caught Sam's attention. Police lights in her rear view mirror. "Gotta go. There's a police cruiser behind me."

She hung up on Dan and immediately dialed 911. She told the operator that she was a single female alone in her car and she didn't feel comfortable stopping for a traffic ticket in the middle of the night. The operator ran Sam's location and queried the units in the vicinity.

None of the patrolmen in the area was trying to pull over a motorist at the moment, the operator said.

Sam felt her insides clench up. *That's no cop.* She matted the accelerator and dove across three lanes to make a hard right turn. The cop car followed, lights flashing insistently. A voice blared at her from the bullhorn atop the police cruiser, warning her to pull over immediately. "He's chasing me. Any ideas?" She asked the 911 dispatcher.

"Don't stop."

"Genius."

"I've already got two units on the way. Stay calm, ma'am."

"Great thinking. How will I know the good cops from the bad cops?"

The operator didn't have an answer, but suggested she drive to the police station to sort it out. She suggested the operator commit an unnatural act with himself.

Then she realized she hadn't told him about the Taser thing. Tasers were controlled items, available only to cops, security firms, and the military. So she told the operator, and then apologized for suggesting self-buggery.

"I understand your concern a bit better now ma'am. Please try not to get in an accident, don't violate any traffic laws, but don't stop your car. You should see another police cruiser soon."

Sam did. It pulled up even with her left rear quarter panel.

Then it swerved into her car, ramming her into a spin.

It's on. Her driving training kicked in.

She steered into the spin, whipping the nose of her car around until it was almost pointing in the right direction down the road. Then she quickly reversed the wheel to stop the rotation. She downshifted into third gear, stood on the accelerator, and felt the twin turbo boosters kick in, pushing her back into the driver's seat. *Not your average douchebag penis-extender sports car, is it boys?*

She accelerated away from the two cop cars. Or non-cop cars. She still didn't know which. She passed 120 miles an hour, then 130, then saw the light turn red two blocks away. Crossing traffic began to crawl through the intersection.

Not stopping.

She didn't. She barely missed a beat-up minivan, and swerved to avoid what would certainly have been a deadly collision with a sedan that had just turned onto the street in front of her. Police lights still flashed behind her, but the distance was growing.

The road curved gently, and Sam accelerated to build more space. 140, then 150. *Do I hear 160?* The police lights disappeared around the bend behind her.

Sam stood on the brakes. The anti-lock system sounded like four jackhammers, and she was thrown into her restraints by the deceleration. She wasn't quite slow enough to make the corner onto the quiet residential street, but she tried anyway, and ended up spending a little time on someone's lawn before chirping her tires back onto the pavement.

She drove half a block, then twirled to a stop behind a gratuitously large pickup truck parked by the curb. She killed the lights just before the two cop cars blazed past on the main road, engines roaring and sirens wailing.

To serve and protect. My tax dollars at work.

Hands shaking, she caught her breath, then realized that she heard a voice coming from the vicinity of her crotch. The 911 operator was still on the line. She hung up with a loud flourish of profanity, and began to disassemble her phone. It would be less than awesome to lose those two cop cars, only to have them locate her using a cell phone signal.

She reached a fingernail to remove the phone's battery when the phone began vibrating. Brock. "Expecting company, baby? There's a cop car in front of our house."

Chapter 2

If Quinn believed in heaven, he would have sworn that it took the form of the two naked nymphs whose undivided attention he had just enjoyed. They lay together, the smell of bodies heavy around them, a satisfied smile on his face. It had been a banner day for Quinn. A bloody, messy job had gone very well, and he now had a pound of pure gold to show for it. He only rarely accepted cash for his work, preferring "real money" instead. The evening's entertainment had cost him an ounce of his bounty, but it was well worth it.

And, he flattered himself, it had obviously been more than just work for the girls, too.

He had just about dozed off to sleep in between the two gorgeous women when his cell phone rang. It was a cheap prepaid phone that wouldn't see more than four more hours' use, if all went well, but the ring wasn't a welcome development.

"Quinn," he lied. It wasn't his name, but that's how his case officer referred to him for this particular job. He listened intently for several seconds, then said, "Got it." He cursed softly to himself after hanging up, and set about quietly gathering his things.

Back to work.

He stopped in the bathroom to relieve himself and put his clothes on, pausing for a look in the mirror. Brilliant eyes blazed back at him; one grey-blue, the other greenish brown, like a wolf or wild dog. He had a long scar beneath his green eye.

He was also very tall, and extremely muscular. It was unusual for a man in his profession to have such distinguishing features, as wet men were traditionally nondescript, but it was testament to his exceptional talent that the Agency had selected him for this particular line of work. He had a gift for it.

And, he occasionally admitted to himself, he enjoyed both the chase and its reward, the feral rush of power and bloodlust that invariably accompanied killing another human.

One of the girls was snoring softly on the bed as he left. He made no sound on the way out of the newly remodeled hotel room in Shirlington, Virginia. He pulled a dark ball cap low on his brow to obscure his facial features from the ubiquitous surveillance cameras. "Good evening, Mr. Quinn," the desk clerk chirped as the assassin strode by on his way to the parking garage. Quinn smiled and returned the greeting.

Minutes later he was on I-395 northbound in his rented Land Rover, en route to a provisioning stop. Unlike the evening's earlier job, which had been what industry professionals refer to as a "scene" – complete with a suicide note, though Quinn didn't believe anyone really took those seriously any more – he was apparently on his way to provide what Agency people euphemistically called "interrogation enhancement."

Torture.

Officially, it didn't happen on American soil. Then again, neither did assassination.

Quinn hated interrogation enhancement jobs. He was a

professional murderer, but he lacked the freakish sadism the really good torturers had, and the jobs tended to haunt him. Howls, screams, begging, sobbing, tearing flesh and snapping bones; they all left their mark on his psyche, which was why he charged so much money for them.

Sure, most of his victims were bad people, but who wasn't a bad person, when it came right down to it? He no longer had a patriot's ideological zeal to soothe his conscience, and knew that he was more mercenary than anything else, which had him contemplating a career change. *But for the gold...*

He exited the highway in a bad part of town, pulled into a warehouse parking lot, lifted up the lid on the third recycling bin from the north end of the wall, grabbed the pre-packed duffel bag his handlers had left for him, and was back on the highway a few minutes later. Clockwork.

He drove quickly toward his destination, an Arlington mansion he'd never seen before. *Hope the guy squeals early.* Quinn had been awake for over 20 hours already, and he didn't have the energy for a prolonged session.

He stopped for coffee, chuckling at the absurdity of needing a caffeine hit to gear up for a torture job.

Just another day in the life, he thought, wondering vaguely who tonight's victim might be. Smart money would bet on a dark-skinned Arabic speaker, but he had removed a few Russian fingernails recently as well. Uncle Sugar had plenty of enemies, and was busy making more all the time. *That couldn't possibly be related to all the murder and torture,* the assassin mused darkly.

He was, quite literally, the pointy end of State policy. As such, he had long since been aware of the cavernous gap between the reality of statecraft and the bright-eyed bullshit the politicos hoped the public would swallow. Mostly the public did swallow it, which kept Quinn well supplied with gold bullion and expensive hookers.

He found the address, entered the gate code, parked in the drive, and rapped on the door, holding an elevated middle finger in view of the peephole. The door opened seconds later, and a familiar face appeared in the doorway. Quinn stepped into the waiting darkness.

Chapter 3

"Baby, whatever you do, stay downstairs in the vault!" Sam knew she was yelling into the phone, but she couldn't stop herself. She felt she had done a good enough job just keeping the hysteria out of her voice.

Brock calmly explained that the police officer had already rung their doorbell several times, and didn't appear to be on the verge of leaving.

She filled him in on the last few minutes of her life, high-speed chase included, hoping Brock would be less inclined to give in to the insistent doorbell. "It might be a real cop, or it might not, and even if it is a cop, he may or may not be planning to screw us over. Please, just sit tight in the panic room."

Brock reluctantly agreed. She knew it went against his Type-A, mess-with-the-bull-and-you'll-get-the-horns personality. He was a career fighter pilot, after all, a subspecies convinced of its own invincibility, high mortality rate notwithstanding. She avoided telling Brock that she would take care of the situation; she knew that would only encourage him to defend his masculinity by doing something stupid.

That settled for the moment, Sam then dialed her boss. "Special Agent In Charge Ekman," he answered after only a couple of rings.

"Lighten up, Francis," she said. His name really was Francis.

"It's midnight on a Saturday. Do we really need all the pomp and circumstance?"

"Hello Sam. Would a little respect for authority kill you?"

"You'd be surprised." She filled him in on how a little respect for police authority almost killed her a few minutes earlier.

"Shit."

"That's your professional assessment?"

"Cool it, Sam. Give me a minute to think this through."

"OK, but while you do, it is my duty to inform you that I am on my way to defend my home from a potential invasion," Sam said, putting the Porsche in gear.

"I can have the response team out the door in two minutes," Ekman offered.

"I was afraid you were going to say something like that."

"You really should have a bit more trust in your coworkers," Ekman chastised.

"You really should hire better coworkers."

Ekman ignored the barb. "I don't have many options here, Sam. Procedures are pretty clear in situations like this. Your wildly arrogant objection is duly noted, but I'm sending the team, and I'll make a few phone calls. In the meantime, stay away from your house."

"Thanks, Francis. Remind me why I bothered calling you?"

"It's your job."

"Says you."

"Sam, seriously, take a drive, and let the team handle the guy at your house. We've got you covered."

"Sure, Francis." She hung up before her boss could challenge her lie, and headed toward the home she and Brock had shared for the past couple of years. She subconsciously patted her Kimber .45 auto in the pancake holster under her jacket, eager for a little reassurance.

Shit. Police lights in her rear view mirror. Though she had every intention of breaking the speed limit, she had just turned the corner and hadn't yet accelerated to speed when the cop appeared.

The damn telephone gave me away. She rolled down the window and threw it out of the car, then stomped on the gas. Her car leapt forward, and the police car gave chase.

Wait a minute. A thought struck. She pulled the portable police light out of her glove compartment, rolled down her window, and slapped the light onto the roof. She fumbled for the electrical cord, which she plugged into the lighter receptacle.

She could tell the light was working, because the cop car behind her immediately slowed down. *Interesting.* The cop thought he was running down a perp, she realized, and the sudden appearance of her police light had caused what the bureaucrats referred to as a paradigm shift.

So the cops in her corner of the world at the moment were behaving as the good guys normally do, which was an important piece of information. They probably weren't rogue police officers moonlighting for someone else, and they probably weren't impostors, either.

She didn't slow down. She was driving at breakneck pace through the surprisingly heavy midnight DC traffic, her analytical mind working as hard as her driving instincts. If the cruiser behind her, which had retreated to a far less aggressive distance behind her car, was indeed driven by a straight-laced cop on the job, it meant one of two things. Either there was a misunderstanding somewhere at the cop shop, or someone higher up at Metro *was* crooked, and looking to do her harm.

That seemed to contrast sharply with her experience during her last high-speed chase, in which the guy in the Metro cruiser apparently wasn't talking to the dispatcher. She didn't quite know what to make of things, but she thought another 911 call might be useful. If not, it would at least be informative.

She suddenly wished she hadn't thrown her work phone out the window. She reluctantly pulled her personal cell phone from her jacket pocket and dialed 911.

Different operator this time, which wasn't unexpected, but it was inconvenient. She spent a couple of minutes telling the dispatcher about her evening. After a few entirely predictable but time-consuming questions, the operator was finally up to speed enough to put the call out to the units in Sam's vicinity.

Déjà vu all over again, Sam thought as she waited impatiently for the answer. She was getting close to home, which was now a real problem. She didn't want to drag the cop behind her into the mess at her house without knowing what the hell was going on.

"Ma'am, I'm in contact with an Officer Davis, who says he's following your car. He's going to move in closer for a look at your license plate to confirm."

Sure enough, the cruiser was closing the gap, and was soon

nearly on her bumper.

"What's your license plate number, ma'am?" The dispatcher's question wasn't unreasonable, but Sam hadn't stayed alive this long in the counterespionage world without avoiding hundreds of stupid-person traps.

"Let's do it this way," Sam said. "I'd like you to read the number to me, and I'll let you know if you're close."

Silence. Sam began to get the sinking feeling she always got when situations turned sour, and she was about to stand on the accelerator to try to lose the cop behind her when the dispatcher's voice crackled over her Bluetooth. "Niner seven x-ray bravo six tango niner," the operator said.

"I'm very glad to hear you say that," Sam said. "I thought I was going to have to add you to the list of people whose ass I plan to kick. Please have your guy follow me. I'm on the way home to head off an intruder."

Hmm. About that intruder. Sam had another thought: "Did anyone dispatch a black and white to 935 Fox Hill Lane about ten minutes ago?"

It took a couple of minutes for the dispatcher to access the digital logs, which apparently required a supervisor's password, and Sam was rounding the corner onto her street when the operator finally came back on the line: "No ma'am. We have no record of a dispatch to that address."

"Thought that might be the case. Stay on the line with me? Who knows what I'll find when I get home. And tell the officer behind me that we'll use a standard pincer to box in the intruder's vehicle, my car in front."

"No problem ma'am."

Sam opted for a full frontal assault, hoping to seize initiative from whoever was lurking outside her front door. She stood on the horn and left her police light flashing as she rounded the lazy curve leading to her larger-than-average brownstone. She pulled her gun from its holster, and was prepared to box the police cruiser in to prevent his escape.

But the street in front of her house was completely empty. No cop car, and no cop, except for the one she brought with her.

She noticed that her call waiting was beeping at her. Brock. He must have been worried when he couldn't get ahold of her on her work phone. "Hi, baby," she answered. "I see that you scared our guest off."

"He left a minute ago," Brock said. "I watched him on the video feed." He was referring to the state-of-the-art Israeli-built video surveillance system that Sam had installed throughout their home, which featured hidden cameras covering almost every square foot of the house and yard. The cameras fed a surveillance control system in the panic room, and every second of footage was compressed and stored on a ridiculously large hard drive.

The system had the added benefit, for which Sam had paid a hefty premium, of not containing the NSA-friendly trapdoors that all surveillance systems sold in the US contained. She had worked for Big Brother long enough to know that she couldn't trust Big Brother.

"Sadness. I was looking forward to whooping some ass."

"I wouldn't mess with you, but I'm glad he slinked off

nonetheless," Brock said with a laugh. "Can I come out yet?" Brock was a big, muscular guy and a minor legend in his own world, but he knew his limits. He wasn't a trained spook, or a trained spook catcher, and Sam was grateful that he was content to leave that kind of business to the pros. Like her. She was also grateful that he was well-hung, which, she believed, made dating a bona fide badass such as herself slightly less emasculating.

"Not yet. I'm not entirely sure that's a real cop behind me."

"I'll bring the shotgun." He hung up. She knew he meant it.

She wasn't wrong. The front door opened about the same time the police officer came up to speak with Sam. Her attention was divided between Brock, stark naked and brandishing a shotgun, and Officer Davis of the DC Metro Police Department.

The badge and cop trimmings all looked real, but she called Davis' badge number in to the DHS duty desk for verification. "I sleep with the naked guy holding the 12-gauge," she reassured Davis while she waited for the DHS duty officer to look up the badge number in the system. The officer nodded, but kept his eye on Brock.

"Thanks," Sam said when the duty officer finally vouched for the patrolman. "Now my boyfriend can get dressed and put his gun away. Or put his gun away by getting dressed. Whatever."

The DHS response team pulled up in their black Suburban, which looked a little ridiculous with its antennae sticking out everywhere. Sam asked them to secure the perimeter, which was polite spook-speak for "stay the hell out of the way." They cooperated by milling about unproductively at the corners of her lot.

She invited Officer Davis in for coffee, and he appeared happy to accept. She quizzed him on the evening's events, hoping he'd heard some snippet of radio chatter or observed something unusual that would help shed some light on the confusing situation.

But Officer Davis hadn't heard or seen anything, and based on his slow uptake, Sam figured that he wasn't a strong candidate for detective any time soon, so the time was largely wasted. Still, a girl had to try.

After Davis drove off, Sam and Brock returned to the panic room to review the video footage for any clues it might hold. They were largely disappointed. The "officer" who parked at their curb and rang their doorbell a hundred times had worn a policeman's wheel cap, which shielded his facial features from the camera's view. The camera angle also prevented them from seeing a license plate number or other markings that might identify the police cruiser, if in fact it was a police cruiser.

But there was something peculiar. As the man approached the walkway leading up to the front door, his arm appeared to make a tossing motion. The camera didn't pick up anything leaving his hand, but Sam felt it was worth investigating.

She and Brock looked through the bushes with a flashlight, fruitlessly, then remembered her multi-spectral camera. She took a few photos of the front of her house, then forwarded them to her deputy to analyze along with the earlier pictures she had taken at John Abrams' place.

There wasn't much else to do. The Stooges, as Sam called them, were guarding the house, which she reckoned meant the house was probably less safe than if nobody were guarding it. So Sam and Brock retreated back to the panic room, cuddled up in the cozy bed in the corner, and dozed off while awaiting the multi-spec photo results.

They hadn't yet reached REM sleep when Dan Gable's call woke them up. It seemed the object the "officer" had tossed into the bushes had shown up terrifically well in the ultraviolet spectrum, because it was a beacon. "For what?" Sam asked.

"Dunno. Satellite maybe, or a handheld transponder. It's tough to say," Gable said. "But we're dealing with someone fairly sophisticated. I'd advise you to evacuate your house for the night, just as a precaution."

"I figured you were going to say that."

"Discretion is the better part of valor," Dan said. "Even for you, Wonder Woman."

Sam started to make a smart-assed response, but an explosion rocked the house on its foundation and rudely cut her off.

Chapter 4

The howls were surreal. Always were. Sometimes they sounded comical in isolation, until Quinn considered that the ridiculous noises were coming from a fellow human being, suffering in unspeakable agony.

Maybe his victims had it coming to them, or maybe they didn't. Quinn had long since stopped trying to assuage his conscience with delusions of some moral rectitude, some higher purpose to justify the barbarism.

He'd caught his employers in too many lies over the years to believe anything they told him, so he had slowly given himself permission to submit to his own inner beast, do what he had to do, and not worry too much about it.

Plus, the pay was outrageously good. That helped.

These particular howls had been caused by applying an electric belt sander to the subject's lower back, then sprinkling salt on the resulting abrasions. It wasn't terribly sophisticated, but it was terribly, terribly painful.

In fact, Quinn was briefly afraid that his subject—forty-something, good shape, expensive clothes, an upscale address, and an ivy league last name Quinn kept forgetting—would pass out from the pain, so he moderated the salt application a bit.

As always, Quinn had a list of questions in need of answers, and he judged his guest to be just about in the right frame of mind for truthful and forthcoming conversation. Salt was magical like that.

"I'm recording our conversation for posterity," Quinn began. He tightened the straps holding his subject spread-eagled and face down on the hard cement of the safe house's basement floor. The heavy leather straps, one for each limb, attached to thick metal loops, which were arranged in an eight-foot square and bolted into the concrete. "Name, please."

"I'm pretty sure you already know my name," the prone and naked man said between gasps.

"Tsk tsk," Quinn chided. "See, you're going to make me lose a bet. My friends said I'd have to remove at least one fingernail, but I told them you were smarter than that."

Quinn noticed that the man's breathing quickened, and his hands involuntarily balled into fists to protect his fingers. Quinn sprinkled a little more salt on the man's back, and said, "Dammit, I can't seem to keep from spilling that salt. So clumsy of me."

The victim's back arched in pain, and he thrashed against his restraints. Quinn let the wave of agony subside before speaking again. "Now, let's start our conversation again, shall we? Your name, please."

Silence, then a long sigh, then, "Peter Kittredge."

"Good. I like the decision you just made. Cooperation is a smart move," Quinn said, absentmindedly feeling the long scar under his eye as he hovered over the naked man lying on the bare concrete floor. "Tell me your job title, Peter Kittredge."

"Deputy Special Assistant to the US Ambassador to Venezuela," Kittredge said, long breaths punctuating his labored speech.

"Sweet. Pete, we're on a roll. Now, don't lose momentum on this one. It's a little bit tricky. You might be tempted to answer a number of different ways, but I would urge you to think of your fingernails. It really, really hurts when someone pulls them out." Quinn watched Kittredge squirm. "Ready for the big question?"

Kittredge didn't move.

"Here goes, Pete. Mind if I call you Pete? I feel like we shared a moment a while ago when I took your clothes off and tied you to the floor." Quinn chuckled as Kittredge's butt cheeks clenched visibly.

"So here's the big question, Pete: what is the name of the Venezuelan man who pays you to spy on the United States?"

Kittredge's breaths came in short, rapid gasps, and Quinn was sure he heard a sob or two thrown in the mix. It was predictable, almost boring, Quinn thought. Lots of guys thought they were tough, but most of them weren't. A little bit of pain, a compromising position that usually involved restraints of some sort, and a hefty secret was all it took to bring all but the biggest badasses to their knees, literally and figuratively. And Kittredge didn't seem much like a badass.

But he also hadn't answered the question.

More salt.

More agonized screams, writhing, twisting, and thrashing.

But still no answer. "I've got all week, Pete. We're going to be good friends, you and me. We've talked about the fingernails already, but sometimes a deep-cycle marine battery hooked up to the gonads is a great conversation starter, too. We'll just have to see what kind of mood we're in later."

There was just something special about a man's balls. Nine times out of ten, just describing testicular torture got some sort of positive movement out of even the most recalcitrant subjects. "Okay," Kittredge finally said. "But I need something first."

"A drink of water? A skinny male hooker? What could you possibly need before you answer the question, Pete?"

"I need a guarantee."

"Okay. I guarantee," Quinn quipped.

"Guarantee what?" Kittredge asked.

"I'm asking the questions," Quinn said, laughing at his own humor. Then he tossed more salt on Kittredge's bleeding, ablated skin.

When the most recent wave of salt-inflicted pain subsided, and Kittredge was again able to speak, he tried a new tack. "I can be useful."

"Not to me," Quinn said. "I'm just the hired help."

"I can be useful at the highest levels of your organization," Kittredge said.

"Ahh, you're asking for a Mephistopheles to your Faust, yes?" Quinn read too much, and fancied himself a Renaissance man. "Through the miracle of modern technology, the devil himself is watching and listening right now. Make your offer."

Kittredge took a deep breath, closed his eyes, and rested his head on the cold, damp concrete. He knew he was about to embark on a path that had a strong chance of ending very poorly.

But it didn't appear that he had many other options at the moment. If he merely sang, he could be executed for treason, depending on who was listening. Worse, he could wind up spending the rest of his life in prison. He was a small, slight man and he wouldn't fare well in a penitentiary, he knew.

On the other hand, if he made a deal, he would likely spend the rest of his days beholden to whoever was currently holding him captive. They'd have the kind of leverage they'd never be willing to relinquish, and he'd find himself doing all kinds of dangerous, unsavory work for them.

Either way, and even in the best possible scenario from this point forward, his treachery would hang forever over his head. It was bitter like bile, all the more so because he had sold out for not nearly enough money.

It was time, he knew, to sell out again. "I'll give you what you want in exchange for the US Attorney General's signature on a lifetime immunity letter."

Quinn laughed, harsh and barking. "That's all?" he quipped. "I thought you were going to ask for something difficult." Another sprinkle of salt drove home his displeasure. "Stop playing games."

"No games," Kittredge said between clenched teeth, the strength of the salt-induced agony still surprising in its brutal intensity even after half an hour of abuse. He felt tears streaming from his eyes, felt his heart pounding in his chest, and felt the impossibly painful fire covering his lower back. He rallied every ounce of his resolve: "Kill me if you want. No immunity, no names."

Quinn snorted derisively. "Pete, you would be surprised at

how many people say things like that, before they really understand how much pain a person is capable of experiencing."

Quinn knew his words had found their mark. Kittredge's body shook, and his tears intensified. But the clenched jaw told Quinn that, for the moment at least, Kittredge remained resolute in his decision.

The assassin pondered his next play. Though he hadn't yet made his presence known, Bill Fredericks, Quinn's CIA case officer, was indeed watching and listening to the interrogation. Quinn knew that the prisoner's offer was an attractive one, despite how outrageous it might have seemed on the face of it. A lifetime of immunity would certainly come with a lifetime of obligation, something the assassin knew from experience that the Agency would salivate over. While the Agency's budget was appallingly, obscenely large, its real currency was leverage.

"It's your lucky night, Pete," Quinn finally said. "In my mercy, I have decided not to hurt you while the devil considers your request." Quinn spoke the words more for Bill Fredericks' benefit than for the prisoner's, in case Fredericks was napping in the observation room and hadn't recognized the juiciness of Kittredge's offer for what amounted to a lifetime of servitude.

The Agency's answer took a little over half a minute. Two knocks on the door.

"Lucifer accepts," Quinn reported.

Kittredge let out a deep breath, and his body stopped shaking.

Chapter 5

"Holy shit," Brock said, looking over Sam's shoulder at the security system monitors in their basement panic room. Whatever had detonated in their front lawn just seconds earlier had left a crater four feet across and several feet deep. The trees and shrubs were all either scorched clean of foliage, or missing altogether. A car parked on the street was windowless and on fire. Their white picket fence was flattened.

There was no sign of the DHS security detail that had been posted at the corners of their property. Had they known about the attack in advance and fled? There was no carnage visible on the video feed, so Sam didn't rule out that hypothesis.

She gritted her teeth and began assessing the damage to their home through the surveillance feed. The heavy stone and mortar construction had held up remarkably well, and it didn't appear that the house was in danger of collapsing on top of them.

But even on the camera monitors, it was obvious that the blast had taken large chunks out of the stone and strewn shrapnel across a wide swath of their homestead. There wasn't a window on the front of the house that wasn't shattered.

Camera views of the interior of their home showed that most of their things in the front two rooms nearest the explosion were a total loss. Blast, heat, and bomb fragments had redecorated. It wasn't a good look.

"Holy shit is right," Sam said. "Half an hour earlier, and we'd still have been upstairs when it exploded. We'd have been minced."

Brock put his arm around her and kissed her cheek. She shook with rage, fear and adrenaline. "Have I mentioned that I have some concerns about your work environment?" he joked. Brock and his fighter pilot buddies always seemed to have a way with gallows humor. She laughed, and a tear escaped, which she quickly wiped away. She hated her human moments, but Brock loved her all the more for them.

"Listen," he said. "I'm no cop or spy catcher, but I've spent my whole adult life dropping bombs and making explosions. That was at least twenty pounds of Tritonal, or an equivalent amount of blast power in another type of explosive material. And I can tell even in the monitors that those fragments aren't screws or nails, like a poor man's anti-personnel weapon. Those fragments are from a steel bomb casing."

Sam connected the dots. "Professional."

"Military," Brock said. "No doubt about it. Or at least paramilitary."

"So we've been attacked by a foreign military on US soil?" Sam asked, incredulous.

Brock shook his head. "I didn't say that. I just said that it's obviously a military weapon. And whoever detonated it on our front lawn didn't care about disguising that fact."

Motion caught their eye, and they both turned to the video surveillance monitors. A police cruiser rolled to a stop in front of the house, and a fire truck stopped near the burning car at the curb.

Seconds later, water doused the smoldering car.

A patrolman got out of his cruiser and made his way tentatively toward the front door, which hung ajar on wrecked hinges.

Sam zoomed the camera in on the patrolman's face. She squinted. "What is it?" Brock asked.

"I can't figure out why that cop's face is familiar," she said.

Then she remembered.

She dialed Dan Gable, and while the phone rang, she ordered Brock to lock the basement vault door. He started to ask why, but she shushed him impatiently.

"Dan, I need your help," she said when her deputy picked up. Gable started a sarcastic retort, but she cut him off. "Shut up a minute. A bomb blew the shit out of my house a minute ago. I think our three Homeland stooges took a powder right before it happened. And do you remember the cop with the Taser I told you about earlier, the one who jumped out of John Abrams' bushes? He's walking in my front door."

Chapter 6

"The United States government hereby accepts your offer," Quinn said to Peter Kittredge, sliding the printed copy of the immunity agreement with the US Attorney General's signature at the bottom. "You're a lucky guy, Pete. They woke the deputy AG up on your account. Should I give you a little immunity idol, just like on that TV show?"

Kittredge didn't appreciate his torturer's humor. He strained his eyes to read the fine print of the agreement, hindered by the wrist and ankle straps that anchored him face-down on the cold basement floor. The small of his back still felt like it was on fire, though Quinn had thankfully stopped sprinkling salt on the belt sander abrasions inflicted earlier in the evening. "Any chance you could untie me so I can read this?"

Quinn complied, releasing Kittredge's wrist straps. Kittredge rose up to his hands and knees, wincing in pain as the ablated skin on his back contorted with his movement. He caught his breath, then moved to sit on his buttocks and peruse the immunity agreement, still feeling naked and vulnerable in addition to the pain.

Kittredge felt something jab his shoulder, and turned to see a fountain pen in Quinn's hand. "Time to seal the deal," Quinn said. "I'm sure you'll come to recall this moment just as pleasantly as I recall my first wedding," he added with a snort. "Only I don't think you'll have a divorce option in this particular arrangement."

Kittredge signed without a word.

* * *

"Arturo Dibiaso," Kittredge said. He was clothed, his raw and bleeding back encased in disinfectant and bandages. He sat in a chair flanked by a two-way interrogation mirror.

Bill Fredericks sat in a chair directly across from Kittredge, taking notes on a yellow legal pad, and Quinn lurked in the corner of the room at the perimeter of Kittredge's vision, just to remind him that things could turn ugly again if he didn't cooperate fully.

"One more time, a little louder, please," Fredericks said. His voice had a grating, nasal quality. He was a fat, balding man with a vicious comb-over, in his late forties or early fifties, Kittredge figured, and he seemed to have a disagreeable sneer frozen permanently on his face.

Fredericks didn't look like much, especially when he hiked his pants up to the middle of his ample belly, but Quinn clearly deferred to Fredericks. *Everyone is someone's bitch,* Kittredge thought.

And now I'm theirs, he realized. "Arturo Dibiaso. My contact's name is Arturo Dibiaso," he repeated, somewhat less meekly than the first time.

"Spell that for me." Fredericks didn't bother to look up from his notepad, writing as Kittredge rattled off letters. Fredericks continued to scribble after Kittredge stopped talking.

After a while, Fredericks stopped writing and looked for a long time at Kittredge, who lost the tacit contest for social dominance by averting his eyes in deference. Fredericks noted the act of submissiveness, and also noted the subsequent flash of annoyance on

Kittredge's face. The fat case officer smiled inwardly. It appeared that Kittredge was in the right frame of mind for a very productive chat. "So, let's talk about the first time you met Arturo Dibiaso," he said.

"I never met Arturo Dibiaso," Kittredge replied.

"I thought you said he was your contact in Venezuela." Fredericks had a puzzled look on his face.

"I said that."

"So now I'm a little confused." Fredericks' voice hardened. "Was Arturo Dibiaso your Venezuela contact, or not?"

"He was. But I never met him. Never even spoke to him, as a matter of fact." Resolve had returned to Kittredge, and he held Fredericks' gaze.

"Then how do you know he was actually your contact, or even a real person at all?"

"I don't know that. I just know what they told me. I know the dead-drop locations, and I know where the payments showed up. I didn't do any sleuthing."

Fredericks frowned, looked sideways at Kittredge, and shook his head. He decided it was a natural opportunity to pursue a secondary purpose of the interrogation: testing Kittredge's mettle.

"I'm inclined to think you're full of shit," Fredericks said. "I'm inclined to think you're keeping something from me." Then he turned to Quinn: "See. And you wanted to leave early. I told you you'd have more work to do on this guy."

Quinn smirked.

Kittredge blanched. He felt his insides knot, and adrenaline crashed uncomfortably in his stomach.

Then he started to feel angry. "Listen," he said, pitch elevated and words tumbling out quickly, "I don't need any more torture. I agreed to help you. You agreed to immunity. We're adults, talking like adults."

"Are we, Pete?"

"Peter. My name is Peter." Kittredge's gaze didn't waver this time.

Fredericks looked intently at him, then nodded. "Fair enough, Peter," he finally said. "So if you never met Arturo Dibiaso, how did it come about that you began selling national security secrets to him?"

"I didn't sell secrets to Arturo. I sold them to his boss. Arturo coordinated the logistics."

"Aw, hell, Pete!"

"Peter."

"Whatever!" Fredericks sat back in his chair and threw his hands in the air. "Are you being cute? What made you think I wanted the name of your lackey?"

Quinn took a silent step forward, and Kittredge stiffened. "Because that's what you asked for. My contact. Arturo Dibiaso was—*is*—my contact."

"Quibbling. You're being cute, and you're quibbling with me!" Fredericks said loudly. He was still testing Kittredge, trying to get a reaction out of his new asset.

Fredericks wasn't disappointed. Kittredge sat up, leaned forward, and looked Fredericks square in the eye. "Actually, I answered your question exactly, just like you demanded."

A little bit of spine, Fredericks thought. That was a good thing. "Fair enough," he said. "Sorry I got a bit irritated there. These hemorrhoids are killing me."

Kittredge relaxed, and Quinn suppressed a laugh in the corner.

"Let's continue, now that I don't have to ask Quinn to twist your nut sack," Fredericks said. "Who, do you think, was your *contact* Arturo working for?"

"Exel Oil."

"What makes you think that?"

"Because that's who approached me looking for the information," Kittredge said.

"What information?"

"Oil policy information. Lobbying efforts. Exploration permit requests. Getting a feel for the other players in the oil landscape, how much they were spending on bribes, if they were making any progress breaking into the Venezuelan production market, if they had embassy support. That sort of thing." Kittredge shifted in his seat, noting that Fredericks was studying him carefully.

"That sounds like bullshit." Fredericks shook his head and dropped his pen on the notebook.

Kittredge sighed. Fredericks was highly unlikeable. "It very well may be, but that's what I was doing," he said quietly, exasperation sneaking into his voice. "Anyway, you know I'm telling you the truth, don't you? Otherwise, if you didn't know what I was doing, we wouldn't be having this pleasant little chat in the wee hours of the morning, and I wouldn't have had the pleasure of meeting your psychopath friend. Right?"

Fredericks shook his head. "No, Peter. We knew you were crooked. But we didn't know what you were peddling."

"But you knew I worked in energy and economic policy at the embassy, right? I mean, what else would I have been selling? Satellite drawings? Missiles? Nukes?"

"Are you saying I'm stupid?" Fredericks asked, testing Kittredge again.

"I don't know. Are you stupid?" Kittredge instantly regretted the retort, and Fredericks flushed with anger.

Kittredge held his hands up in a conciliatory gesture. "Sorry," he said. "You were baiting me, and I bit. But I don't know what you thought I was doing. I'm an economist, not a ninja."

"Okay," Fredericks said. "Fair enough. Maybe you did risk spending the rest of your life in jail to sell diplomatic secrets about the oil industry in Venezuela. I mean, I suppose that's possible, and I suppose there's a market for it. And maybe it jibes with the fact that you were a really shitty spy, which is why we sniffed you out and hauled you in."

"Fair enough," Kittredge said, irritated, imitating Fredericks' annoying affectation. Fredericks pretended not to notice.

"So tell me, who is the guy at Exel that convinced you to sell your soul?"

Kittredge bristled. "Listen, my soul was never for sale," he said. "I sold information, and not even the important kind. And I sold it to an American company. After which, you hauled me into a house in the United States of Fucking America and tortured me, which makes you a little bit of a bastard yourself. So maybe you can spare me the moralizing."

Fredericks put on a thoughtful look, then nodded. "Fair enough. But, technically, because it was a foreign-owned subsidiary of an American company, you're still guilty of espionage. Which is a capital offense."

"Maybe. But fortunately, we now have an agreement."

"A contingent agreement," Fredericks admonished. "If we decide you're being uncooperative, we'll leg-sweep you."

"I'm not being uncooperative."

"Okay. Fair enough."

"Please stop saying that," Kittredge said.

"What?"

"*Fair enough.*" Kittredge imitated Fredericks' nasal tone and jowly expression. Quinn couldn't hide his amusement.

"Listen, you little shit—"

Kittredge held up his hands again. "I'm sorry. You've caught me at something less than my best. You kidnapped me, pulled skin off my back with a belt sander, and poured salt on me. Do you have any idea how much that hurts? Forgive me if I'm a little less than cordial, but you can maybe see where I'm coming from."

A long moment passed, then Fredericks smiled. "Fair enough."

Kittredge cracked a smile and laughed in spite of himself.

Fredericks spoke again: "I think we're going to get along just fine, Peter Kittredge."

Then a thoughtful look crossed his face. "Listen, something's bugging me. Why did you make so many trips back up to the States?

I mean, you were up here almost twice as often as anyone else in your division, always with a diplomatic pouch. What gives?"

"Well, I actually did have State Department business up here."

"Anything I could corroborate?" Fredericks asked.

"Not without arousing suspicion," Kittredge replied. "But I'm on the courier rotation. It used to be a job all its own back in the old days, but after the budget cuts, now we rotate the duty between four embassy officers. I'm the only one in the economics division pulling courier duty, but there are three people from other divisions."

"Convenient. It gave you plenty of opportunity for a little entrepreneurship, didn't it?" Fredericks arched his eyebrows and gave Kittredge a sideways glance.

"It did. That's how I met the Exel people," Kittredge said.

"Which Exel people did you meet?"

"Lots of them. They're really racking up the frequent flyer miles."

"Who recruited you to sell information?"

"Charley Arlinghaus. He's not in charge of the operation down there, but he works as an aide to the Exel wigs."

"Arlinghaus, you say. Can you spell that?"

"You're killing me with the gumshoe routine, you know that?"

"I'm a gumshoe. Spell the damn name."

"H-A-U-S. Like house, but German," Kittredge said.

"Tell me how you met Arlinghaus."

"I just told you. On one of my courier trips."

"Describe your relationship with him."

"Intimate."

"As in, you're good friends?" Fredericks arched his eyebrows.

"As in, we have sex."

"You're gay?"

"You're sharp."

"How long?"

"My whole life."

Fredericks grimaced. "I mean, how long have you and Charley Arlinghaus been, um, *intimate*?"

"Two years, give or take. Just fun at first, more serious later."

"Serious as in relationship-serious?"

"Isn't that what people usually mean?"

"I just didn't know how it worked for, well, you know."

"Humans?" Kittredge asked. "We have relationships, some of which become serious. Charley and I are somewhat serious."

"So maybe one night after, um, *intimacy*, Charley suggests you start selling secrets?" Fredericks asked. "That must have been some interesting pillow talk."

"It didn't quite work like that," Kittredge said. "It happened over time. We discussed our jobs a lot at home, and somewhere along the way I figured out that Exel was pretty interested in learning the kinds of things that I knew. So one thing led to another."

"And that's when you decided to seal the deal?"

"Sort of. Charley gave me Arturo's name and number, and we negotiated it all by text. Untraceable, they said."

Fredericks laughed. "Did they read that on a blog somewhere? Master spies passing secrets by text message?"

"Maybe it was a little naïve."

"You think?"

"Is that how you figured it out?" Kittredge asked.

"No, but that's how we confirmed it," Fredericks said.

"Beautiful. I'm going to kill Arturo if I ever meet him." Kittredge paused, then asked, "Can I go now?"

"Almost. But one more thing is confusing to me," Fredericks said. "How did you get the information out of the embassy? Don't they have a zero-transfer policy? No paper or magnetic media passes in or out without being searched and logged, right? And the diplomatic pouches are sealed up before they hand them to you, right?"

"Do you really want to know?" Kittredge asked.

"I really do."

"Let's just say that my sexual orientation makes me less averse than average to certain transportation methods," Kittredge explained.

"Sort of wish I hadn't asked," Fredericks said, unable to disguise a look of disgust. "So to sum it up, you walked out of the embassy with oil industry information stuck in your tailpipe, and you dead-dropped it for Arturo to pick up?"

"Maybe," Kittredge said. "I mean, everything you said is true, except, as you pointed out, I can't actually verify the last part. I don't actually know who picked the information up out of the dead-drops. But I do know that Arturo told me where to drop the information, and he acknowledged receipt, again by text. He also told me where and how to pick up the payments."

"Could you get me a copy of the info you gave them?"

"No. I gave Exel real-time stuff that matched their criteria, but that kind of daily traffic piles up and has to be put in cold storage on the server. It's all been archived, and I'd have to ask for it specifically, which would set off alarms like nobody's business."

"Fair enough."

"You're killing me."

"You don't say."

"Can I go to a hospital now?"

"No. You'll be fine. Quinn will take you home. You guys should get to know each other better. You're going to be working together quite a bit," Fredericks said. Quinn winked.

"I don't think so, Mr. Fredericks. We're two very different kinds of people," Kittredge said.

"Maybe so. But you two have a very important thing in common. I own you both."

Chapter 7

Brock turned the lock on the heavy steel door of the basement panic room, hidden from view behind a bookcase mounted on a hinge, which itself opened and closed like a door. He and Sam were sealed in, protected first by concealment and then by three inches of solid steel.

He was pretty sure the room's reinforced concrete walls and ceiling could survive another bomb attack, but he was also sure that the rest of the house would not.

Sam watched intently through the video monitors as the cop – at least he was dressed like a cop – walked up the entryway steps and toward the broken front door of her house. The man passed close by the video camera hidden in the porch light, and Sam got a good look at his face. It was definitely the same guy who had emerged from the bushes at the scene of John Abrams' death.

Not a coincidence, she concluded.

She had just ended the call with her deputy, Dan Gable, charging him with figuring out where the DHS security detail had gone, and who the hell the "cop" walking into her house with a drawn weapon might be.

Her face tightened as she watched the video feed, and she subconsciously felt the grip of her holstered Kimber .45, wondering whether to charge out of the panic room and take matters into her own hands. She hated the idea of hiding in the basement shelter while some goon strolled through her home upstairs.

On the other hand, she didn't want to get ambushed by an unseen accomplice. And she still wasn't sure if the guy was a real cop or some sort of impostor. She stayed put, eyes glued to the video monitors as the man strode through her broken front door, his pistol drawn.

The man took three paces into the entryway, then stopped. His head turned as if he was summoned from outside, and Sam switched views to the driveway camera to see what the intruder in police garb might be responding to.

It didn't take long for her to figure it out. The camera showed another police officer on her driveway, standing in the Weaver firing stance with his own service pistol trained in the direction of her front door. *This could get interesting,* she thought.

She commanded a split-screen view of both the entryway and driveway cameras, which gave her a ringside seat for what was beginning to look very much like a standoff between two uniformed police officers.

With his pistol pointed at the floor, the man in her house turned to face the policeman on her driveway. She saw them talking to each other, but cursed herself for not having installed audio surveillance equipment. She couldn't read lips, so she had no idea what the conversation might be about, but their body language was decidedly unfriendly.

Brock voiced the obvious question, "What the hell are these guys doing?"

"No idea," Sam replied, "but it's safe to say that it's not

standard procedure for cops to point guns at each other."

Out on the driveway, another man in a suit sidled up and also settled into a firing position, aiming what could only be described as a small cannon at the man standing in Sam's entryway. "It's a party now," Brock observed.

Suddenly, a blur of motion erupted on the screen as the interloper raised his sidearm to fire. The *pop-pop-pop* of gunfire was barely audible through the thick cement walls of the basement panic room. Sam counted at least half a dozen shots before the exchange ended, leaving the man in her entryway lying motionless on the hardwood in a growing pool of crimson around his head.

"Holy shit!" Brock exclaimed. "They smoked that dude!"

Sam's reply was interrupted by her ringing cell phone. "Hi, Dan," she answered. "You're missing quite a party at my house this morning."

"I wouldn't say I'm missing it," Dan replied. "Anyway, I have it on good authority that there's a dead guy in your entryway."

"Who told you?"

"Ekman."

"How the hell did he know?"

"I don't know, but it seemed awful quick to me, too."

"I suppose he's on his way?" Sam asked. Despite his shortcomings, their boss did care about his employees. And explosions and shootouts certainly justified a visit from one's supervisor.

"He is. He also told me that our guys had been following your cop for a while. Over a year in fact. He's a real cop."

"*Was* a real cop," Sam corrected. "That'll be a messy situation for Metro."

"It gets messier. His name is – was – Everett Cooper, and he was part of a group of about five Metro guys who picked up some moonlighting work that got a little, well, *involved* shall we say."

"Involved how?" Sam asked.

"Well, DC Metro's Internal Affairs guys obviously caught wind of it, and they had a money laundering and evidence tampering file going. But someone over in our financial crimes division sniffed out a national security angle."

"Homeland's involved too? Interesting. Anybody we're tracking?" Sam ran the Department of Homeland Security's counterintelligence division, a small but well-funded group of spooks and quasi-spooks who were trained to catch other spooks. She was surprised she hadn't heard about the investigation into the Metro police department.

"Ekman was pretty tight-lipped on that subject," Dan said. "It had that 'embarrassing to the department' vibe about it. You know how he is." Ekman had well-tuned political whiskers, and he almost never spoke out of turn.

"I'll wring him out when he gets here," Sam said. "Did you find anything in those multi-spectral photos I took at Abrams' house?"

"Strange you should ask. I found another one of those ultraviolet beacons in the bushes."

"There's got to be a connection," Sam observed.

"I tend to think you're right," Dan agreed. "Those are unusual items. But that's not all I found. One of your photos imaged our friend, the late cop, hiding in the bushes. He stood out like a sore thumb in the infrared picture because of his body heat."

"That's not unexpected," Sam said. "I took the photos right before I got in the car, which was right before he jumped out of the bushes."

"Right. But what *is* unexpected is that he was standing over a corpse."

"Wow," Sam said. "It *was* a big night. But are you sure the second person in the photo was dead?"

Dan chuckled. "If he's not dead, he's the coldest living human on the planet. Judging by the color differences in the IR photo, the second guy's body temp was a good ten degrees lower than the cop's. He'd been dead for a while."

Sam let out a low whistle. "This is turning into a serious ball of yarn. I assume you called back over to the crime scene to let them know what you found in the photo, yes?"

"No, this is my first day on the job," Dan deadpanned. "Yes, of course I called them. But this is where things get seriously freaky. Want to guess what they found when they checked the bushes?"

"A stiff."

"Wrong. No stiff, no signs of a stiff, and no signs of a struggle, either. At least that's what they're claiming."

"My head hurts."

"Mine too," Dan said. "And Sara is bitching at me to get back home. As much fun as this is on a Sunday morning, I need to go mow the lawn and try to stay married."

"Sure thing. Thanks again, Dan. I don't tell you this enough, but you're one hell of an asset."

"You're right. You don't tell me that enough. But you can make it up to me with a pay raise."

Sam laughed, then hung up.

Motion caught her eye on the video monitors, and she turned to see the two officers on her driveway move into the house to examine Everett Cooper's dead body. As she squinted for a look at the two men's faces, the driveway camera diverted her attention. Francis Ekman's SUV pulled into the drive, and she instantly recognized the improbably curly mane of dark hair as Ekman got out of the truck and made his way toward the door.

She turned to Brock. "Want to hang out with my boss for a while? He showed up unannounced."

"Sure," Brock said, twisting the deadbolts and opening the heavy steel door that led out from the panic room and into the basement. "It's always entertaining to watch him make doe eyes at you."

* * *

Sam poured coffee for Brock, Ekman, and the two officers who had shot Everett Cooper just minutes before. Two separate forensics teams – one for the bomb that exploded in her lawn, and one for the policeman lying dead in her entryway – worked busily but noiselessly on their respective crime scenes in the other room.

The two shooters, one a beat cop and the other an Internal Affairs officer, took their coffee into the next room to join the forensics investigators.

Sam and Brock were quarantined to the kitchen, forbidden from traversing either scene for fear of contaminating or destroying evidence. Ekman stayed with them, and the three of them sat down at the kitchen table.

Brock noticed the same dynamic he always noticed when Ekman and Sam spent time together. Ekman stared intently at Sam when she wasn't looking directly at him, but he glanced quickly away whenever her eyes landed on him. It was obvious to Brock that Sam's boss was afraid of her, and he also wanted to sleep with her.

Poor guy, Brock thought. He certainly understood Ekman's attraction – even after having been up all night, Sam was strikingly beautiful with her fire-red hair and blazing green eyes.

Ekman started talking in his slow, steady, bureaucratic cadence, but Sam's mind wandered even as she watched his mouth move. She was tired and strung out, having had no sleep over the past twenty-four hours, and her mind was reeling as she tried to put the wild series of events into some semblance of order.

An awkward silence brought her back into the present. It appeared that Ekman had asked her something. "I'm sorry, Francis, what did you say?"

"I just asked if you wouldn't mind recounting the events leading up to right now."

"Sure thing. Brock and I had just finished having sex when you called last night." She watched Ekman's cheeks turn red. Brock chuckled. Sam smiled. She enjoyed making her boss feel uncomfortable.

Ekman's blush faded. "I'm not sure I needed to know that. Go on, please."

"After you called," Sam said, "I put on yesterday's underwear and went to the residence of the late John Abrams. He was a CIA agent and, if I'm a betting girl, a double. I worked the scene with Phil Quartermain—"

"Isn't that the guy who got booted from the FBI?" Ekman interrupted.

"One and the same. Probably the best crime scene guy in the district, but apparently it's still 1962 in the Bureau. Gayness isn't kosher."

"No comment," Ekman said.

"Lighten up, Francis," Sam chided. "You're not running for office just yet. You can have an opinion." Brock sniggered again.

"Go on, Sam. We have a lot to cover, and I have a long day ahead." Ekman looked impatient and uncomfortable.

"Poor thing," Sam said. "I guess I'm lucky. All I have on my agenda is a little housecleaning. You know, a hole in the front wall, a dozen broken windows, a corpse on the floor. . . Nothing big."

"I'm sorry," Ekman said. "I'm just due at the deputy director's office in an hour and I want to have my stuff together."

"In that case, you should be taking notes," Sam said. Ekman started to reply, then simply grabbed a notebook from his jacket pocket and began scrawling.

When he looked up at her, Sam continued. "So the Abrams scene is possibly the worst staged-suicide I've ever seen. It's like they were doing some sort of parody on the whole staged-suicide thing."

"What do you mean?" asked Ekman.

"They didn't just slit his wrists. They dug trenches down almost the whole length of both forearms. I don't care how despondent or stoned Abrams might have been. There's no way he would have done that to himself. And then they scrawled some bullshit note that looked like it was written by a fourth grader."

Ekman wrote on his notepad, Brock listened, and Sam took a sip of coffee. "Abrams was sitting on some sort of a key," she said after a few seconds. "Quartermain thought it belonged to a music box or something similar. Not a very specific clue, because the same key opens multiple locks of the same design. And it was just attached to a chain, with nothing else to identify it."

Ekman nodded, but didn't say anything. When he stopped writing, Sam continued. "I walked the house while Phil worked forensics around the body. The place didn't have a safe house vibe to it. It was more like a sex pad. The downstairs was decorated in early douchebag, and there were way too many of Abrams' personal items. The black light confirmed my suspicions. DNA everywhere."

"Tell me about the notepad with your name and address on it," Ekman said.

What the hell? Sam was taken aback. She had only told Dan Gable about the notepad on John Abrams' nightstand, and she had sworn Dan to secrecy. She had no idea how Ekman found out about it.

She made a mental note to revisit that little riddle, then considered how she should answer Ekman in light of what his question revealed. He obviously knew more about the situation than he was letting on, and Sam wasn't sure she was comfortable with that.

But she wasn't about to lie to him, particularly since it was the note on the dead spy's nightstand with her name on it that had catapulted her into the ridiculous car chase with the local cops, which Ekman had undoubtedly also heard about.

So she played it straight. "Yeah, that definitely got my attention," she said. "That's when I started to think that the scene might still be live."

"So you called Gable and me," Ekman said.

"Yeah. After I called Brock."

"Why did you call Brock?"

Sam noticed that the conversation had changed from Ekman listening to her explain the evening's events, to Ekman interviewing her as if she were a suspect or person of interest. It was an unwritten rule that you didn't interrogate your colleagues, even when you were squeezing them for information. She didn't like the sudden change in the temperature of the conversation. "Umm, I don't know, Francis. What would you do if you thought someone might be on their way to your place with guns and sharp objects?"

Ekman didn't answer.

"Oh, that's right - you're not banging anybody," Sam said. Ekman flushed again. Brock chuckled under his breath.

"But if you *were* banging somebody, wouldn't you call and warn them?" she asked.

"Yes, Sam, I would call home," Ekman said, a little sheepishly. Her inappropriately personal comment had had the desired effect. Ekman was no longer on the offensive, and he was no longer in charge of the conversation.

Sam sipped her coffee, then continued. "I left the scene when I discovered the note. I assessed that it was possibly still an active scene, and that I might have been a target."

"And that's when you ran into Cooper?" Ekman asked.

"Yes. I was getting into my car, and he scared the living shit out of me. He came out of the bushes. No flashlight, no radio squawking, nothing."

"What did you do?" Ekman asked.

"I squealed my tires backing out of the driveway, like some scared rookie. But like I said, he scared me to death."

"Did you see that he was a cop?"

"Before he came out of the bushes? No," Sam said pointedly. "After that? Yes."

"So why did you drive off like a perp?" Ekman asked.

That was a weird way to phrase things, Sam thought. It definitely felt as though Ekman had her under the microscope. *Does he think I'm culpable for something?*

She decided to take the offensive again. "Listen, Francis, I'm not sure I like the direction you're heading. If you have something to say, work up the balls to say it. Otherwise, let's be on the same team, shall we?"

"Sam, I'm just trying to figure out what happened."

"Funny, it sounds to me like you think you already *know* what happened," she said.

"I'm sorry, I just want to make sure I have your version

straight."

"How many other versions are there?" she asked, her agitation evident.

"Don't bust my chops, Sam. You know I have to get the facts together."

"Then shut the hell up and write," Sam said. "I'm telling you the facts."

Brock broke the tension: "More coffee, Francis?"

"I would love another cup of coffee. Thank you, Brock. And I actually prefer to be called Frank. Sam knows that, but she likes to aggravate me."

"Listen, I'm tired and hungry," Sam said, "and I'm only going to make one pass through the rest of this. So write fast."

Sam told him how Everett Cooper, the cop who jumped out of the bushes, had reached for his Taser as he approached her car in front of the John Abrams murder scene. She explained how she drove off in a heightened state of awareness – "completely freaked out," as she described it – and picked up a police tail within a couple of blocks of Abrams' place.

She recounted how the emergency dispatcher couldn't get in touch with the officer in the police cruiser behind her, which made her wonder whether it was a real cop, a real-but-crooked cop, or an impostor *pretending* to be a cop, chasing after her.

She also relayed how a second police cruiser appeared behind her and rammed her car into a spin, after which she decided to stand on the accelerator and let the twin turbo boosters save the day.

"One-sixty, for your report," she said. Ekman looked puzzled.

"One hundred and sixty miles an hour," Sam clarified. "That's how fast I was going when I lost them." Ekman shook his head and wrote it down.

"Meanwhile, back at the homestead," Brock interjected, "someone in a police uniform wouldn't stop ringing our doorbell."

"Did you answer?" Ekman asked.

"Hell no. I always obey my better half," Brock said. "She has a vicious uppercut."

"So you didn't answer the door when a police officer rang the bell?" Ekman asked again, eyebrows raised.

"That's what he said," Sam said.

"Why did you tell him not to answer the door for the police?" Ekman asked Sam.

"Is something the matter with you?" Sam asked. "Have you listened to anything I've told you?"

"I'm sorry, I just want to make sure I have it all straight, that's all."

"You're about to get it straight. Straight up a dark place!" Sam said. "Now stop being difficult, Francis." She watched Ekman's eye twitch. He really did dislike being called by his given name. And he really did put up with too much shit from her, she knew, but she couldn't help herself sometimes. Few things annoyed her like bureaucracy and officiousness.

"Then what happened?" Ekman asked, after a deep breath bolstered his composure.

"A real Metro patrolman showed up and escorted me home," Sam said. "Davis was his name. I verified his badge number with the

Homeland dispatcher. When we got here, the other cop, the guy who kept ringing the doorbell, was already gone. Brock and I were trying to piece together what the hell had happened when the explosion went off in the front yard."

She left off the part about the Homeland team disappearing moments before the bomb went off. Even though he had a right to know that extremely important detail, she didn't trust Ekman enough to share it with him, particularly given the interrogation-like vibe Sam was picking up from him.

"A couple of minutes later," Sam continued while Ekman took notes, "Everett Cooper showed up here. And another minute after that, those two gentlemen in the other room splattered Cooper's brains on my Monet knock-off."

Ekman scrawled on his notepad for a while, then stopped. He looked pensively into the distance as if formulating a question, opened his mouth to speak, then abruptly stopped, thinking better of it. "Thank you, Sam," he finally said. "Please stay available. I have to go see the deputy director, and I'll call you if he asks me anything I can't answer."

Sam looked at him for a long moment, thinking things through. The tenor of the conversation led her to believe that Ekman suspected her of something. And even if he didn't suspect her of wrongdoing, the tone of his questions made her feel as though he certainly wouldn't stand up for her in case the deputy director decided he might want to discipline her for leaving a scene prematurely, or running from police cruisers at ludicrous speeds.

"I have an idea," she said. "Why don't I go with you? That

way, if the boss has questions, he'll get his answers straight from the source."

Ekman started to argue, but decided against resisting her. "Okay," he said. "Against my better judgment, and only if you agree not to speak unless spoken to," he added.

"Deal," Sam lied.

Chapter 8

Peter Kittredge, Deputy Special Assistant to the US Ambassador to Venezuela, was in a sublime state of drunkenness. It was barely ten o'clock in the morning, and on a Sunday no less, but Kittredge had made a substantial dent in the bottle of Stolichnaya he kept chilling in the freezer at his DC flat.

Because of his frequent trips up from South America, which were due in part to his duties as a courier for the US embassy, and also due to his duties as a spy for Exel Oil, Kittredge kept a crash pad in Washington. It was far enough away from Embassy Row that Kittredge could afford the rent – but only if the Exel Oil payments continued. DC was a tough town on a budget.

But it was a terrific city in which to be a gay man, particularly a gay man in a fulfilling but extremely open relationship with someone who lived in Venezuela. Sure, Charley made his share of trips up north from Venezuela, but not nearly as frequently as Kittredge. Par-tay.

The previous night had begun just as many other hookups had begun. Kittredge had bellied up to his favorite spot near Crystal City. "Festive" was an out-and-proud place, festooned with rainbow curtains and featuring a wait staff comprised exclusively of women with flat-top haircuts and extremely effeminate boys.

Beautiful, promiscuous boys, at least in Kittredge's experience. They hired well at Festive, and Kittredge was grateful that the old maxim about never trying to pick up a cocktail server while they were working didn't apply in the gay world. He had enjoyed more than his share of evenings with more than his share of the waiters.

The previous evening was to have been another memorable adventure with a very pretty blonde named Daniel. Daniel was slight, athletic, and very flirtatious. He had let Kittredge make the first move, as Kittredge was a bit more butch, but Daniel had responded enthusiastically in kind. Everything had been terrific, and Kittredge was looking forward to enjoying Daniel back in his apartment.

They had made their way to Daniel's car and were about to leave when Daniel realized he had left his sweater under the bar.

At least, that's what Daniel had said. Kittredge didn't know for sure if that was true or not, because as soon as Daniel had disappeared back in the bar's alley entrance, two men had opened the passenger door of Daniel's car, and dragged Kittredge, kicking and howling, into a waiting minivan.

He had subsequently become a torture victim at the hands of a giant, wolf-looking knee-capper. And, a little later, Kittredge had become an asset of the Central Intelligence Agency, after which his new "boss," Bill Fredericks, had conducted a decidedly unpleasant and confrontational interview.

It wasn't his libido that had created the situation in which he now found himself, Kittredge realized, but his sex drive was certainly the catalyst. His little brain had also led him into Charley Arlinghaus' bed, which had led to his very brief and not-very-lucrative career as a low-level spy for Exel, one of the world's largest oil conglomerates.

Kittredge drunkenly celebrated the way his sexual appetite had ruined his life by pleasuring himself while watching his favorite boy flick. He had scarcely finished when the phone rang. He let it go to voicemail, but the same number popped up again. And again. Finally, he answered.

"I especially like the way the blonde guy keeps his sunglasses on while he's performing oral services," a now-familiar voice said as soon as Kittredge put the phone to his ear.

"What the f—"

"Settle down," Quinn said. "Does it really surprise you that we're looking in on you?"

Kittredge felt violated and deeply vulnerable. "You're watching me?"

"Watching you jerk off. Nice Prince Albert, by the way. That had to have hurt."

Kittredge looked around frantically to find the source of the video feed that was obviously coming from his flat. He heard Quinn chuckle on the other end of the line, and he felt his throat constrict and his chest tighten. "My God," he said.

"Flattery will get you everywhere," Quinn quipped. "Don't bother trying to find the cameras. They'll just put new ones in if you rip them out. Welcome to the team."

"I can't believe this. What a nightmare." Kittredge felt cold and dirty, unable to shake the sense that his world had turned inside out over the past twelve hours. It was as if a parasite had burrowed into the center of him and announced its intention to stay, forever.

"I know. You have a new reality now," Quinn said. "Five stages of grief and all. Or is it six? I should have paid closer attention in sensitivity school," Quinn laughed. "Anyway, you'll get used to your own private Truman Show soon enough. For now, I need you to put away the vodka, towel off your puppet, and meet me downstairs in ten minutes. We're taking a ride."

Kittredge shivered, feeling naked and victimized. He showered and dressed hastily, eager to get out of his bugged apartment, but acutely aware that they had probably been watching him elsewhere, too.

He had no idea where he might go to hide from the watchful eye of the Agency. Privacy wasn't a thing most people valued until it was stolen. After that, the world took on a much different hue, and Kittredge knew that his life had changed irrevocably. And certainly not for the better, judging by how little he cared for Quinn and Fredericks.

He rode the elevator to the lobby, and found Quinn waiting for him.

Gawd, that guy is huge, Kittredge thought. Quinn was six-three or more, Kittredge guessed, and at least two hundred and thirty pounds of pure muscle. And he was handsome, in a rugged, scares-the-shit-out-of-you kind of way, with his crazy wolf eyes, square jaw, and that uber-masculine scar beneath one eye. *Too bad he's an asshole,* Kittredge thought.

"Partner!" Quinn beamed, crushing Kittredge's hand in a vice-like grip. Kittredge couldn't think of anything to say. "Aw, don't be scared, Pete. We're friends now."

"Peter," Kittredge corrected. "My name is Peter."

"That's right," Quinn said. He motioned toward the parking garage, and they made their way out of the lobby. "Anyway, Peter, I thought you and I should get to know each other, given that we're teammates now."

"Teammates who spy on each other?" Kittredge asked testily.

"Are you spying on us?" Quinn asked.

"Of course not!"

"Well, then, it just looks like *we* are spying on *you*."

"That's what I said."

"No it isn't. You said we're spying on *each other*. That's false."

"Thanks for clarifying," Kittredge said. Quinn struck Kittredge as the kind of guy who didn't have many friends. "Do you have any friends?" he asked, realizing immediately that the shock of the morning's events hadn't completely sobered him up.

"I do now, Peter. You signed on the dotted line, which makes us pals, remember? Ergo, our little outing this morning." After a small pause, Quinn said, "You're still a little drunk, aren't you?"

"That's not illegal, I don't think. Even though it seems like we are much closer to living in a police state than I had ever imagined," Kittredge said.

"Ha ha! Police state! Good one." Quinn guffawed a bit, then stopped. "But the term 'police' implies some sort of rule of law. I'm here to tell you that we really don't care much about stuff like that in our little corner of the organization."

Kittredge saw something mean and feral in the large man's eyes, and his uneasiness, which had started to fade a bit, returned with a vengeance.

"Aw, don't sweat it, partner. Nothing you can't handle. You're a ninja-spy, remember?" More guffaws.

Kittredge struggled to wrap his mind around the situation. Was he really going for a ride with the guy who had tortured him the night before? Was he out of his mind?

And where the hell were they going?

That seemed like something he should figure out before getting into a car with the giant freak who, just a few hours earlier, had peeled the skin off of his back with a belt sander. "Where are we headed?" he asked.

"I was thinking earlier, it's such a nice day for a drive," Quinn said. "So I said to myself, 'I should invite my new friend Pete along.'"

"It's Peter."

"I know, but when I was talking to myself earlier, saying I should invite you along for a drive, I forgot you didn't like to be called Pete."

"Who *are* you?"

"Your new partner," Quinn said, motioning toward a silver Land Rover. "Hop in."

"I'm not getting in that car until you tell me where we're going."

Quinn let out a long breath. "Okay, Peter. I was going to break this to you later, but here goes. We're going to visit Charley

Arlinghaus. In the hospital."

"What?" Kittredge felt himself reeling. "Charley is here?"

"No. He's in the hospital," Quinn said. "That's where we're going."

"What the–"

"Get in the car, please."

* * *

Charley Arlinghaus lay in a coma, intubated. The right side of his head had been shaved, and a long row of stitches traced a line from above his ear to a point just beneath his temple. His face was swollen, and his eye was black and puffy.

Tears streamed down Kittredge's face as he sat beside Arlinghaus' inert form. Quinn kept a respectful distance, but didn't leave the room.

"Are you Peter?" a nurse asked. "He was awake for a moment earlier, and he asked about you, just before he went into surgery."

"What happened?"

"He was attacked in the parking garage at the airport this morning," Quinn said from the corner of the room. "Tire iron. Fractured his skull. He's lucky to be alive. Bill Fredericks called me this morning and told me to come get you."

"Oh my God, Charley" Kittredge cried. "What in the world happened to you?" He stroked the comatose man's face tenderly.

"His brain is swelling due to the trauma, and we may have to reopen the wound to relieve the pressure," the nurse said.

"Oh my God," Kittredge said again. "Is he going to be okay?"

"We'll see to it that he gets the best possible medical care," the nurse said. "He's stable for the moment, but the next two days are important."

"My God. . . Charley, who would do this to you?" Kittredge gave in to anguished sobs.

"I'm really sorry, Peter," Quinn said, after the wave of emotion passed. Kittredge could tell he meant it. Maybe the beast was human, after all.

Then again, maybe Quinn did this to Charley, Kittredge thought suddenly. He realized that he had absolutely no idea what to believe or who to trust. Charley was his emotional anchor, and now he was in a coma with his head bashed in.

And what the hell was Charley doing in DC this weekend? He was supposed to be staying in Venezuela! Did something pop up at work? He would've called, certainly.

Another boyfriend? They were open enough not to have to sneak around. If Charley wanted someone else, he could have him. He knew that.

And why would the CIA goons be the ones to come get me? Wouldn't the police do that?

Kittredge felt panic rise up within him. The alcohol, sleep deprivation, emotional trauma, and torture all caught up with him at once, and Kittredge felt the room start to swim. He vaguely registered Quinn's voice saying "Easy, big guy," as he slipped from consciousness.

Chapter 9

"Listen, Frank, I'm sorry for being so hard on you earlier," Sam said to Ekman when they met in the parking garage at DHS headquarters in DC. It took concentration for her not to call him "Francis." It had become a habit.

Ekman was silent, so Sam went on. "It was a bit of a rough night, and I was a little cranky, and a little out of line," she added. "Sorry."

"I'm used to your abuse," Ekman said. Sam couldn't tell whether he was joking or not. He didn't sound angry, though it was tough to tell with him. He was a good enough guy, but he usually had all the personality of an ashtray, although he sometimes surprised her with a wry remark.

She didn't think she had pushed him too far during their somewhat heated conversation at her house earlier in the morning, but she wasn't certain either way.

Sam had decided that she needed to keep Ekman close while she sleuthed out his agenda. Doing so required an apology for her sharp tongue, which was the easy part.

It also required her to remain on her best behavior in front of the deputy director, which was going to be hard. She wasn't the president of the Deputy Director Tom Jarvis fan club. As far as she could tell, the feeling was mutual.

But she needed to change the game up. Ekman had clearly had

an idea in his head when he questioned her earlier in the morning, and Sam needed to figure out his angle. She had the distinct impression that he was withholding information from her. She hated that on principle, but more than that, being kept in the dark was a potential health issue given all that had transpired in the preceding twelve hours.

She had realized that she suddenly didn't know who was on her side. And obviously, judging by her banged-up Porsche and the bomb crater in her front yard, at least a few people were playing for the opposition. It would be nice to know who was who.

Ekman held the door for her – chivalry before rank – and they walked through the dingy hallway and into Jarvis' spacious office. The décor screamed, "Fed." The furniture looked like it came straight out of the Dick Van Dyke Show. The air smelled vaguely of mothballs, which turned Sam's stomach.

"You've had quite a morning, haven't you, Sam?" Tom Jarvis was a career bureaucrat in his early fifties. He had bovine eyes and a bulldog's jowls, but none of the latter's tenacity. If there was a decision to be made, Jarvis generally felt that it ought to be made at a later date, and by someone else. He treated his charges with kindness, but rarely stuck his neck out for anyone. He liked memos, meetings, calendars, and keeping the stakeholders informed, whatever that meant.

He didn't motion for Sam and Ekman to take a seat, which wasn't a good sign.

"Yes, I have," Sam said with a small smile. "In fact, I can't recall a more eventful Saturday night. At least since my sorority days." Jarvis laughed politely.

Out of the corner of her eye, Sam saw Ekman squirm a little. She wondered if there was some agenda at play other than just giving the big boss a rundown of the evening's kerfuffle.

"Can you tell me how you came to be mixed up in all of this?" Jarvis asked.

That's one hell of a strange question. "I'm not quite sure what you mean," Sam said. "Frank called me last night at about eleven to work the John Abrams scene. What else am I mixed up in?"

She saw Ekman squirm again.

"Sam, it's not a good idea to act dumb," Jarvis said.

"It's no act, Tom," Sam said. "In fact, I'm starting to get the distinct impression that it's *you* who probably owes *me* an explanation."

Jarvis looked at Ekman, who took the cue to reign in his employee. "Sam, let's keep our cool, shall we?"

"I'm cool as a cucumber," Sam said. "Especially considering you guys dispatched me to a fake suicide, where I discovered my name and address on the victim's nightstand, and after which I was chased by crooked cops. And I probably don't need to mention the explosion that remodeled my house this morning."

"Another way to look at those events," Jarvis said, "would be to say that you left a scene prematurely, then led police on a high-speed chase through the city."

"Police?" Sam asked, incredulous. "Oh, you mean the dead cop in my entryway who was moonlighting as a gangster or something? And maybe the policeman who tried to run my car off the road? Those police? You need to open a window and let some fresh air in here. All the fumes from that pile of bullshit on your desk have affected your brain."

"That's enough, Sam," Jarvis said. "We're looking into the facts. I have not yet ruled out administrative leave while we sort this out."

"Are you serious?"

"I can't have agents running rogue out there. Consider yourself on notice."

Consider yourself a jackass. "Unbelievable," Sam said.

Ekman chimed in. "Sam, I think you should go home, take some time to get your house put back together, and let us sort through this."

"Sure thing, Frank. Just as soon as you tell me what you should have told me hours ago. You know something about why I'm suddenly so popular. I'm not leaving until I hear it."

"I'm afraid that's above your pay grade at the moment," Jarvis said.

"Then earn your paycheck and make the decision to lower the classification. These people attacked me *at my home*, Tom."

Unbidden, Sam sat down in a chair across from Jarvis' desk. "And if either of you knew something beforehand and didn't warn me," she said in a low tone, "that's a hell of a lot more than just a bad decision. It's a crime."

Sam watched Jarvis stew. Jarvis had the power to cause problems for her, but she was mindful that the party who cared the least held the power in any relationship. She cared a great deal about figuring out who was wreaking havoc in her world, but she cared far less than Ekman or Jarvis about office politics, niceties, and the formal rank and protocol structure of the Department of Homeland Security. She wasn't afraid to make a mess.

She also knew that she could easily create the kind of problem that kept both of her supervisors awake at night. It would take no more than ten minutes of her time to file an Inspector General complaint. Both Jarvis and Ekman were in line for promotion, which would be frozen for the duration of the IG investigation – easily half a year, sometimes longer.

If the IG found against them, their careers would be redlined. In the federal government, an IG complaint was the nuclear option. Both men knew that she wasn't afraid to go there. She had done it before.

Jarvis exhaled heavily. "Okay, Sam. Let me make a phone call. We do owe you some information."

"Damn right you do. And an apology."

Jarvis frowned. "Don't push it, Sam."

* * *

"What would you like to know?" Jarvis asked after returning to his office from the top-secret vault down the hall.

In his five-minute absence, Ekman and Sam had exchanged scarcely a word, except for Ekman's tongue-in-cheek thanks to Sam for having kept to her best behavior in front of the boss.

Sam thought for a second before replying to Jarvis. "I think you should tell me what you know you should tell me. Whatever that is."

"Cute, Sam." Jarvis observed.

"I'm not being cute, Tom." No one but Sam called Jarvis by his first name, and she knew her insolence hadn't gone unnoticed.

"Frank gave me the third degree already this morning," Sam said. "And your first response to my near-death experiences of the past evening was to critique my adherence to chapter and verse of the damned rule book. I mean, are we on the same team here, or aren't we?"

"Of course we are," Jarvis said. Something in the way he said it made Sam's bullshit alarm go off. It was the answer a boss obviously had to give, but Jarvis hadn't quite made enough eye contact to be convincing. *Something's up,* Sam thought.

"It's just that sometimes," Jarvis explained, "I don't have the ability to let people in the organization in on things that I know they would be interested in."

"Like who is trying to kill them? Because I would be interested in hearing a thing like that." Sam smiled to take the edge off her barb.

"Sam, if we had had any warning, or even if we suspected anything might be amiss, you have to know that we'd have moved mountains to stop it." Jarvis did make eye contact this time. Maybe he meant it.

Or maybe he knew that it was an important lie, and he was a little more deliberate about his delivery.

"I know, Tom. This isn't the CIA, after all."

That was a bit of a low blow. A while back, someone had started a rumor that Jarvis was actually an Agency plant, placed in

Homeland to keep tabs on the fastest-growing bureaucracy since the Soviet Communist Party.

Whether or not the Agency was engaging in domestic espionage had been largely academic. People *believed* the CIA was shady enough to do something like that, and Jarvis had protested a bit too much for some people's tastes, giving life and legs to what would otherwise have been idle water cooler gossip.

Sam saw his eyes narrow, and knew she had made her point.

She smiled again, and made a demand, disguised as an olive branch: "It's hard to piece things together in advance, and I know it's hard to manage need-to-know to protect your sources and minimize risk of exposure." Jarvis nodded, and Sam went on. "But I think we can all probably agree that even if I didn't have a need to know before, it's safe to say that I do now. And hell," she added, "I've even been known to solve these kinds of cases from time to time. Maybe I can be helpful."

"This stays between the three of us," Jarvis said. "I don't have permission to brief your deputy. Just you."

Sam suspected that was bullshit – Dan Gable held all the same clearances she held, and by virtue of his involvement in the morning's insanity, the same need-to-know. *They want to keep us from comparing notes,* she thought.

"Understood," she said. *My fingers were crossed.*

"Operation Bolero," Jarvis said.

"Bad movie with Bo Derek?"

"Funny. No. But a plot line just as awful. American mob meets Venezuelan mob, or government – we think it's kind of the same thing – and it looks like they're teaming up for some Stateside shenanigans."

"Everett Cooper?" Sam asked.

"Yes, and a few others, though it's not certain that the Metro cops fully understood who they were actually in bed with," Jarvis said. "By all accounts, these guys are loyal Americans and good cops. On the job, I mean. They maybe could have picked a better hobby."

"So they're good guys, except for the thuggery and espionage? I'm with you so far," Sam said.

"Like I said, it all looks a bit more tangled up than that."

"Why do you think I'm in with them?"

"I didn't say I thought you were in with them," Jarvis said.

"I know you didn't say it." Sam eyeballed Jarvis. She liked the hardball game, and she was good at it. She saw Jarvis flinch just a little bit. "Tell me why you *think* it."

"I can't comment on who we might be looking at."

"I thought you were going to let me peek up your skirt, Tom. Just between the three of us, and all of that. Did I misunderstand?"

"No, Sam, you didn't misunderstand. But you know as well as anyone that there are limits."

That didn't take long, Sam thought. It only took a couple of questions to run smack into the stonewall tactic again.

"No, Tom, I don't know that," she said. "See, when there are limits to how much you're willing to let me find out about a case that almost killed me, that tells me that we're really not playing on the same team. If you have something against me, you need to make your move. Otherwise, you need to cut the bullshit. Either way, there's a corpse stinking up my house right now, which means that we're miles beyond the point where it's okay for you to mushroom me."

Jarvis was clearly unaccustomed to anyone handing him an ultimatum, least of all a subordinate, and it was evident to Sam that his patience was wearing thin. *That makes two of us,* she thought.

Jarvis spun his pen, mulling.

Sam glanced at Ekman. Always uncomfortable with confrontation, he had faded into the furniture.

She shifted her gaze back to Jarvis and sat patiently, legs crossed, one foot swinging rhythmically.

Jarvis finally broke the silence. "Do you know that Brock James is married?"

The left-field question took her aback.

She blinked twice before regaining her mental footing. "Legally separated, and divorce pending. Did you know that the price of tea rose in China?"

"Not yet divorced means married," Jarvis said. "Technically, you're both guilty of conduct unbecoming an officer."

"I'm sorry, Tom. You must feel so disappointed in me. I'm having sex with a soon-to-be-divorced guy, who's been separated for a couple of years. What the hell does that have to do with Venezuela, the dent in my rear quarter panel, and the brains on my wall?"

"They're related, Sam. We caught wind of your affair—"

"Brilliant work. We have the same mailing address."

"As I was saying, your affair—"

"It's a relationship, Tom. Not an *affair*."

"Legally, it's an affair. The end of the sentence I keep trying to complete goes like this: we had an obligation to investigate your affair in order to make sure you're not vulnerable to blackmail. As you know, that's a byproduct of having a top-secret security clearance. In the process of that investigation, we found some things that might connect you to Bolero via Brock."

Sam sat dumbstruck. She couldn't fathom what connection Brock might have to the Venezuelan government or American organized crime. He had spent twenty-three years in the Air Force— not exactly the kind of environment that would have exposed him to mobsters and spies.

And Brock probably couldn't find Venezuela on a map, she thought. He religiously ignored international politics. *All* politics, for that matter.

"I'm pretty sure Brock hasn't been any further south than Cancun," Sam said.

"I think you're mistaken," Jarvis said.

"Tom, Brock is a no-shit hero. They gave him a Silver Star after Kosovo. You'd damn well better have something more than rumor and innuendo behind what you just said."

Jarvis' voice was quiet. "I do, Sam."

Her heart pounded in her chest, and a surge of adrenaline slammed her stomach. The suggestion that Brock might be hiding something important from her awakened deep-seated trust issues. Her throat constricted and she fought tears. "Tell me, Tom."

"Arturo Dibiaso," Jarvis said.

Chapter 10

Peter Kittredge rocked pensively on the chair in the hospital room, transfixed by the EKG readout that punctuated his boyfriend's heartbeat. Except for the steady beeping of the monitor and the mechanically induced rise and fall of his chest, Charley Arlinghaus' body showed little sign of life. He was still in a coma, demonstrating few positive signs of recovery.

The doctors had warned Kittredge to prepare for "diminished cognitive function," which Kittredge reckoned was as sterile a euphemism as possible for the loss of a loved one's personality.

But it certainly wasn't time to give up hope. It had only been a matter of hours since the attack in the airport parking lot had left Charley with traumatic brain injury and a fractured skull. And the doctors had been sure to mention that while he remained unresponsive to stimulus, the rate of swelling had slowed. Charley wasn't yet getting better, but at least he had stopped accelerating downhill.

Quinn had finally left, but Kittredge still felt, or imagined, a watchful Agency presence, a byproduct of the gross violation of privacy he experienced earlier in the morning. *As if espionage weren't enough—now they have plenty of compromising footage to blackmail me with,* he mused darkly.

They. CIA, they had told him, and he was inclined to believe it. His five years in the Diplomatic Corps had taught him a healthy respect for the reach and resources of the Agency. He had known that US spies surrounded him on the embassy staff, and he'd had his suspicions about which of his colleagues might also have been Agency assets, but none of his suspicions were ever confirmed, and he certainly never voiced them to any of his colleagues. Doing so was strictly forbidden. It wouldn't do to have embassy personnel speculating aloud about which among them might really be spooks.

In retrospect, selling information as an embassy employee was an exceptionally stupid move on his part. Had he thought more about it, he would certainly have realized that there were probably as many *counter*intelligence agents at work in any given embassy as regular intelligence officers. After all, embassy personnel spent their days living in the belly of the beast, as it were, and there were few other jobs whose hazards included being the target of regular recruitment pitches to switch sides and spy for a foreign interest.

In the end, despite his respect for the CIA's capability and presence, he had grossly underestimated them. They'd probably been watching him for months. They probably had weeks of video footage. They probably knew his favorite positions and his favorite boy-toys.

I'm well and truly screwed, he thought for the hundredth time in the past twelve hours. He shuddered again, unable to shake the feeling of violation.

His eyes refocused on Charley's heart monitor, and he thought again about how strange and disorienting the situation had become. *You're supposed to be in Caracas, you bastard.*

As his Exel responsibilities had grown, Charley had made

fewer and fewer trips back home. While the workdays were a bit longer, Charley's life as a deputy section chief was a thousand times more predictable than when he was a lower-level functionary, and there were almost never any emergency trips back Stateside these days. So it was beyond strange that Charley should turn up in a DC hospital with a broken melon.

And it was stranger still for Charley not to have told him about the change in schedule. It contributed to Kittredge's sense of violation, and had at least as much emotional impact as the CIA's invasion of his privacy.

Kittredge did his best to control his thoughts, but he couldn't stop himself from imagining that Charley had found a new relationship, which caused him to wrestle for long minutes with feelings of deep betrayal and isolation. Then a calmer voice momentarily prevailed, and he allowed himself to believe that a perfectly logical explanation must exist.

Those voices competed for prominence, and he wavered between anger, despair, humiliation, betrayal, and concern for Charley's prognosis.

Kittredge also found himself replaying various episodes in their relationship over the past months, scouring his memory for clues that might betray a betrayal. Kittredge now wondered whether deception had become a characteristic of his relationship with Charley, which cast everything in an ominous light.

Kittredge knew that the human mind had nearly infinite capacity to stew over past events, and he even believed that such worry-in-retrospect was grossly counterproductive, but he couldn't stop himself. Every askew glance or incomplete answer Charley had given him over the past several months had suddenly turned into a potential smoking gun.

Kittredge didn't know what was going on, but he did know that *something* was off. He could have believed that Charley was the victim of a mugging or random act of violence in the airport parking lot, except that Quinn, the CIA thug, had been the one to inform him of the attack.

Plus, whoever had attacked Charley hadn't bothered to take his wallet or cash.

It was beyond suspicious. Was the attack on Charley some sort of a warning? If so, why go to the trouble of bringing him to DC? Or was Charley's presence in DC a separate but related thing, and someone just took advantage of the opportunity?

And who was the warning meant for? *If it is about me,* Kittredge thought, *I can't imagine what they might be trying to say now that they couldn't have said when they had me strapped to the concrete last night.*

It's probably not about me, he concluded. But if the attack was about something going on in Charley's world, what was it? That line of thinking brought him back to fruitless and neurotic re-examination of their recent history together, and the vicious cycle repeated.

It was interrupted by the ringing of a telephone. Kittredge looked around to find the source, and located a wall phone adjacent to the door in Charley's intensive care room. Kittredge expected the phone to stop ringing at any moment, but it droned on insistently.

Finally, on what must have been the twentieth ring, Kittredge answered the phone.

"How's he doing?" asked a gravelly voice that Kittredge didn't recognize.

"Who is this?" he asked.

"Jim Bishop, Exel Oil."

"Charley's boss?" Kittredge was taken aback. He straightened up involuntarily at the realization that he was speaking with a big wig.

"That's right," Bishop said. "Peter Kittredge, isn't it? How's Charley?"

Kittredge said. "Charley's had better mornings, but they say he's stabilizing. He's in a coma." Kittredge's voice broke, and he fought back tears.

"What a damn shame. Do they have any leads on the bastards who did this?"

"I'm not sure. I haven't seen any police officers, but a. . . well. . . A federal agent let me know about the attack." Kittredge didn't know what to call Quinn, and he certainly didn't want to have a conversation with Charley's boss about his recently-acquired Agency acquaintances – particularly since Exel Oil had been paying Kittredge a stipend in exchange for certain tasty tidbits culled from embassy message traffic.

Does Bishop know I'm Exel's guy inside the embassy? Probably, but there was no easy way to find out for sure.

"Interesting," Bishop said. "What kind of a federal agent?"

Shit. I have no poker face. How did I ever think I could be a spy? "Well, I'm not quite sure." That wasn't a lie. He still couldn't quite bring himself to believe that the CIA employed agents to kidnap and torture US citizens on US soil, so he really didn't know for certain what Quinn was.

"Strange," Bishop observed.

"It *was* weird." The initial shock of the oil executive's call had started to wear off, and Kittredge's mind reawakened. "Mr. Bishop, if you don't mind my asking, who let you know about the attack?"

"The embassy duty officer called me at home. I've asked them to notify me of anything serious going on with any of the folks in our Venezuelan contingent." Bishop paused. "Such a tragedy, with Charley's father in the hospital, too."

"Charley's father?"

"Yes, the heart condition and all."

What the hell? "Heart condition?" Kittredge asked before he could stop himself.

An awkward pause. "I'm sorry," the oil exec said. "I thought for certain you knew, given that the two of you are, well, close."

"No, sir," Kittredge said, feeling his insides churn. "I didn't know."

"Well, I'm sure he just didn't have time to call you before he caught his flight."

In the cell phone age? Not likely, Kittredge thought. "Yes, sir. I'm sure you're probably right." *Something is seriously messed up here,* he thought. His heart raced, and his head swum.

"Anyway, Peter, I'm so very sorry that this happened, and please, do give Charley my regards and well-wishes when he wakes up, will you?"

"Of course. I'm sure he'll appreciate knowing that you called."

"And you'll let us know as soon as anything changes with him?"

"I will."

"And please, take care of yourself too, will you, Peter?"

"I will, sir."

Bishop signed off. Kittredge slumped into a nearby chair, feeling nauseous. It just kept getting weirder. Charley had taken the time to tell his bosses about the trip to DC, but he hadn't bothered to tell his live-in boyfriend? Kittredge shook his head.

And Charley's dad lives in Baltimore, he recalled. *And what heart condition? The man runs marathons!*

It was now obvious that Charley Arlinghaus had a few secrets he'd been keeping, and Kittredge felt anger and bile rising. He looked at Charley's inanimate form and swollen, blackening eye. *Have we been living a lie, Charley?*

He felt as though he might be sick. Nothing isolates like betrayal, and he couldn't remember a time when he had felt quite so alone in the world.

Another troubling question arose in Kittredge's mind: who had called the embassy's duty desk to tell them about the attack on Charley? Kittredge cursed himself for not having thought to ask Bishop.

Then he realized the answer probably wouldn't have been terribly instructive – if the CIA had thought to pick him up and bring him to the hospital, they would certainly also have thought of calling the embassy. And they would have played a pretty convincing role no matter who they chose to impersonate.

Kittredge felt despondency settling in. In twelve short hours, his life had come apart at the seams. The first wave of sobs took him by surprise, but he quickly gave himself over to paroxysms of fear and rage.

Chapter 11

"Arturo who?" Sam asked Tom Jarvis.

"Dibiaso," Jarvis said. "Arturo Dibiaso. Known Venezuelan spy."

"Working for whom?"

"Arturo Dibiaso is a Venezuelan spy working for the Venezuelan government," Jarvis said a little testily. "We have credible evidence linking Brock James to Dibiaso."

Deputy Director Tom Jarvis' accusation made Sam's blood run cold.

The rational side of her, the side responsible for her rapid rise through the ranks to the top of the DHS Counterintelligence Investigations division, knew that Jarvis and his brood of sycophants had even odds of being wrong about both assertions: Arturo Dibiaso might not *really* be a spy, and Brock James, the first man to whom she had ever fully given her heart, might not *really* be involved with Dibiaso.

Sam had a very short list of people whose conclusions on such matters she trusted. It was a list of one. Herself. She had long ago discovered that almost everyone in the lumbering DHS bureaucracy was an idiot, on the take, or both.

But the rational side of her also knew that even if Jarvis' conclusion about Brock was wrong, it was still an idea that could have a very grave pragmatic impact on their reality.

And the emotional side of her was scared shitless.

The Department of Homeland Security didn't often move quickly or smartly, but God help you if it moved against *you*. Draconian didn't begin to describe how thoroughly DHS could screw with someone. Sam had seen it on more than one occasion, and she had personally brought Homeland's wrath to bear on more than a dozen people, with uniformly devastating effect.

It occurred to Sam that under the current set of circumstances, right or wrong, Jarvis was a staggeringly dangerous man. She locked her eyes onto his, hoping that the trembling she felt beneath her skin didn't show on her face. She forced herself to take two deep breaths.

"Tom, I have no doubt that you thoroughly investigated your claims. I—"

"Wrong, Sam," Jarvis interrupted. "They're not claims. They're facts."

"In that case, you will probably have no problem demonstrating their validity to me," Sam said, hoping she sounded much more even-keeled than she felt.

"You're not in a position to make demands like that."

"And this is not a police state, Tom. At least not yet. It's one thing to play coy with information about a suspect, but it's something else entirely to do that to one of your own. I almost became a martyr for the cause today. Twice. I think that's worth something."

"Not if the situation is of your own making, Sam."

"You know it isn't."

"Do I?" Jarvis leaned forward. "How do I know that? You

asked me earlier if I was on your team. How the hell do I know whose team *you* are on?"

Anger flashed. The words "Go to hell, Jarvis!" formed in her mind, and they were well on their way toward her mouth when a different thought struck: *he's got a point.*

She realized that despite her stellar record and rock-star performance over the past several years, there was no way for Jarvis to know for certain about her true motivation and affiliations. Particularly if something had given them reason to doubt her.

What do they know? Or think *they know?* Sam wondered. And could she really blame Jarvis for a bit of mistrust when she harbored so much skepticism herself?

For what seemed like the hundredth time in the last deeply-aggravating hour, Sam took a deep breath. If Ekman and Jarvis refused to show their hand outright, she would have to get at things another way.

Judo, she thought. *Use your opponent's momentum against him.* Even if they wouldn't make statements, they probably couldn't help but to ask questions. And a person could learn a lot just by listening to the questions.

"Hook me up to the poly," she said.

The lie detector. It was almost never advisable to volunteer for a polygraph, but Sam needed to know what Jarvis and Ekman were sitting on. And she wasn't making much progress using the straightforward approach.

Ekman and Jarvis looked at each other, raised their eyebrows, and cocked their heads slightly. She could tell they wanted to take her offer, but were straining to figure out her angle. *Nobody* volunteered for the polygraph.

She gave them a nudge. "We obviously have a trust gap," she said. "I want to remove your doubts."

Jarvis wrinkled his lip, spun his pen, and glanced at Ekman again. Finally, he nodded. "Let's go downstairs. Frank, call in the polygraph tech, please."

* * *

It took the technician forty minutes to arrive, time that Sam used to take a nap on the couch in the lobby facing the polygraph room. Her nap was part necessity – she had been awake for twenty-seven hours straight – and part strategy. Sleeping communicated calmness and ease, attributes that someone with something to hide would likely find difficult to fake right before a lie detector test. She knew that her display of calmness wouldn't be lost on her superiors.

It took another half hour to hook Sam up to the electrodes and get the perfunctory questions out of the way. To baseline her responses, the tech asked for Sam's name, address, educational background, and other factual sundries, then moved on to the "emotional baseline," questions which weren't directly related to the investigation at hand but still caused an emotional response: have you ever told a lie? Have you ever stolen anything? Have you ever cheated on your taxes? The questions were sneaky but useful, and provided the physiological response threshold above which the subject was likely lying.

The first real question was a doozy: "When did you know that Colonel James was married?"

"On our first date." Sam felt her heart rate increase. She was telling the truth, but felt apprehensive about where the question was pointing.

"So you chose to violate regulations by continuing to see each other?"

Sam forced herself to breathe slowly. "With his divorce pending and his future ex-wife a thousand miles away, we chose to see each other. Discreetly, I might add."

"Did you know it was against the regulations?"

Another pause. "Yes," Sam answered.

"Do you routinely violate regulations?"

Sam felt her eyes narrow. "Only the stupid ones."

"Excuse me?"

"I skip mandatory gender sensitivity training," Sam said. "And I don't get the damned flu shot."

"Are you saying that you selectively adhere to the regulations?" the tech asked with raised eyebrows.

"I wouldn't lie to you," Sam said.

The polygraph technician put on a poker face and made a note before continuing. "How long has Colonel James known Arturo Dibiaso?"

She had expected a bullshit question like that one, but she was still angry about it. "Do you still beat your wife?" she asked the tech.

"Ms. Jameson, how long has Colonel James known Mr. Dibiaso?" The tech's voice was a bit firmer.

"What makes you think he *does* know anyone by that name?"

"Please answer the question, ma'am."

"I don't know whether Brock knows Arturo Dibiaso. If he does know someone by that name, I've never heard him speak of it. And *I* don't know that person."

"When was Colonel James last in Venezuela?"

"To my knowledge? Never."

"Are you sure, ma'am?"

"Quite."

More writing, then the tech continued, "Do you own stock in any oil company?"

Left field.

Oil. She didn't know why she was surprised. Of course it was about oil. What else was in Venezuela that the US might give a shit about? It wasn't like American companies were opening factories down there, smack in the middle of a personality-cult quasi-dictatorship.

"I don't own any stock," she said.

"You own no oil stock?"

"I own *no* stock."

"You don't invest?"

"I didn't say that. I said I didn't own stock."

The tech looked puzzled. Sam chuckled inwardly. *Lemming. Probably fell off the August cliff with every other Wall Street sucker.* The crash a few months ago had sent a few brokers leaping from fiftieth-floor windows.

"Do you have any oil-related investments at all?"

"A Porsche. But that investment is largely hedonic."

"Ma'am?"

"Never mind. I own no oil investments of any kind," Sam said.

"Does Colonel James own any oil stock?"

"I don't know."

"How long has Colonel James associated with Edward Minton?"

Interesting. Sam and Brock actually *did* know Edward Minton. Brock called him "Fatso," a humorous nickname that the rail-thin Minton had picked up as a young lieutenant in a fighter squadron in Korea. Minton had also been bald since his early twenties, which made him look like a chemo patient.

"They've known each other for a long time, but I'm not sure exactly how long. I think Brock mentioned they were stationed together in Germany in the late 90's, but don't quote me."

"Can you give me an estimate of how long they've been friends?"

"I just did. Please try to pay attention," Sam said, smiling to take the edge off her barb.

"Ma'am, please give me a year, if you can."

"Late 90's is as good as I can do, and I'm not even sure about that. Anyway, what does it matter?"

The technician didn't acknowledge Sam's question. "Are you sure ma'am?" he asked, a little too stridently.

Note to self: the polygraph tech turned amateur over the Fatso date, Sam thought. *Probably not a bad direction to start looking.*

"No. That's what I'm telling you," she said. "I'm *not* sure of the exact year that Brock and Fatso met each other. But they did meet each other at some point, and they're friends today. Fatso sends a disgusting joke about once a month."

Sometimes what you *didn't* hear was just as important as what you *did*. The tech didn't ask her about Minton's nickname, Fatso. That was interesting, because Fatso had gotten out of the Air Force a decade earlier, and his new civilian friends and coworkers were unlikely to call him by an old fighter pilot moniker. The tech's non-reaction probably meant that Homeland had already started digging into Fatso's background.

The tech was silent for a while, turning pages in his notes. *Recomposing himself.* They obviously had a whole line of questions centered on the date Brock and Fatso became friends, and her inability to give a firm answer had thrown them off track.

She looked toward the two-way mirror and smiled, then gestured toward the still-silent polygraph technician and shrugged her shoulders with an exaggerated look of confusion on her face. She knew Ekman and Jarvis were watching the interrogation from behind the mirror, and she couldn't resist toying with them a bit.

She shouldn't have. A faint buzzer sounded twice in quick succession, and the polygraph technician abruptly thanked her for her time and candor, and began unhooking her from the machine.

"Was it something I said?" she asked.

Wordlessly, the tech unstuck electrodes from her.

"Don't leave," she prodded again. "We were having such a good chat."

Sarcasm aside, she was disappointed that the interview had come to an end. She had found it very useful. *Venezuelan oil, Fatso Minton, some guy named Dibiaso, and something about the late nineties,* she recited to herself. She would write it all down as soon as she got back to her desk.

And Jowly Jarvis was frightened enough to pull the plug as soon as I turned things around on them a bit. That also seemed important. Was Jarvis' stake professional or personal? And what is Ekman's role in this whole thing?

It was far from a complete picture, but for the first time all morning, Sam felt like she had something solid to follow up on.

She knew that Jarvis would have further browbeating in store for her, but she also knew that she had crushed the lie detector test. If they tried to force an administrative leave of absence on her, it would blow up in their faces. *I might start feeling sexually harassed, and be forced to report the hostile work environment,* she thought with a wicked smile.

Chapter 12

"The nurse asked me to tell you that visiting hours are over," Quinn said. "They need to wheel him off for some more tests."

Peter Kittredge composed himself. He had been loudly lamenting the unraveling of his world, curled up in a chair in Charley Arlinghaus' hospital room when Quinn arrived. Quinn's reappearance had brought the cathartic fit of crying to a premature and embarrassing end, adding to Kittredge's growing resentment of the giant man with crazy wolf's eyes who had tortured and then spied on him.

Kittredge realized that he was at Quinn's mercy yet again, having ridden to the hospital with him. "Where are we headed?" he asked.

"The world is our oyster," Quinn said. "Anywhere you want to go. As long as I want to go there, too."

"Would you mind dropping me off at my apartment? I need some sleep."

"Sure thing," Quinn said. "Actually, on second thought, I have some business at the National Mall. Mind if we stop on the way?"

Who has business at the freaking National Mall? Then Kittredge reminded himself that Quinn was in no ordinary business, as the salted wounds on his back could attest.

Is that my business now, too? Kittredge again lamented the greed and boredom that had prompted him to moonlight for Exel, and felt a flash of anger as he looked one last time at Charley's comatose frame. *What have you gotten me into?*

* * *

The sun shone brightly and the temperature was perfect. The leaves had turned but had not yet fallen, and Kittredge sat on a bench between the Lincoln and War Memorials, watching ripples traverse the reflecting pool beneath a brilliant autumn kaleidoscope.

A few hundred meters to his right, the gigantic figure of Abraham Lincoln sat perched like royalty in what had to be the world's largest stone chair. Roughly the same distance to his left, the long, arcing wall of the nation's War Memorial, which Kittredge viewed as an overdone homage to the grisly human cost of the military-industrial-political complex, sat bathed in mid-morning sunlight.

Waterfowl approached him for handouts, and tourists paraded past, snapping photos and chattering. It was a gorgeous fall day, the kind of interlude between the crushing summers and the bone-chilling winters that made living in DC bearable.

Quinn had left him on the bench with clear instructions: "Do whatever you want. I'll be back."

Kittredge was taking yet another ride on the emotional roller coaster, departing hope and rapidly descending toward despair, when an elderly gentleman sat next to him on the park bench. "Gorgeous day, no?" he said in a native Spanish speaker's accent.

Kittredge wasn't much in the mood for idle banter with strangers. "Sure is," he said.

"But if our minds and hearts are noisy, we cannot see what is before our eyes," the old man said.

Kittredge turned. The old man was looking at him, his eyes startlingly intense and his gaze presumptuously direct. The man wore a tan leather jacket and a bright red scarf. "Do I know you?" Kittredge asked.

"I think not," he said. "I am an old man and you are a young man, and our paths have not crossed."

Creepy.

Kittredge wasn't in the mood for another intrusion into his life. He started to stand up, but felt the old man's surprisingly firm grip on his arm keeping him down. "What do you want from me?" Kittredge asked.

"Nothing. But you may want something from me," the old man said. It wasn't just a Spanish accent, Kittredge realized. The man had a *Venezuelan* Spanish accent.

"I'm sorry, sir, I think you might have—"

"I haven't made a mistake. But *you* have. And you have new, unwelcome acquaintances in your life as a consequence."

Kittredge tried to rise again, but the old man tightened the grip on his arm. "Listen," Kittredge said.

"No, Peter Kittredge, please listen to me." The old man's stare intensified. "Your new friends are not friendly people. I do not like them, and neither do *my* friends. And, I think, *you* do not like them, either. So we all have something in common – you, and me, and my friends, that is."

The old man reached into his pocket and took out a small piece of paper, and handed it to Kittredge. On it, a phone number was scrawled in shaky script. "Call anytime you need assistance."

With that, the old man rose and quickly blended into the stream of passersby.

* * *

Kittredge paced back and forth inside his DC apartment, keenly aware that a hidden camera recorded his every move. The car ride back from the National Mall with Quinn had been uneventful, and the two men had exchanged scarcely a word during the fifteen-minute commute through the Sunday DC tourist traffic.

But Kittredge had noticed something unusual. Despite the cool autumn day, Quinn was perspiring. And he had seemed somewhat out of breath when he collected Kittredge from the park bench at the reflecting pond. Quinn wasn't dressed for exercise, so Kittredge wondered what Quinn had been up to during the time the strange old man had spoken with him near the reflecting pond.

But he didn't ask, because he realized he'd rather not know.

He stopped his pacing long enough to refill his glass of vodka. They were watching him get buzzed again, he knew, but he didn't care. He had to figure out what the hell was going on, and he had to figure out what the hell to do next. He felt the alcohol beginning to work its magic, and the apprehension and fear were beginning to loosen their grip on his psyche.

Let's try this one out: Charley's an innocent victim of a random crime. Maybe. DC still wasn't a terribly safe city if you went more than a block or two in the wrong direction.

But muggings in the airport parking lot were almost unheard of. *And he wasn't mugged.* The attackers hadn't even taken

Charley's cash. That meant that they didn't even try to disguise the attack as anything other than a targeted, deliberate act.

Plus, there was still the riddle of what Charley was doing in DC in the first place. Booty call? Business? Charley had lied to his bosses at Exel, and he had kept Kittredge completely in the dark about the trip.

Is Charley crooked?

Or, more precisely, was he more crooked than average? He was fond of observing that business, war, and politics were nothing but influence at the end of the day, and influence was about leverage, or the art of using what someone wants or needs in order to get what *you* want or need.

Over the course of their relationship, Kittredge had come to understand that Charley's thoughts along these lines were more personal credos than mere observations. Charley was no bright-eyed idealist, and Kittredge had seen him work angles with the best of them.

There's a word for that, Kittredge realized. *Manipulation.*

Charley was a manipulator. He'd never really thought about it in such stark terms before, but it was certainly the truth. Charley pushed and pulled a person's levers to gradually bring them around to working for his own interests. He was patient and subtle about it, but, Kittredge realized, there was an ulterior motive behind almost everything Charley did.

So where does that leave us? Or leave me?

Was the relationship a lie? Kittredge felt there were genuinely soul-baring moments, and the day-to-day stuff wasn't difficult, either, in the grand scheme of things.

Minus the manipulation. There was a lot of it, he started to realize, and usually over simple and silly shit, like emptying the dishwasher, doing the laundry, paying the bills. There was a thin layer of drama that covered things. Nothing too overt, but it was definitely there.

So, Charley Arlinghaus is undoubtedly a player. But in what game? And on whose side?

And do I want to keep letting him ball me? Undoubtedly, yes, Kittredge realized. Charley was amazing in bed, and he smelled good, in a way that never failed to get Kittredge turned on. That made up for many, many ills.

Kittredge called the nurse's station in Charley's hospital wing for an update. No news is good news, she told him. No more swelling, but no less swelling, either, and he was welcome to return during evening visiting hours.

As he ended the call, he felt his phone vibrate with a new text message. He looked at the small screen, and his blood ran cold. It was Arturo Dibiaso, demanding a dead drop at location four in Caracas. *Tomorrow evening.*

Chapter 13

Sam parked her dented Porsche in front of her bombed-out front lawn, and walked wearily past the plastic tarp covering the gaping hole in the front of her house. The front door had also been wrecked, and workers were busily clearing debris from the inside of the house through the large portal where the door used to be. She brushed past them with a grunt of acknowledgement and made her way upstairs to the bedroom.

She badly needed a shower and a change of clothes. And she needed some sleep. But first, she badly needed some answers from the man who shared her home and her bed.

Brock had just emerged from the shower when she walked into the bedroom. He was stark naked, muscular, and well-endowed. Sam felt a visceral wave of desire, but the excitement wasn't strong enough to penetrate the fog of her fatigue, and her worry over what Jarvis had told her about Brock.

"Hi baby," Brock said, leaning in for a kiss. "You look tired. We should take a nap." That was code for "we should copulate like rabbits, then fall asleep together."

She welcomed his embrace, but knew she could do neither of the things Brock implied without some answers first. "Who is Arturo Dibiaso?" she asked.

"Sounds like the start of a bad joke," Brock said.

"I wish it was. Do you know him?"

"Never heard of anybody by that name." Brock continued to towel off.

"Are you sure?"

"Pretty sure. I mean, if he's someone I've met somewhere along the way, I've certainly forgotten about it." He perched a leg atop the bed and dried his undercarriage, but stopped when he noticed Sam's intense gaze and troubled expression. "You look upset. What's up?"

Sam searched his eyes. They didn't waver. She'd never known Brock to lie to her, and she wouldn't have any idea what his giveaways might be if he ever did try to deceive her, but she didn't notice anything in his face. And Special Agent Sam Jameson was really good at catching liars.

She decided to honor their tacit but ironclad agreement not to pull punches or keep secrets. "Jarvis says he has phone records linking you to some Venezuelan guy named Arturo Dibiaso."

"Venezuela? Home of the hater?"

"Yeah, Hugo Chavez. Not a big fan of Uncle Sam these days."

"That describes just about everyone on the planet who isn't us," Brock observed. "What phone records? I mean, I don't think I've ever met a Venezuelan in my life. Plenty of Mexicans, though I don't have any of their phone numbers."

"I don't know. He didn't show me. But that's the reason they're suspicious of me. They think the dirty cops were linked to some Venezuelan gang, which is linked to someone in Chavez's regime, and they think you're linked to all of the above via Arturo Dibiaso."

"Sweet Jesus. What the hell gave them that idea?"

"The phone records, Brock. At least that's what Jarvis told me. After I sat through a damned polygraph test."

"Whoa! A lie detector? Aren't you on the A-team? What the hell were you doing taking a lie detector test?"

"They thought I was in on the thing, too."

"What *thing*?"

"I told you – that thing with the Venezuelans."

Brock sat down on the edge of the bed. "I know you said that, but I'm trying to figure out who the hell they think I'm talking to. I mean, I'm happy to talk to them, maybe set them straight."

"I don't know if that's a great idea right now. We have no idea what they really have on us."

"How the hell could they have anything on us? We haven't done anything?"

Sam cursed herself for feeling like she had to ask. But she had to ask: "Are you sure?"

"Baby, yes, I'm sure. I work in the Pentagon in military acquisitions. How many Venezuelans do you suppose there are, running around a US military weapons program?"

He looked at her. She seemed uncertain whether to believe him.

"And they have a military of, like, four donkeys and a biplane, don't they?" he went on. "I mean, I don't even know if they have an army. We could probably hand them everything we're working on, and they wouldn't have the first clue what to do with it."

Her eyes continued to search him. The part of her who knew

Brock James very, very well believed that he was telling her the truth.

The paranoid side of her was tough to ignore, though.

She felt that familiar panicky feeling begin again, the one that reared its ugly head whenever she started feeling vulnerable to a breach of trust by an important male in her life. *My bastard old man. Why won't he stay dead?*

Brock saw it coming on. "Baby, I don't know what the hell is going on, but I didn't find you and turn my life upside down to keep you, just to lose you by lying to you. I don't know Arturo whoever. Or if I know him, it sure as hell isn't by that name." He pulled her onto his lap and wrapped his arms around her. She felt stiff and distant. Afraid.

"Sam," he said, "I want you to trust me because I'm trustworthy and I'm telling you the truth. But failing that, I want you to dig through everything in my life, if you have to, in order to figure out that I'm shooting straight."

"Brock, I do trust you. I mean, I always have. And I don't know what they think they know, and half the time they're full of shit anyway. But it scared me. It *does* scare me."

"*I'm* not scared, baby."

"You should be. Big Brother thinks you're spying."

"Why? Tell them to dig through all my shit." Brock's voice rose. "You have all of my passwords. Use them. And I never go anywhere without one of my two phones, except inside the security vault, and even then, the phones are right outside the door. So you can track everything, can't you? Where I've been, who I've been with. I mean, they can do that, right?"

"I'm sure they already have. That's what worries me, because they think they've found something."

"Then let's figure out what's up. I don't want to pussyfoot around this. I haven't done anything wrong."

She looked at him a long moment. *Which voice to trust?* She felt certain he wasn't lying to her, but she couldn't tell if that was just because she desperately *wanted* him to be telling the truth.

Her own motivations aside, she knew that there was no such thing as fact without interpretation, especially in the counterespionage world. And there was no way to know whether Jarvis and Ekman were lying about there being some connection between Brock and Dibiaso. It could all have been a smokescreen. They could be chasing some other agenda she had no idea about, and they could easily have invented the Brock connection to get her out of their way.

She made her decision. "I trust you, and I love you. Or maybe I trust you because I love you. I don't know. But let's stay on the same team, okay?"

* * *

Sam and Brock had no sooner fallen asleep when her personal cell phone rang. "Hi, Dan." Her voice sounded groggy and thick with sleep.

"Guess it's *my* turn to wake *you* up. Isn't that a nice change of pace?" Dan Gable's voice was annoyingly loud and cheery.

Sam checked the number. Gable was calling from work. "Didn't I send you home hours ago?" she asked.

"Yes, but I got a call from the lab guys. I brought them in to analyze the bomb fragments. Are you sitting down?"

"Actually, I'm lying down."

"Right. Sorry. Anyway, it was definitely a military bomb, but not from anything in the US stockpile."

"That's a relief. I think. I don't know what I really expected. A bomb is a bomb, but it's nice to know that nobody in the US military wants to blow me up in my home in the burbs."

"I wouldn't go quite that far," Dan said. "We're pretty sure it's a US-made guidance kit. But we're tracking down whether it's a version that's used exclusively by our guys, or if it's an export version."

"Guidance kit? What are you talking about?" Sam asked.

"Sam, someone dropped that bomb from an airplane or helicopter," Dan said.

"And it guided to the ultraviolet beacon you found on the multi-specs?"

"We think so. Like I said, I don't know if it's an export version or not," Dan said. "We'll know more tomorrow, after the military makes it in to work."

"Export version? What do you mean?" Sam asked.

"Have you been living in a cave? Uncle Sugar is the biggest gun runner in the world. We make almost as many weapons to sell to other people as we make for ourselves."

Sam thought about this. Foreign bomb, US guidance kit, dropped from an airplane or chopper in US airspace, with an explosion in a US neighborhood. Terrorism? If so, it was the seriously ballsy variety of terrorism, the kind that says *I have access to government-only toys and I'm not afraid to rub your nose in it.*

It seemed outrageous on the face of it – a military bomb exploding in a US city? Unheard of. Sam would never have believed it in a million years. Except that it was *her* front lawn the bomb had rearranged.

And the guidance kit may or may not have been sold to another country. Either somebody in the US had gotten their hands on a foreign bomb and strapped a US guidance kit on it, or another country had used a bomb it had purchased from the US to commit an act of war on American soil.

More than likely, a third party was in the mix. It would explain the in-your-faceness of the move if a fringe group was behind the hole in her house. And it would leave plenty of plausible deniability if there was a foreign government somehow pulling the strings. Very sorry, they could say – rogue actor, and our best people are investigating, etc.

"Okay, thanks Dan. I've got to get some sleep, and then I'll chew on this some more."

"One more thing first, if you don't mind. Who's Fatso?"

Whoa. Sam knew her pause was too long, but she couldn't help it. She hadn't expected Dan to have any knowledge of what her polygraph test had revealed hours earlier, and she wasn't allowed to talk to Dan about it, anyway. It was asinine, but if she violated Jarvis' security order, it could land her in jail. "Why do you ask?"

"I walked by Ekman's office on my way to the pisser a minute ago. I overheard the name, and he looked like he'd been caught with his hand in the cookie jar when he saw me looking at him."

"I don't know what's going on," Sam said, knowing that her dodge was insufficient but unable to think of anything better to say to her deputy.

"Obviously. But who's Fatso?" Dan asked again.

"Nobody. Nothing to worry about. At least, nobody to worry about over an open phone line. You follow?"

Dan got the message, and changed the subject: "Where are you staying? You're not at home, are you?"

"Where else would I be? It's not like I'd be hiding from anyone, wherever I went."

"You could stay in a safe house."

"Sure, Dan. But that would require me to make up my mind about who the good guys were."

"Always paranoid."

"Can you think of a good reason not to be?"

Dan couldn't. He signed off, promising to update her as soon as he heard anything new. For the second time on the same Sunday, Sam told her deputy to go home to his family.

She collected Brock and went downstairs into the basement strong room. She shut and locked the door, and turned a recording of the surf on the stereo to drown out the noise of the construction upstairs. Workers had been called in to remove the shattered remnants of her bombed-out entryway and seal the opening from the elements.

Sam and Brock crawled in bed in the panic room and slept like the dead.

Chapter 14

El Jerga – The Shiv – boarded his flight in Caracas, Venezuela. He took his seat without so much as a nod to the person next to him. He wasn't big on conversation with strangers.

It wasn't that he wasn't talkative. It was just that he couldn't talk. A smashed trachea and larynx had almost killed him, a decade ago last spring. Injured on the job, but he couldn't exactly collect worker's comp. His reward for the excruciating suffering and the gruesome scar on his neck had been the privilege of more work for the same employer.

It wasn't like he could quit, though. Venezuela was a small country, and Caracas was not nearly big enough to hide a man like El Jerga. He was, consequently, a lifer. His work would end when *he* ended.

Scar tissue covered most of his damaged and deformed larynx, and his voice was a horrible croak, like tires on gravel mixed with an emphysema patient's death rattle. He didn't use it much. He let his hands do the talking.

He checked his messages one last time before the flight attendants began chirping about cell phone use. Just one message, from El Grande: stay on schedule.

As if I'd do anything else, El Jerga snorted quietly to himself. *Puta.* He pictured El Grande in his fancy office building with his young, nubile secretaries taking turns sucking him off while he stared out at the Caracas skyline. Even the Venezuelan Special Service, known for its ruthlessness and swiftness of action, had its strap-hanging bureaucrats.

But unlike most office-dwellers, El Grande had teeth and balls to go along with his occasional officiousness. It didn't stop him from grating on El Jerga's nerves, though.

He popped another pill to help him settle in for the five-hour ordeal to North America. The flight route would take them over millions of square miles of open ocean. Drowning in the ocean was El Jerga's second greatest fear.

Flying was his first. Pigeon, they sometimes called him. They had to throw a rock at him to get him to fly. He'd rather drive for two days than fly for two hours. El Jerga could easily look a man in the eyes while choking him to death, or blithely slit the throat of a pretty young *doncella* and watch the spark of life leave her body in bloody spurts, but he needed beta blockers to climb aboard an airplane.

The phone vibrated again. El Grande: don't wet your pants, Pigeon.

Puta.

The flight attendant began her scripted harangue, and El Jerga turned off his phone, closed his eyes, and tried to think of something pleasant. Like the upcoming job. He would get paid handsomely to unleash the nastiness at the center of him. What could be more pleasing?

Chapter 15

Peter Kittredge, Deputy Special Assistant to the US Ambassador to Venezuela and sometime-spy for Exel Oil, gazed absently out the large picture window of his eighth-floor DC flat. The view was spectacular, encompassing the Washington Monument and the Capitol, but he barely noticed. He was busy trying to figure out what to do.

He hadn't yet replied to Arturo Dibiaso's text requesting another dead-drop. It was a problem for a few tiny little reasons. First, the dead-drop location was in Caracas, Venezuela, and his boyfriend, Charley Arlinghaus, was lying in a coma in a DC hospital; second, the Central Intelligence Agency – or a couple of guys who did a damn convincing impersonation – were wise to his little moonlighting gig with Exel, and would undoubtedly want to play along in any Exel-related activities.

Third, he didn't have any of the information that Dibiaso wanted. He would have to collect it from the embassy before making the drop. That would be tough to pull off without raising suspicions.

Kittredge had less than twenty-four hours to figure a way through all of those snags, then fly back down to Caracas to collect the information from the embassy servers and make the drop across town for Dibiaso.

So you're saying there's a chance, Kittredge mused glumly.

Kittredge had always believed that problems and challenges

were often gifts that helped you think of new and better solutions, and you often ended up much better off for having dealt with them. But Peter Kittredge had never built himself a set of problems quite as prickly as this one.

So what to do from here?

He swilled his vodka. Fourth glass? Fifth? He couldn't remember. He was getting hungry, and knew he would have to venture out for food before heading back to the hospital to sit with Charley. For the moment, though, he took comfort in the burn of the booze in his empty gut, and let his growing buzz buff a few of the jagged edges off of his fouled-up world.

He briefly considered playing along with Dibiaso without telling his new Agency handlers, but quickly dismissed the idea. After all, Fredericks and Quinn had made him their reluctant guest precisely because they knew what he was up to. It was stupid to think that he could do anything without their knowledge.

And what was Dibiaso's rush, anyway? He had to know the situation with Charley, didn't he? After all, *they worked for the same damned company.* Charley had given Dibiaso's number to him way back at the beginning of this mess, eighteen lifetimes ago, so it wasn't like they didn't know each other at least a little bit.

So that meant that Dibiaso's hurry had a strong chance of being *related* to the attack on Charley. Which made Kittredge want to follow the string and see where it led.

But he didn't want to leave DC. Not with Charley lying in an intensive care ward with a smashed-in dome and a swollen brain. He wanted to be there when Charley woke up, to hold him, to hug him, to kiss his cheek. And to ask him *what the holy hell was going on.*

His phone rang. The caller ID displayed a number that brought instant adrenaline. "What do you want, Quinn?"

"Hello to you too, Peter. Hitting the bottle a little hard, aren't we?"

"I can't imagine why," Kittredge replied.

"Fredericks and I have an idea for what to do about the Dibiaso text."

Kittredge made a dumb decision to play dumb. "What text?"

Of course the Agency knew about the text from Dibiaso, but Kittredge was hoping for some clue about *how* they knew about it. Did they read his phone display via the video cameras planted in his apartment? Or were they tapped directly into his phone account?

Quinn didn't bite. "So anyway, as I was saying," Quinn said, "we think you ought to scoot back down to Caracas for a while. Make the drop, pick up the payment. Bing, bang, business as usual."

"Sure thing, Quinn. I'll just leave Charley in a coma, fly home, breeze into my office to pick up a few secrets, then hustle on over to make the drop while you and Fat Bill lurk in the shadows. I'm sure nobody will figure anything out, right?"

Quinn laughed. "My, you're a theatrical little gay guy when you've knocked back a few drinks, aren't you? But yes, that actually sums it all up very nicely. We've taken the liberty of making plane reservations for you. Your flight leaves tonight."

Kittredge slumped back down into a chair and noticed that the sky had started to grow dark. He let out a heavy breath. "Well, why the hell not, then? I'll do it. And you'll pull me out of jail when I get caught during my little smash-and-grab at the embassy?"

"Don't be so dramatic, Petunia."

"My name is Peter."

"How could I forget? Clean yourself up, pack a bag, and I'll pick you up in ten minutes. Food, hospital, airport. That's our plan." Quinn hung up.

Kittredge cursed, gritted his teeth, balled his fists, and cursed again.

Then he did what he was told.

* * *

The flight to Caracas lifted off thirty minutes behind schedule. Kittredge's buzz was rapidly turning to a hangover. He'd had a double vodka with dinner to help fortify himself for the view of Charley's black eye and swollen head, and he was relieved to discover that his strategy worked well. Mild drunkenness was a perfectly viable and largely painless way to endure life's difficult moments.

Quinn had dropped him off at the airport, and handed him a slip of paper as he climbed out of the Range Rover. It was another telephone number. Kittredge rolled his eyes. Before he could stop himself, he had blurted, "What is it with you guys and your freaking notes? It's like high school."

Quinn looked at him a moment, then burst into laughter. "What's so funny?" Kittredge asked.

"You. Thinking you could ever survive as a spy. It's hilarious." Quinn cackled. His features crinkled comically, and his huge shoulders shook up and down. "When your dick isn't getting you into trouble, your boozing picks up the slack."

"What are you talking about?"

"You just made a comment about people handing notes to you. I assume you mean the old Venezuelan guy in the red scarf on the park bench, right?"

Kittredge felt a little foolish, but not surprised. He had slowly resigned himself to the Agency having visibility into every one of his moments, and they had demonstrated their reach convincingly. Apparently his strange meeting with the old man on the park bench was no exception.

"I think it's probably obvious to you now that it wouldn't be a good idea to dial the number the old man gave you," Quinn said.

Though the vodka placed a pleasant patina on Kittredge's world, he couldn't mistake the note of menace in Quinn's voice. He bristled with alcohol-induced bravado. "Of course, Quinn. You and I. And Fat Fredericks. All the way. There's no 'I' in 'team.'"

"That's the spirit. And if you have any doubts about the right team to be on, Google 'National Mall' and see what pops up."

After clearing security, Kittredge had done just that. Apparently, an elderly man was the victim of a stabbing. Punctured aorta, the news report said. The reporter wondered, when would the district toughen up on crimes against tourists?

Could this get any crazier? He had wanted to belly up to one of the over-priced bars at Reagan International, but his flight was boarding. He had hustled to the gate, plopped in his seat, and pushed the "call" button above his head the instant the captain turned off the seat belt sign as the jet turned south into the night.

"Two vodkas, please," he asked the visibly annoyed stewardess when she found his seat. "And a cup of ice."

Chapter 16

Monday morning arrived with a vengeance. Brock and Sam awoke to a ringing telephone. The clock read 4:30 a.m. This time, it wasn't Sam's telephone disturbing the peace. Brock groaned when he saw the caller ID: Major General Charles W. Landers. His asshole of a boss.

"Morning, sir. What's the good news?" Brock sounded far more charitable than he felt, an art military men mastered over years of dealing with inconveniences and annoying superiors.

Brock listened for a while, then sat upright in bed. "Yes, sir," Brock finally said through clenched teeth. "I'm on my way."

"What was that about?" Sam asked.

"You," Brock said, climbing out of bed. "Landers wants to talk about a moral problem I seem to have."

Sam was instantly livid. "That little prick. I'm going to murder Jarvis."

"I understand that our living arrangement came up in casual conversation with your superiors yesterday," Brock said with forced civility. "Were you going to tell me about that?"

"Shit, baby, I forgot all about it," Sam said. "And it never occurred to me that those two ball-lickers would dime you out to your boss over something like this."

Brock disappeared into the small bathroom in the panic room, and Sam heard the shower. Several minutes later, Brock reappeared in his uniform, and leaned in to kiss her goodbye.

"It's four-thirty. What does Landers want at this hour?"

"To screw with me. And, apparently, he feels he has plenty of ammunition."

"I can't believe this," Sam said.

"We're held to a 'higher standard,' and all that," Brock said. "To the bureaucrats, 'almost divorced' is another way of saying 'married.' It's complete chickenshit, and only a chickenshit boss would think about it for a second. But that's Landers for you."

"Landers and Jarvis. I'm going to choke the life out of both of them," Sam said.

"Don't forget Ekman," Brock said. "Anyway, I'm sure it'll fade away soon enough. Don't sweat it."

"I forgot to tell you, that's the whole reason they started digging into our lives. It was over your pending divorce, and you and I living together before it's finalized. That's why they started all of this, and the pretext for finding this supposed connection with Arturo Dibiaso."

"I'm sure you'll crack the appropriate skulls. I'm due in Landers' office by five-thirty."

He kissed her and started to leave, but she stopped him, thinking of something from the prior day's events. "Baby, when did you first meet Fatso?"

"Germany," he said. "Why?"

"I know it was Germany, but what year? They seemed really hung up on the exact timing of when you met Fatso."

"Late 1997, early 1998 maybe. I don't know for sure. Anyway, why do they care about Fatso? I haven't seen him for years. And I get kind of sick of those jokes he always sends."

"Maybe you should leave me his number and address. I'll see what I can dig up."

"Okay. Go back to sleep, baby. I'll be home as soon as I can."

She smiled at him and pulled him in for a kiss. When he pulled away, he said, "I don't care what the bureaucrats say. Having you in my life is worth any price."

"I love you too," Sam said. "Come home for lunch. Let's roll around naked." Brock smiled, kissed her again, and left.

"And punch Landers in the throat for me," she yelled as he disappeared up the stairs.

* * *

Sam had just started to doze off again when her phone rang.

"Jesus, Dan. It's five a.m. No wonder Sara wants a divorce."

"Did she say that to you?" Dan Gable asked.

"No, but I can tell. You'd better get your act together. What are you doing in the office at this hour?"

"The bomb guys called. Definitely an American-made guidance kit, and it's definitely the American version."

"You mean it's not an export version?"

"Nope. One of our own. And Ekman asked about you already. Wants you to stop by his office when you get in, which he hopes is sooner rather than later."

Sam groaned. "Great." So much for catching up on a little more sleep.

* * *

"Hi Francis," Sam chirped with manufactured cheer as she walked into his office. She took pleasure in the look of annoyance that crossed Ekman's face. She didn't know why she pushed his buttons. Maybe it was because at times, he struck her as a bona fide douchebag. She hated douchebags.

Without a word, he handed her two pieces of paper. Each page had two columns. The left column contained what looked like times, arranged vertically in chronological order, and the right-hand column was full of what looked like map coordinates. "What am I looking at?" Sam asked.

"One page is Arturo Dibiaso's cell phone position data. The other page is from Brock James' phone. Look closely, and you'll see why Mr. Jarvis and I are concerned."

Sam looked closely at the numbers, and her heart sank. The position coordinates overlapped at multiple points, down to the second decimal place, for up to thirty minutes at a time.

It was clear that Brock and Dibiaso had spent some quality time in close proximity to each other.

She felt a lump form in her throat, and tears welled. She turned on her heel and walked out of Ekman's office, determined not to let him see her cry.

Chapter 17

Kittredge awoke to the airliner's cabin lights coming back on near the end of the redeye flight to Caracas, and some sort of inane announcement blaring over the PA system. The stewardess' nasal voice sounded like a bugle in a dumpster, and it clanged around viciously inside his pounding skull.

He smacked his lips and sensed the disgustingness of his breath. *Did a rat die in my mouth?* He felt awful, head spinning and heart pounding from the solid day of drinking. He hadn't slept long enough, and he awoke smack in the middle of a horrible hangover. He was certain that he smelled like a distillery, with the prior day's liquid courage off-gassing through his pores.

Fighting incipient nausea, he gathered his bag and trundled off of the airplane amidst the gaggle of passengers, feeling like livestock. Livestock with a crushing headache.

He passed a bar en route to the airport exit, and stopped briefly for a Bloody Mary to put a little bit of a shine back on. He couldn't possibly endure what lay ahead while fighting a hangover, he reasoned.

Constitutional complete, he stopped in the airport bathroom to brush his teeth, and picked up a coffee to go on his way to the taxi stand.

Caracas wasn't a large city by modern standards, but the cabbies knew where to find fares at four in the morning, and it didn't take long before Kittredge was on his way back to his Caracas flat for a shower and a change of clothes. And maybe one more little drink to keep his nerves in check.

Kittredge noticed headlights in the rearview mirror and turned to see a black SUV driving behind them. "Are we being followed?" he asked the cabbie.

The cabbie flashed a toothy grin. "Si. By many cars. And also we are following many cars."

Everyone's a comedian.

"You are nervous, Señor? Maybe you have diamonds in your pocket? Or you are *espia?* A spy?" The cabbie laughed. "Or maybe *paranoico.* Watch too many movies, eh?"

Kittredge didn't answer. He rode along in silence, and the cabbie dropped him off presently at the apartment he shared with Charley Arlinghaus. "Bye bye, Señor Bond," the cabbie said after counting the paltry tip Kittredge left him.

He climbed the stairs to the third floor and opened the door to his flat.

What the hell?

It looked like a war zone. Pictures hung at odd angles on the walls or lay shattered on the hardwood. Every book they owned was strewn on the floor, and Charley's beloved bric-a-brac had been tossed and shattered. The kitchen cabinets were wide open, and the floor looked like the aftermath of a Greek wedding. Shards of dishware covered most of the tile floor.

"Bastards," Kittredge repeated over and over as he surveyed the damage. He made his way slowly into the bedroom, where all of their clothes lay in a pile on the center of the bed. Every drawer had been removed from the dresser, and nothing remained hung in the closet. The master bathroom was similarly destroyed, with the contents of every pill bottle in the medicine cabinet now floating in the toilet.

Kittredge moved a pile of clothes and sat down heavily on the bed. Would calling the *policia* do any good? Would it make any sense? And which department would he even call? No fewer than four jurisdictions laid claim to this section of Caracas, a remnant of the 1989 Venezuelan decentralization that gave rise to a number of entrepreneurially-minded police entities that all competed with each other. Venezuela was a terrible place to be the victim of a crime.

And it wouldn't have surprised him if one of those police units was behind the redecorating effort.

He debated telling someone at the embassy, but quickly realized that the last thing he needed was embassy attention on his recent activities.

Looks like I suck it up, he concluded.

A thought struck. *What if Charley came home and found the place like this, and decided he had to get out of the country?* It wasn't entirely implausible. It might even account for the lie Charley told to his bosses. If he had gotten himself into a compromising position that led to his apartment being ransacked, he probably didn't want to jeopardize his position at Exel by letting the cat out of the bag.

But that wasn't a new revelation. Charley obviously lied to his bosses for a reason. It was a dumb lie, too, one that wouldn't stand up to even a cursory investigation. His dad in a DC hospital? It would take less than a minute to disprove the claim.

Or maybe it was completely different than that. *Maybe Charley was running from Exel Oil.* Maybe he hadn't called them at all. Maybe he had just fled, and they caught up to him in DC.

Or, more likely, Exel had someone waiting for him. It wouldn't take Nostradamus to figure out that Charley would likely make a stop at home before setting out on the lam.

That was an interesting scenario. Maybe Exel was the key.

But that still didn't solve the riddle of how Quinn and Fredericks found out about Charley's attack as quickly as they did.

The Agency and Exel. . . Are they in bed together? That would certainly explain a few things.

Kittredge sifted through the pile of clothes on the floor to find something clean to wear, located a towel, and showered. Moments later, he made his way down to the street for his one-mile walk to the US embassy.

* * *

It went like clockwork. No one at the embassy had heard about Charley's attack, which made Kittredge wonder whether Jim Bishop was full of shit when he said that he had heard about it from the embassy duty officer. But it worked to Kittredge's advantage, as he wasn't badgered by endless questions about Charley's condition, how the attack happened, or if the police had any leads. He was able to slip into his office without much notice from his coworkers.

He was senior enough to get his own office, which was really the random detail that made his brief and unsuccessful foray into espionage remotely possible. He shut the door, turned on his computer, and inserted the thumb drive into the USB slot.

That was highly illegal, of course. Every computer belonging to the US State Department flashed a warning screen on login that wagged a virtual finger in users' faces, warning them against inserting portable disk drives into government-owned computers.

For one thing, computer viruses often lurked in thumb drives. For another, using thumb drives made it relatively easy to do what Peter Kittredge was about to do.

He downloaded the week's message traffic on high-level economic developments with the Chavez government and its various quasi-governmental arms.

In true Latin- and South-American fashion, it was necessary to grease the palms of various Venezuelan functionaries and adjunct offices in order to receive the permits, licenses, and judiciary findings that allowed commerce. Bureaucracy was its own industry, and bribery was its conveyor belt. So the embassy kept tabs, to the best of its ability, on the most relevant crooked officials to approach in order to get anything done.

This was the information that Kittredge provided to Exel Oil. The message traffic was basically gossip. It was stupid, really, that any of that kind of information should be classified "SECRET." But it was most definitely classified, and that's what made Kittredge's next act fall unambiguously in the category of treason against the United States government.

He saved the relevant traffic streams to the thumb drive, which he placed in a small, smooth, cylindrical plastic container. Then he dropped his pants and hid the container where the sun didn't shine.

He breezed through the embassy's security checkpoint with nothing in his hands and walked out into the warm Caracas afternoon.

His hands shook and he felt adrenaline in his stomach as he did his best impersonation of a nonchalant pedestrian, and he had a moment of insight: he enjoyed the rush.

Exel had paid him reasonably well for his trouble, but they sure as hell hadn't paid him enough to be suitable compensation for the hellish nightmare he had endured over the past couple of days. But the satisfaction and enjoyment of a secret, the knowledge that he was getting over on his government and employer, gave him a perverse thrill. For a brief moment, he felt that the adrenaline rush might really be the thing his life had been missing.

Then a passing car's horn startled him, and he twisted quickly toward the sound. The sudden movement tore at the scabs that had begun to form on his lower back, where Quinn had used the belt sander and the table salt, and Kittredge was reminded that they called it cloak-and-*dagger* for a reason. And sometimes the dagger was in your own back. It wasn't a game for pussies.

Deep down, though he enjoyed the thrill of secrecy and the fun of running around acting like a spy, Kittredge knew that he was a lightweight. Everyone was a pussy at the right level of pain, but he suspected that his threshold was lower than average. That made him scared.

So he stopped for a drink at his local hangout.

It wasn't strange by Caracas standards, but it was definitely unusual behavior for a US government employee in the middle of a workday, and Kittredge wasn't smart enough to be concerned about his profile. He sat at a sidewalk table, ordered stuffed Arepa, a bread cake filled with fish and cheese, and sipped vodka while he waited for his food.

Movement caught his eye, and he looked up to see Bill Fredericks staring at him from across the street. His blood ran cold, and he flashed back to his unpleasant interrogation with Fredericks just a little more than twenty-four hours earlier. It seemed like a lifetime ago.

Fredericks walked across the street and approached Kittredge's table. "Hello, Peter. Helluva nice day, isn't it? A little muggy for my taste, but at least the temperature is agreeable."

"Hi Bill. Fancy meeting you here."

"I was in the neighborhood and thought I'd say hi to my newest friend. How's Company life treating you?"

"Go fuck yourself, Bill."

"You're still sore about the cameras, aren't you?"

"Yes. And my back hurts. And I don't appreciate what you did to my apartment. But thanks for asking."

"Well, I understand your anger, but I won't claim all of that antisocial behavior you just listed. And I'm glad we're friends now."

He smiled, but Kittredge didn't reciprocate.

"Anyway, just saying hi," Fredericks said. "We're here if you need anything."

"Making sure I behave myself?"

"Obviously. But here to help, too. Quinn gave you the number, right? Don't be afraid to use it if you need to."

"What a mensch," Kittredge said.

"Hey, no hard feelings, okay? Lunch is on me. Take care of yourself, Peter." Fredericks left the table, handed cash to Kittredge's waiter, and walked out of the café.

* * *

Kittredge finished lunch and wandered aimlessly until the appointed hour. Always between one and one-thirty in the afternoon. That was when foot traffic was heavy enough to cover the drop, but not heavy enough to interfere. Dibiaso likely wanted to be able to watch the whole thing unfold, and too thick a throng at the El Valle Metro station would obstruct the view.

The time finally came. The whole thing was ridiculously unsophisticated. Kittredge stepped into the men's room, pulled the container out of his ass and washed it off, and removed the thumb drive from the container.

Then he walked to the bank of pay-per-day lockers, deposited change in locker number sixty-nine (Kittredge always appreciated the innuendo), and locked the USB drive inside. That was it. Dead-drop, done. It went without a hitch.

He could return any time after three p.m. to retrieve the duffel bag full of silver bullion. He stopped at a bar to pass the time. Mental miscellany accompanied a double-vodka on the rocks, and helped Kittredge while away the two hours before he could collect his silver. Same-day pay was nice, but it contributed to his delinquency by giving him idle time across town from the rest of his life, time that he filled with booze.

He thought about the silver, and about how much he liked to pick it up, feel its heft, exalt in the shiny richness of it.

Oh, no. The silver! Was it still there?

He paid his tab and walked hurriedly out the door and around the corner to the Metro station. He rode to the end of the Blue Line at Plaza Venezuela, dashed through the turnstile and up the stairs, and bounded up the long escalator to the street. One half-block of Olympic sprint-walking, which was his interpretation of being in a hurry without being in a panic, brought him to el Banco de Caracas.

Sweating, he badged into the safety deposit room, found his locker, and inserted the key with trembling hands.

Empty. Fourteen pounds of pure sterling silver, the sum of his remuneration for selling US State Department secrets to Exel Oil, was gone. In its place was a note: *We'll keep this safe for you. Kisses, BF.*

Kittredge pounded his fist into the lockers and hollered curses. Women and children stared at him as he slumped to the floor. He fought back tears, progeny of his exhaustion, intoxication, and utter defeat.

They had bent him over in every way possible.

He sat leaning against the wall, arms folded over his knees, and cried quietly into his sleeve. He felt helpless, completely powerless to exert any control over any facet of his life. Friday night's booty quest had quickly morphed into a complete calamity.

Was there any corner of his existence that hadn't been violated over the past two days? He couldn't think of one. *My life is a shambles,* he repeated over and over to himself.

Despair turned to anger. Kittredge may not have been the most butch of men, but he was no milquetoast, either. He had picked himself up and dusted himself off plenty of times before. Granted, he had never before had his entire life reduced to rubble in front of him. But he knew how to persevere.

Sitting on the safety deposit room floor, Kittredge's anger hardened into resolve. He would find a way out of the situation. He would find a way to shove it up Fredericks' ass, he decided. And Quinn's too.

Chapter 18

Special Agent Samantha Jameson left her office at seven a.m., retrieved her dented Porsche from the parking garage at the Department of Homeland Security, and headed toward her bombed-out home.

As she drove in angry impatience, one thought occupied her mind, clouded her vision, and tore at her heart: *he lied.*

They didn't have any rules in their relationship except honesty. They'd both survived awful relationships, and had been stripped entirely of their patience for head games or manipulation. They had told each other viciously difficult truths about themselves, and some of those truths had caused pain for the other. But they had done it, because above all, they valued having no secrets between them. They always delivered it with love, but bare-naked, bare-knuckled honesty was the cornerstone of their relationship.

Until now. If Ekman's cell phone triangulation printouts were correct, it looked like Brock had taken miles-long car rides with a man he claimed not to know, on several different occasions.

Why would he lie to me about that? And who the hell is Arturo Dibiaso?

She knew that if it was true – if Brock had lied to her – it was over between them. Life was too short to wonder whether the man she loved was somehow playing her.

And it was pretty clear that he had lied to her. *Convincingly, too. Bastard.*

She had grown up in an environment like that. She could always tell that her old man was lying, because it happened just about every time his lips moved. Missed birthdays, all-night benders, promises long forgotten – they all took their toll on Sam's psyche, and she had lived the clichéd troubled teenager lifestyle to compensate.

She had let more douchebags than she could count climb all over her body and heart. All the while, she had vehemently denied her need for male affirmation even while seeking it desperately.

She had put herself together professionally, gone to a great school, caught the eye of the spook recruiters, and risen rapidly through the ranks at Homeland, but that was all elaborate overcompensation for the brokenness she felt.

She had endured shitty relationships with horrible men, most of them older, many of them married, all of them completely wrong for her. Her pinup model looks and razor intellect made her trophy material, and she had no shortage of attention. She hated them, but hated herself more.

She had been lying to herself and she knew it, but truthfulness seemed too bitter a pill. To acknowledge the truth would have meant the end of the life she had constructed. It was a horrible life, but change took courage. While Sam was a balls-to-the-wall counterespionage agent, her no-prisoners style had its limits. She knew that making the choice to see herself clearly would inevitably have demanded a life overhaul that she lacked the strength to undertake.

Unsurprisingly, she drank. A lot. Trembles and shakes were a daily reality toward the end. She almost didn't survive. One Tuesday morning, after returning from the convenience store with a fresh bottle of vodka, she had sat in her garage with the car motor running, daring herself to do nothing while the fumes overtook her.

Then, improbably and at a deep, wordless level within her, a will to live intervened. She turned off the car, went inside, and began living.

She hadn't thought that she could endure reality unvarnished by an insulating layer of inebriation, but she had beaten the odds and beaten the addiction. And she had thrived. Her sobriety was hard-won, but she did it all by herself. And she stuck to it. Thirty-eight months and counting.

She learned that life was precious, brutally short, and never to be wasted by putting up with bullshit. Especially from a lover. She lived with abandon and rolled with the punches in almost every other area of life, but she could never compromise on honesty. It was the center of her existence and the mechanism of her mental health.

I trusted you. She felt nauseous thinking of Brock's deception. *You were the one, you fucking bastard.* She loved him wildly and madly. She couldn't imagine walking the earth without him.

But she couldn't stay with him. He had lied. It would never, ever be the same between them.

Sam wiped her eyes and hardened her heart as she arrived home. She had to park across the street from her house, as the cleanup crew had placed a dumpster in her drive to collect the remnants of her bombed-out entryway.

She walked past the workers without a word, lost in her own private apocalypse. She packed a duffel bag full of clothes and sundries, and threw in three full clips of hollow-point .45-caliber ammunition for her Kimber semi-automatic.

She found a notepad and scrawled a note: "You broke our only rule, and you broke my heart." She pasted it to the bathroom mirror, walked back to her car, and drove away.

Chapter 19

Sam's phone vibrated. Phil Quartermain. The last time she had thought about him was when she left the John Abrams scene, which seemed like seven decades ago. Apparently, the crooked cop who had tried to Taser her hadn't gone inside the house to mess with Phil.

Or, maybe Phil was in on the thing, whatever the thing was.

She took a deep breath to try to cleanse the sobs from her voice. "Hi Phil."

"Darling, you sound positively awful," Phil said. She couldn't tell if the overt gayness was an affectation he had acquired since being fired from the FBI – for his gayness, everyone said – or if it was a natural part of himself that he had stopped suppressing.

"Rough day," she said.

"Boy troubles?"

"Among other things. How can I help?"

"Do you remember that key we found under John Abrams' flabby ass? I found a suitable lockbox for it."

"Where?"

"Can you come over? We'll talk then."

"Sure. You're at Metro?"

"No, I'm taking a sick day. I'll text you my address."

"See you in a few," Sam said.

The text with Quartermain's address arrived seconds later, and she left the parking spot by the greenbelt near her house, where she had gone to think and suffer in private. She rounded the corner and headed toward 395 Southbound, which would take her to the Shirlington address.

Shirlington was a hip little micro-development with a couple of high-rise apartment complexes and a number of trendy shops, stores, restaurants, and boutiques. Like all of DC, it was overpriced, but not pretentiously so. Probably a great place for a single guy to live.

As she accelerated up the on-ramp onto the highway, she noticed a DC Metro police cruiser tuck in behind her. Her pulse quickened. *Not this again.*

She only had a couple of miles to go before the Shirlington exit, but Sam got all the way over in the far left lane. The police cruiser remained a dozen car lengths behind her, but followed her lane changes. *I'm so over all of this,* she thought.

She moved back over into the right lane and slowed to a crawl. The cruiser followed her lane changes, but came up on her quickly as she lowered her speed. Her move was designed to force the issue – either the cop would have to slow down below the flow of traffic to remain behind her, making it excruciatingly obvious what was going on, or he would have to go around her.

The policeman did a little of both. He stayed behind her for a while, until he realized how drastically she had slowed. Then he went around. She noted the car number as he drove past, and jotted it down on a parking garage receipt. She left a message for Dan Gable to track down the officer behind the wheel. Following her was a pretty brash move in light of the weekend's events, and Sam planned to find a way to get her boot on the guy's throat.

Her heart rate had almost returned to normal by the time she arrived at Phil Quartermain's building. She rode the elevator to the twelfth floor and walked around to find apartment #1223.

It was a nice building – relatively new, well-appointed even by DC standards, and very clean. *Maybe Brock will move down here.* She realized that she really did think it was over between them. Lies were deal-breakers. But she knew that breaking up with Brock was going to be like losing a limb. She would never be the same.

Apartment #1223 was as far away from the elevators as possible, and she walked the entire length of a long hallway before arriving. The door was ajar. "Hi Phil," she said, rapping lightly.

When she didn't get a response, she called out and knocked a bit louder, but with the same result. She started to get a feeling of dread, like she knew what she was about to discover. She inhaled deeply to steady herself, and smelled the unmistakable, metallic scent she had come to recognize all too well.

She drew her .45, chambered a round, removed the safety, and announced her presence: "Federal agent. Hands up!"

Hearing no response, she kicked the door open, then immediately moved for cover around the jamb and listened intently for any movement. Backup would be ideal – necessary, most would say – but it was a luxury she didn't have. Quartermain might still be alive, but if there was enough blood for her to smell it from the entryway, he wouldn't be alive for long.

Sam ducked through the doorway and rolled quickly to her right, crouching behind the kitchenette counter. She peered around the edge and saw that the apartment opened beyond the kitchenette into a large room, but her view was obstructed by a large L-shaped couch. She listened again for movement, shouted again for hands up, and made her way toward the edge of the couch, being careful to stay low.

She peered around an end table and was instantly revolted by what she saw. Phil's throat had been slit from ear to ear. The cut was catastrophically deep, and she could see the white cartilage of his exposed trachea. The carpet was soaked in his blood.

It took discipline to clear the rest of the flat, but it wouldn't be healthy to be caught off guard by the killer if he was still on the scene. So she took her time.

The killer was long gone, and she returned to the great room to snap photos of the scene.

The large ottoman had been displaced from its carpet indentations, and a lamp had been knocked over, indicating a brief struggle. Quartermain had fought, but it hadn't taken the killer long to subdue him, and saw the knife through his throat. Either the killer was a strong guy, or he had gotten the jump on Quartermain. Maybe both.

Sam realized that she had a problem: she didn't know who she should call to report the murder. She wasn't about to give the Metro guys unfettered access to her, especially after her most recent encounter moments ago on the freeway.

But until there was a bureaucratically compelling reason for Homeland to assert jurisdiction, the Metro guys called the shots, and they always got first dibs on a scene.

Safety over protocol, she decided, dialing Dan Gable's number. As the phone rang, she looked absently around the apartment. A bright pink box caught her eye on the kitchen counter.

A music box.

The music box. Evidence in two crimes, and maybe an act of international terrorism. Or an act of war.

No way was she going to let Metro screw it up. *Or cover it up.*

Gable's voicemail picked up, and Sam cursed her luck. She really needed to talk to Dan about the events of the last half hour, and about the music box. Subconsciously, she hoped he would talk her out of doing what she was about to do, which was either a misdemeanor or a felony, depending upon how pissed off the attorney general got about it.

"Dan, please call me right away," she said to his voicemail, then hung up her phone, realizing instantly how screwed she would be if Big Brother played the "where is Sam Jameson's iPhone?" game using the same technology that had earlier revealed Brock's deception. *No turning back now.*

She made her way to Quartermain's closet, looking for a duffel bag or backpack she could use to abscond with the music box. She wrapped her hand in her shirt before touching anything to avoid leaving prints.

She found what she was looking for behind a raincoat, and quickly zipped the music box inside a black backpack, again being careful not to leave fingerprints.

As she hooked the backpack over her shoulder and made for the door, movement caught her eye. Red and blue emergency lights reflected rhythmically off the high-rise across the street, and Sam rushed to the window. Two Metro cruisers were parked at the curb.

She dashed for the stairwell, not bothering to shut the door to Quartermain's apartment on her way out. She ran down the hallway toward the elevators, arriving just in time to hear the *ding* of an arriving elevator car.

The door hadn't opened a third when she recognized the black uniform and shiny metallic flair. Cops.

The nearest cop had his head turned away from Sam, and spoke into the radio transmitter clipped to his shoulder epaulet as he stepped out of the elevator. The far policeman turned to look in Sam's direction, but was distracted by another resident getting in the elevator.

With every ounce of nonchalance Sam could muster, she put her phone to her ear and walked casually toward the open elevator door. She held her breath as she walked past the policemen, and prayed silently as she stepped into the elevator.

The doors closed. Sam breathed a sigh of relief as the elevator descended toward the lobby.

She glanced at the man in the elevator with her. She noticed the cleaning company logo on his shirt. Her eye was drawn to a horrific scar on the man's neck, but she looked quickly at his eyes as he turned to greet her.

"Buenos dias," croaked El Jerga.

Part 2

Chapter 20

Hector Yosue Alejandro Javier Mendoza – El Jerga, The Shiv
– looked at the tall, strikingly beautiful woman in the elevator next
to him. She had flame-red hair, brilliant green eyes, a strong but
feminine jaw, and a tall, athletic frame.

He was instantly captivated. If she were for sale or rent, he
would gladly pay a premium for her. He wished that his favorite
brothel stocked such quality. He had long ago resigned himself to the
role of a frequent customer; it was how men as ugly as El Jerga had
satisfied their carnal needs since the dawn of time.

The woman looked nervous, El Jerga noticed. His adrenaline
was still up from the job he had just completed – there was a
struggle, and those killings were always interesting – but this woman
seemed far more unsettled than he felt. Her brow was furrowed with
worry.

When the elevator reached the ground floor of the Diplomat
Tower, El Jerga let the woman exit first. This polite gesture afforded
him the opportunity to watch her exquisite ass as she walked away.
She rounded the corner, out of sight. *Pity.*

Watching a man's life squirt from his severed jugular had
awakened a dark and primal arousal, and the sight of the gorgeous
redhead had amplified the effect. Death was a sexual pleasure for El
Jerga, which placed him in the enviable category of those who dearly
loved their chosen profession.

El Jerga decided that he would ply his DC contacts for the right kind of companionship to channel his awakened energy and pass the time until his next job.

* * *

Sam rounded the corner of the Shirlington apartment lobby quickly. Something about the short man with the ruddy complexion and grisly scar on his neck had creeped her out. It seemed as though the man was leering, even while he stared straight ahead.

Thoughts of the unpleasant elevator ride faded quickly. She had bigger things on her mind.

She was surprised that whoever had killed Phil hadn't taken the music box with them. It was evidence in the John Abrams murder, the staged suicide that she and Phil had investigated in the middle of the night.

She rounded the corner in the lobby, and caught sight of the blue and red Metro DC police lights. Her thoughts snapped back to the present, and the new rush of adrenaline in her veins washed away the fatigue.

Dan Gable had told her about the gang of crooked Metro cops who were moonlighting for some unsavory people. But she had no idea why those crooked cops might be targeting *her*.

And she also had no idea which team the individual cops on the scene, whose cruisers were now parked outside the Shirlington residential high-rise, happened to be playing for.

Should she do the right thing by approaching one of the Metro guys with an offer to help work the scene of Quartermain's murder, or provide them with some background on what she and

Quartermain had been working on?

Not in a million lifetimes. The opposition had already demonstrated a willingness to use deadly force, and she wasn't eager to further test their resolve.

That narrowed her options down to one: *time to get the hell out of here.*

Sam retreated back around the corner toward the elevators, hugging the far wall to stay out of the line of vision from the street through the large wall of windows at the tower's entrance. It was an art form to sneak around without appearing to sneak around, and Sam's years as a counterespionage agent had taught her well.

She found her cell phone and turned it off – no sense making it easy on the bastards – and located the doorway leading to a stairwell.

Locked.

You've got to be kidding me. Fire codes demanded stairwell entrances remain open at all times, but the increase in vagrancy after the recession had led some upper-end residences to risk a citation in order to keep people from sleeping in the stairwells.

Sam fumbled in her pocket for her keychain, which had a stylized red heart charm. She gave the charm a twist, and a lock pick snapped open from the side of the heart, much like a switchblade knife.

The lock yielded in seconds, and Sam descended the stairs to the first level of below-ground parking, dodging a snoozing bum. *The way my week's going, I might be joining you soon, buddy,* Sam thought.

She opened the door to the parking garage and was instantly

assaulted by more flashing police lights. There was a line of cars leading up the ramp to the parking garage exit, and a police cruiser was stationed at the top of the ramp. The police were either searching cars, or had completely closed off the exit.

Either way, it was clear that she wasn't going anywhere by car. And if these particular Metro guys were in cahoots with Everett Cooper and company, it was a safe bet that they already had her Porsche under surveillance.

All of that had happened extremely quickly. She was pretty sure that she had been the first person on the scene of Phil Quartermain's murder, so it was uncanny that Metro had responded so quickly, and in such force. It reinforced her decision to get the hell away from the scene as quickly as possible.

It's a nice day for a walk, Sam thought with a gallows chuckle. But there was the small problem of how to exit a subterranean parking level without getting nabbed.

The answer, of course, was to exit via a non-subterranean parking level. Many buildings had them, usually bordered by a waist-high concrete wall. Sam hoped the Diplomat Towers had hired the same architects. She retreated back into the stairwell, climbed a half-level above the lobby, and tried her luck by opening the door.

Hallelujah. She reemerged into the parking structure, and her insides unclenched at the sight of daylight spilling over the low wall.

She held her breath as she walked past a bank of elevators and peered over the wall. It wasn't quite ground level, but it was low enough to jump to the alleyway below.

She surveyed the area as she tightened the backpack straps. No one was looking at her. She heaved herself over the wall, dangled briefly by her fingertips, and jumped to the pavement below.

She found herself next to the Harris Teeter grocery store loading dock, and walked past an open doorway. Smelling opportunity, she looked inside, then walked quickly through the back door to the popular big-city grocery chain.

Seven steps forward took her to the retail floor, and she joined lunchtime shoppers in the deli section. She bought a ham sandwich, extra jalapeños.

En route to the checkout counter, she picked up a pair of oversized sunglasses and a white scarf, paid, put the scarf over her head to hide her blazing red locks, and walked out of the grocer onto the street, doing her best imitation of someone who wasn't on the lam.

Always assume you're being watched, she coached herself, *and act appropriately.* It would have been unusual for someone *not* to stare at the police cars parked on the street one half-block away, so Sam paused briefly to watch the spectacle.

Then she took off at a medium pace in the other direction, passed the Shirlington Public Library, walked around an in-sidewalk fountain, and followed the southeasterly bend in the road. Moments later, the Diplomat Towers were out of view behind her. She felt her heart rate begin to slow.

Now what? She was alone and on foot in what had become occupied territory. She needed information and help, but using her cell phone for any appreciable length of time was out of the question – they would triangulate her position, and she would be rolled up within minutes.

That gave her an idea. She turned the power on to her phone.

A message from Brock popped up: "I can't wait to see you." Her heart sank. They had made a lunch date for today, a ritual they had enjoyed since their fiery romance had begun two years earlier.

Another notification chimed: six missed calls and three voicemails, all from Brock. As she walked down the street away from the commotion behind her, she listened to the first message: "Baby, what's going on? I got your note and I'm really confused. I don't know what you're talking about – I'm completely yours in every way, and I don't know what rule I broke or what you're upset about. Are you still coming home for lunch? Let's figure this out, okay? I love you, Sam, and I want to work this out, whatever it is, okay? I mean, anything at all – let's just figure it out. I love you."

The next message was more urgent, and she heard panic in his voice in the third message: "Sam, I don't know what the hell is going on, but I just noticed that your overnight bag is gone. Baby, what is this? Is there someone else? I thought this was something special, and I turned my life upside down for you, and I'm not giving up. . ." She stopped listening, the tears falling from behind her sunglasses. *He still isn't coming clean.*

She took a deep breath and felt her diaphragm flutter with emotion. *Get your shit together,* she admonished. *Play the hand you're dealt, and cry about it later.*

She looked up Dan Gable's contact information in her phone and wrote his office and home digits on a receipt she retrieved from her wallet. She talked to Gable by phone a hundred times every week, but in the digital age, when smart devices remembered everything humans used to remember, she had no idea what the numbers were.

Sam quickened her pace, barely noticing the hip restaurants, bars, and boutique shops on the way to the traffic intersection. She approached the end of the line of vehicles waiting for the light to change, and found what she was looking for: a pickup truck.

It was exceedingly large, and the small man in the driver's seat barely saw over the steering wheel. *Standard,* Sam thought. *Big truck, tiny johnson.* Loud music blared from the speakers inside the truck.

She crossed the street before the intersection, directly behind the big pickup waiting at the light, palming her cell phone. In one smooth motion that would have made her spook school instructors proud, she wedged her phone on the waist-high bumper between the chrome trailer hitch and the license plate holder.

Sam reached the other side of the street as the light changed, and she watched the truck drive away and turn right onto the highway on-ramp. They – whoever the hell was trying to track her down this particular minute – would certainly be watching her cell phone signal move away from Shirlington on I-395 Southbound.

Throwing away her cell phone was like losing a piece of herself, but she knew it was necessary. *And it's probably time to quit wasting so much time playing that stupid bird game.*

A new problem to solve: connectivity. She surveyed the street and found a convenience store, and paid cash for three prepaid burner phones. They weren't untraceable, of course, but the burners had no associated account information, so if she used them carefully, it would be exceedingly difficult to trace them back to her.

She unwrapped the phones and threw them into her backpack, then walked across the street to the Sherwood Indie Theater. *Breakfast at Tiffany's* was showing at 1:00 p.m. *Random, but convenient.*

She bought a ticket from the bored cashier and sat down in the dark theater, alone, with eleven minutes to spare.

Sam cried through the previews, thinking of Brock and what his deceit had taken from her. She loved him fiercely, until several hours ago at least, and she couldn't imagine life without him.

But it was her new reality, and as Audrey Hepburn made her dramatic appearance, Sam resolved to adapt.

Chapter 21

The assassin called Quinn was on his knees, gag in his mouth, naked, with burgeoning whip welts on his backside. His dominatrix stood behind him.

She released his feet from their shackles. He stood shakily, still breathless. Quinn towered over her petite frame, but despite her diminutive stature, he still felt thoroughly dominated in her presence. It was surely an art.

Perhaps this kind of liaison fulfilled a deep need to experience some semblance of temporary retribution for all of the submission he had forcibly inflicted on his many victims over the years.

Or maybe he was just a kinky bastard.

Some people preferred a couch, soft music, and a therapist. Quinn preferred a riding crop and a ball gag. He didn't give it too much thought.

Quinn had paid in advance, customary terms in the oldest profession, so there was only the awkward business of dressing and getting ready for the rest of the day.

His pants were barely zipped when he felt the all-too-familiar vibration in his pocket. Fredericks. He sighed. "Hi, Bill," he answered. "Working on your sun tan?"

"Funny," Fredericks said. "Actually, I'm really working my ass off down here. Speaking of which, how about getting on a plane?"

"No, thanks. It's my day off."

"We need you down here in cucarachas, or whatever the hell they call this dump."

"Caracas."

"Right," Fredericks said. "So, you'll be on the first flight out then?"

"What's the rush?"

"Curmudgeon is pissed, says we're not moving quickly enough, says the Intermediary is breathing down his neck."

"The usual, in other words."

"You're too young to be cynical."

"I blame you," Quinn said.

"Sorry to have taken the idealistic gleam out of your eye. So, I'll see you in a few hours?"

Quinn sighed again. He enjoyed frequent changes of scenery, but he also enjoyed a day off every now and then. "Which account do you want me to use?"

"Use the OS dossier."

Holy shit. Operation Syphilis? Rumored to be the brainchild of the Facilitator himself, distasteful moniker notwithstanding. "Are you sure?"

"No, I'm making all this up," Fredericks deadpanned. "Of course I'm sure. Stop thinking and start traveling." Fredericks hung up.

Quinn found himself feeling nervous. Operation Syphilis was serious business, at least the portion of the op that he knew about. He finished dressing and was almost to his Land Rover when the phone buzzed again. "I forgot to tell you that I need you to bring the dry cleaning," Fredericks said, then hung up before Quinn could reply.

It was code, of course, for a pickup. Not a dead drop, which usually went quickly, but a meeting at a safe house with a live agent. It meant he was supposed to pick up something that came with special handling instructions. *There goes the afternoon.*

* * *

Quinn returned to his hotel, paid cash for two more nights, collected his belongings, and left the room empty with the "do not disturb" sign hanging on the door. The room still smelled a little bit like sex and perfume, remnants of the two women whose company he'd enjoyed a couple of nights earlier, and the recollection left a lingering pleasantness that put a rosy patina on the excruciatingly boring procedure he now undertook.

He drove south of town and parked his Land Rover at a park-and-ride facility, then caught the northbound train back into the city, overnight bag slung over his shoulder.

He bought a newspaper from a kid on the train, discarded everything but the fashion section, and pretended to read the inane articles covering hem height, appropriate neckline depth, and all sides of the question of whether cheetah-patterned high heels were appropriate for the workplace. Forcing him to read the fashion section was undoubtedly a cruel joke perpetrated by Fredericks, and Quinn vowed revenge.

His discomfort was rewarded when he exited the underground Metro station to find a cab waiting at the curb. The cab number – 12114 – corresponded to the rendezvous instructions.

"Helluva day," the cabbie said. "I should be at the game."

Quinn finished the challenge-and-response ritual: "Are the Senators playing today? I've been too busy to keep up with their schedule."

The cabbie shut the door for Quinn and wedged his cab back into the growing DC gridlock. The two Agency men made small talk during the hour-long journey to the meeting place, a nondescript unit in a Falls Church condominium complex.

Quinn had long ago stopped wondering how many such places the Agency maintained, but he was sure it was an impressive number. He had never used the same safe house for more than one operation. *Dirty institutions do paranoia pretty damn well,* he thought with an internal chuckle. He surmised that it also helped to have a bottomless budget and almost no public scrutiny.

"Keep the change," Quinn said as he exited the cab, loudly enough for the microphones hidden in the bushes to pick up over the traffic noise. It was never smart to surprise anyone at a safe house. He rang the doorbell twice and knocked once.

Seconds later, Quinn heard heavy footfalls, and the door opened to reveal a portly, bookish fellow four hairs taller than five-seven. Another challenge-and-response sequence preceded Quinn's entry into the dark eighties-era condo.

"Whatcha got for me?" Quinn asked as he plopped himself onto a sofa that predated the condo by at least a decade.

"The name's Alfredson," said the slightly rotund fellow with the academician's face. "Thanks for stopping by. Don't get much activity these days, with things winding down overseas."

"Winding down? We're killing more people than the plague," Quinn said.

"By drone," Alfredson lamented. "Not much work for the biologicals department anymore."

"Biologicals? I'm not getting paid nearly enough to haul that shit around."

"That's what guys like you usually say," Alfredson said, obviously sizing Quinn up and placing him in the appropriate mental category. "But you'll probably want to pay attention. It's a little nasty."

"So I shouldn't mix it in my cocktail on the plane?"

Alfredson didn't laugh. "You shouldn't open the package at all until you're in the approved environment for the operation."

"Did you memorize that sentence just for me?"

"And you shouldn't open the exterior package, either, until you're in the approved environment." Alfredson looked stern.

"You're all business, aren't you?" Quinn said. "Why all this trouble for syphilis?"

Alfredson snorted. "Who told you this was syphilis?"

"I assumed that since this is Operation Syphilis. . ." Quinn said, shrugging his shoulders.

"Fredericks," Alfredson said, shaking his head. "He thinks he's much funnier than he really is. This is definitely *not* syphilis, though it is a strain of a disease that is sometimes transmitted sexually."

"AIDS? No way will I transport that shit on a plane, I don't care who's asking," Quinn said.

Alfredson rolled his eyes. "It's an engineered variant of Hepatitis C." Noticing the relief on Quinn's face, Alfredson said, "You shouldn't be relieved. This stuff will kill you much, much faster, and there's no drug cocktail around that will make any of the suffering go away."

Quinn let out a long sigh. Whatever happened to a good old fashioned knife hit, or a bullet to the temple? The world was going to hell. It was all satellites, germs, and remote-controlled drones these days. Quinn had the acute awareness that his was a dying breed.

"Are you listening? This is important." The germ scientist looked intensely at Quinn.

"Sure, sorry," Quinn said.

"This virus causes cirrhosis of the liver. Normal Hepatitis C infection causes a similar result, but it acts slowly, over a number of years. We've tweaked the replication proteins to remove some reproductive inefficiency, and this particular virus acts several million times faster."

"Aren't you afraid you're going to wipe out the human race?" Quinn asked.

"No. It's not possible. The disease kills too efficiently to spread that far. People don't stay alive long enough to infect each other in large enough quantities."

"Like Ebola," Quinn said.

"Exactly." Alfredson held out what looked like an expensive fountain pen. Quinn noticed the distinctive Montblanc logo. The letters *HC* were monogrammed in gold lettering.

"What do I do with this thing when the time comes? Do I stab him with it?"

"No. This is a normal pen. You hand him the box," Alfredson said, brandishing a Montblanc pen case. "The virus is skin-permeable, and it's embedded in the felt. When he removes the pen, the virus seeps into his body through his fingertips."

Quinn shook his head. "You bastards are evil."

"You should talk," Alfredson said.

"Touché. Shouldn't we be wearing a breathing thingy right now?"

"Not necessary. The virus is chemically bonded to the felt, and will only break free by abrasion. Just keep the case closed, and keep it in its wrapping paper until the time comes."

Quinn shivered. "This freaks me out."

"I thought you were a steely-eyed killer," Alfredson chided. "Just keep the thing closed until it's time, and you'll be fine. Everyone around you will be fine, unless you let them paw the interior of the pen case."

"If you're wrong, I will hunt you down," Quinn said.

Alfredson smiled. "If I'm wrong, you won't have time to hunt me down."

"What if he doesn't open the pen case?"

"Then I guess we hire a real assassin," Alfredson said.

Quinn erupted in laughter. "A real assassin. That's the funniest thing I've heard in weeks."

Chapter 22

Peter Kittredge was drunk again. He had left the bank's safety deposit room, which used to contain every last ounce of silver Arturo Dibiaso had paid him, but now contained just a note from "BF" promising safekeeping of the ill-gotten bounty. Kittredge had bellied up at the nearest bar, serious about drowning his sorrows.

"BF" was undoubtedly Bill Fredericks, and after a brief emotional meltdown that had caused bank patrons to stare at him, Kittredge had vowed to find a way to make Fredericks pay for the innumerable indecencies he'd inflicted over the past forty-eight hours.

Fredericks and Quinn had tortured him and broken into his DC apartment to install hidden cameras.

And they had probably also trashed the Venezuela flat that he and Charley Arlinghaus shared together.

Charley. In his anguish over the missing silver, the missing skin on his lower back, and his ransacked apartment, Kittredge had momentarily forgotten about his lover of two years, who was still in a DC hospital, lying in a coma.

The Agency goons had been the ones to inform Kittredge about the incident, which made him wonder whether they weren't behind *that,* too. He felt a sudden, desperate urge for an update on Charley's condition, but couldn't work out a way to get more information without alerting Fredericks or Quinn. And at the moment, Kittredge felt that he would rather murder both of them than have a conversation of any sort.

Kittredge waved to the bartender and was ready to shout out his order above the growing din of the Monday afternoon crowd when he felt a clap on his shoulder. "Hi, Peter," said a now-familiar voice.

"Fredericks." Kittredge slurred.

"You should slow down, Pete."

"It's Peter, asshole."

"Right. You should let up on the booze, *Peter Asshole*. You have work to do, and I don't have time to dry you out."

Kittredge's annoyance reached a boiling point. "I'm not doing a damned thing for you, Bill."

"That's the booze talking," Fredericks said with a smile. "Of course you're going to do things for me. Have you forgotten our little written arrangement? I'm sure you remember – it gave you immunity from punishment for your *capital crime of treason*." He paused for effect, then said, "With a couple of tiny strings attached."

"Strings?" Kittredge bellowed. Fredericks shushed him.

"Strings?" Kittredge started again in a more subdued voice. "You've put my boyfriend in a coma, torn up my apartment, and now you've robbed me!"

Fredericks shook his head, laughing. "You give me way too much credit. And you're accusing me of *robbing* you? That's a little dramatic, don't you think? I mean, did you really think we were going to let you keep the money you earned by spying?"

He has a point, Kittredge realized.

He felt his anger subside a bit. Fredericks *did* have him over a barrel, to be sure, but things could be much worse. He could be facing a trial for treason, for example. It occurred to Kittredge that in the current context, doing a few odd jobs for a decidedly disagreeable CIA case officer wouldn't be the end of the world.

At least until I can figure out how to turn the tables.

"Okay," he finally said. "What do you want?"

"Go home. Sober up. I'll call you." With that, Fredericks was gone.

* * *

Kittredge wandered slowly back toward his apartment, in no hurry to face the disaster that awaited him. They had left almost nothing untouched, and had gone out of their way to break his and Charley's belongings, as if they were making a point.

Fredericks hadn't actually denied ransacking their place. He had merely accused Kittredge of giving him too much credit. Kittredge fumed anew, cursing that smug torturing deviant Quinn, and that fat bastard Fredericks.

An ocean breeze whistled through the mountain valley, gaining strength, and the Caracas air grew chilly. Kittredge stuffed his hands in his pockets. Two slips of paper grabbed his attention, and he pulled them out to examine them.

One had a US telephone number written on it, followed by the words "XOXO, Quinn." *Go to hell, Quinn.*

Kittredge examined the other slip of paper. It contained a Venezuelan number. It was given to him the previous afternoon, on the park bench in the National Mall, by the old man in the red scarf.

Whom Quinn had subsequently killed, Kittredge thought with a shudder.

Quinn and Fredericks were fantastically horrible people, Kittredge decided, and they badly needed someone to kick their asses for them. A good ass-kicking restores an appropriate level of humility, which a man could easily lose when he tortures and kills other people for a living.

To hell with both of you.

It was likely due to the combination of his rage, inebriation, and the pervasive but incorrect sense that he didn't have much left to lose, but Kittredge felt emboldened. He pulled a few *centimos* from his pocket, stopped at the next pay phone, and dialed the Venezuelan number.

His heart pounded as the phone rang, and he felt himself sobering up with each passing second. He imagined the potential ramifications if Fredericks or Quinn caught him.

And there was a very good chance that they would catch him, he realized.

He had nearly lost his nerve, and was just about to hang up the phone when a voice came on the line, sealing his fate. "Buenos noches. We have been waiting for your call," the man said.

"Buenos noches," Kittredge replied. "I, uh—"

"Do not speak, Peter Kittredge," said the man at the other end of the phone line. "Do not go back to your apartment. Throw away your cell phone. Take the Red Line to the Santa Marta station. Wait for a man in a John Deere hat. He will ask you a question. The answer is five-thirty."

The line went dead.

Kittredge did as he was told, with one exception. Instead of throwing away his cell phone, he placed it in the safety deposit box at the bank. That made it impossible for Fredericks and Quinn to track him using the phone, but it also left his options open.

When he opened the deposit box, he was surprised to discover a pound of silver in the place where, hours earlier, there had only been a note from Bill Fredericks.

I want off of this crazy ride, Kittredge thought, thoroughly and hopelessly confused.

But he knew that was impossible. His ride was just beginning.

Chapter 23

Quinn sat folded uncomfortably in his airline seat in sardine class, doing his best to ignore the shrill voice of the flight attendant amplified by the tinny speaker inches from his head. He hated flying.

More accurately, he hated *riding* in an airplane. Quinn was a pilot himself, and he loved flying himself around, though he didn't fly airplanes big enough to make the trip from DC to Caracas. The Agency had an impressively large fleet of aircraft, but the powers-that-be had not yet seen fit to check him out in anything larger than a Cessna Citation.

And despite their ridiculous budget, they'd never spring for business class tickets, so Quinn sat with his huge frame wedged into the undersized seat in coach class with the rest of the human cattle.

He was in a characteristically expansive mood. While his job required continuous travel and he rarely stayed in one place for more than a few days at a time, it did afford him plenty of mental down time.

It was both blessing and curse. Some Agency assets found themselves sinking further into a black hole of their own making, with drug and alcohol abuse and other mental instabilities an all-too-common occupational hazard.

Quinn had tried those on for size, perhaps just to see whether he enjoyed embodying the cliché, but he had ultimately decided to take a more philosophical approach to things. Drunkenness, he discovered, was frequently followed by a hangover, and he failed to see the point of the cycle.

So he became something of a savant-assassin, reading widely from all sorts of subjects, to occupy his capacious brain during the frequent periods of inactivity that came along with his job. It also helped him to come to grips with the heinousness of his chosen profession, which required that he inflict pain, suffering, and death on his unfortunate subjects.

Earlier in his career, he had spent time trying to convince himself that his targets deserved the fate he brought them, but he had learned over the years that his employers, and even his nation, didn't quite occupy the moral high ground they claimed. Were some of the poor bastards really bad people? Unquestionably. Did that mean they deserved their death at his hands? Maybe.

But it was largely a useless question. The fact was, Quinn killed them because he *could* kill them. The Agency ordered him to kill people, only because they *could* order him to kill people.

And they thought up bullshit ideological euphemisms to justify these murders only because they *could* justify them, and the public – or Congress, or whoever happened to express a passing interest in the disgusting underbelly of statecraft – chose to believe the bullshit because they had the luxury of believing it.

Except in the rarest of circumstances, when bloody failures became too public to ignore, nobody really had to account to anyone but themselves for the savagery. So savagery had become an instrument of quotidian utility, which also made it prosaic and unremarkable.

Quinn's dogged self-education had rapidly disabused him of the notion that his employers used assassins to protect the US Republic and The People. Really, the Agency was far less an extension of state interests than business interests. The functionaries he'd killed over the years were frequently employees of foreign governments, but they met their end only because they proved too recalcitrant to get out of the way of American Enterprise.

In short, Quinn assassinated people mostly because they hindered corporate profits. It wasn't an uplifting truth, but it was impossible to look honestly at the situation and arrive at any other conclusion.

"Economic terrorism," one author had called it. The author knew whereof he spoke – he had been an Agency asset for a couple of decades, and had personally trained Quinn, before a Saul-on-the-road-to-Damascus-like conversion compelled him to unburden his soul in a tell-all book.

So it didn't take much in the way of mental gymnastics for Quinn to arrive at the conclusion that he owed his trip to Caracas to the desire of a particular oil company to expand their portfolio of oil fields into the state-controlled Venezuelan countryside, and the desire of the Agency to help.

It wasn't quite right to say that the CIA was infiltrated by powerful economic interests. It was far more correct to say that the CIA was created, sustained, and populated by such interests, at least at the policy levels.

Still, it was highly unusual for Fredericks to throw Curmudgeon's name around, as he had done during their recent phone conversation, and it was even more unusual to hear anything at all about the Intermediary. The latter was supposedly some ultra-deep, ultra-connected operator with a godlike grip on the big levers of commerce and policy, but Quinn wondered whether the guy even existed.

But he wouldn't be surprised if there was such an animal lurking behind the curtain. Individual worker bees in the Agency hive might be ideologues fighting for truth and God and justice, Quinn had discovered, but the big boys didn't give half a damn about those things. It was all about greenbacks.

And he was okay with that. Life was nothing if not the continuous process of consuming other life. But for the chlorophyll, the little guys who turned sunlight into energy, just about every other living thing on the planet stayed alive only by destroying other living things.

Quinn didn't kill people to eat them, of course, but he recognized the role of death in life, and he wasn't too squeamish to do his part.

In fact, he usually enjoyed it.

And why not make a living doing what you enjoy? Sure, he'd never tell his grandmother how he snapped bones and sliced throats for a paycheck. But in the dark corners of his soul, he liked who and what he was.

That made Quinn at least a sociopath, and probably a psychopath.

He didn't mind. *Everybody has a little space to fill,* he thought. If the robber barons found him useful enough to keep him on the payroll, all the better. He was happy to lead an interesting life doing enjoyable – if horrific – things.

As the jet taxied toward the runway, Quinn opened his book and started reading. More Faust, as imagined by Goethe. He laughed inwardly at the implicit joke. But there was an important difference: unlike Faust, Quinn hadn't really sold his soul to the devil.

Rather, he had merely discovered that he and the devil had a lot in common.

Chapter 24

Sam exited the Village Theater just after dusk. Her eyes were red and puffy, indicative of the early stage of the grief cycle in which she found herself.

She still couldn't believe that Brock had lied to her about Arturo Dibiaso. She wondered whether the reason she found herself targeted by a fringe group of crooked Metro cops might be hidden behind that lie, and she resolved to put the pieces together into a coherent picture. It's what she did for a living, and she was damn good at it.

But she had never before had to piece the facts of a case together while simultaneously piecing together the fragments of her heart. Maybe there was another woman involved, which had fueled Brock's deceit, or maybe not. Either way, his lie cut deep. She had organized her life around naked honesty, and long ago discovered that there was no place in her world for anything else.

Sam returned her focus to more immediately pressing concerns. She wandered slowly toward the Diplomat Towers, wondering whether the police had grown weary of waiting for her to emerge. She hadn't walked more than half a block before she caught the reflection of flashing police lights off of the library building's windows. Apparently, they hadn't yet lost interest. She had no idea how many policemen might still be in the neighborhood, and she had no intention of finding out.

Of course, it was entirely possible that the Metro guys were simply still mopping up the mess in Phil Quartermain's apartment, and had no interest in her whatsoever. But those odds weren't great, and trying to get at her car in the apartment building's parking garage was a huge risk without much upside.

She crossed the street, entered a coffee shop, and ordered a latte to go, then meandered past the gas station at the far end of the urban center. She nonchalantly rounded the corner and left the enclave of chic shops, restaurants, and condo high-rises behind her as she made her way to the bus stop two blocks south.

Minutes later, aboard a crowded Metrobus connector, Sam turned on one of her burner phones and dialed Dan Gable's number. Voicemail.

She tried his home number; a haggard Sara answered with a crying baby in the background. Sam cringed as she asked to speak with Dan.

Sara was cordial to Sam, but there was palpable tension as Sara summoned Dan to the phone. "Your office wife," Sam overheard her say.

"I'm really sorry to disturb the peace, Dan," she said when her deputy picked up.

"No problem. There's not much peace to disturb. And I'm actually glad you called. Are you somewhere secure?"

"I'm on a bus. Quartermain's dead. A Metro guy followed me over here a few hours ago, and they showed up about four nanoseconds after Phil was murdered. I've spent the afternoon holed up and trying to avoid them."

Dan whistled. "This just keeps getting more and more messed up."

"No argument here. Listen, I need you to work something for me on the down-low. I need to find a crime scene investigator who's willing to do some work off the grid."

Dan laughed. "You mean, you want me to find a CSI who's willing to commit a felony for you? Sure thing – I've got 'em lined up around the block."

"I'm aware that it won't be easy, but I can't run the risk of the evidence leaking. It already seems like the Metro gang is always a step ahead of me. One of these times, they're going to catch me."

"So you want to find an investigator to sneak back into a sealed scene or something?"

"No. I. . . *found* something in Quartermain's apartment."

"Jesus, Sam. Have you lost your mind?" Removing evidence from a scene was a great way to lose one's liberty.

"Maybe. But who do you call when your deputy is taking a powder and the cops are playing for the wrong team? I couldn't exactly spell things out on your voicemail. And I had to make a decision quickly."

Dan was silent for a while, then sighed. "Let me work on it. No promises though. And this might be none of my business, but is something going on?"

"You mean aside from dead people and crooked cops?"

"I mean at home. Brock has called the office about fifty times looking for you."

Sam had successfully compartmentalized that particular

problem over the past several minutes, but she felt herself choking up again as she tried to think of a reply.

"I don't know what's going on," she finally said. It wasn't false – she really didn't know what Brock was up to, why he hadn't come clean with her, and what his connection with Dibiaso might be.

"You might consider calling him, before he starts to become a real pain in the ass. And I have something else you need to hear about."

"Hit me."

"I overheard Ekman and Jarvis talking about verifying a death certificate for a life insurance policy. I don't have any evidence, but I think it's related to the stiff we saw in the multi-spec photo of John Abrams' front yard."

"The one that Everett Cooper was leaning over before he jumped out at me?"

"Yep. That's what I think anyway."

"You think a Homeland guy got whacked by the Metro thugs?" Sam asked.

"I think so. Either that, or he got whacked earlier, and the Metro guys found him in the bushes. I asked Ekman about it—"

"You did *what?*" Sam interrupted.

"Ekman. I talked to him."

Sam cursed.

"I know. But what else could I do?" Dan asked. "He's our boss, and I still have a duty to report potential connections to open cases. Anyway, he got a look on his face like I had caught him whacking off, if you'll pardon the expression. It was pretty clear that he and Jarvis are keeping us in the dark and feeding us shit."

"I'm glad it's not just me," Sam said. "Let me know if you learn anything more on that front, but I wouldn't press Ekman or Jarvis for anything else."

"I'll back off but keep you posted."

"Dan, I really need that CSI help. I'm carrying around the souvenir in a backpack, and need this thing analyzed before I accidentally destroy evidence. Can you work on it tonight?"

"Okay. I'll call you soon."

"And please be careful, Dan. I think Phil Quartermain was on to something, and that's why he got smoked."

"I'll be quiet like a mouse," Dan said.

Chapter 25

The evening breeze felt cool and stark, like reality forcing itself on Kittredge's still-reeling, still-inebriated consciousness.

He stood on the platform of the Santa Marta station on the Red Line in Caracas, and felt the rumble of a train approaching. There were numerous clocks in view, and each expressed a slightly different idea of the time. It was indicative of the Venezuelan approach to scheduling, Kittredge thought.

"Don't turn around," said a voice in quiet tones, very near to Kittredge's ear. He immediately tried to turn around, but a practiced hand on his elbow stopped him. "You didn't follow instructions very well," said the man, annoyance apparent in his voice. "When did you get here?"

"Uh," Kittredge said, "I dunno. Few minutes ago, maybe?"

"Think carefully about your instructions, and then I will ask you again," the man said impatiently.

"Oh. Right. Sorry. Five-thirty," Kittredge said, recalling his earlier instructions: *you will be asked a question. The answer is five-thirty.*

"That's better."

The man sidled up, and Kittredge turned to see a wiry man of medium height in dirty brown overalls and a John Deere hat. "Mauricio," he said, extending his hand and speaking loudly over the sound of the arriving train.

Kittredge shook it, and felt a card pressed against his palm. He looked down to find a train ticket.

"Join me," Mauricio said, stepping through the open train door.

Kittredge followed, heart beating fast.

* * *

An announcement in Spanish told Kittredge that the train had reached the southeastern-most station on the Red Line. Mauricio had deposited him in a seat immediately after boarding, and had disappeared into a different car, leaving Kittredge to wonder anxiously at each subsequent stop whether he was supposed to exit the train or stay put.

He also wondered anxiously whether it would be best just to walk off the train and disappear into the sunset. He had just thrown his fate upon complete strangers, and he was having second thoughts about the wisdom of that decision.

In the end, indecision, curiosity, and residual liquid courage had kept him in his seat.

Mauricio reappeared as the train ground to a halt at the Red Line's last stop. The sinewy Venezuelan gave Kittredge a toothy smile, and beckoned him to follow with a flip of his chin.

A dilapidated Toyota pickup truck awaited them. Mauricio jumped into the bed, and motioned for Kittredge to ride shotgun.

A large brick of a man sat in the driver's seat. He nodded as Kittredge climbed in and looked for a seatbelt, but the driver said nothing and remained expressionless. He jammed the truck into gear and made his way slowly through the crowd of workers returning home from a day at work in the city.

Several miles later, the pavement ended, and the truck bucked wildly as the driver drove indifferently over ruts and potholes on what had become a dirt road at best, a donkey trail at worst. "Where are we going?" Kittredge asked, feeling increasingly claustrophobic as the South American jungle thickened around him.

In reply, the driver opened the glove compartment, removed a wad of black cloth, and handed it to Kittredge. It was a hood. The driver motioned for Kittredge to don it.

"Seriously?" Kittredge's protest sounded a little whiny, even to himself.

The driver nodded. His stern facial expression needed no translation, and Kittredge thought it best to do as he was told.

The oppressive jungle heat, the lack of air conditioning in the truck, the jostling, his nerves and claustrophobia, and the onset of a mini-hangover all conspired to make Kittredge feel nauseous. He lifted the hood to increase the airflow to his face, but immediately received a whack from the driver.

Fear and dread replaced nausea in the forefront of his consciousness, and he wondered for the hundredth time what lay ahead, and what the hell he had been thinking when he called the number in his pocket. Quinn and Fredericks were certainly bastards, but at least they were somewhat known quantities, and Kittredge wondered whether he had made a grievous mistake.

He stewed in his worry for the better part of an hour before the truck ride ended. He heard Mauricio jump out of the bed – *had he ridden way back there the entire way? His skinny ass must be beyond repair,* Kittredge thought – and felt the passenger door jerk open. "This way, Señor Kittredge," Mauricio said, leading him by the arm. "Watch your step."

Kittredge felt afraid, but also a little ridiculous. He was stumbling around someplace in the jungle with a hood over his head, like a prisoner of war, or a criminal of some sort. "What the hell are we doing?" he asked.

"We are almost there, Señor Kittredge," Mauricio said. "Just a little further. Maybe a mile."

"A *mile*?"

"Yes, just a little one. You are a city gringo, Señor Kittredge, but you will survive, I think."

Kittredge felt perspiration drip down his face. *At least I'm out of that damned truck,* he thought. "Really, Mauricio, where are you taking me?"

"You asked for help, no? I am taking you to help."

Ask for help? Is that what he had done? Kittredge wasn't sure. The old man in the red scarf had given him the telephone number during their brief and very unusual conversation on the park bench, halfway between the Lincoln and War Memorials in DC. It seemed like seven light-years away and two lifetimes ago. In a moment of anger and rebellion, Kittredge had simply dialed the number. A disembodied voice had given him instructions, and he had followed them.

It was a reckless thing to have done, he knew. *As reckless as becoming a spy in the first place?* He wondered to himself, suddenly aware of a glaring personality flaw. It seemed that he had systematically created ever-riskier situations for himself over the past few months, but he had no idea why. Even things like having unprotected sex. *Do I have a death wish? Or am I just bored?*

"Duck your head, Señor Kittredge," Mauricio said. Kittredge heard the screech of rusty hinges, felt a hand on his head urging him to stoop lower, and stepped forward as Mauricio prodded his arm. He tried to stand up, but cracked his head against a solid ceiling. He heard the rusty gate slam shut. "You may take off your hood," Mauricio said, his footsteps retreating through the jungle.

Kittredge pulled off the hood. He was surprised by the darkness outside. The sun had long since set, and he wasn't sure how Mauricio and the driver had navigated through the jungle in the dark. His eyes were already dark-adapted from the hood, and it became instantly clear to him that he was in a cage of some sort, like an animal.

Discomfort turned to fear. "Mauricio?" he queried the darkness. "What is this? What's going on? Mauricio!"

He heard only the sounds of the jungle.

* * *

Kittredge heard a horrific screech, which he incorporated into his nightmare – he was being chased through a dark passageway by some unknown evil presence, with people lined up on both sides to watch him. The evil behind him screeched and howled, and his fear was visceral. Each person he passed became a pursuer, and he ran faster and faster, but only wound up with more angry people chasing him.

Something sharp poked his chest, and he awoke. "Señor

Kittredge, it is time," said an unfamiliar voice with a thick Spanish accent. "Come this way."

He felt a tug on his arm, stood up too quickly, hit his head against the top of the cage, and unleashed a stream of curses. "What is the deal with the damned cage?"

The man ignored the question. "This way, Señor Kittredge." More trudging through the jungle in the darkness. More thorns, bug bites, dripping perspiration, and more apprehension.

Then a flickering light appeared through the trees. Campfire. Subdued voices, then a little laughter. Kittredge saw three men encircling the campfire, Kalashnikov rifles slung across their chests, beer bottles in their hands. They straightened up when they heard Kittredge and his captor approach.

Kittredge heard what sounded like a bird's shrill call, but was surprised to hear an equivalent response from the man who had led him through the jungle. The noise was apparently some sort of code.

A fourth man emerged from within a large military-looking canvas tent adjacent to the campfire. "Ahh, Señor Peter Kittredge, if I am not mistaken," the man said as Kittredge and his guide rounded the last turn through the jungle and reached the camp.

"That's right," Kittredge said, doing his best to keep the trepidation out of his voice. "You have me at a disadvantage, I'm afraid," he said. "I have no idea who you are."

"My friends call me El Grande. And my enemies, too." He extended his hand.

El Grande. The Big. Completely absurd. "El Grande. I hope I fall in the friend category," Kittredge said, wiping the perspiration from his face.

"I hope so, too. I don't have enemies for long," El Grande said. The three men laughed, as if El Grande had made a joke. Kittredge wondered if that was some kind of a threat.

"Please, come inside." El Grande motioned toward the tent, and Kittredge complied.

Inside, Kittredge found a hookah, a woman of obvious Slavic descent wearing nothing but her panties, and another henchman, curled up and snoring. A lamp hung suspended by a nail driven into the tent's center support. "Sorry to crash the party," he said, surprised by his own boldness.

"Not at all. We are honored to have you as our guest. I am very sorry about the bumpy ride and the dark hood and the animal's cage. But these are necessary precautions, I am afraid."

Kittredge didn't reply. It all seemed a bit over the top, like big boys playing little boys' games out in the jungle, but with real women and guns. And narcotics, judging by the torpor of the passed-out henchman.

"You are uncertain about your choice to call us. Maybe skeptical of us," El Grande observed.

I really have to work on my poker face, Kittredge thought. "I don't know what I am. Mostly confused, I think."

"That is understandable," El Grande said, sitting down at a chair in the middle of the large tent.

As he sat, his face became bathed in the lamplight, and Kittredge felt something familiar yet strange: attraction. El Grande had a chiseled jaw, strong shoulders, and dark skin. He was mildly but not objectionably swarthy. And Kittredge was a sucker for the accent.

He quickly put those thoughts aside, however, in favor of figuring out whether he had just made the biggest mistake of his life – next to committing treason, of course.

El Grande was still speaking, and Kittredge did his best to focus on the words. "I think that you do not like your new CIA friends. I do not like your new CIA friends. They are old enemies. They want our oil, then our women, then our lives. Si?"

"They have me by the balls," Kittredge said.

"Si. Quite so. Exel Oil, no? You sold them things?"

Kittredge nodded.

"You got a big price for these things?" El Grande asked, as if he already knew the answer.

Kittredge shook his head.

"Yes," El Grande said. "It is hard to get paid enough for our troubles, no?"

Something didn't seem quite right. Kittredge had sold economic secrets to an American oil company, and the CIA had caught him. Yet El Grande accused the *CIA* of going after Venezuelan oil. It made Kittredge think back to the way he had found out about the attack on Charley. *Quinn and Fredericks.*

CIA.

Was Charley connected with them, too?

"You are much confused." El Grande pointed a finger at his temple, made a twisting motion, and laughed. "La maquina, your machine, it is turning fast, no? But it is simple, really. You think there are two things, but there is just one thing."

"I'm not sure I follow," Kittredge said.

"The oil brings gringos. Always."

"I'm still not with you."

"They are the same. Exel. CIA. Solamente uno." He held up one finger.

Then he pointed it at Kittredge. "But you are a different kind of gringo. You do not like puta. You like hombres and their pepinos. You have made small money and big enemies. And you are afraid that you will never be free of these enemies."

Kittredge nodded. *That pretty much sums it up.*

"And you are afraid at this moment, because you have helped gringo oil companies, and now you help the gringo CIA. And you have heard me say that I do not like them." El Grande stared at Kittredge, eyes unwavering.

After a moment, he looked away from Kittredge, and smiled at the girl. She rose and sat on his lap, and he wrapped his arm around her waist.

"But do not worry, Peter Kittredge," El Grande said. "The jihadists have a saying: The enemy of my enemies, he is my friend."

El Grande puffed on the hookah. "And you could use a friend, I think."

Chapter 26

Tuesday morning dawned in Caracas, and sunlight crept into Bill Fredericks' hotel room. He had failed to close the curtains all the way the night before, and a beam of light found his eyelids as if by magic.

He stirred, and asked himself the same two questions that groggy salesmen and spies had asked for eons: What city am I in, and which direction is the bathroom?

Both answers came to him slowly, and he rolled out of bed and found his way to the toilet without stubbing a toe. He was nearly finished with the first order of business when his cell phone clattered on the dresser. Fredericks waddled with his underwear around his ankles to reach the phone.

Curmudgeon. "Twice in one week? People will start to talk," he said.

"Hello, Bill," a deep, calm voice replied. "It's always a pleasure. I hope I didn't wake you up."

"Nope. But I am in the middle of something," Fredericks said, making his way back to the bathroom, wondering for the thousandth time how a Catholic priest ever came to be mixed up with the Central Intelligence Agency.

At least, Fredericks *thought* Curmudgeon was an Agency asset. He didn't know for sure.

"I'll make it quick. This is just a heads up that people aren't happy with the pace of things down there."

Fredericks felt defensive. "Then maybe *people* should come down here and take a swing at this themselves," he said.

"That wasn't meant as a personal affront," Curmudgeon said with a practiced, disarming ease. Fredericks could easily imagine him in front of a congregation, exhorting his flock to turn away from intrigue, greed, and murder. *But they'd have to quit their federal jobs.*

"Besides, you're not yet green-lighted for the op, are you?" Curmudgeon asked.

"You would know better than I," Fredericks said pointedly. Curmudgeon didn't reply.

"Anyway," Fredericks said, after the silence had grown a little uncomfortable, "Quinn just picked the package up yesterday and flew down here last night. I'm not sure how we could possibly speed things up."

"As I mentioned, I don't think the sentiment is directed at you, per se," the priest-cum-spy said, his voice reminding Fredericks of a radio host on a classical music station. "I just wanted you to be aware that your work has the attention of the very highest levels."

"The director?"

Curmudgeon laughed. "No. I said 'highest levels.'"

Shit. The Intermediary.

"That is good to know, because there wasn't enough pressure on this thing already," Fredericks said.

"You have my full support," Curmudgeon said.

"Do I *need* your support? I mean, I just got the call yesterday telling me to make this thing happen. I wasn't aware I was already screwing it up."

"You're not. That is to say, if you *are* making a mess of things, I'm not aware of it. I'm just saying that you have my support in a very high profile operation, and there's significant interest in making it happen quickly."

"Thanks for the pep talk, padre. Shouldn't you be molesting a young boy?"

"Low blow."

"Sorry. Guess the pressure got to me. And, my pants are around my ankles, which makes me feel a little more vulnerable than normal. Anyway, I appreciate the head's up. I'll keep you posted."

"Please do. I get about one phone call every hour asking about this op, so it'll be helpful if you can keep me in a steady supply of mundane details, which I will dutifully feed to the old men."

"Is that all?"

"No," Curmudgeon said. "Don't forget to take your heart medicine."

* * *

Quinn parked his rental car illegally on the street in front of the apartment building where Kittredge and Arlinghaus lived. His attempts to reach Kittredge by phone had failed, and he had left a number of messages urging Kittredge to call as soon as he saw fit to remove the penis from his mouth.

Fredericks had insisted that Kittredge be rounded up, if for no other reason than to confirm that the troubled new Agency asset hadn't caved beneath the emotional turmoil of the past few days, or otherwise taken leave of his senses.

Quinn turned on the car's hazard flashers, bounded up the stairs, and knocked on Kittredge's door. Hearing no movement, he tried the handle. Locked. He picked the lock using a credit card. He always wondered why there weren't more burglaries in the world. It really was easy to break into just about any residence, with just a little training.

The door yielded, and Quinn let out a low whistle when he saw the disaster inside the apartment. "Peter!" he yelled, suddenly concerned that Kittredge might have been whacked.

He did a quick search of the apartment, noting the lowbrow thoroughness employed by whoever had done the job, but didn't find Kittredge or his rotting corpse.

He dialed Fredericks. *Fat Freddie's going to need some more heartburn medicine when he hears this,* Quinn thought as the phone rang.

Chapter 27

Sam awoke in a sweat. As grogginess left her consciousness and the reality of the past three days rushed back to her mind, a sickening heaviness settled in her stomach. She took a deep breath and shuddered as she exhaled, feeling her body's response to the extreme stress of having her life turned upside down.

Sunlight peeked through the hotel's windows. She had paid cash, of course, and had checked into the hotel using identification cards belonging to one of her work legends, the name Jennifer Garman captioning the deliberately unflattering photo on her fake driver's license.

The hotel desk clerk had demanded two forms of ID, and Sam had produced a Jennifer Garman passport as well. It struck her as odd that she was required to present two forms of American identification to the North African hotel desk clerk in order to pay cash for a night in a cheap DC flop house. But such was the modern world. It was interconnected in absurd ways.

The way to stay alive in extreme situations was to keep moving forward, Sam knew. When the shit hit the fan, it rarely turned out well for those who simply stayed holed up, hoping for the best. Sitting still was a good way to wind up with even bigger problems.

She turned on one of the three burner phones she had bought after her escape from the scene of Phil Quartermain's murder, and dialed Dan Gable's number.

Sam cringed as Sara answered. "Hello."

"Hi, Sara," Sam said. "You're probably extremely tired of me disturbing you guys at home."

"It's okay." Her tone said it wasn't.

Awkward silence.

"Um, is Dan available?" Sam asked.

"Just a minute."

Sam heard a shrill "Dan!" along with muffled but strained conversation, and then Dan's voice: "Happy Tuesday, boss."

"Sorry, Dan. I need to quit getting you in trouble with your better half."

"If it wasn't work, it would be something else. Anyway, got a pen handy? I have some info for you."

Gable gave her a phone number, address, and a name: Jeff Jensen. "I think I've seen him around," Sam said. "Younger guy, looks tired a lot?"

"Yep. He doesn't yet know he's a volunteer for some work on the side, but there's a fairly compelling angle you can work." Dan filled her in on the details.

She showered, called a cab from her room, and stopped in the lobby for the free "continental breakfast," which would have been barely edible on a good day but was nearly unbearable with a queasy stomach.

She stepped out into the DC dawn, and her cab arrived seconds later. Sam climbed in the back seat, and set Phil Quartermain's backpack, containing what she suspected was John Abrams' music box, on the seat next to her.

Traffic was light but picking up steadily, and she fretted about whether she would arrive at Jeff Jensen's residence before he left for work.

In fact, she made it with a couple of seconds to spare. Jensen recognized Sam as he opened the door – there weren't many people in the DHS headquarters office who wouldn't recognize Sam instantly, as a five-ten redhead with Playboy looks tended to attract more attention than the average employee – and his surprise was evident. "Uh, hello?"

"Hey Jeff. Sam Jameson." She extended her hand. "I think we've worked a case or two in the past. Sorry to drop in unannounced."

"Of course. Come on in. Sorry about the mess." Jensen had dark circles beneath his eyes. He had showered and shaved, but somehow still looked disheveled. His apartment had a mild bachelor funk, making it clear to Sam that there wasn't a woman in his life.

"To what do I owe the pleasure?" he asked.

"Well, it probably won't be a pleasure, unfortunately." She unhooked the backpack from her shoulder and took a seat on the couch nearby, suppressing the slightly grossed-out feeling brought on by the mess.

She took a deep breath. *Here goes nothing.* "I need a little on-the-side work for a case that's taken a bit of an interesting turn."

Jensen stiffened, and a look of concern crossed his face. "I don't think there's any such thing as forensics work 'on the side.' At least, not if I'm interested in keeping my job."

"I understand your reticence—"

Jensen cut her off. "It isn't reticence. Collecting evidence without a warrant is a misdemeanor at best. Processing evidence outside the normal chain of custody will get me fired. And you could never use any of the info for an arrest or conviction, anyway."

Sam nodded.

"But I'm sure you knew all of that already," Jensen said.

She nodded again.

"I'm sorry, Jeff. I should have explained this a bit better. . . It's not what it sounds like," Sam said. *I screwed this up,* she thought. *I should have taken my time with him.*

"I'm sure it isn't," Jensen said. "But I think we'd both have a hard time explaining it to a jury, or to our bosses."

"That's just the thing," Sam said. "I think this evidence may point toward someone inside Homeland, and I don't want to tip them off."

"So you have a warrant, then?"

"No. Same problem – it would be impossible to get one without alerting the parties in question."

Jensen shook his head. "So what you really have is a hunch."

Sam decided to take a risk. "Yes. And a group of police officers trying to kill me."

She watched Jensen carefully. He cocked his head to the side and narrowed his eyes, which Sam recognized as the universal human signal for skepticism, so she added a few details: "They chased me from a scene on Saturday night. One of them broke into my house, and was gunned down in my entryway. Another one followed me yesterday."

Jensen shook his head. "No way am I sticking my nose in the middle of whatever *that* is all about," he said. "Unless you bring something into the lab via the normal channels, no sane man would go near it."

"Isn't there any way you can think of to examine a couple of things without logging them into the database? People really are in danger, and I'm afraid that DHS might be compromised."

Jensen shook his head. "I worked my ass off for this job and I need to keep it. I don't have much of a life, but it's the only life I've got, and I don't want to screw it up by getting fired. Or thrown in jail."

Sam sighed. She felt a heaviness descend. Without a bit of forensic help with the music box, Sam knew that she was dead in the water.

She knew what she had to do, but she hated doing it.

"Jeff, I was hoping it wouldn't come to this—"

"I think you should leave. I have to get to work. You've already jammed me up by asking me to do this. You know we're supposed to report stuff like this."

Sam sighed again, suddenly feeling extremely tired.

"Methadone," she said.

Jensen's eyebrows raised and an expression of fear came over his face.

"I know about the clinic, Jeff," she said softly.

She saw his eyes moisten, and she turned away to give him some psychological space. Sam had used human frailty as leverage more times than she could count. It was often enjoyable – it was satisfying to watch a blustering bastard reduced to rubble by a meltdown of his own creation – but other times, like this one, when she was forced to use a good person's demons against him, she felt only weight.

"I know you're getting your life together and you're managing your issues," she said, softness in her gaze. "But you can't be a drug-addicted CSI. And you must have perjured yourself during your security investigation, didn't you? They ask you about drugs while you're under oath."

Jensen shook his head. "How did you find out?"

"You work for an intelligence agency, Jeff."

The silence lingered. "Trust me, if I had any other option, I'd use it," Sam said. She felt awful.

"I've been clean for three months."

"I know how hard that is. Booze was my thing. One addict to another, you can beat it."

Jensen kept shaking his head. "They give me take-home doses now. I don't have to go to the clinic every night anymore."

"You've worked hard to get here. You should be proud of your progress."

She stayed quiet for a while, letting Jensen begin to drown in a sea of imagined consequences before throwing out the life preserver: "One music box. That's what I need dusted and analyzed. That's it. If you can do that, the other thing will remain between us."

Jensen pondered. Sam sweetened the deal. "And I'll give you a few hints to help keep other people from figuring out your secret, too."

He finally nodded. "Okay."

* * *

Crime scene investigators were often called upon to perform their duties at odd hours, so most of them kept a briefcase full of rudimentary supplies handy. Sample containers were chain-of-custody items, meaning that the investigator in charge of the scene was responsible for bringing them from the clean vault to the scene, and they couldn't be kept in a CSI's personal kit. But nearly every CSI eventually ended up with a briefcase full of items like fingerprint powder, blood die, lock picks, and DNA tape.

Jensen cleared a space on his kitchen table, set down some newsprint, and got to work. It took him less than fifteen minutes to examine the exterior of the music box, and his efforts produced over two dozen full or partial prints.

He set them aside, and picked the lock on the front of the music box. Inside was a slip of paper and an unlabeled CD ROM disc, which Jensen also dusted for prints. Sam saw the circular striations, like rings on a tree trunk, and knew that the disc contained data. She talked Jensen into letting her borrow his laptop for the day in order to examine the CD ROM's contents.

Jensen next removed the curled piece of paper. Turning it over, he realized it was a photograph.

Sam's heart stopped when she saw the photo's subject.

Herself.

The photo was actually a shard torn from a larger photo, one that Sam didn't recognize. It looked like it might have been taken at a recent office Christmas party, or some other event, but Sam couldn't be sure. There was an arm around her shoulder – undoubtedly Brock's, a realization that brought yet another wave of grief and anxiety – but no other faces to provide context for the photo or a clue to who might have taken it.

Her hands shook, and she must have done a poor job of hiding her apprehension, because Jensen asked if she needed a drink of water. She did, along with something solid to lean against.

This is messed up like polio.

Jensen got a couple of prints off of the photo and added them to the pile for analysis, used a pair of surgeon's glasses to find and collect fibers from the music box interior, and declared himself as done as he could possibly be without doing a real workup in the lab.

"You realize, all of this work is meaningless without running the prints through the system to get names," he said to Sam. "That requires associating them with a particular case file."

Sam nodded. "I trust you to think of something."

She collected Jensen's laptop and placed it in Quartermain's backpack, along with the music box. Then she added, "Just don't associate it with any of my cases. I'm sure I'm flagged in the system, and everything with my name on it will turn to shit before your very eyes."

Jensen smiled.

"Thank you, Jeff. Believe it or not, you've done a good thing." Sam gave him the number to one of her burners, asked him to call as soon as he had any results, and stepped out of the front door into the growing daylight.

She held out her hand, and Jensen shook it. "One day at a time," she said. The recovering addict's creed.

One day at a time, she repeated to herself as she set off on foot toward the corner coffee shop.

Especially when the world crumbles around you.

* * *

Jensen's MacBook whirred, ingesting the contents of the CD ROM that she and Jensen had found locked in the music box.

Sam still had no idea how Phil Quartermain had come to be in possession of the box, and she had no idea whether it would contain anything useful. She was desperately searching for a link between John Abrams, the murdered CIA agent whose fake suicide she'd investigated on Saturday night, the gang of crooked Metro cops who had been following her around, and some character named Arturo Dibiaso.

Sam forced herself to relax. Her deep breath brought in the soothing aroma of coffee, and she took another sip of her Americano while the contents of the CD ROM popped up on the screen.

There were only two files, and she opened them both. They looked like payment records. Each file contained dozens of transactions, most into unique account numbers that didn't repeat.

But all of the payments shared just two origins, tracked by what looked to Sam like employer identification numbers, or EINs, the corporate equivalent of social security numbers. The IRS kept track of corporate taxes through EINs, and reconciled claimed expenditures with individual employees' income tax records to ensure that no dollar went untaxed, and no expense went unverified.

Sam logged into the coffee shop's free Wi-Fi. A quick search of the IRS' public database revealed that the two numbers common to all of the transactions contained in the CD ROM files were indeed EINs, belonging to two corporations.

The first was called Executive Strategies. It didn't ring a bell for Sam, but it felt like it was a name that she should have been familiar with. *Where have I heard of Executive Strategies before?* She wasn't sure, but felt a strong suspicion that she would recognize the connection when it appeared. And the connection would inevitably reveal itself, she knew, if she applied the right amount of doggedness and patience.

The second EIN belonged to JIE Associates, a name that meant nothing to her.

She called Dan Gable at the office and asked him to research the two companies, and she read off a few of the recipients' account numbers from the list of financial transactions for him to investigate as well. "Follow the cash" was a hackneyed investigative truism for a reason. It usually worked.

"I'm on it, boss," Dan said. "And FYI, Ekman's already asked about you."

Sam groaned. "I feel a fever coming on."

"I'll tell him you're taking a personal day."

She thanked Dan and signed off, just in time to receive a call from Jeff Jensen on one of her other burner phones. "That was quick," she said. "What did you find?"

"The matches came back quickly because they're all federal or state employees," Jensen said.

Interesting. "Hit me," Sam said.

"Phil Quartermain, and. . . sorry, I just lost the slip of paper. . ."

Sam tapped her finger impatiently while Jensen shuffled papers. Quartermain's prints weren't a surprise – the music box had been in his possession, and he had actually called her minutes before his murder to invite her over for a discussion. She assumed he wanted to talk about evidence germane to the Abrams scene, but she would never know for sure.

"Here it is," Jensen said. "Sorry about that. John Abrams and Everett Cooper are the other two names."

Holy shit. Abrams and Cooper? Abrams was the dead Agency guy, suspected to be a double agent of some sort. And Everett Cooper was the creepy cop who had jumped out of the bushes in front of Abrams' house, and later, whose brains had been splattered all over her entryway.

So they knew each other?

That wasn't a conclusion she could yet draw, Sam knew, because it wasn't fully supported by the prints – both Abrams and Cooper clearly handled the music box and its contents, but it was possible that they did so at separate times, which meant they didn't have to know of each other's existence.

Still, it was worth further investigation, and there was clearly a link of some sort between the two of them.

"Thanks, Jeff. That's really interesting. What else did you find?"

"There's also a fourth set of prints, but I only got partials and wasn't able to match them. The system's still grinding away on it, but the partials were small, and I don't expect a match any time soon."

"That's interesting too." There was evidently a fourth player, one who had been careful not to leave a full set of prints, but who had also chosen not to wipe things clean. *The fourth guy wanted us to ID the other three,* she thought.

She thanked Jensen for his trouble. He asked, somewhat timidly, that she not discuss his involvement in the case with anyone.

Sam laughed. *Office workers. So naïve.* "Jeff, you realize that we're in a mutually assured destruction situation, right? If one of us talks, we both go down. I don't have any more desire for a jail sentence than you do." Jensen's anxiety seemed assuaged, and Sam thanked him again before hanging up.

Her mind churned over what she had just learned, and she had an important realization: There was another key connection between Cooper and Abrams, and *she* was that connection.

Her name and address were on Abrams' night stand, her photo was in the music box with fingerprints from both of them, and Cooper had attempted to ruin her night on numerous occasions before he met his demise in her entryway, shot by a fellow beat cop and an Internal Affairs officer.

So Cooper and Abrams were working the same job. That seemed pretty clear.

But on whose dime? Agency? If the CIA was behind an attempted murder of a fellow federal officer, it really wouldn't be all that surprising. *No one alive has plumbed the full depths of the*

Agency's intrigue, Sam thought.

But it *would* be highly unusual, on the other hand, if the Agency was working with a DC Metro cop to get the dirty work done. The Agency didn't outsource from other organizations, and Cooper wasn't some impostor in a cop's uniform – he was a full-fledged Metro officer. At least, he was a bona-fide cop until he clocked out permanently a few nights earlier.

But if Ekman and Jarvis were correct, Cooper was also moonlighting for someone with Venezuelan ties.

Random. Who works for Venezuelans?

Who even knows *a Venezuelan?* Sam wondered.

Then it struck her. *Maybe Abrams!* While it made no sense for Cooper to be working with the Agency, it would make much more sense if Abrams were moonlighting as well. In fact, there were significant rumors to that effect, even before Abrams had turned up in a pool of his own blood.

So maybe Cooper and Abrams share an employer of convenience. . . but who whacked Abrams? The job they both seemed to be working on together – getting rid of Special Agent Samantha Jameson, for some reason she couldn't yet wrap her mind around – wasn't nearly complete, so it wouldn't make much sense for the Venezuelans to snuff Abrams. If, indeed, they were both in fact on the Venezuelans' payroll.

Of course. CIA.

The Agency was a jealous employer. Double agents only occasionally went to jail, because trials were public and embarrassing. More often, when discovered, double agents met an end similar to Abrams' recent outro. So she surmised that Abrams and Cooper *were* likely on the Venezuelan payroll, and both the Agency and Metro Internal Affairs were wise to it.

At least those loose ends seemed to tie neatly together, and Sam felt marginally better. The landscape wasn't so thoroughly foggy any more.

But she still had no idea why anyone from Venezuela – or, for that matter, why anyone who knew any Spanish whatsoever – might want her dead. She'd locked up or smoked plenty of bad people, but none of them were from anywhere further south than Florida.

The paranoid voice in the back of her head warned her that she had already spent too long in the same place, so she slammed Jensen's laptop shut, gathered her things, and walked out of the coffee shop toward the bus stop.

She had another important question in need of answers.

Chapter 28

Sam exited the L'Enfant Plaza Metro station on C Street, one block south of the National Mall, and headed west on foot. The late morning sun warmed her back uncomfortably, and she sweated beneath the scarf she had bought in Shirlington the day prior to cover her blazing red hair.

Being on the lam sucks, she lamented, suddenly annoyed to no end by the unfairness of everything that had gone wrong in her life since Ekman's call late Saturday night.

It had only been a little over seventy-two hours since she had exchanged witty banter with Phil Quartermain while sniffing around the Abrams scene. Now, two days later, Sam found herself betrayed by her lover, on the run from a faction of Metro cops who apparently had orders to do her harm, and distrusted by her two bosses at Homeland, who were themselves clearly hiding something important from her.

She stepped off of the curb to cross the street and was almost run over by a taxi. *Wake up,* she chided herself as the cab's horn blared.

A phrase from a book she read recently popped into her head: *Never let your life situation ruin your life.* She knew from experience that it was almost always best to live in the moment, tackle just one issue at a time, and let the bullshit sort itself out.

She knew better than to fret, but she also knew that she could be forgiven for sweating things at the moment, because she was in one hell of a pickle. But the only way out of the mess was to keep calm and focused.

The light changed. Sam crossed C Street, and walked into the Federal Aviation Administration's national headquarters.

"May I help you, ma'am?" The desk clerk was rail-thin, and his smile didn't reach all the way to his eyes.

Sam flashed her badge, and mentioned that she was just following up on a case, and needed some information about all of the aircraft that happened to be airborne over Alexandria around three a.m. on Saturday morning.

"Oh. Are you with the other guy?" the clerk asked.

Shit. Someone else thought of this too, Sam realized. "Maybe. What was his name?"

"I don't remember. But he had curly black hair. He was here yesterday about this time."

Ekman. Her heart sank. "That sounds about right," she said, hoping she had successfully concealed her chagrin. "I'm just double-checking a couple of things. Can you point me to the flight records room?"

The clerk walked toward a large set of double doors and motioned for Sam to follow. He waved his badge in front of a keypad, which beeped. He typed a few digits, and the doors opened. "Third left. Just knock, and tell them I sent you."

She did as the front desk clerk suggested, and soon found herself sifting through computer-generated logs of the air traffic into and out of DC during the preceding weekend.

Sam wasn't certain that the bomb that had exploded in her front yard in the wee hours Sunday morning had been dropped from an airplane or helicopter, but the video surveillance footage hadn't revealed any other clues, so it was the most logical hypothesis to explore.

At three-seventeen on Sunday morning, the minute prior to the bomb explosion that had rocked her house on its foundation, there were three aircraft flying in the airspace above.

Sam copied down the flight plan and aircraft registration information she thought might be relevant, then took it to the records clerk. "May I get the owner registration and flight crew manifest for these flights, please?" She showed her badge to help incentivize the clerk.

"Sure thing. You brought the warrant, right?"

Warrant? "Um, I thought Special Agent Ekman brought that by yesterday."

"Yes, ma'am. But *you* need to have a warrant, or I can't release the information to *you*. See what I'm sayin'?"

Unfortunately, she did. "Of course. Silly of me. May I borrow your phone?"

She dialed Dan Gable's office phone, and felt relief when he answered. She passed the information on to him, charging him with finding out who owned the planes, and who was flying them at the time the bomb exploded in her yard.

"Sure thing. I have nothing else to do, because I finished playing forensic accountant, and I'm all done conspiring to help people commit felonies by tampering with evidence."

Sam rolled her eyes. "Count your blessings. You could be Ekman's deputy instead of mine. You'd be straightening his tie all day." She heard Dan chortle. "Anyway, you said you're done playing forensic accountant – what did you find out about those two companies?"

"Is this a clean line?"

"FAA phone."

"Close enough. JIE Associates is a US subsidiary of a foreign thing," Dan began.

"Wait. Don't tell me. Venezuelan?"

"That's right. You should consider becoming an investigator."

"I'll consider it," Sam said. "And Executive Strategies?"

"I'm waiting on a call from a guy I know. Had to call in a favor. The records are sealed."

"Interesting," Sam said. "Call me when you hear something?"

"No, I plan to keep it a secret from you," Dan deadpanned.

He waited for a laugh that didn't come, then said, "Sam, listen, don't take this the wrong way, but you should really keep your private business private, okay? Brock stopped by the office this morning looking for you. He wouldn't stop asking questions. I was this close to giving him the number to your burner, just to get him to go away. He mentioned he was going to try to find Ekman because he's worried about you."

Sam was silent, and her eyes moistened. She hadn't had the time or energy to process what had happened between her and Brock. He had told her he didn't know Arturo Dibiaso, yet his cell phone records demonstrated unequivocally that he and Dibiaso had spent time together, probably while driving somewhere. She had no idea why he would lie about something like that, but she was sure that there was no room for deception in the most important relationship in her life.

"I'm sorry, Dan. It's, uh. . ." She paused to compose herself a bit. "It's complicated."

"Can I help? Do you need something?"

"It's kind of you to ask, but I wouldn't dream of asking any more of you. I can handle crooked cops and Venezuelan gangs, but your wife scares the shit out of me."

Dan laughed. "God, me too! She's a ball buster, isn't she?"

"I haven't exactly let you two enjoy a normal home life over the past few days."

"Past few years," Dan corrected.

"Yeah, that."

"Really, whatever is going on, I think you should talk to him. You've had your house blown up, and a guy got shot in your doorway. There's probably a few things to discuss."

Sam was quiet again, mulling whether to tell Dan what was going on. She trusted Dan. *But I trusted Brock, too, and look how that worked out,* she thought. Plus, Ekman and Jarvis had specifically told her *not* to tell Dan about what they had discussed in Jarvis' office on Sunday.

Thinking of Jarvis's jowly, officious stare and Ekman's refusal to stand up for her settled it for Sam. She decided to let Dan know what was going on. Speaking in hushed tones on the office phone in the FAA records branch, Sam filled him in.

"Wow," Dan said when she finished. "That's a gut punch. I don't know what to say. Is there any chance there's a logical explanation?"

"Yeah. Brock lied. That's logical enough, I think. I haven't had time to snoop around our finances to figure out exactly what's going on with the Dibiaso thing, but I know all I need to know from a personal standpoint."

"I'm sorry, Sam. I always thought you guys were great together."

"Me too."

"Will you let me do some digging for you? A fresh set of eyes can be helpful."

"Okay. Thanks, Dan."

"Please be careful. I would ask you where you're staying, but I don't want to have to lie about it later," Dan said.

"Good plan. Call me on the burner when you hear something about Executive Strategies, and maybe dig around the Homeland database for that flight plan information. I'm pretty sure DHS keeps a copy of aircraft ownership registrations, and I'm mildly curious about who the hell might have dropped that bomb on my house."

"I'm on it."

Chapter 29

Peter Kittredge wiped sweat from his brow, widened his stance, and straightened his elbow as he lined up the front and rear sights of the .45 caliber pistol. He did his best to superimpose the sights together over the center of the target several meters away. The black circles scribed on a piece of paper nailed to a tree in the Venezuelan jungle seemed blurry, and his hands couldn't seem to steady themselves.

"You are a natural, Señor Kittredge," El Grande said, chuckling.

It was far from true. Kittredge had initially resisted learning how to shoot a firearm, but El Grande had pointed out the obvious: Kittredge needed all the protection he could get his hands on.

"You have heard about the scorpion and the frog crossing the river, no?" El Grande had asked. Kittredge had nodded – it was a familiar old saw, the one about the scorpion convincing the frog to carry him across the river, then suddenly stinging him to death before they could reach the other side. "Your new friends, they are scorpions. They will hurt you because that is their nature."

Kittredge didn't need further convincing. His relationship with the CIA had started with a belt sander and a bag of salt. The scabbed abrasions on his back still hurt like hell every time he sat down, stood up, or twisted his torso too far.

He held his breath and tried to pull the pistol trigger slowly and steadily. He missed the target entirely. "You try too hard," El Grande said. "Do not pull the trigger. Just *think* about pulling the trigger, and let it surprise you. Try again."

Another miss. "Now, breathe deeply, and relax. Tense mind makes crooked bullets." El Grande was like Yoda with a Spanish accent, Kittredge thought. He did as instructed, and was rewarded with a small hole appearing on the edge of the paper.

"You have wounded his shoulder. Now, shoot his heart," El Grande coached. Kittredge tried again, scoring a hit closer to the center of the target. "Good! More."

The lesson continued until the heel of Kittredge's hand felt bruised and numb. He handed the pistol back to El Grande, but the Venezuelan refused. "It is yours now. Keep it close by. Use this—" El Grande handed Kittredge a shoulder holster and strap—"and hide it with a jacket. Always loaded. Your one true friend, as we say in our business." El Grande laughed.

El Grande motioned for Kittredge to follow him back into the canvas tent. "Food for the body, food for the mind," he said. *More Yoda shit.*

Kittredge did as instructed, and discovered the nubile young lady arranging a tray of food on a makeshift table surrounded by a semicircle of camping chairs. She was still topless, and Kittredge wondered with a chuckle whether that was a clause in her employment contract.

The food was incongruously delicious, equal parts traditional Venezuelan rural cuisine and modern urban tapas. It made Kittredge wonder whether the canvas tent in the middle of the jungle was a security necessity or an act put on for his benefit. He ate in silence, still wondering whose hospitality he was enjoying.

He didn't have to wonder for long. "So. You have questions, no?" El Grande said. "Ask."

Kittredge considered for a second. "Who are you?" he asked.

El Grande smiled. "Si, a good question. I will answer with another question: Do you like it here in Venezuela?"

Kittredge nodded, playing along.

"So do I," El Grande continued. "It is a beautiful country. We have beautiful jungles, beautiful beaches, and beautiful women." He smiled at the topless nymph. "It is my desire for Venezuela to stay this way. That is who I am."

Interesting but irrelevant, Kittredge thought. "Maybe I should ask a different way. Who pays you?"

The question brought a laugh. "Si, si. Already you think like a spy. Follow the money, no?" He lit a cigar, inhaled, and blew rings.

A Che Guevara wannabe. How perfectly cliché. All he needs is a beret.

After pondering for a moment, El Grande continued. "I am an instrument of state security. I have many resources at my disposal. Some of them you would walk right past and not think about. And others, well, I think that they would grab your attention."

"Why all the cloak-and-dagger?"

"What do you mean?"

"Tents in the middle of the jungle and secret telephone numbers. That kind of thing."

El Grande nodded and puffed more smoke. "Why? It is simple.

Cars."

Kittredge furrowed his brow. "I'm not following."

"You gringos love cars. Cars drink oil. We have oil. We are simple and unsophisticated, and we are vulnerable as a result. Your bankers want to help us build, how you say, *infrastructures*, but we have seen what has happened to other countries when they take the loans. Loan payments will increase and soon, American companies will take our oil from under our soil. I do not want this for my country."

"Isn't that all political? I mean, isn't that for men in suits to decide?"

"They have decided. We have refused the loans and turned away the oil companies. But the gringos do not like the decision, so they make, how you say, *small wars*. With spies and companies and embassies."

"That really happens? It all sounds like Hollywood bullshit."

"Bullshit, maybe. But very real. I have lost another friend this week. The one who gave you the number to dial. But you know this already, I think, no?"

Quinn had intimated that the old man in the red scarf had met an untimely end, and Kittredge had checked the online news story while waiting for his flight to Caracas. Kittredge nodded, suddenly feeling guilty, as if the old man's death were somehow his fault.

So this is the other end of the game? he wondered. *Hiding in the jungle from the Agency goons and the oil guys?*

El Grande's mien darkened, his thoughts far away. "Many others have already died in this cause. But for the moment, we are not yet your slaves."

"I've never heard anything at all about this."

"Si. Of course not. It would not sound very American to the American people. Truths and justices, no? You gringos think you are a different thing than the thing you really are. This is a big problem for small countries like mine. But it is the way of things, no?"

Was it really? Kittredge had no idea. He didn't doubt the CIA was capable of all manner of unpleasantness, and he also didn't doubt that US oil companies had a greedy eye on Venezuelan crude. He supposed that together, those two realities could combine to cause problems.

El Grande was right, he realized – it didn't sound very American to show up in another country and bully people around. But El Grande had another good point: most Americans only see one side of what it means to be American. It might mean something else entirely to outsiders with resources to protect.

Kittredge certainly wasn't surprised to hear that the pervasive commuter economy had implications outside US borders. Only a jackass would conclude that Western interest in Persian Gulf politics was anything other than oil-based. Other than sand, backwards and brutal theocracies, and an occasional camel, what the hell else was over there?

He thought about a statistic that Charley had once quoted, something about the United States having spent three dollars protecting the flow of Persian Gulf oil for every one dollar spent *buying the damned Persian Gulf oil*.

He remembered his offhanded reply: *Only a government*

would do something that stupid.

Are we starting something similar here? It was a chilling thought for Kittredge. The Persian Gulf was on the opposite side of the globe. But Caracas was only a couple of hours away from Florida, and the entire East Coast was within striking distance for a determined enemy. It wouldn't make much sense to kick over a hornet's nest, but if what El Grande said was true, the Agency might already be doing just that.

And he knew that Venezuela was already the fourth-largest supplier of oil to the American juggernaut. The US bought twice as much Venezuelan oil as Iraqi oil. *And we already annexed Iraq,* he thought. Maybe El Grande and his crowd weren't so crazy to think they had a bulls-eye on their backs.

"You are doing much thinking, no?" El Grande was looking at him.

Kittredge nodded.

"Maybe you are thinking, this is a big and dangerous thing, and maybe it's not so good to get involved, si?" El Grande exhaled smoke while he spoke.

Kittredge nodded again. *It certainly has an unhealthy vibe about it,* he mused.

El Grande smiled and took another long drag of his cigar. "Of course, Señor Kittredge, you must know that you are already involved."

He exhaled a thick cloud of smoke, and fixed a hard eye on Kittredge. "And you have already chosen sides."

* * *

Kittredge found himself again in the passenger's seat of a dilapidated pickup, this one a Datsun. He wouldn't have guessed there were any operational Datsun trucks left on the planet, and he was certain the one that was currently rattling his teeth loose on a jungle trail didn't have many miles left before it too fell completely apart.

El Grande drove, and treated the travel time back to Caracas as an indoctrination opportunity. "You must learn a new mentality," he was saying. "It is not a pleasant thing, but your life is not the same any more. You must be careful about everything. Everything that you say, everything that you do, it must be done carefully. Otherwise?" He squeezed his hand into a fist. "They will squash your cojones."

"You talk as if I've decided something," Kittredge said. "I haven't."

El Grande laughed. "You are young, no? Maybe you have not seen the world in this way before. Let me assure you, you have most definitely made decisions."

He stopped speaking to negotiate a particularly tricky rut in the road, then continued. "You are having confusion, I think. You must choose a way forward, but you think that going backward is also a choice."

El Grande shook his head. "There is no going backward for you. You cannot make unseen what you have already seen."

Yes, Jedi Master. Kittredge didn't appreciate being patronized.

But he was also aware that he lacked perspective on El Grande's world.

And he knew that he was in a very precarious position. Quinn and Fredericks had already demonstrated a surprising degree of ruthlessness; El Grande and his people had already demonstrated a surprising degree of organized opposition. Kittredge got the sense that he had stepped into a mature conflict. It was not yet large, but it certainly wasn't new.

And he wasn't particularly enthused about joining either side. Jungles and campfires were tolerable in small doses, but Kittredge knew that he wasn't cut out for life as a guerrilla, even part-time.

On the other hand, Fredericks and Quinn had crawled so far up his ass that they could undoubtedly see daylight, and Kittredge's resentment had only grown deeper over the past day.

He had signed the immunity agreement, naked and shackled to the cement in the Virginia safe house, and he had understood in an abstract sense that he had merely exchanged one type of prison sentence for another. But over the past few days, he had glimpsed the nature and extent of his indenture, and also the extent of the Agency's brutality.

The iconoclast in Kittredge rooted for El Grande and his ragged band of little guys against the giant, grinding American machine.

The pragmatist in him recognized that El Grande didn't stand a chance. Big Oil would summon its military and political servants, and it would win. Just like always.

He couldn't really make up his mind to cast his lot with either side, but he couldn't easily hedge his bets, either. He wasn't a fool, and he knew that he lacked the skill and subtlety to play one side against the other.

And, as El Grande had annoyingly spelled out, there was no going back.

In the end, Kittredge tentatively decided on a middle course, at least until a better option presented itself. He knew that a friendship with El Grande could be very helpful, maybe even life-saving. But he also knew that it wasn't possible to walk away from the deal he had made with the Agency.

But wouldn't it be great to cause a bit of pain for Fredericks and Quinn?

He still had some pride, some gumption, and Kittredge vowed not to roll over and take a beating without dishing out a little punishment himself.

* * *

Quinn watched the tired, dusty pickup truck pull up to the Santa Marta station on the Red Line, and watched the passenger climb out. He adjusted the focus on his binoculars, and scanned back and forth between the truck's driver and his quarry.

"You're sure?" Fredericks' voice crackled in Quinn's phone earpiece.

"Of course not. I'm staring through 1950's binoculars from a hundred yards. I called you because I'm *pretty* sure. Kittredge and a VSS guy, most likely."

"El Grande?"

"Maybe. Hard to say. But I picked them up coming in on the road from the boonies. I don't think there's much out that direction that doesn't belong to either the Venezuelan Special Services or the cocaine cartels."

"Either way, it's a situation."

"How so? You want access to the VSS crowd. Kittredge has obviously made friends with them. Done." *Idiot*, Quinn didn't add. *How is it that I work for this guy, and not the other way around?*

"I like where your head's at," Fredericks said.

"You should."

"Stick with him for the moment."

"Did you think of that all by yourself?"

"I'll call you in a while," Fredericks said. "I have bigger fish for you to fry, and your replacement should be arriving soon to keep tabs on Kittredge."

Chapter 30

Special Agent Sam Jameson sat on a bench at the edge of the greenbelt, in view of her house. It appeared from a distance that the cleanup and reconstruction from the weekend's bombing was progressing well. The dumpster in her drive was rapidly filling, and she anticipated that within a few days, the crews would transition to rebuilding the exterior wall that had been largely demolished by the military-style bomb that had exploded in her front yard just after three a.m. on Sunday morning.

Sam hoped Brock was still staying at their house. If not, there was no one to keep tabs on things, and Sam didn't dare risk a trip home to speak with the construction crew.

On the way back from the FAA, Sam had stopped by the Shirlington parking garage in the hope that she would be able to collect her car, but a bright orange wheel boot had dashed her hopes. The Metro guys were apparently still interested in smoking her out, and they would undoubtedly have her house under surveillance, too.

She wondered how long the Homeland and Internal Affairs people would take to build a case against the group of rogue cops. She would have thought that Everett Cooper's outrageous actions over the weekend would have forced the authorities' hand, and they'd have swooped in to arrest the remaining players in what was apparently a gang of crooked Metro cops, working for some sort of Venezuelan concern.

But if the previous day's encounter on I-395 was any indication, when yet another Metro cruiser had followed her briefly en route to Quartermain's house, not much had changed.

Perhaps Internal Affairs and DHS needed more evidence for an indictment. If so, it meant that Ekman and Jarvis were using Sam as bait.

Those bastards. They would never endanger a private citizen in order to gather more evidence, but they evidently felt little compunction about leaving Sam in harm's way.

Another thought struck: *Was Brock now a target, too?* There was no way to know, especially since she still had no idea why *she* had been targeted in the first place.

But she clearly *had* been targeted – her name and address had shown up at John Abrams' house, and her photo was in the music box containing Abrams' and Coopers' fingerprints. Whoever *they* were, they certainly had her in their crosshairs.

She adjusted the burka she had purchased from the specialty shop a couple of blocks south of the Mall. DC's Muslim population, especially of North African descent, had exploded over the past decade, and it wasn't unusual to see women clad in traditional garb throughout the city. She was certain that her unusual attire attracted more than a few stares, but it would be a disorienting change of context for anyone looking specifically for a tall redhead. It was a clever way to hide in plain sight.

The late afternoon traffic picked up, and Sam glanced at her watch. If Brock had gone to work today, he would be returning home soon. A part of her hoped that she would find something of interest, some piece of information that would explain his dishonesty and his apparent association with Arturo Dibiaso.

A different part of her just wanted to see him, if even from a distance.

It was weakness, she knew, and there was no place for weakness when a group of very bad people seemed to be bearing down on her, but she was still reeling from what she felt was a death blow to her relationship with Brock.

He was everything she had wanted – handsome, brilliant, mature, fun, funny, big heart, big johnson, big sense of humor. . .

And honest.

That was the kicker. She had declared her life a no-bullshit zone, and Brock had professed to have done the same, so it felt like a match made in heaven. Everything was easy between them. Sure, they had their share of problems to work through, but they were always external problems. No difficulty ever arose between them that they couldn't resolve within seconds.

Until now.

Sam shook her head, still incredulous. She tried to think of a reason that Brock might have been compelled to keep the Dibiaso connection from her, but she failed.

They both had security clearances for their work, and they both had things they weren't allowed to discuss with each other because of need-to-know restrictions. But they had always been honest about them. Some programs had "cover stories," or officially-sanctioned lies that those with access were supposed to tell their spouses in order to keep unwanted attention away from secret information, but Brock and Sam had explicitly agreed not to use *any* cover stories with each other. If they couldn't talk about something, they simply said so. In addition to keeping them out of trouble at work, it kept their hearts and consciences clean.

She felt the now-familiar lump form in her throat, and battled tears for what felt like the thousandth time.

One of her burner phones buzzed, and Sam fumbled to remove it from the folds of the burka. She recognized Dan Gable's office number. "Hi Dan."

"Everything okay? Your voice sounds muffled, like you're gagged," Dan said.

"I'm wearing a burka."

"The Muslim thingy? Did you lose a bet?"

"I sure as hell did. A big one, apparently. So what's up?"

As Dan started talking, Brock's car drove up and parked in front of their house. Sam's insides stirred as she saw him climb out and walk toward the flurry of construction activity. More tears tried to work their way out.

"Did you hear what I said?" Dan's question snapped her back to their phone conversation.

"Sorry, no."

"I said, I got that information on Executive Strategies. They're like Blackwater, only not yet on steroids."

"Shit." Blackwater was an American contracting company that employed mercenaries, usually ex-military guys. They were paid incredible amounts of money by the US government, and their primary business was to do the things that international law and public scrutiny prevented the US military from doing itself. Those were usually very unsavory things.

A gaggle of me-too companies had also sprung up around the same business model, and, apparently, Executive Strategies was one of them.

"Who received all those payments?" Sam asked, referring to the long list of financial transactions contained on the CD ROM inside the music box.

"I have the financial crimes guys doing some digging, but right now, it looks like all of those different accounts belong to Everett Cooper and John Abrams. They were trying to hide their association with Executive Strategies and JIE Associates, the Venezuelan firm we found earlier. But Swiss accounts aren't what they used to be."

Sam pondered for a moment. "Why would Abrams and Cooper create a box full of evidence against themselves?"

"Because you have to have some way of keeping track of all of your accounts. Otherwise, the money is as good as lost. They probably created the file, then hid the file and destroyed the computer they used to create it. That's what I would do, anyway."

"So it was bad luck that Abrams happened to get killed while holding the key to the music box?"

"I think it was a message," Dan said. "Somebody got wise, found the box, and smoked Abrams in a pretty spectacular way, as a warning. Like Henry the Eighth hanging skulls on posts outside London."

That sounded reasonable to Sam. "So what does that mean for us?"

"Strange you should ask," Dan said. "Are you sitting down?"

Sam rolled her eyes. Dan had a dramatic flair at times. It was occasionally humorous, but often tiresome. "Yes, Dan. Out with it."

"Executive Strategies is owned, in part, by Edward Minton."

Sam was momentarily disoriented. *Minton was a familiar name. . .* Then it came to her: "Fatso?"

"Yep. Fatso Minton is part owner of Executive Strategies."

"How do you know Fatso Minton?" Sam asked, still confused.

"I don't. I hacked into the system and read your lie detector transcript."

"Jesus, Dan."

"I know, right? But Ekman and Jarvis have a seriously strange air about them these days, and I was tired of being in the dark. Anyway, not only is Minton part owner of Executive Strategies, he's actually one of the founders. They started out in 1998, and they're still based in Dayton, Ohio. He registered the company while he was still on active duty in the Air Force, right before he got out. Does Brock know him?"

Sam thought back to the lie detector technician's strange line of questioning during Sunday's test, which she had volunteered to take in the hopes that it would demonstrate to Ekman and Jarvis that she wasn't mixed up in whatever they thought she was mixed up in.

The technician had become a little too insistent that Sam provide an accurate date about when Brock and Fatso had met each other. She obviously couldn't, since that era in Brock's life predated their relationship by more than a decade, and it was never a topic of detailed conversation between them.

The technician had pressed for a precise answer, which meant that Jarvis and Ekman were looking into Brock's past. Or Minton's. Either way, it was a strong indication that she needed to investigate the connection, too.

Unfortunately, events had conspired against her since then, and she hadn't been able to look into it. *Looks like that particular answer found me,* she thought. Usually it worked the other way around.

"Brock does know Minton," Sam said, feeling heaviness as she spoke the words. If there's a Dibiaso connection that Brock was keeping from her, it was likely the Minton thing was equally important.

What the hell did you drag me into, Brock?

"I hear Dayton is nice this time of year," Dan said.

"Dayton is like Siberia this time of year."

"Maybe your new burka will keep you warm."

Part 3

Chapter 31

Sam woke up feeling remarkably peaceful. She'd had the first good night's sleep in four days, since Ekman's Saturday night call dispatching her to the scene of John Abrams' bloody demise.

Life had roundly kicked her ass over the ensuing four days. Biology had finally taken over, leaving her too exhausted to lay awake worrying, and she had slept dreamlessly for nine straight hours.

And then, daylight, and a flood of recollection, and her stomach was soon awash in adrenaline as she pondered her next move.

It was important to prioritize her efforts, she realized. Priority one: figure out who the hell was trying to kill her, and why.

Priority two: figure out how to stop them.

Easy. A short to-do list for a run-of-the-mill Wednesday.

Except that both tasks seemed nearly insurmountable.

But, she realized for the thousandth time in her life, the best way to accomplish anything at all was to first begin, and then to keep going until finished. *Thanks, grandpa.* It was a piece of Zen pith, a non-financial inheritance from her mom's dad, that had proven annoyingly prescient and remarkably useful.

She turned on all three burner phones, which she'd been using chiefly to communicate with Dan since she had bought them in a shop around the corner from the scene of Philip Quartermain's murder.

As the phones powered up and began communicating with their various cell networks, Sam turned the situation over in her head again. Abrams. Cooper. Brock. Arturo Dibiaso. Phil Quartermain. Fatso Minton and Executive Strategies. JIE Associates. Ekman. Jarvis. They were all linked. But how?

Her next step was pretty clear. She had to travel to Dayton, Ohio, and have a chat with Fatso Minton. A phone call or email was out of the question – because Homeland was interested in Fatso, there wouldn't be a safe way to communicate with him except in person, and even that would be tricky.

There was also the small problem of Jarvis and Ekman. They'd asked about her repeatedly since the weekend's events, and Dan had so far been able to put them off, but that wasn't going to last forever.

Reluctantly, she called and left a message on Dan's phone at work, asking him to leave a note on Frank Ekman's desk, to the effect that Sam would call with an update at 9 a.m.

How screwed up is it that I have to play cloak and dagger with my own boss?

Another of her grandfather's many epigrams came to mind: *no use wishing a thing was what it wasn't.* The gamesmanship was necessary because the moment Ekman had a phone number, he would soon have her location. That was unacceptable, because she still wasn't sure whose team Ekman and Jarvis were on. If they were indeed on her team, they sure had a funny way of showing it.

Her mind next turned back to Fatso. Sam had to get to Dayton, as soon as humanly possible.

That wasn't a pleasant prospect, because Dayton wasn't like most other places. It had summer, which sucked, and winter, which sucked more. There wasn't much in the way of an interstitial period, what other parts of the country referred to as spring and fall. While she was still perspiring in DC's late fall warmth, folks in Dayton were already shivering and shoveling snow.

That was inconvenient, because it meant that she'd have to invest in winter clothing before traveling to Ohio. She sure as hell wasn't going home any time soon to pick up any of her own things.

Getting to Ohio meant leaving a trail. One decade after 9/11, it was possible to pay cash for airfare, but only if one wanted the Transportation Security Administration, adjunct office of the Department of Homeland Security, to crawl up one's ass. Sam didn't want that.

She had broken out her Jennifer Garman legend to check in to both of her hotels over the past two nights. Unlike her other legends, which came complete with credit cards, birth certificates, passports, drivers' licenses, and registration in the DHS database, her Garman legend was "off the books." It didn't officially exist, mostly because it was highly illegal – Sam had purchased the legend herself, using the Tor online anonymity network and a website called "Silk Road."

At the time, it had been a huge risk, but one that Sam thought was worth taking. Nobody could destroy you like the US Federal Government, and Sam knew there might be a time when she found herself on the receiving end of all that nastiness.

Like now, for instance.

She fished the Jennifer Garman credit card out of her purse, made her way down the hotel's dank, dark hallway to the "business center" – though what kind of business people might care to conduct in a cramped closet with an ages-old computer and an even older printer, Sam wasn't certain – and booked herself on the next available flight to Dayton.

She knew that a same-day booking automatically invited extra screening by the bovine TSA people, and she groaned at the thought. Traveling was unpleasant enough, and she wasn't in the mood for extra bullshit.

She stopped by the lobby, grabbed a donut and a cup of coffee, and asked to visit the lost and found, where she found a jacket heavy enough to stave off death in frigid Dayton.

Then she packed, checked out of the hotel, and hopped on the dilapidated airport shuttle for the thirty-minute commute to Reagan International.

On the way, she made small talk with the driver, a refugee from Ethiopia who lamented what his homeland had become, lamented having to live in an apartment with eleven other adults and three kids, lamented the large skim that the informal currency network took from the payments he sent back to his family in the old country.

But the driver never stopped smiling. "At least, in this country, I am free," he said.

He memorized the brochure, she thought. It brought to mind that old quote, something about no one being more thoroughly enslaved than those who falsely think they're free.

At least I know I'm screwed, she thought grimly.

* * *

Sam managed to keep her phone appointment with Ekman, calling from Reagan International to let him know that she was going to work swing shifts for a couple of days to allow her time to oversee reconstruction of her bombed-out house.

She was pretty sure Ekman didn't buy her lie, and was pretty sure that an airport announcement in the background gave her whereabouts away, but he didn't press her on either issue.

She thought that Ekman and Jarvis maybe preferred that she not hang around the office. It would be much more difficult for them to snoop around in her life if she were there, looking over their shoulders. But they wouldn't dare place her on administrative leave, because they thought, correctly, that she would eviscerate them with an IG complaint.

So the conversation had amounted to an uneasy and momentary truce. But Sam knew it would be of limited duration. She hoped her discussion with Fatso Minton would be productive.

The airport hassle was annoying but tolerable, as was the flight, the rental car counter, and the traffic from the Dayton airport to Wright Patterson Air Force Base, home of Fatso Minton's Executive Strategies Corporation.

She had thrown her three burner phones away at Reagan, and bought two more at a Verizon store in Dayton. She used one of them to ask Dan to arrange a visitor pass at the Wright Patterson gate for Jennifer Garman.

It was a huge risk – Dan now knew of her off-the-grid alias, and while she trusted him more than anyone else in the world at the moment, she generally trusted no one further than she could throw them.

But Sam knew that she would soon have to discard the legend, anyway. She had broken the seal and created a trail, and she would no longer be able to use her Jennifer Garman identity for a completely anonymous getaway if she needed one in the future. So, if Dan *did* dime her out for some reason, she would certainly lose a brief tactical advantage, but little more.

Sam exited the highway, grateful for the change in direction so she could stop staring into the setting sun. She followed the wide curve to the access road that led to Wright Patterson's main gate. The road skirted the perimeter of the base for a couple of miles, taking Sam past the largest aircraft hangars she'd ever seen.

Her visitor's pass was waiting for her, and the process of gaining admittance to the base caused her surprisingly little aggravation.

Being careful to obey the posted speed limit, which seemed ludicrously slow, she made her way past the main part of the base and toward the older, disused buildings on the other side of the runway. Checking the building numbers, which were arranged in no logical order that Sam could discern, she finally found the Executive Strategies address.

Immediately, her heart sank. Video surveillance cameras surrounded the facility, and a guard was posted at a shack at the entrance to the complex. There were no signs to identify the building, which was another bad sign. All of the surveillance – the fortress-within-a-fortress of extra security on an already-secure Air

Force base – meant that Executive Strategies was involved in something very sensitive.

It also meant that nothing happened at Executive Strategies that the whiz kids at Homeland couldn't observe, in real-time, just by hacking into the security servers.

If Fatso Minton were under surveillance, which he undoubtedly was, then a couple of pimply-faced hackers were surely watching him right now. Ekman and Jarvis would know within minutes if she set foot on the Executive Strategies campus. She had nothing to hide, but they had expressed a keen interest in any sort of connection that she and Brock might have had with Fatso. She wasn't anxious to fuel the fire.

The gate guard spotted her, and walked toward her car. He motioned for her to roll down the window, and asked to see her identification.

"I'm very sorry, sir," she said, putting on a respectable Southern accent. "I was looking for the base library, and I seem to have gotten myself lost." She gave him a slightly pathetic smile, and he dutifully described the route back across the base to the library.

She thanked him, turned the car around, and drove away. *Time for Plan B. Whatever the hell that might be.*

* * *

Sam did in fact drive to the Wright Patterson Air Force Base library. She used a library computer to access the Deep Web, which comprised ninety-six percent of the Internet, but was accessed by fewer than one percent of Internet users. It was mostly comprised of junk web pages that nobody needed to access, but there were certainly gems buried among them.

The Deep Web also contained some frighteningly efficient tools to ferret out some frighteningly personal information about almost anyone in the Western world. She had needed to install some temporary software, which she accomplished by faking a printer driver problem and watching the computer administrator's fingers as he typed in his password. Then she replicated the password to give permission to the Tor browser's installer program.

Once inside the Deep Web, Sam began surfing through mountains of account information, the subterranean raw material of modern commerce. It hadn't taken her long to discover that, unlike the vast majority of Americans, Fatso Minton had an extremely small digital signature.

Most of his account information was contained offline, and she wasn't able to employ any of her usual tricks to access bank account numbers, credit cards, mortgages, or anything else that might also come with an address. Someone very good had hidden Fatso's records from prying eyes.

But very good was rarely good enough, and Sam got what she needed by going about things a different way. She searched the records of common service providers, such as cable television, utilities, and the like, for accounts belonging or relating to Edward Minton.

Those obvious places yielded no results, but she only had to widen her search a little bit to get what she needed.

She tracked down Fatso Minton by, of all things, his automotive service records. She found an invoice from just two weeks earlier, something about a torque converter for his BMW X5, which also contained Fatso's telephone number and address.

She wrote down the address and phone number, printed a map and directions to Fatso's place, erased the Tor application she had illegally installed on the library's computer a few minutes earlier, and walked out into the frigid Ohio evening.

The chill was startlingly earnest, and she hunkered down into the slightly-oversized coat she had liberated hours earlier from the DC flop house's lost-and-found.

If I lived here, I would move, she thought as she started her rental car.

* * *

Fatso Minton's house wasn't a fortress, but it was a reasonably well-secured private residence, set back in the woods on the outskirts of town. There were motion detectors around the perimeter of the yard, but no video surveillance that Sam could detect. She was something of an expert in the field, having installed a state-of-the-art Israeli system in her own home during a paranoid episode following a particularly nasty case.

It was clear that Fatso had done well for himself. So well, in fact, that he didn't really live in a neighborhood, but on something of an estate. It was well north of conspicuous consumption but just shy of ostentation.

More importantly for Sam, his castle didn't include a moat, wall, or fence, and she simply circled around to the backyard on foot, and waited.

It wasn't so much that careful people made mistakes. It was

more that life was such a messy and entangled business that it was impossible to live an airtight existence. The Minton's security situation was compromised by their beloved pug, who wandered out into the backyard through a doggy door. If the back yard motion detectors were on, Sam reasoned, they were certainly ignored.

She simply walked across the lawn to the back door. It was locked, but the doggy door was large enough for her to reach an arm through, and her arm was long enough to unlock the door from the inside. If the Mintons had teenagers, Sam thought, they would undoubtedly have discovered the same technique to sneak back in the house after an evening on the prowl.

Sam calmly walked into the Minton's house, noting the two beeps of the security system that announced the opening and closing of the back door, and also noting the utter lack of response the beeps produced. The human mind has an impressive intrinsic capacity to ignore repeated stimuli, even those it shouldn't ignore.

She found Fatso's rail-thin frame hunched over a computer keyboard, his face scrunched into a scowl as he tried to make out some small detail on the computer display.

"Need glasses?" Sam asked by way of introduction.

Fatso jumped out of his chair, then reached awkwardly for a desk drawer – clearly it contained a gun, Sam noted – but he soon recognized Sam's face and smile, and his panic subsided. "Holy sweet baby Jesus, you scared the piss out of me!"

"I'm so sorry to startle you, Fatso. And it's been ages. How are you?" She moved forward and held her arms out for a hug.

Fatso obliged eagerly, but was still obviously disoriented by

Sam's sudden appearance in his study.

"So you were just in the neighborhood and thought you'd break in?" Minton laughed. "You government types think you own everything."

"If the shoe fits," Sam said, grateful for his warm reception despite her having startled him nearly to death.

"Actually, I barged in on you *because* of those annoying government types," she said. "I was hoping I could have a conversation with you."

Chapter 32

"Fredericks, I can actually feel the change in gravity when you walk by," Quinn said. "You really gotta lay off the ho-ho's."

Quinn clapped his boss on the back as he took his seat at the kitchen table in the Caracas safe house. It wasn't a house as much as an apartment, and its position twenty-five floors up a thirty-floor high-rise meant that its air conditioner, which came off the assembly line no earlier than 1987, had to work extra hard to expel the late evening heat.

It wasn't doing a great job, and Fredericks' corpulent face glistened. He flipped Quinn the bird, revealing soggy armpits. "Case in point," Quinn said. "You're sweating like a gay Republican."

Fredericks waved him off. "Not everyone can be a steroid-gobbling freak, Quinn. Where's our freshman? I wanted him here for this."

"Not my day to watch him, Bill." Really, it wasn't. Quinn had stopped tailing Kittredge the afternoon prior, handing the duty over to another Agency guy Quinn had never met. "But it looks like you had the blind watch the stupid. How come you haven't been fired yet?"

Fredericks ignored Quinn's barbs as the room continued to fill with Agency players.

Quinn recognized none of them, which always made him nervous. The CIA was a big place, on paper, but just like everything else in life, it worked on personal relationships. Quinn didn't trust anyone he didn't know, and a roomful of unknown players in his op made him uneasy.

And this particular operation was too large and high-profile to take any chances, which Quinn had earlier observed to Fredericks in a typically undiplomatic fashion. Fredericks had assured him that they *weren't* taking any chances, and that Quinn didn't know anybody on the Operation Syphilis team because, up until a few days ago, *Quinn* had been on the B-Team. *Touché.*

Fredericks had a way of putting people in their place, and Quinn was still a bit stung. Hence the fat jokes.

As the last of the attendees appeared, Fredericks turned on a radio, tuned to some horrific mariachi station, to drown out their conversation. Perhaps the horrendous music would be enough to defeat an unsophisticated adversary's surveillance equipment, though there wasn't much evidence to suggest that the Venezuelan Special Service was anything but a modern state security apparatus, to the extent that any second-world power possessed such an animal.

"So, welcome," Fredericks began. "No introductions yet, for obvious reasons, but I've arranged private meetings afterwards between the parties who need to have more detailed conversations. And, as always, no questions. The shitheads in DC have already decided what you can and can't know about this op, so there's no use trying to get me in trouble by asking for more." A few chuckles sounded around the table.

Quinn looked at the faces, tuning Fredericks' voice out. It was an unlikely crowd, comprised of Fredericks, who could have starred in a bad gangster movie, a frumpy middle-aged woman, a guy in a three-piece suit who looked like a banker, a sixty-ish fossil with thick glasses and an even thicker German accent, and three twenty-somethings in jeans and t-shirts. And one hot chick, a petite blonde that Quinn couldn't stop looking at.

"Don't let me interrupt your sexual fantasy, Quinn," Fredericks said. Quinn felt himself blush, a human response that seemed not to fit an assassin's image, and the attractive girl smiled coyly.

"As I was saying before I was so rudely ignored," Fredericks continued, "the op has four phases. Phase one is what I like to call 'getting our shit together.'" Fredericks made quotation marks in the air, and Quinn rolled his eyes, drawing another smile from the hottie across the table.

"Once you're all settled in to your respective accommodations, we'll begin the surveillance phase in earnest. Spotters, scopes, video cameras, parabolic mikes, the whole nine."

"Isn't that going to be tough to pull off? It isn't like that stuff is common around here," one of the twenty-somethings asked.

"Yeah, not optimum, as the bureaucrats say," Fredericks said. "But it's pretty high profile, as you can imagine, which means I have to send a bunch of bullshit back home before they'll green-light us."

"Pussies," the girl said. Quinn was certain that he was falling in love.

"Anyway," Fredericks continued, "that's probably three or four days, all told, before the go-team gets here and we execute. So it's going to be a big pain in the ass for those three or four days, and you're going to have to play dress-up, like, sixteen times a day to keep the surveillance presence fresh and unrecognizable. Which reminds me, make sure to check your wardrobes and supplies when you get to your safe houses. It should all be pre-positioned, but let me know right away if the admin people screwed anything up."

"Weapons?" the frumpy lady asked.

"Also at your safe houses."

"Gear?" Another of the twenty-somethings.

"You know what I'm going to tell you, right? It's all at the safe houses already, give me a call if anything's missing, please fucking try to pay attention." The kid who'd asked the question slumped into his chair, and Quinn chuckled at Fredericks' Tourette's-like outburst. Fredericks wasn't famous for his patience.

"So, contingencies," Fredericks continued. "If you think they made you, or even if you have the slightest inkling that you might have been compromised, go to the collection point and wait. On even numbered dates, the collection point is the National Parthenon."

"Pantheon," Quinn corrected.

Fredericks looked confused.

"It's the National *Pantheon*," Quinn repeated. "Not the Parthenon. That's in Greece."

"Right. Whatever." Sniggers around the table, which Fredericks ignored. "And on odd days, go to the Caracas Cathedral. The magic number is nine. It will be an embassy puke picking you up, so don't cock it up. If they say 'six,' Quinn, what will you say?"

Quinn rolled his eyes. "Three."

"Yep. You see how he did that?" Fredericks looked directly at the twenty-somethings. They also nodded, somewhat annoyed at Fredericks' patronizing condescension.

"What if they say 'fourteen'?" Fredericks asked.

"Five," the frumpy-looking lady said, with obvious aggravation. "I think we're pretty well versed in our addition and subtraction rules."

Fredericks reddened. "You guys think I'm a pain in the ass with this stuff, but I have a few stories about guys who honked up their meeting codes and never got picked up, except by the Russkies and the Hajjis. They didn't make it home for dinner. So you'd better know that stuff cold, even when your brain is mush and you're ready to piss yourself because you're scared."

"Thanks for the pep talk, Gipper," Quinn quipped.

"You're welcome. You get the first shift, sweetheart. Starts at midnight." Fredericks smiled at Quinn, who raised the bird in response.

Chapter 33

Sam smiled at Fatso Minton. "I'm sorry again to barge in on you like this," she said. "If I promise not to get too nosy, would you mind talking a little shop with me?"

"It's the least I could do," Minton said, "seeing as you went through all the trouble to show up in my house unannounced. Really, you're lucky I still have a crush on you. Otherwise, I'd have sent my attack pug after you."

Sam laughed. "Brock sends his best."

"That bastard! What is he up to these days? Still in the Air Force, isn't he?"

"Yeah, but I think the bloom's off the rose. He's been at a desk for a few years, and it's making him perpetually cranky."

"Yep," Minton said. "It's the great bait-and-switch. One day, you wake up and figure out that they've turned you into a bureaucrat. He should've taken me up on the job offer. He'd still be flying jets if he had."

"I think he regrets not having done that," Sam said. "But I don't think he has much interest in the places you guys spend all of your time."

Minton laughed. "Like Dayton?"

"Yes, without a doubt," Sam said with a smile. "But also the third-world garden spots."

"Yeah, but the fun more than makes up for the geography,"

Minton said. "And the cash ain't bad, either."

Sam nodded. "I was admiring your place as I was breaking in. It's absolutely gorgeous."

"Thank you," Fatso said. "Mostly Deenie's work, of course. She's visiting her sister, which is probably a good thing – if she'd seen you sneaking in the house, I'd never have been able to convince her I wasn't having an affair."

Another affair, Sam thought. Fidelity wasn't exactly a strong suit, if Brock's recollection was accurate. And she wasn't sure how Minton pulled the wool, either. He was kind of gangly and a little bit ugly in the face.

Maybe it's the personality that does them in, she thought. *Or maybe he goes for fat chicks with low standards.*

She followed Minton's gesture and took a seat in a plush leather chair, and he took his place opposite her, an expensive coffee table between them. "Drink?" he asked.

"I'm fine, thanks." She began her interview, which was most artfully done when it didn't feel like an interview at all. Sam was terrific at turning such meetings into friendly and extremely productive conversations.

It was actually fairly easy. She usually began with an innocuous topic, such as sports or the weather, to get the subject used to talking. Then she'd move to questions that asked for the subject's opinions on various things. These questions were deceptively personal, because they forced the subject to reveal something of themselves in their answers.

Then, only after a solid rapport developed, which sometimes

took an hour or longer, Sam would slowly move into more sensitive topics.

It helped that Fatso wasn't shy. She emerged from his house two hours later, just before ten p.m., with a head full of interesting details.

Fatso had indeed overlapped with Brock at Spangdahlem Air Base, in the Eifel region of Germany. It was Fatso's last assignment, as he put in his papers to separate from the Air Force in 1998. He knew all that remained as he got older was more email and more meetings, the gristle of endless layers of middle management in large organizations the world over, and Fatso wanted nothing to do with it.

People viewed the pre-9/11 world as delightfully simple, but the reality was quite the opposite, and Fatso's time in the 52nd Fighter Wing, the pointy end of the American spear and one of the closest US air units to any Middle Eastern trouble, had shown him that the world was continually at war.

He smelled opportunity, and he started Executive Strategies even before he had officially separated from the Air Force.

It was ever so slightly illegal, but it wasn't Fatso's idea to start his new business before his separation from the Air Force. He had simply made a few inquiries into whether a special air service, the kind that provided special-needs transportation like Air America had provided during the Vietnam war, might be a useful thing to have. By the time he left Germany, Fatso had a fat federal contract in hand.

He called all of his flying buddies, and a few of them got out of the Air Force to join Fatso's Flying Circus, as he affectionately called his new enterprise. Brock had elected to stay on his promising career track in the Air Force, but Sam knew he secretly wished he'd joined Fatso when he had the chance.

Fatso soon expanded from simple transportation of paramilitary goods and people into far more active areas. He was able to parlay his huge profits into an ever-expanding fleet of foreign-built light attack aircraft, which allowed the American CIA and other agencies to apply direct military force in any region of choice while leaving the US government with plausible deniability of any involvement whatsoever.

It was a truly elegant solution for the dozens of small wars that the US started, and sometimes finished, without any public knowledge or debate. Because Fatso and his men were contractors, and not military members, there was no requirement for the Executive Branch to report anything to Congress whenever they sent Fatso and his guys to raise hell in some third-world country.

It became clear to Sam during their lengthy conversation that Fatso was a true believer. He felt that while his company had been involved in a number of what he termed "blowback situations," where things hadn't gone nearly as neatly as planned, he and his guys had nevertheless spared countless American lives by averting much larger and costlier conflicts.

Sam didn't share his optimistic appraisal of the efficacy of the many low-intensity conflicts in America's recent history. Fatso had hinted at a few places where Executive Strategies may or may not be involved, and those places were all net exporters of some natural resource. It was usually oil, but sometimes precious metals or rare earth elements, useful to the cell phone and computer industries.

Fatso spoke often of helping to ensure "energy and economic security," which Sam translated into a more bare-knuckled term: empire.

But she had kept her cynicism to herself. She was there to absorb, and, hopefully, to figure out why she and Brock had ended up in the middle of what had turned into a giant mess.

It was an important data point that Fatso was a true patriot, as far as she could tell. He had put his money and his life where his mouth was.

Sure, it paid him extremely well, but he still flew combat missions in shitholes, and the bullets were very real. She felt that, in his heart, Fatso believed he continued to serve the greater good of the United States of America.

So she didn't know what to expect when she brought up the names Everett Cooper and John Abrams, two people she was sure were on the Executive Strategies payroll with apparent Venezuelan ties.

Fatso didn't confirm that ES employed either Cooper or Abrams, citing privacy and security, but neither did he flinch. In fact, Sam got the impression that while Fatso was speaking the words, his head was nodding up and down, as if to tell Sam without actually telling her that he had employed both men.

She pressed him for more detail about how foreign funding might be involved in Executive Strategies' operations, expecting him to dodge the question, but he surprised her with his forthrightness.

"Uncle Sugar likes to launder his money before he gives it to me. Keeps things out of the news." She asked him about Venezuela in particular, and he shrugged. "The payments could have been routed through anywhere," he had said.

Her next question had surprised Fatso: was Brock on his payroll? "You should know! Aren't you two living together?" Fatso had asked in response, but Sam pressed him for a straight answer.

"I sure as hell wish Brock was with us," he eventually said. "I tried probably five different times over the years to get him to jump the fence and join us. But he never would. I think he never liked the idea in the first place. He never really was a joiner, you know."

Sam agreed. It's one of the reasons she loved him as wildly as she did. Brock always did his own thinking. Thinking of him had brought painful barbs to her heart, but she had to understand the extent of Brock's involvement.

One last agenda item: Arturo Dibiaso. Fatso gave her the same spiel, about privacy and all that, but shook his head this time. The message was clear: there's no Dibiaso on the Executive Services payroll, at least to Fatso's knowledge.

Interesting.

She left Fatso's house convinced that Brock and Executive Strategies were not in league together. She was undecided about whether Executive Strategies was involved in any anti-American activity, though it would certainly have surprised her, given Fatso's idealistic approach to the dirty work he and his compatriots performed at the behest of the US government.

It was obviously possible that Fatso's overarching ideology

was profit, and that he was therefore open to doing shady work for foreign thugs in addition to doing shady work for American thugs, but she doubted that was the case. It would have been bad long-term strategy. Sooner or later, the Agency would figure it out, and that would be the end of Executive Strategies.

She also decided to provisionally believe Fatso's claim that there was no Arturo Dibiaso on the ES payroll, at least until she uncovered evidence to the contrary. Dibiaso was Homeland's remaining link to Brock, which made Dibiaso Priority Numero Uno for Sam, so she was disappointed not to have learned more about him.

In the end, she had spent a very long day chasing after what appeared to be a dead-end lead. But even dead ends taught you something, she knew, and a part of her was relieved to learn that Brock wasn't involved in Fatso's world. It meant that there wasn't another lie between them, and that made her feel better about having invested her heart and her life into her relationship with Brock.

Unfortunately, it also meant that she wasn't any closer to figuring out who was barking up her tree, or why.

And Brock had still lied to her about Arturo Dibiaso. She got angry at him again as she thought about it, gripped the steering wheel tightly as she felt herself descending into the familiar emotional vortex, and drove eastward into the darkness, fighting tears once again.

She held imaginary conversations with Brock, in which she gave him a piece of her mind in no uncertain terms.

She realized that over the past two days, she had returned to her earlier worldview, the one she held before Brock swept her off her feet two years earlier: *All men are bastards.*

Chapter 34

The Thursday sun rose in a quiet fury, its light reflected off a high layer of clouds that painted the sky a gorgeous crimson. It was amazing to be alive, Sam thought as she cruised along with the eastbound traffic on I-70.

She had rested for a few hours at a Dayton flop house, again paying cash and using her Jennifer Garman identification, then rose several hours before dawn to get a head start on the drive back to DC.

She had elected not to buy a return airline ticket simply because she thought Ekman might have circulated a watch order through the TSA network. She was pretty sure he didn't know about her Jennifer Garman alias, but that wouldn't help her get past the facial recognition software in use at almost all airports in the US. She wasn't sure whether Dayton had one, but Reagan International certainly did.

So she guzzled coffee and rolled down the window to help her stay awake on the long drive east, and her mind gnawed on the confusing events of the past five days, searching for possible connections.

Dibiaso wasn't an Executive Strategies guy, and neither was Brock. That was good, she thought, but it left her back at square one trying to figure out what Brock and Dibiaso were involved in.

Also, Fatso Minton's company may have been paid by a

Venezuelan company – Fatso wasn't sure – but if that were the case, it was more than likely nothing more than a shill corporation used to launder CIA money. It didn't seem logical for Executive Strategies to become involved with a real-life Venezuelan concern on the side. The profit couldn't possibly be large enough to justify jeopardizing a long and very lucrative relationship with the Agency and its satellite organizations. Fatso was keenly aware of where his bread was buttered.

So that left another mystery: why the hell did Executive Strategies pay John Abrams and Everett Cooper, who, if Ekman and Jarvis were to be believed, were dancing to a Venezuelan tune?

But were Ekman and Jarvis to be believed?

They were both careerists, which meant they were reeds in the wind. That wasn't necessarily bad, as long as the wind blew from the right direction. But Sam still had no idea what pressures they were responding to at the moment, and what was fueling their suspicion of her and Brock. Obviously, it was somehow connected to Dibiaso, but all of her efforts to figure out the Dibiaso connection had so far produced bupkis.

Then an idea struck. Really, it was a realization of her own weakness. When Ekman had shown her the cell phone location data that proved Brock and Dibiaso had spent time together, she had let her emotions cloud her investigative judgment. She was instantly overcome by the horror of Brock having lied to her, and she failed to ask the obvious question: *where the hell were Brock and Dibiaso going together?*

Time for another chat with her deputy. She turned on one of

her new burners and dialed his office. It was still early, but she had no desire to anger Sara, Dan's tired and long-suffering wife, so she didn't dare call Gable at home. To her surprise, he answered his office phone. "Are you hiding at work?" she asked.

"Is it that obvious?" He chuckled.

"Good luck with that time bomb. Anyway, I'm a jackass, and I thought of a question I should have asked four days ago. Where did Brock and Dibiaso meet each other those times when they were together?"

"Holy shit, Sam, I thought you knew that already. The first thing I did when you sent me the data was to plot it on a map. I'd have sent it over right away, but I thought it was old news for you."

Sam cursed under her breath. *That's what I get for acting like a lovesick chick.*

"Hit me," she said.

"Both times, they met at the Pentagon and drove south together. Brock's line ends in Arlington a couple of blocks away from your house, while Dibiaso's line goes all the way to the park-n-ride at the end of the HOV lanes."

"Down in Triangle?" It was a town built around a daily traffic jam. Brock used to joke that the whole town would declare bankruptcy if Virginia ever added another southbound lane, because people wouldn't have to pull out of the bumper-to-bumper traffic to go to the bathroom or get food.

"Yeah. It's a dump. Anyway, whatever they were doing, they only did it during those car rides together, at least as far as I can tell."

Sam's mind churned. She realized that she had seen only two episodes of Brock's and Dibiaso's locations overlapping. She had assumed that they were representative episodes, chosen by Ekman to illustrate a larger pattern of Brock and Dibiaso doing business of some sort, but she realized that might not be the case at all. What if the two times that Ekman had showed to her were the *only* times?

Two episodes were surely enough to demonstrate a connection, but it was worth knowing how deep the rabbit hole might have gone.

She asked Dan to assemble a location map for Brock and Dibiaso's phones over a three-month period. Dan raised the issue of not having a warrant, but Sam pointed out that Brock was in the military, which meant that he did not enjoy the same constitutional protections as ordinary citizens. Strange, and a bit sad, but true.

And Dibiaso probably wasn't a US citizen, which made him fair game – at least with some degree of plausible deniability.

Dan wasn't a stranger to legally ambiguous territory, but that didn't make him excited about skirting the line. He voiced his displeasure, and Sam promised an extra smiley face on his year-end report card. Dan reluctantly agreed, and Sam thanked him with due fervency.

Something else was important, she realized as she tossed the phone into the passenger seat. If Dibiaso were indeed Venezuelan, what was he doing at the US Pentagon? While the Pentagon was a famously overpopulated place, Sam was fairly certain its Venezuelan constituency was approximately zero.

Venezuela was on several State Department tourism alert lists because of its officially unfriendly position vis-a-vis Uncle Sugar, and Sam felt certain that any spare Pentagon office space was reserved for America's Inner Circle – the UK, Canada, and maybe Australia. There might be a few others, but the list surely didn't contain openly truculent governments.

So what gives? Sam checked her watch. If the traffic gods smiled on her, she'd arrive back in DC before the mass Pentagon exodus at the end of the day. Maybe she would be able to find out for herself what Dibiaso was up to.

It felt good to finally be moving forward, although she was still angry at herself for ignoring such an obvious question days before. How much closer to figuring out this mess would she have been if she hadn't let her emotions get the better of her?

Flashing lights caught her eye, and she looked in her rear-view mirror. A state trooper was on her bumper. She looked down at the speedometer, and realized that her impatience and frustration had manifested in a lead foot.

Balls.

Her first instinct was to run like hell, but her little rental car was no Porsche. And she realized that she wasn't anywhere near the Metro DC jurisdiction – she was in Pennsylvania, to be precise – which significantly lowered the odds that this particular patrolman was interested in anything more than meeting his monthly ticket revenue quotas.

Sam sighed heavily and pulled over.

Gotta quit making rookie mistakes, she thought. *One of these days, my luck is going to run out.*

Chapter 35

El Jerga waited in an upscale coffee shop, the kind with six-dollar lattes and four-dollar percolator swill, and watched the suits come and go.

It was a strange town, he thought. Nobody smiled at anyone else. Even in the toughest parts of Caracas, there was some basic human courtesy passed between random strangers. But not here, in the Mecca of Democracy, with its towering monuments to the common man, built by history's greatest oligarchs and religious kooks.

How can they be anything but crooked? It wasn't that the system was corrupted. The problem was that the system was *corruption itself.* And it was administered by an army of anonymous bureaucrats, with only their egregiously inflated sense of self-importance held in common with each other.

And nothing held in common with the governed. *How dare the gringos wag their fingers at us,* he thought.

The exchange went nothing like the movies. El Jerga rested the appropriate book face-up on his table for two, and a stranger in a three-piece suit sat down without warning in the opposite chair. "Finally cooling off," the stranger said.

"About time," El Jerga croaked. His voice sounded like gravel in a clothes dryer, and the well-dressed stranger immediately looked to El Jerga's grievously scarred throat. El Jerga had long ago stopped viewing such reactions as impolite. It was human nature, and he had grown used to the common reaction to the sound of his voice, as well as the pained facial expressions that inevitably followed.

Regardless of its horrific sound, El Jerga's voice had delivered the appropriate identification code, and the man in the suit crossed one leg over the other, slouched in the coffee shop chair, and nonchalantly tossed a folded newspaper onto the table. "I know you're following the stock market," he said, "so I saved the business section for you."

El Jerga nodded and smiled in thanks, in lieu of attracting more attention with his wrecked voice box.

He waited the appropriate amount of time, then retreated to a restroom stall to check the delivery. He unfolded the business section to find a clear plastic bag with a few grams of chalky white powder. He put a little on his tongue. Satisfied, he re-wrapped the substance in the newspaper and left the coffee shop.

* * *

El Jerga waited in an idling minivan in a curbside parking spot outside the Department of Agriculture, surveying the stream of pedestrians exiting the Department of Homeland Security's national headquarters building across the street. It was a stone's throw from Congress and the Washington Monument, the world's largest obelisk.

Lunchtime was a horrible time to find a particular individual in Washington, DC, but it was otherwise a terrific time to do what El Jerga needed to do. He divided his attention between watching the doorway of the building across the street and cooking the bag of heroin, by holding a lighter beneath a large spoonful of the white powder.

It didn't take long for the powder to liquefy, and El Jerga placed a needle in the center of the liquid and withdrew the syringe plunger. The liquid filled most of the syringe. He wasn't a user himself, but he figured it would have been enough heroin for a house full of addicts. And more than enough for his purposes.

He replaced the cap on the needle, tucked it into his pocket, and resumed his surveillance of DHS' front door.

His quarry appeared right on time. El Jerga's source had provided detailed information about the Thursday lunch attended by everyone in his target's office. They didn't always go to the same restaurant, but they always ate together, and they usually left a half hour before noon to beat the lunchtime rush.

El Jerga exited the minivan, patted his pocket for reassurance, and joined the rush of self-absorbed, unsmiling pedestrians crossing the street with the light. The timing worked serendipitously well, and El Jerga found himself just a dozen paces behind his target.

The gaggle rounded the corner onto a street full of restaurants, and El Jerga had to find creative ways to avoid detection as the group of office workers paused to view the menus. It was interesting to watch a group of people come to a decision, El Jerga thought with professional detachment. It happened in stops and starts, and it was much more about social dynamics than about the substance of the decision at hand, he thought.

Indian food eventually won out, and the dozen Homeland workers took over a corner of Najeeb's Finest in L'Enfant Plaza. El

Jerga pulled his ball cap low over his face and took a seat at a table for two near the hallway leading to the restrooms.

He ordered food, monitored the table of Homeland employees, and did his best to control the growing impatience he felt. He didn't have long before the syringe cooled and the drug condensed, making it impossible to inject.

The waiter had just brought a basketful of naan bread when motion in the vicinity of the pack of bureaucrats caught El Jerga's eye. A tired-looking man in his mid-thirties stood up. He had dark circles under his eyes, and he seemed rumpled and too thin for his clothes.

El Jerga cross-referenced the photo on his phone to remove all doubt. *He's the one.*

The man walked past El Jerga's table and down the hall toward the men's room. El Jerga followed.

The door was locked, and his quarry waited patiently, so El Jerga did the same, smiling at the tired-looking man when their eyes met. They heard a toilet flush, and soon the door opened.

"It's a two-holer," the tall, thin man said to El Jerga. "I just need the urinal, so no need to wait."

El Jerga croaked his thanks and followed the thin government employee into the restroom, locking the door behind him.

As his target stood before the urinal and unzipped his fly, El Jerga reached into his jacket pocket and removed a handkerchief from a sealed Ziploc bag. The unmistakable stench of chloroform assaulted his nose.

In a flash, El Jerga approached from behind and pressed the

handkerchief tightly over his target's mouth and nose. The man was too taken aback to struggle at first, but soon began to thrash. El Jerga dragged him to the center of the small bathroom to prevent him from kicking the walls and alerting passersby.

The exertion rapidly depleted his target's oxygen supply, and he gasped for breath, ingesting a lungful of chloroform fumes. Several seconds later, his skinny body went completely limp in El Jerga's arms.

El Jerga hefted his target into the toilet stall, set him on the toilet, and propped his torso upright against the toilet paper dispenser while he unbuttoned the man's sleeve. He pushed the sleeve up above the elbow and wrapped a phlebotomist's band around the too-skinny arm.

It took several seconds for a suitable vein to expose itself, and it took two attempts with the syringe before El Jerga was rewarded with a surge of blood as he withdrew the plunger ever so slightly. He watched his victim's blood mix with the drug, and wondered how many times the skinny addict had performed the same ritual on himself.

Never again, hombre, he thought to himself as he slowly pressed the plunger toward the needle, forcing the deadly dose of heroin into Jeff Jensen's veins. He felt his victim's body shudder, and watched cyanosis spread from the man's lips to the rest of his face.

Less than a minute later, El Jerga witnessed the last breath of Homeland CSI Jensen.

He wiped the syringe free of his own fingerprints, and used

Jensen's lifeless hand to create the appropriate evidence of a self-inflicted overdose, then exited the restroom and returned to his lunch.

As his curry arrived, El Jerga sent a text message: addiction kills.

El Grande's reply was swift: nice work…stay ready…more to come.

El Jerga smiled. He thought that with his fat cigars and his skinny Russian prostitutes, El Grande was far more poseur than bona fide heavy, and his ostentatious pistolero-and-freedom-fighter affectation would likely lead to a painful demise. But El Jerga hoped it wouldn't happen any time soon, because he thoroughly enjoyed all the business El Grande brought him.

It took a surprisingly long time for anyone to discover the late Jeff Jensen's corpse. When it finally happened, El Jerga left cash on the table for his lunch and took his place among the open-mouthed gawkers.

Chapter 36

But for a $200 traffic ticket and a brief slowdown due to road construction in Eastern Pennsylvania, Sam's car trip from Dayton to DC was uneventful. She skirted around the southeastern edge of the city via the Beltway, jumped onto I-395 northbound, and took Exit 8C for Army Navy Drive and the Pentagon.

She turned left and headed toward the vast Pentagon parking lot, but was greeted by a slovenly and surly rent-a-cop who informed her that she lacked the appropriate sticker to gain entrance. Apparently, nobody but the three-stars were allowed to park next to The Building, as it was affectionately known, so Sam set about trying to find a place to park her rental car.

Half an hour later, with the sun threatening to duck behind the Crystal City office buildings, Sam settled for leaving her car in an underground lot beneath the Doubletree Hotel.

She ventured across Army Navy Drive on foot, dodging speeding cars as they rounded the blind curve with a crowded city's reckless abandon. This section of road must have been what Brock meant when he talked about "playing Frogger" on the way to the Pentagon, she thought. The old-school car-dodging video game predated her popular culture awareness, but Brock had brought her up to speed on the joke.

She walked briskly beneath the 395 overpass, past the same surly traffic cop, and toward the Metro entrance of the Pentagon. It

was easily a two-mile walk. She finally arrived at the entrance, only
to discover a lengthy line of people waiting to pass through a
security screening station. It looked just like an airport security
setup, complete with metal detectors and seven underemployed
guards milling about.

She took her place at the end of the line and surveyed the long,
serpentine procession of humanity. Sam only had an hour before the
place turned into a ghost town. The daily Pentagon exodus was
famously fast, much like the way large factories disgorged their
employees during the Industrial Revolution, and she didn't have time
to waste.

She held her DHS badge above her head, called out, "Pardon
me, folks," and made her way to the front of the line, as if *her*
official business were naturally more important than *their* official
business. Her advance garnered a few angry looks, but people mostly
just got out of her way.

As she arrived at the front of the line, she made a curious
observation: *The headquarters of the most powerful military in
human history is guarded by. . . rent-a-cops?*

She shook her head at the absurdity, emptied her pockets,
passed through the metal detector, and emerged seconds later in
front of the vast bank of escalators leading up into what was once the
world's largest office building.

She was instantly overwhelmed. Another rent-a-cop stationed
at the escalators instantly recognized her look of confusion, and
pointed her to another ridiculously long line of dour-faced people
waiting beneath a sign that said "Visitor Check-In."

Sam employed the badge trick once again, and soon found herself leaning over the counter to hear a slightly mouse-faced security administrator provide mumbled half-answers to her repeated requests to see the visitor log for two particular dates in the recent past.

The clerk eventually handed her a clipboard containing a form with dozens of fill-in-the-blank fields, and mumbled that Sam should get back in line when she had finished filling out the form.

Sam rarely responded well to low-level bureaucratic bullshit, and she was even less charitable than normal after suffering through what had to have been the world's longest week. "Point to the place where your supervisor sits," she told the clerk through clenched teeth. The clerk pointed to the chair next to her, occupied by an equally dull-looking human. "Thanks. Now, point to *that* person's supervisor," Sam said.

The clerk rolled his droopy eyes, sighed, and pointed a stubby finger toward a glassed-in office, also with a long line of people waiting to be seen.

You've got to be kidding me, Sam thought. She recalled Brock's frequent jokes to the effect that the country was wasting its money on military weapons; the surest way to kill an enemy would be to subject him to American military bureaucracy, thereby instantly removing his will to live.

By the time Sam reached the uber-rent-a-cop's office and used her badge to elbow her way to the front of the line for a third time, she was feeling stressed and far less than courteous.

Fortunately, the supervisory clerk had above-average

situational awareness, and recognized that the combination of Sam's DHS credentials and her foul mood could spell trouble. He wrote down the two dates she was interested in, disappeared behind some modular office furniture, and emerged several minutes later with a computerized printout of the visitor's logs.

Finally.

Sam referenced the precise times when Arturo Dibiaso's cell phone data appeared to pause at the Metro entrance to the Pentagon. Over a hundred people signed in during the thirty minutes Dibiaso's cell phone signal was stationary. *Not much help.*

She figured that signing the visitor's log would be the last thing Dibiaso did before venturing into the bowels of the Pentagon, so she narrowed her search to within three minutes of when Dibiaso's location moved deeper into the complex.

Six names. *Much better.*

But none of them were Arturo Dibiaso.

She hadn't expected Dibiaso to use his own name to sign in to the Pentagon, if he had indeed visited the Building, but it would have been a welcome break. Alas.

Sam took a closer look at the remaining fields on the visitor form, hoping for something to guide her search of the remaining six names. Each visitor required an escort, who was required to both print and sign his or her name, along with an office symbol and telephone number.

She scanned the list of escorts, and one jumped out at her immediately: Major General Charles W. Landers. *Brock's boss!* He had escorted someone named Avery Martinson, which didn't ring any bells for Sam. But the timing matched up almost exactly, *on both days in question.*

Sam's spirits lifted, but she realized she had very little time before Landers would be joining the throng of Pentagon refugees on their daily pilgrimage from the bowels of the world's ugliest building, back to civilized society.

Chapter 37

The Caracas sun had begun its descent, casting the city in the nostalgic light of day's end. Peter Kittredge glimpsed the deepening hues through the window of a street cafe and bar.

The Eurotrash music was already pounding as if it were 1999 in Berlin, adding further ammunition to his side of a running discussion with Charley about exactly how many years behind North America their South American counterparts chose to remain. Charley said five years, but Kittredge maintained it was a decade if it was a day.

Thoughts of Charley were hard to keep from his mind. He still wavered between sadness, anger, and fear. And he was still horribly confused about just what he and Charley were together. A couple? Partners? Or sex-buddies of convenience, one of whom happened to be playing the other like a marionette. It was not an uplifting line of thought, and Kittredge felt emotionally worn out.

Thankfully, his rumination was cut short by the arrival of his arranged date for the evening. She looked to be in her very, very early twenties. Her bare legs were exquisite, leading to a heart-shaped tush barely covered by a skirt. She had large breasts, and big, expressive Latin eyes, along with perfectly smooth, olive skin. She had a beautiful face and a perfect mouth, which delivered the agreed-upon opening phrase: "You must be angry with me for keeping you waiting so long."

He had been practicing his rejoinder. "I couldn't possibly be angry at you," he said. In the moment, it felt wooden and rehearsed, possibly because he had been rehearsing, and he was still scared witless about his deepening affiliation with El Grande's Venezuelan Special Services friends.

Fortunately for Kittredge, a comfortable alcohol buzz had set in, and he soon forgot his nervousness. The bar was apparently a very popular place on Thursday afternoons, which made it extremely public but also a terrific place to have a private conversation. Nobody could hear a thing anyone else said, unless they hollered directly into each other's ear drums.

"You're beautiful, and I would definitely try to pick you up if I wasn't gay," Kittredge shouted into his new friend's ear.

She laughed. "I have toys we can both play with, in that case." Kittredge's turn to laugh.

Maybe the VSS thing wasn't such a bad deal after all, he thought. Except it seemed like a great way to make enemies out of the the Agency, which Kittredge had come to view as one of the world's most vicious clandestine services.

But Kittredge had already managed to do that without much help. Maybe Quinn and Fredericks weren't his outright enemies, but they certainly weren't better than frenemies. He got angry all over again about their invasion of his privacy, and their violation of his person with a belt sander.

And they had ripped him off. He had conveniently forgotten Fredericks' point regarding the silver, namely that Kittredge had "earned" it by selling embassy secrets, and therefore the Agency hadn't technically stolen from him.

Details.

It felt good to be taking back control. He felt that was the overarching purpose for having dialed the number given to him in the National Mall in DC, by a guy who was now very dead. And regaining control was also the reason he had allowed El Grande and the VSS to continue to cultivate a relationship with him.

He also realized that he was at least as interested in the VSS as they were in him, which made theirs the kind of mutual neediness that would either lead to a successful relationship, or to abject dysfunction.

Not much to lose by seeing what happens, Kittredge decided, but he knew instantly that such a choice was undoubtedly progeny of alcohol-induced hubris, and possibly a little carelessness.

Living dangerously again. Guess I'm a born operator. He chuckled. James Bond, minus the machismo, and with a limp wrist and the faint trace of a lisp.

The girl was shouting in his ear again. "You have to assume they're watching you," she was yelling, as if her twenty-one-ish years of life experience had bestowed this pearl upon her, which she now dutifully passed on to the feckless protégé almost twice her age.

He bristled a little.

"Did you read that in a LeCarré book?" he shouted in her ear with a wicked grin.

"Clancy," she corrected.

"I didn't know anyone still reads him."

"It's 1995 here in Caracas, even though the calendar says

something different."

"Ha!" he bellowed. "Yes! I keep telling Charley that same thing. He says 2005 though."

"Not even close. We're still worried about Y2K."

Kittredge laughed. "Were you even alive then?"

"I was giving head to my boyfriend at the turn of the century."

"You must be very proud. And hopefully older than you look."

"Si. Thirty-one."

"I never would have guessed."

"We have no petrochemicals in our water. We don't age as fast. But I think you gringos want to change that for us."

"It's called progress. Get on board." It drew a laugh from his pretty companion.

Kittredge began to seriously entertain heterosexual notions. He'd dabbled before, always returning to the male end of the sexual spectrum but certainly enjoying the change of pace.

"I like you, Peter Kittredge," she said. "Buy me another drink."

"If I wasn't mistaken, I'd think you were coming on to me."

"Maybe I'm trying to help you see the error of your ways," she said playfully. He was sure her flirtation was brought on by the universal notion among women that gay guys were safe to flirt with, but he wondered how "safe" he actually was – he felt the beginnings of arousal.

"Maybe I'm open to alternative points of view," he said, matching her playful tone, his mouth next to her ear, his hand on her thigh for good measure.

"You can't put it in my ass no matter how much you beg."

He laughed until tears came out of his eyes. Then, "Is that why they sent you to meet me? To put me in a compromising position?"

She smelled *good*. Not in a perfumed way, but in a visceral, biological way.

"You mean more compromising than already? I don't see how that could happen, super-spy." Her lips brushed his ear, and she nibbled his earlobe.

Was he really about to have sex with a *woman,* and one he'd met just moments before?

His crotch voted "yes." There were worse things in the world than female favors, even for a middle-aged, ostensibly-gay guy.

"Seriously, they sent you to have sex with me?"

"No. They sent me to keep an eye on you. Sex was my idea."

It didn't take Kittredge long to decide. "Barkeep! Tab, please."

* * *

She was absolutely wild. She left teeth marks on his thigh, bit his nipple, and rode him with abandon.

Round one complete, Kittredge and his new friend watched the sun track further toward the horizon. She ran her fingers tenderly along his scabbed-over lower back, and asked him about the injury.

"My new friends," he said.

"You need better friends."

"I think I just made one," he said. She smiled.

He wasn't sure whose apartment they had used for their unlikely rendezvous, but it was clear that at least some of the things were hers. It was probably a safe house, but one she'd been inhabiting for a few days.

"Now that we share the same diseases, what's your name?" he asked.

"Maria," she said.

"Really?"

"No. But that's what you should call me."

"I can live with that."

"Of course you can," she said.

It was all thoroughly disorienting for Kittredge.

"You are confused, no? Like, where has this girl been my whole life, and why have I wasted all these years with hombres?"

"Maybe. But maybe it's just that I'd hate to have to give up my gay card if anyone found out."

She laughed. "Sex and politics."

"They're one and the same," Kittredge agreed.

"Uh-oh," she said, suddenly serious. "Time for us to move."

"Why?"

She pointed out the window to a car parked on the curb across the street, twelve stories below. "Your friends are here."

* * *

Kittredge slipped on his underwear and pants and stood next to Maria, peering through the bars of the balcony and down at the opposite curb, where a white sedan was parked illegally.

An unbelievably intense flash of red light had a blinding effect on his vision, and he instinctively turned his head. The intense light appeared to be coming from the high-rise across the street, but he was too disoriented by the painfully intense beam to figure out its import.

He felt Maria's shoulder crash into his side, and felt his body hurtled backwards toward the bed. He heard her yell, and then heard the deafening crash of glass as the balcony door shattered into pieces.

"Sniper!" she yelled. She rolled off the bed and moved on all fours along the far wall, hidden for a moment behind the bed.

"Bathroom, now!" she commanded, and Kittredge obeyed. They low-crawled against a wall, using the furniture to obstruct the sniper's line of vision.

Kittredge looked up to follow Maria into the bathroom, and he got an eyeful of her still-naked derriere. *This is craziness, all of it.*

Maria scooped up enough clothing on her way to the refuge of the bathroom to cover all the appropriate parts of her, and she dressed with a speed and nimbleness that instantly impressed Kittredge. It was clear that she was far more than just a pretty face sent to occupy his time to keep him from getting in more serious trouble. She was actually in charge of keeping him alive.

"When I tell you, you're going to crawl. Keep low. Turn right, wait for me at the apartment door," she said.

She opened the bathroom cabinet door, moved aside a box of tampons beneath the sink, and retrieved the largest handgun he'd ever seen. She also grabbed a snub-nosed Glock .45, and threw it at him. He missed, and the handgun clattered on the tile floor. She beat him to it, grabbed his right hand, and forcibly placed the gun in his palm. "You should have brought the gun El Grande gave you. Don't lose this one. It has my prints on it."

She peered around the corner and studied the scene for several seconds. "Go Kittredge!" she shouted suddenly. She was still the same animal who'd had her way with him moments earlier, but now that feral energy was channeled in a much different direction.

As he exited the bathroom on his hands and knees, he saw the red flash out of the corner of his eye again, and instinctively flattened himself to the carpet. A bullet tore into the wall just above his torso, and his mind registered in a strangely detached way the scant few inches that delineated between drawing another breath and having a rifle slug destroy his heart and lungs.

"Move! Crawl! You have to get out of the line of sight!" She shouted. "Around the corner, now!" Kittredge scampered in what he imagined was an Army low-crawl, pulling his body forward over the carpet with his elbows and knees flayed out to either side.

More glass shattered as a bullet tore into the bathroom mirror, and Kittredge heard an explosion that sounded like a cannon's report. Shocked by its incredible loudness, Kittredge turned to find its source, and saw the giant .50 caliber handgun in Maria's hands roar for a second time, belching flames out the front and moving her entire body backwards with the force of its recoil.

"Vamanos!" she commanded, and Kittredge resumed his panicked scramble toward the apartment's front door.

As they crawled deeper into the flat and away from the balcony, the laser sight crept its way along the hallway wall above them, but it disappeared abruptly each time it descended toward them. Kittredge realized that the shooter must have been on a lower floor across the street, and as he and Maria moved further into the apartment, the shooter was unable to draw a bead on them because his firing line was obstructed by the balcony floor.

They gathered their breath at the doorway, Maria straightening the tee shirt she had collected from the floor moments earlier.

"What now?" he asked, breathless with fright and exertion.

"Now, it gets difficult," she said, tucking an extra clip of .50 ammunition in her pocket.

She reached up, unlocked the front door, swung it wide open, and somersaulted out into the hallway, coming to rest on one knee with the giant handgun pointed in the direction of the elevators. Finding no one, she rolled again, this time ending up in a prone firing position pointing the opposite direction down the hallway.

"Come!" she hollered for the second time in the last few minutes, meaning something far different this time than the first.

Kittredge scrambled to his feet and lurched clumsily after her as she ran downy he hallway. "The elevators are the other way!" he shouted.

"Exactly!" She leapt feet-first at the fire door beneath a lighted sign depicting a staircase. Her heel caught the horizontal door bar, and the door exploded open, crashing into the cement wall on the stairway landing and slamming shut again. Now certain no one was behind the door, she opened it for a second time, and admonished Kittredge to keep up with her.

He entered the stairwell a few paces behind her, and was shocked to find her climbing *up* the stairs, bounding two at a time. "We'll be trapped!" he yelled.

"They are already on their way up! Just trust me."

He didn't have a better idea, so he followed her up two more flights of stairs and onto the fourteenth floor landing, his lungs suddenly burning. He felt lightheaded from fear, exertion, and the kind of dehydration that only a three-day bender can inflict.

Kittredge heard pounding feet climbing the stairs beneath them. "Hurry!" she hissed.

He reached her as she opened the doorway to the fourteenth floor hallway, and she repeated the Hollywood-esque procedure of rolling around on the floor with her gun drawn.

Twenty paces down the hallway, a resident had just opened the door into her apartment, and had reached back down toward the floor to retrieve a basket of laundry. Kittredge heard Maria bark terse instructions in Spanish, and the woman let out a feeble screech of alarm.

More barking from Maria served to encourage the woman's silence, and Maria closed the gap to the open apartment doorway in what looked like three giant steps, her hand waving behind her for Kittredge to follow.

As Kittredge approached, Maria grabbed his unbuttoned shirt and dragged him into the apartment, slamming and locking the door behind him. Kittredge heard soft crying, and turned to see the poor woman who was now their reluctant host. She shook with fright, and tears streamed from her face as she babbled a stream of pleading Spanish, which Kittredge only caught half of.

Maria spoke in machine-gun Spanish and walked through the apartment's entryway, stopping to stroke the woman's face and hair gently with her free hand. The woman stopped her sobbing.

Whatever Maria had said, it had apparently convinced their host that her life wasn't in danger.

In a flash, Maria had the sliding glass balcony door open and had stepped out onto the small landing, clearly searching for something.

"You'll be shot!" Kittredge hollered, but then realized that they were on the other side of the building from Maria's apartment. Wide open space greeted him as he looked beyond the balcony railing. If there was another sniper stationed at the back of the building, he would have a much more difficult job without an adjacent high-rise to shoot from.

Maria took off her shoe and began pounding it against something.

Kittredge heard a metallic clang with each of Maria's strikes, and then the horrible screech of rusting metal, followed by what sounded like an avalanche. Maria had loosed the fire escape.

Before Kittredge could request a different plan of action, on account of his irrational yet debilitating fear of heights, Maria had flung herself over the balcony railing and started clanging her way down toward the street, fourteen stories below.

"I really can't do this!" Kittredge protested.

"Then you will be shot!"

"I'm afraid of heights!"

"But not bullets?" He heard what sounded like curse words coming from over the balcony, and could have sworn he distinctly heard the word *puta*.

He peered over the railing at Maria, now perched five rungs

below him, and felt himself swoon.

"Kittredge, climb, now!" It was clear she was losing her patience with him. He shook his head. "You *must climb down!*" she said.

He shifted his weight, preparing to throw his leg over the balcony railing, then faltered. "I can't do it," he said.

He looked back down at Maria, and was shocked to find the barrel of her hand-cannon point at him. "Climb, or I will shoot you in the face."

Kittredge shifted his weight again, raised his heel three or four times, but again failed to throw his leg over the railing and alight on the fire escape ladder.

He heard the explosion of Maria's gun, and thought he might piss himself.

"You have been to El Grande's," Maria hissed. "You have seen our training camp. You are coming with me down this ladder, or I will kill you where you stand. I will *not* let you lead the gringos to us!"

Kittredge shook with fright, closed his eyes, and made his decision. He climbed out over the edge of the railing, white-knuckling each rung of the ladder as he followed Maria shakily down the fire escape.

"Faster," Maria commanded. Kittredge forced his arms and legs to work more quickly, but he was hamstrung by fear, and he descended painfully slowly.

"Kittredge, it's only a matter of time before they find us, and we're very exposed. You must go faster!"

"I'm trying," Kittredge said.

Maria cursed quietly in Spanish.

He settled into a rhythm, hand under hand, foot under foot, and felt he was finally making good time down the fire escape ladder.

"They rounded the corner!" Maria called out from below him. Kittredge glanced beneath him and felt his innards clinch with fear as he glimpsed a man in a suit on the sidewalk, stopping to raise a pistol toward them.

He heard the thud of feet on a hard surface nearby, and realized that Maria had jumped from the fire escape onto a third- or fourth-floor balcony.

Kittredge moved with a speed and agility that surprised him, whirling around the fire escape ladder and landing in a crouch on the balcony next to Maria.

She tried to open the glass door, but cursed as she found it locked.

She picked up a metal hibachi grill at her feet on the balcony floor and swung wildly at the glass door. Kittredge dodged her swing to avoid being hit, and the grill clanged noisily against the glass, causing it to spider.

The unmistakable sound of a bullet ricochet added urgency to Maria's next swing, and the glass yielded in a shower of shards.

Maria used the grill to pound away the remaining jagged edges, then bound through the opening, exhorting Kittredge to stay close behind her. She reached the apartment's entrance after passing a wide-eyed child wearing a diaper.

Kittredge stopped Maria from turning the knob to open the

door to the hallway. "What if they're out there?"

"Of course they're out there," she said irritably. "But probably not yet on this floor."

His protest died in his throat as Maria bounded out of the apartment and down the hallway toward the elevators. "Time for another gamble," she said, pushing the button to summon the elevator.

Four eternities passed while they crouched in the hallway, breathing hard, guns trained at the bank of elevator doors.

An elevator finally appeared. It had come from the first floor, and Kittredge felt his heart pounding as he pointed the small snub-nosed .45 in the vicinity of the opening doors. Maria held a kneeling firing position, her comically large pistol trained in the same direction.

The bell dinged, and the doors opened at a tectonic pace.

Kittredge found himself holding his breath, and realized that he had the trigger half-squeezed. Maria shifted her weight, and the suddenness of it almost made him shoot his gun. He regained his composure and looked intently into the elevator.

Empty.

"Come on!" Maria grabbed his arm and pulled him into the elevator with her. She mashed the button for the second below-ground parking level, the doors crawled shut, and a century later, the elevator began to move.

They held their breath as the car stopped on the second floor. The doors parted to reveal a tuft of white hair atop a flowery sun dress. The old woman's eyes grew wide as saucers when she saw

Maria's gun.

Maria held her a finger over her mouth, indicating silence, and the woman complied. The doors shut again, and the cab didn't stop until they reached the underground parking structure.

Maria grabbed Kittredge's arm again, and he found himself dashing after her along the parking garage wall. "Are we driving out of here?" he asked, out of breath.

"You'll see. Hurry!" She quickened the pace, now heading toward two large swinging doors beneath an illuminated sign warning of an electric shock hazard. The doors were locked, but Maria produced a key from her jeans pocket, and they were soon inside a musty room filled with the deafening roar of equipment.

It was hot, cramped, loud, and dark, a combination that Kittredge enjoyed only slightly more than he enjoyed heights, and he felt the familiar closed-in feeling descend on him.

Maria felt him hesitate, and tugged harder on his arm, keeping him close to her.

They followed the wall, stepping over a cluster of pipes and electrical conduit, and soon found their way to the back of the machinery room. It was strewn with disused tools and scraps of metal.

Maria swung her arm through the air and found what she was looking for: a string, connected to a bare overhead bulb. She tugged, and the weak light chased the darkness from the damp, dirty corner of the room.

She hefted and tossed the scraps out of the way to reveal a heavy metal doorframe, situated in the floor of the mechanical room.

She stood, placed both hands through the metal loop opposite the door's hinges, and gave it a mighty pull. Several Spanish curses later, the trapdoor opened, and Kittredge found himself staring down at another ladder, this one descending into nothing but darkness.

"Now, you find out the answer," Maria said.

"What answer?"

"How deep is the rabbit hole."

Chapter 38

Getting in touch with Landers turned out to be remarkably easy, once Sam figured out which of the seven prefixes to place in front of the extension. Sam was reminded about some superlative relating to the number of miles of telephone lines encircling the Pentagon. To the moon and back? Around the globe six-point-nine times? She couldn't recall, but it was quite telling that there were enough numbers in that building to require seven telephone prefixes.

"General Landers' office, how may I direct your call?" answered a chirpy female voice, which cooled dramatically when Sam mentioned her desire to speak directly with Landers himself.

The receptionist, who turned out to be a lieutenant colonel, suggested a half-hour slot five days in the future, and Sam laughed. She mentioned she was working on a high-profile Homeland investigation, and the receptionist sounded even less impressed.

Then Sam floated the idea of returning in the morning with a warrant, which she would ensure was addressed to the Air Force Chief of Staff, suggesting that one of his hundred-plus two-star generals was a person of interest in a national security investigation.

Landers' receptionist found fifteen minutes on the General's calendar, commencing immediately.

* * *

"Thank you for seeing me on such short notice," Sam said with a smile as she shook Landers' outstretched hand.

"You made a compelling case," Landers deadpanned, motioning toward a plain-looking chair in a surprisingly spartan and cramped office.

This is two-star digs? Not impressive, Sam thought.

She mused that all of these people must really love their jobs to put up with such shitty accommodations in the world's dreariest office building, but the parade of frowns and angst-filled faces she had passed en route to Landers' office told her that she was probably dead wrong on that account. It seemed like life in a salt mine might have been preferable to life in the Pentagon.

Sam sized Landers up. He was ridiculously short, and bald to boot. He was forced to hold his head at an awkward angle to look Sam in the eye, and she almost stooped down to reach his hand. It was like she was shaking hands with a child, except the general had the pear-shaped physique of a sedentary middle-aged bureaucrat.

The total package, Sam thought to herself. *No wonder he's no fun to work for.* Brock wasn't a Charlie Landers fan, and it didn't sound like Brock was alone in his dim assessment.

"National security and all that," Sam said. "I won't take much of your time. I was just wondering about a person you escorted into the Pentagon on the 18th of last month, goes by the name Avery Martinson."

"Sure. How can I help?" Landers seemed friendly enough, despite the fact that he had recently expressed his intention to punish Brock for his "affair" with Sam. She did her best not to think about that particular issue, because it made her want to stab Landers in his chubby little throat, along with the two castrati above her in her own

DHS supervision chain. And she happened to need Landers' help at the moment.

"Can you tell me what your meeting was about?"

"I really can't." He didn't offer anything else.

Sam looked at him and let the silence linger a bit. Sometimes the social pressure of silence induced people to talk when they'd otherwise rather not. But Landers didn't say a word. In fact, he put a mildly arrogant, expectant expression on his face, as if to say, "Now what?"

"Where did you meet him?"

"You don't need me to answer that for you. It's in the visitor logs."

"You're right. Thanks."

Asshole.

Landers was beginning to live up to his reputation. She felt like tearing into him a bit, but she was completely at his mercy, because she had zero information on him. That meant she had no leverage to apply, and that she had to rely entirely upon his good graces. Informed by his nasty reputation, her expectations were low.

"And which organization is Martinson with?"

"Can't say."

"Is that because you don't know, or don't want to say?"

"Does it matter?"

"It does to me," Sam said, smiling sweetly, hoping that a particular vein in her temple wasn't bulging, the one that always gave her away when she wanted to wrap her hands around someone's throat and squeeze.

More silence, which Landers handled like an old pro.

Sam tried another tack. "Brock tells me that you're affiliated with the Council on Foreign Relations. They have quite a reputation. It must be exciting to rub shoulders in that crowd."

"Not terribly," Landers said. "Were you making a point just now, or was that investigative small talk?"

Sam was pretty sure her vein was pulsing, and she was pretty sure her face had turned slightly red.

She took a moment to bridle her growing anger, and decided to level with him. "General Landers, I was hoping for a bit more to help us with our investigation. As I mentioned, this is an issue of national security, as there's already been an attack on US soil, which we think might have been perpetrated by an organization with operatives who've spent a lot of time here in the States."

Big law enforcement words sounded very official, and she hoped they'd help play down the fact that she didn't have a warrant compelling Landers to disclose any of the information she wanted from him.

Landers shrugged his shoulders. He sat ramrod straight, which was likely a habit cultivated over the years to keep his short body from sinking below sight during meetings, like a little kid at the dinner table.

He crossed one leg over another, which Sam knew usually indicated a defensive mental posture.

Asshole-ness aside, Sam realized, it was possible that Landers was genuinely not permitted to talk about the meeting he had held with the guy whose cell phone locations and times overlapped nicely with Arturo Dibiaso's. *Twice.*

Landers smiled, a little smugly for Sam's taste, which triggered her bastard-radar.

"You also met with this gentleman, Mr. Martinson, on the eleventh. One week earlier. Is that something you can discuss?"

"Nope."

"General Landers, if you'd like, I can return with a warrant."

"That might be best," he said, calling her bluff. He smiled pointedly.

Then he looked impatiently at his watch. "Listen, Ms. Jameson, I'm sorry I can't be more helpful. If you have more questions in this vein, I'm afraid I'm going to have to demur. It's almost five, and I need to get out of here."

Sam was used to the brush-off, but "it's quitting time" was a new one on her. "You have an appointment this evening?"

"No. The slug line."

Sam cocked her head, confused.

"It's Pentagon-speak for carpooling with random strangers," Landers elaborated, "to take advantage of the HOV lane. It's as fun as it sounds, but I don't want to have to take the train home. I hate missing dinner. Now, if you'll excuse me, I have to wrap up and get out of here."

Sam shook his hand and left the office, dejected.

Chapter 39

Kittredge smelled damp, musty air, and felt a mild sliminess on the ladder's rungs. He held his breath in prim disgust, but descended after Maria into the yawning darkness beneath the floor of the mechanical room, itself tucked within a parking level two floors beneath the Caracas street.

She called up to him to close the trapdoor after him, which took no small effort, and showered him with rust and filth as the door slammed shut above his head. He shuddered, then concentrated on not falling on top of Maria as he negotiated the slippery ladder.

"Where are we going?" he asked when he reached the bottom. He couldn't see anything, but the close echoes of his own voice told him that he was in a short, narrow passageway.

"Our evening plans have changed slightly," Maria said, grabbing his hand and leading him along through the darkness, using her other hand to feel her way along the damp wall of the earthen passageway.

"It will be a while before we reach a light," she said. "We're close to the mechanical room, so there are no lights until a safe distance away. Duck your head, because there's–"

She was interrupted by a dull metallic clang, caused by Kittredge's skull impacting a support beam.

". . . A low ceiling," Maria finished.

"Thanks for the warning," Kittredge said sorely. His forehead hurt with a sharp pain, and he was sure it would turn into a headache. He felt something warm and liquid dripping down toward his eyebrow, and realized that he was bleeding. He gritted his teeth.

The path narrowed in places, so that Kittredge had to turn sideways to pass, and he felt the earthen floor beneath him slope downward. They descended deeper beneath the apartment building, and the damp darkness and closed-in space caused a feeling of panic in his chest. "How much further?"

His voice betrayed his anxiety, and Maria laughed. "My brave spy." She squeezed his hand. "We have a long way to go. This is not a new tunnel and it is not very well maintained. It must be that way, for safety reasons."

Kittredge was confused. "Wouldn't it be safer to maintain it? I mean, is this thing going to collapse on us?"

She laughed again. "Maybe. But probably not."

Kittredge felt the slope even out beneath his feet, and heard the splash of water with their footfalls.

"Maintenance requires activity," Maria continued, "and activity draws attention. Attention is not safe. So we weigh one risk against another risk and we hope for the best."

"Life in a microcosm," he observed.

"Ahh, here we are," she said. He heard her hand searching along the wall in the darkness, and then heard a loud click, followed by buzzing. Lights flickered to life, spaced every dozen feet or so for what seemed like an infinite distance in front of them.

Kittredge thought he would feel better when the lights came on, but he actually felt worse – it was a horribly confined space, and his mild panic returned.

He forced himself to breathe deeply, and Maria heard him. "Deep breaths, Super-Spy."

"What is this place, anyway?" he asked.

"It is exactly what it looks like. A tunnel to someplace secret."

"Did you guys dig it?"

"You mean, El Grande and his people? No. This tunnel was here long before we came of age. You could say we inherited it from a long line of concerned citizens."

An interesting way to put it.

Kittredge didn't know nearly as much about Venezuelan history as he felt he should, but he was aware of the basics. Because the country was blessed with oil beneath its land, its problems were of a far different nature than the poorer Central and South American countries.

Oil brought interest, intrigue, and all manner of deals with the devil that left the populace whipsawed between increasingly shrill political entrepreneurs, who crafted a self-sustaining system where oil money bought political influence, which protected oil money. Synergy.

It had gotten nasty at times, of course, and party politics had infiltrated the neighborhoods in a very palpable way. Unlike in the US, where political debates were usually about abstract issues that rarely impacted the common man, every kind of real event in a Venezuelan neighborhood became a potential division bell between opposing parties.

Kittredge recalled one particularly grisly story involving a basketball court, which the local politico had agreed to put in for a group of interested teens, in exchange for some election day get-out-the-vote activity. The teens weren't innately interested in the political process, but were interested in a new basketball court. So they agreed to back the local public works official when the time came.

Most of the teenagers walked around the neighborhood holding the right signs and knocking on the right doors when election time came around, but a few of them didn't. In all probability, they didn't abstain on principle; they were just lazy teenagers.

They were beaten, one of them to death. The survivor suffered permanent brain damage.

There was a saying at the embassy: *Every councilman is a gangster in a suit.* Kittredge got the idea that there weren't many minor issues in Venezuelan politics. Every issue was a loyalty check.

A thought occurred to him. "Was this tunnel built for drugs?" Kittredge asked.

"No. At least, I don't think so. Maybe it was used for that purpose for a time, but I think probably not. But to my knowledge, it's always belonged to members of the special services."

"The *government* special services? Why would they need to sneak around in a cave, like rats?"

He heard Maria chuckle. "You are a little bit naive, I think. It's cute, and very American."

Kittredge bristled. "Maybe. But I really am interested in knowing what the caves are all about."

"We have a long walk, so I will tell you. In Venezuela, wealth is not a problem. It is beneath the ground. If you want it, you drill a hole, collect it, and sell it. Voila. Wealth."

"Must be nice."

"Ahh, more naive American thinking," Maria chided. "You see, the problem is removed one layer. Nobody worries about *finding* the wealth. The trouble is always over how to *distribute* the wealth."

Kittredge understood. It certainly explained the elaborate patronage system that Chavez was ostensibly elected to upend. Getting one's hands on fistfuls of oil money still required skill and hard work. It was just that the required skills were political, not entrepreneurial or administrative. If you wanted to reach into the big bag of oil cash, you had to gain favor with the right people.

In many ways, a ready supply of wealth created the worst kinds of problems. "I bet you see a lot of ugliness," he said.

"Of course. And not just from each other. Also from people like you." She squeezed his hand, which reminded him that she was still leading him along, even though a dim string of lights illuminated the narrow subterranean passageway.

"I think it is probably the same everywhere," she went on. "Powerful people attract supplicants. But in Venezuela, even more so."

"That still doesn't explain the sneaking around."

"Sure it does. When everyone owes favors to everyone else, it is easy for two people to want the same payback," Maria said. "When this happens, one of them will be unhappy. And we have long memories."

"So why is everyone pissed off at Chavez?"

Maria groaned. "*Everyone* isn't. And you're lucky we've already had sex," she said. "Discussing politics is such a turnoff."

"Sorry. I'm just trying to figure out who the hell you guys are, and what the hell I'm doing in the middle of all of this."

She laughed. "The existential struggle of the pawn, as El Grande says."

"Should I be offended?"

"Only if you prefer. But you *are* a pawn, no? Your Agency friends, they don't ask you for strategic advice, do they?"

He shook his head. "Good point. So if I'm a pawn, why are you risking your life to keep me out of trouble?" He turned his shoulders to squeeze through a narrow section.

"It's your physique," she said with a playful squeeze.

"Obviously." She hadn't really answered any of his recent questions, and he found himself a little annoyed. "Really, why are you doing this?"

"El Grande has already told you. The enemy of my enemy is my friend."

"But you know that I work for the CIA."

"No. We know that they have *forced* you to work for them. That is very different."

"True."

"And there's Charley."

Kittredge stopped. "How the hell do you know about Charley?"

"*I* know because *we* know," she said. "And we just know, the same way we knew to hand you a phone number."

"And you knew I would call?"

She laughed. "You are cute, Peter Kittredge. A cute baby boy in a big, bad world. Of course not. We knew only that you would certainly *not* call if you did not have our number. So we gave you our number."

Something bothered Kittredge. The old man in the red scarf had given him the phone number *on the same day* that Charley was beaten up, and just hours after his horrible and painful introduction to Quinn and Fredericks. How did the Venezuelans find out so quickly about his unpleasant introduction to the Agency, and how did they know about Charley?

It was also troubling that the old man had been killed – probably by Quinn – just moments after handing Kittredge the slip of paper with the Caracas phone number scrawled on it.

"Does the Agency have a leak?"

"Other than you?"

"I don't know any secrets to tell."

"But I think you would tell them if you knew them."

"I think you're right," he said. "Seriously, Maria, I need to know how you guys figured out what was going on so quickly. You gave me the phone number right after I visited Charley in the hospital."

"I think only El Grande knows that. And I think I would never *want* to know the answer. Safer that way. Watch your head." She ducked beneath an especially low support beam, which was obviously installed to repair the damage from a cave-in.

Kittredge ducked, and had to twist to squeeze through the narrowed walls around the area of the collapse. He shuddered again, anxious to end the spelunking adventure.

"So how did you know to find me at the Mall? I mean, Quinn stopped there on a whim after we saw Charley."

"You ask a lot of questions. You should stop, or El Grande may change his mind about you."

Kittredge thought about El Grande. "That night when I met him out in the boonies, he said something about not having many enemies."

"That is true. El Grande has few enemies because he has the right friends."

"Like who?"

"Like ones with tunnels."

Kittredge started to press, but she cut him off. "Enough questions. Really, it's unhealthy. Besides, we're getting close, and it's time to be quiet."

He reluctantly obliged, but felt more unsettled than before the question-and-non-answer session with Maria. It wasn't that she didn't want him to have the answers, he sensed, but more that she didn't want to be the one to give them to him. It was undoubtedly a byproduct of living for too many years in a hyper-political society.

But there was probably a much more pragmatic reason, too. Kittredge realized that El Grande, Maria, and their interesting coterie of guerrilla goat farmers had a difficult task where he was concerned. They had to keep him interested in their organization, yet tactically distant enough not to be a threat, because of his lingering

Agency ties. If he returned to Quinn and Fredericks, it would certainly be catastrophic for El Grande's group.

Which is who, exactly?

"One more question," he said.

"No."

"Yes. El Grande said that he was an instrument of state security, which sounds very official. But he said that in a tent in the damned jungle, and now you and I are playing Indiana Jones in a cave. So who are you guys, really?"

She sighed. "You will come to regret all these questions, I think."

"Are you government employees?"

"Of a fashion."

Aha. Contractors. Blackwater, but Latin style. "It's all much clearer now. Thank you." He was only half kidding.

"Quiet," she said. He heard a click, and they were plunged once again into darkness.

* * *

The last several hundred meters of the subterranean passageway were even worse then the first. The ceiling was lower, and Kittredge had to stoop to avoid adding another welt to the growing collection of bruises on his skull, one of which was still bleeding.

Maria pulled him along by the hand, pausing every few steps to listen carefully for anyone else approaching in the cave. As they continued onward in the stifling darkness, Kittredge heard the faint hum of distant machinery growing louder with each step.

The passageway's floor sloped upwards over the last few steps, and the cave ended at the foot of another ladder, this one leading up a circular shaft capped by what looked like a manhole cover.

Kittredge offered to be the first up the ladder to remove the heavy cover, but Maria declined, favoring trade craft over chivalry. She climbed the ladder and listened intently.

Kittredge wasn't sure she could have heard much, as the noise of machinery had grown almost unbearably loud, amplified by the tight confines of the passageway. He had grown impatient by the time she lifted the manhole cover several inches and peered into the darkness of another unlit mechanical room.

Several seconds later, she slid the cover aside, and motioned for Kittredge to follow up the ladder.

They inched their way around the machinery and came to a set of double doors, with slatted ventilation openings at the bottom. Maria ducked down to the floor and peered through the ventilation slats for several long moments while Kittredge waited.

Finally, Maria turned the handle on one of the doors, and opened it several inches to peer outside. Satisfied, she opened the door all the way.

Kittredge gasped. *Holy shit!* "I know this place!"

"Shh!"

In fact, Kittredge had been in this very building just days earlier, before meeting El Grande for the first time. It was the lobby of the Banco de Caracas, situated at the ground floor of a modern high-rise building. The bank had long since closed, and the lobby was dark.

Maria grabbed his hand, and they stole quietly from the mechanical room, past a bank of idle elevators with their doors open, stopping at a stairwell entrance.

Maria produced another key, and Kittredge soon found himself following her curvaceous frame up flight after flight of stairs. He had begun to sweat and pant, but Maria seemed unaffected by the exertion.

She slowed politely to allow him to keep pace. "What's wrong with the elevators?" he asked, but she simply laughed in reply. Security cameras, he figured.

The climb ended at the eighteenth floor. The building had twenty-five floors, so Kittredge counted his blessings, which numbered seven unclimbed flights, he figured.

Maria again found the right key and gained entrance to yet another locked door, this one leading to what appeared to be the foyer of a very expensive apartment. They exited the stairwell and walked past a single elevator, which he surmised wasn't available for public use.

They stopped at a set of large oak double doors, each adorned with an ornate eagle's head encircled in an elaborate coat of arms, all carved in relief from the heavy oak. Burnished silver hardware graced the edges, and an ordinary telephone keypad, surrounded by an extraordinary silver frame, protruded from the wall to the right of the doors.

Maria punched nine digits into the keypad, and Kittredge heard a metallic click as the magnetic lock yielded. "Wait here," she instructed.

She disappeared inside the doors, gun drawn.

Moments passed, which afforded Kittredge the opportunity to ruminate further on his situation, resulting in a fresh swell of anxiety and apprehension.

He wanted another drink, which made him feel more anxious. He'd spent the better part of the past five days in varying degrees of inebriation, and he realized that he'd become very used to dealing with the substance of his problems by turning to a problematic substance.

Time to slow down.

Moments later, the door opened, and Maria handed him a drink. "Vodka on the rocks," she said with a smile.

Maybe tomorrow for the sobriety thing, he thought, taking the glass gratefully.

He stepped into what was possibly the most upscale apartment he'd ever seen. He took in the marble floors, Persian carpets, leather and oak furnishings, and a giant wall of windows framing a breathtaking view of the Caracas skyline.

Maria noticed his reaction and smiled. "Good friends are important, and important friends are good," she said.

Venezuelan life summed up nicely.

"This is as secure as we can make you for the moment," she told him. "The windows are mirrored, so no one can see inside. Machines vibrate them so that laser listening devices have a tough time picking out conversations. The phone lines are VOIP with proxy masks, but don't call anyone you know. Your friends will have them under surveillance. The Internet connection is also secure, but you shouldn't access any of your accounts for the same reason."

Kittredge raised his eyebrows, impressed by the thoroughness of the preparations. He'd been in secure facilities at the embassy before, and they had nothing on the apartment. And they sure as hell had nothing on the decor.

Kittredge opened his mouth to ask a question, and Maria held her finger to his lips. "No more questions, Peter. Now we wait, and relax."

She lied. She didn't want to relax. She wanted activity that involved exertion, gasping for breath, and orgasmic convulsions.

Then they relaxed. "Will your boyfriend be upset?" she asked, running her hand through the hair on his chest, her head resting on his shoulder atop silken bed sheets.

He hadn't thought much about Charley, and her mention of him brought a cloud over Kittredge's thoughts. He shook his head. "We have an open relationship, but I think he'd be surprised that you're a woman."

"You're worried about him," she observed.

"Among other things."

"And you wonder why he was beat up."

"And by whom."

"Those are good questions."

He looked at her, troubled by a thought. "Was it you guys?"

She held his gaze. "Your Charley is more than he seems."

That was a whale of an answer, but to a vastly different question. And it was a telling dodge. Kittredge sat upright in bed, jarring Maria off of him, and walked naked to the kitchen to refill his drink, cursing under his breath.

She followed, naked and exquisite, catching his eye in spite of his sated sexual appetite and his sudden emotional turmoil. "You knew that already, but maybe the words were difficult for you to hear," she said gently.

He nodded. "Yeah, a lot of things between Charley and me haven't made much sense, looking back on them. I feel like a fool."

Maria smiled. "Everyone is someone's fool. Maybe now, I am yours?"

"You give me too much credit."

"I've learned never to underestimate anyone. For example," she said, with a devilish smile and a playful caress of his reproductive gear, "you told me you were gay."

"I was. I mean, *I am*."

"Right," she said. "Whatever you are, it is working for me. Now come back to bed."

* * *

Hours later, while Maria snored softly in the vast, luxurious bed, Kittredge stole away to the kitchen table, poured another glass of vodka to stave off the burgeoning hangover, and turned on the computer in the luxuriously appointed study.

Kittredge didn't know much about IP encryption, except that it was supposed to make it look like you were using a different computer than the one you were really using. His intuition told him that it would be very difficult to pull a trick like that off, with the ubiquity of data and the cheapness of data storage combining to leave unexpected clues that would undoubtedly betray any clandestine browsing.

Intuition notwithstanding, Kittredge needed some information about Charley's condition. He wanted to be the first person to speak with his erstwhile lover and flat-mate when Charley regained consciousness, in the hope that Charley would be maximally forthcoming before his cognitive defenses fully returned.

Kittredge browsed for the intensive care desk phone number at DC General Hospital.

A few minutes and a dozen clicks later, he picked up the phone from its cradle on the wall and dialed the number displayed on the screen. He heard clunking as the call routed through several terrestrial trunks, and a more rapid clicking as the voice-over-Internet system synchronized.

A tired voice spewed a stream of nearly unintelligible sounds, but Kittredge thought he made out the words "DC General" and "intensive care." He identified himself and asked for an update on Charley Arlinghaus' condition.

The tired nurse asked him for his phone password, established during the emotional moments at the end of his one and only visit to Charley's room in the hospital on Sunday morning, an eternity ago.

Kittredge struggled to recall the password he'd given them.

"Sir?" The nurse sounded impatient.

"Boilermakers," Kittredge finally said. In honor of Charley's alma mater. It was a random password to think of, and honestly not all that secure, but he wasn't thinking all that clearly at the time.

"Just a second while I pull up his chart," she said.

Kittredge heard a thud as the nurse set the receiver unceremoniously on her desk. He also heard clicks and pops in the background, and he got the same feeling he used to get when his younger sister eavesdropped on his telephone conversations on another extension in their house.

This is probably a huge mistake, he thought, and he briefly considered hanging up.

The nurse's return interrupted his indecision. She relayed that Charley was still unconscious, but his swelling had receded, his pupils responded well to light, and he was demonstrating positive signs of cognitive function, but that Kittredge should still be prepared for permanent changes.

He asked her for a prognosis for when Charley might regain consciousness, hoping for a timeframe to help him wrap things up in Caracas and return to DC in time for Charley's awakening, but the nurse demurred. "Predicting the future is the job of a doctor, not a mortal. I haven't been taught how to read the chicken bones," she said. Kittredge chuckled, thanked her, and hung up.

He sipped his vodka and stared at the midnight lights of Caracas. He had always loved this city, with its own local twist on the universal themes of conspicuous consumption cohabiting with grinding poverty, and the lights comforted him as he mulled his situation.

Kittredge knew that he had not yet made a rational decision about which associations to keep, and he had no idea how to cleanly and permanently sever the others.

He had the feeling that he was deeply entangled in two

diametrically opposed worlds. Quinn and Fredericks considered him their property; El Grande's people could also lay roughly equal claim to him, by virtue of his insider knowledge of their operation.

Beholden to both sides. What could possibly go wrong?

He shook his head and sighed, fearing the train wreck that would inevitably unfold, then tossed back the last of his vodka. He eyed the bottle, momentarily tempted to pour another drink, but he had a sense that the morning would already arrive far too quickly for his liking.

Kittredge walked quietly back into the bedroom and slipped in the bed next to Maria's warm, naked body. His foray into life as a sexual omnivore wasn't unpleasant in the least, he thought to himself. He closed his eyes and enjoyed the sound of Maria's rhythmic breathing.

Chapter 40

Quinn phoned Fredericks at first light. "I noticed that the back of your neck is starting to look like a pack of hot dogs. You should really lay off the sugar and starch."

"You woke me up for that?" Fredericks wasn't amused.

"Yes. And to tell you that I got a message from our flunky monitoring the hospital switchboard. Kittredge called around midnight last night, asking about Arlinghaus."

"That little shit," Fredericks said.

"What'd you expect? They're lovers."

"You say that like it's not even an abomination."

Quinn laughed. "You've been listening to that pedophile priest again, haven't you?"

Fredericks chuckled. "I'm beginning to think Kittredge is going to be a problem for us."

"He was fine, until your amateur-hour stunt. Speaking of which, your guys did a great job last night with their OK Corral routine. I think there might still be two or three Venezuelans left who don't know that the CIA's in town."

"Go to hell, Quinn."

"And you called *me* B-team."

"What would *you* have done?" Fredericks asked, making no attempt to hide his anger. "He made contact with the VSS guys, then broke contact with us."

"He left you his cell phone, Bill. In the safe deposit box. Do you think he'd have done that if he wanted to go permanently off the reservation?"

"He's not the world's brightest operator."

"He'll fit right in with your team."

"Go to hell," Fredericks repeated. "Did our guys trace his call to the hospital?"

"Not yet. IP encryption. The nerds think it'll take a few days. I suggest we sit tight."

"I suggest you don't make suggestions."

"You're not a very good supervisor, Bill. I don't feel very empowered."

Fredericks didn't reply.

"Seriously," Quinn pressed. "Just relax, let his crisis of conscience subside, and let him calculate his odds. I bet we hear from him."

Fredericks snorted. "Even after last night?"

"*Especially* after last night."

Chapter 41

Special Agent Sam Jameson drove her rental car aimlessly through the Old Town streets. She loved the feel of the city, with its quaint old buildings and real, one-off shops and restaurants. Sure, the chain stores and restaurants had invaded, just like everywhere else, but there was still plenty of local flavor. Alexandria wasn't yet homogenized, and Sam hoped it never got that way.

She had left Landers' office in the Pentagon a little over fourteen hours ago, and since then, she'd thought about nothing but the dead ends she'd discovered, which had knotted themselves together to form an impossibly tangled mess.

She was growing weary of living on the lam. Each hotel stay was another risk, and she had spent the night in the back seat of her rental car, just in case someone had circulated a warning about her, or had the area flophouses under surveillance. It was a bit of a paranoid move, but she knew better than almost anyone alive that once Big Brother decided to bear down on someone, it was all over but the crying.

And it was certainly her turn under the microscope, because of the Brock/Dibiaso thing, and because of the Brock/Minton thing, though the latter appeared not to be a thing at all. Brock and Fatso were fighter squadron buddies from years ago, but evidently not much else, so that had left her with only the Dibiaso connection.

She hadn't necessarily expected to find a smoking gun at the

Pentagon, but she had certainly hoped for *something* to help piece things together. Dibiaso hadn't signed the visitor log using his own name, and Landers had said nothing at all about their business together, which was more than frustrating, so the trip wasn't terribly educational.

All of that had made for a melancholy morning.

And I got Jensen killed yesterday, too. It was a melodramatic thought, she knew, and it wasn't entirely accurate. But it contained a kernel of truth, and hearing the news about Jensen during a brief phone conversation with Dan Gable as she left the Pentagon the previous afternoon had turned her dejection into something just shy of despair.

Gable had also mentioned that his search for Dibiaso's phone records had come up empty. The number was apparently only in use for a couple of weeks, and it hadn't appeared on the network before or since the period of time when Dibiaso's movements coincided with Brock's.

So Dibiaso was using a burner. It was telling, but it was yet another dead end.

Sam churned things over in her head. She was pretty sure that Jensen, the young CSI, hadn't committed suicide in a restaurant bathroom, and she was also pretty sure that he wasn't stupid enough to have made a lethal dosage error.

And, while people fell off the wagon all the time, Jeff was probably too smart to get high at lunchtime, with all of his coworkers around to watch his intoxicated antics.

So the deadly *thing,* whatever the hell it was, had claimed another victim.

Abrams, Cooper, Quartermain, and now Jensen.

I was within seconds of joining them, she noted. But for a bit of good luck, Sunday morning's bomb would surely have killed her and Brock.

And what if she had shown up a few minutes earlier to Quartermain's apartment? Would she have been Phil's morgue-drawer neighbor? Random chance had saved her a few times over the past week.

Random chance.

Randomness made her think of what Landers had said at the end of their interview at the Pentagon. *Random strangers* was the phrase he used. He was talking about waiting in the so-called "slug line," a strange Pentagon euphemism for a slightly creepy carpool arrangement, to jump into a car with people he didn't know.

The meme got Sam thinking about the way the slug line worked. It was a symbiotic relationship, it occurred to her, as adding passengers allowed the drivers to use the HOV lanes, and the passengers avoided the expense, hassle, and stench of the subway system.

It seemed odd to Sam that they wouldn't organize steady carpools, but maybe there was a bit of wisdom to it. Under the slug line concept, if one guy's boss decided to keep him late, the whole carful of people wouldn't have to miss dinner.

It probably worked because the Pentagon was such a huge place, and nobody wanted to stay a nanosecond longer than necessary, so there was probably always someone to carpool with.

Sam thought more about the size of the building, with its thirty thousand employees. The carpool was probably an interesting numbers study, she thought. You could probably go months without getting in the same car twice, and probably at least that long before ending up in a car with another passenger for a second time.

The whole thing didn't sound terribly appealing on a personal level, and Sam thought it would be awkward to climb into a car full of complete strangers twice a day.

Complete strangers.

It hit her like a freight train.

Of course!

Complete strangers!

Sam fumbled with her new burner phone. It took ages to turn on, and she punched a wrong number trying to dial Dan Gable's office number. She cursed, almost ran a red light, and finally redialed.

It rang forever before Gable picked up.

"Dan, maybe Brock isn't lying!" she shouted before he could even get a word out.

"Huh?"

"The slug line! He carpooled home from the Pentagon!"

"I'm not following," Dan said. "And Ekman's asking about you again. I can't keep pretending I'm not helping you."

"Dan, Brock might not be lying about Arturo Dibiaso!"

Dan sighed. "Sam, his cell phone data matched Dibiaso's exactly." His voice sounded tired. "I'm sorry, but they were in the same car, twice."

"That's what I'm saying! People at the Pentagon carpool with random strangers all the time!"

Dan thought this over. "So you're saying he randomly rode in the same car with Dibiaso, twice in two weeks?"

"Yeah. I mean, maybe. You told me that he got off at his normal spot both times, and Dibiaso continued on all the way to Triangle both times."

"Are you sure this isn't just wishful thinking on your part?"

"It sounds impossible on the face of it," Sam said, "which is why I was convinced he was lying. But I was just thinking, what did they teach us during IB?" Sam asked. Investigation Basics was the entry-level course all Homeland counterespionage agents cut their teeth on.

"Nothing useful," Dan said.

"They taught us that random events don't space themselves evenly. And random events sometimes bunch together, making it look like they're connected when it's really just coincidence."

It got silent on the other end of the phone while Dan considered Sam's idea. "You might be right," he said. "It sure would explain why Brock wouldn't leave us alone. Up until yesterday, he kept calling, trying to plead his case with anyone who would listen. Guilty people don't usually do that."

Sam thought about this. Brock's behavior seemed to support her notion that the connection with Dibiaso was, in fact, pure coincidence.

Something gnawed at her. "You said, 'up until yesterday.' What did you mean?"

"Jarvis finally got good and ready to interview Brock. Even set up an appointment and everything."

"And?"

"Brock didn't show. We have people looking for him. . ."

"Oh, Jesus," Sam said.

Had something happened to Brock?

Her blood ran cold thinking of the awful things that had happened to four different people associated with this case over the past few days, and of the horrible things that had almost happened to her and Brock over the weekend.

"I tried to call you a few times," Dan said, "but you'd changed out your burners again and I didn't have a number."

"Oh, Jesus," Sam repeated.

"I'm afraid there's more. They found his car at home, with his cell phone in the glove box. The construction crew working on your house said the car hadn't moved all day, and they never saw Brock."

The tears came.

"I'm sorry, Sam. They searched your house," Dan said, speaking with the air of a physician bearing news of a terminal disease.

He paused before continuing. "I hate having to tell you this, but there was some blood."

Sam choked back a sob.

"The lab results aren't back yet on the blood from your kitchen," Dan said. "But they haven't found any sign of Brock."

Part 4

Chapter 42

Peter Kittredge awoke to sunlight penetrating the room. The posh surroundings reminded him of the Cayman resort where he and Charley had vacationed during their early days together.

He heard soft snoring, and turned to see Maria lying next to him. She was on her side facing away from him, and he followed the exquisite line of her shoulders and back as they gave way to her trim waist, and rose again to her perfect hips, barely covered by the silk sheets.

Something primal stirred in Kittredge. He sidled up to Maria's body, kissed her neck softly, and moved provocatively against her.

She responded in kind.

The animal pleasure of it surprised him again, and he soon found himself blissfully entangled, drinking her in, devouring her.

Afterward, they lay together, conjoined. He kissed her neck, feeling none of the mild post-coital revulsion his previous heterosexual conquests had engendered.

That was interesting, and new. With every other woman in his life, his desire for sex had lasted precisely until climax, after which his desire shifted instantly to escape and evasion, longing to return to the comfort of male companionship.

"Good morning," she finally said.

"Quite."

"If your boyfriend could see you now," she teased.

"You might have ruined me for boys."

"I hope not. I think there are many fun possibilities we could explore."

His response was interrupted by the ringing telephone. He reached to grab it, but she held his hand. "Wait. Count the rings."

Four rings of the phone, then silence.

It rang again, twice, then more silence.

Thirty seconds later, it rang again, and this time Maria picked up the receiver. "Si."

Kittredge overheard a male voice speaking in staccato Spanish, and watched Maria's face harden. "Si," she said again, and hung up.

She looked at Kittredge for a long moment.

Without warning, she slapped his face, the sharp smack echoing off the marble floor. "Fucking idiot. Get dressed. We must go."

* * *

Kittredge joined Maria in the shower. Despite their shared nudity and the novelty of their new sexual relationship, she was all business. She moved quickly out of the shower, dried off, and rummaged in the expansive closet.

"Wear this," she said, tossing a black two-piece suit on the bed as he toweled off.

"To what do I owe the pleasure?" he asked. No reply, other than a frosty glance and a thin black tie thrown at him from the recesses of the walk-in closet, which was stocked with enough quality clothing to make the urbane cosmopolitan in him insanely jealous.

He set about getting ready.

"So you made a little phone call last night," she said a few minutes later. Kittredge got the impression it had taken a while for her to muster the limited civility evident in her tone.

"Yes." He was unapologetic.

"You couldn't have asked me to find out what you wanted to know?"

"I needed to trust the answer."

She turned from the mirror. "What's between us," she said. "That's not trust?"

"Maybe," he said. "Or maybe it's manipulation. There seems to be a lot of that in my life these days. And I still don't know what you want with me."

He debated telling her what was really on his mind. He decided to take a chance, and maybe inflict a wound in the process. "And I think the VSS put Charley in the hospital in the first place."

She wasn't wounded. "I think you're a brilliant spy," she said with obvious sarcasm. "Of course we did. You're lucky he's not dead. Get dressed."

It wasn't a surprising revelation. Her eyes had told him nearly as much when he'd asked a similar question the previous evening.

He had an idea of why the VSS had attacked Charley, but a part of him needed it spelled out. "Why?" he asked.

"Wear the black shoes on the floor," Maria said. She disappeared into the other room and shut the door behind her.

* * *

Kittredge sat at the kitchen counter, staring out the window at the Caracas skyline while nursing a Bloody Mary he'd concocted from ingredients stocked in the gorgeously apportioned kitchen. He'd considered a sober morning, but quickly dismissed the thought. Maria's sudden turn from minx to jungle cat was all the excuse he needed to start the day with a shine on.

So the VSS had put Charley into a coma. He was surprised that he wasn't surprised.

But it *was* surprising that he wasn't terribly angry about it, and he attributed that to the inchoate knowledge that there was much more to Charley than Charley had let him see. His lover, whom Kittredge had even thought of as his partner, had hidden a few terribly important things from him, and that felt very much like a betrayal.

What next, then? It all felt like an amusement park ride. He was strapped in, unable to climb off, and thoroughly apprehensive.

But it wasn't accurate to say that he wanted it to stop. There was a sizable portion of his psyche that craved the attention, intrigue, and extremes of his precarious position, perched between two powerful interests that seemed to be at war with each other.

Sure, he might end up dead, but that wasn't terribly different than the semi-stasis of his cubicle at the embassy, shuffling sterile and boring economic reports around while ignoring barrages of meaningless email from his coworkers.

He knew that his burgeoning buzz gave him a much more stoic attitude toward the risks and unpleasantness, and he needed only to twist his torso to remind himself just how uncomfortable things could become. His lower back was still covered in painful scars from his introduction to Quinn a few nights earlier.

But as the alcohol helped remove the sharp edges from his situation, his wounds served only to punctuate the relative excitement of his new reality, unreal as it might be.

It could always be worse, he thought. *I could be sitting at my desk.*

Which reminded him that he needed to call his supervisor at the embassy to extend his sick leave. He eyed the telephone, but immediately thought better of it. Maria had been more than a little angry about his ill-advised phone call the evening prior. He made a mental note to bring it up with her, whenever she emerged from her sequestration in the apartment's second master suite.

It didn't take long. The door opened, and Maria stepped into the hallway, transformed. She had been gorgeous when he met her, wearing tight-fitting casual clothing that had stirred his dormant heterosexual appetite, but she was resplendent now.

She wore a long, black gown that followed her body's perfect contours to just below the knees, then flared elegantly toward the ankle. An improbably large diamond teardrop hung suspended just above her décolletage, punctuating the gown's plunging neckline and threatening to disappear between her breasts at any moment. Her dark eyes smoldered, framed by long, dark lashes and smoky shadows.

Kittredge was taken aback. Hidden inside yesterday's tomboy was a true international beauty. "Oh my God," he said.

"I'll take that as a compliment," she said, offering a slight but reluctant smile. She straightened his tie as she walked past him toward the coffee pot. "You clean up nicely yourself."

Kittredge heard the sound of the apartment door opening, and saw a blur of motion where Maria stood. He had no idea where she'd hidden it, but she produced a snub-nosed pistol and trained it at the hallway opening.

A deep male voice spoke in Spanish, which Kittredge translated roughly as, "The only pace is a suicide pace." The phrase made no sense to him.

Maria responded instantly, however. "And today is a good day to die." More spy shit, Kittredge realized.

Four men rounded the corner into the apartment's posh kitchen. They wore suits identical to the one Maria had picked out for him.

A fifth man, older, grayer, and more distinguished, followed in something that was more formal than normal business attire, but somehow not quite a tuxedo. Extremely stylish, in a throwback sort of way, the gay man in Kittredge observed instantly.

All five men embraced Maria warmly, as if they were old friends who hadn't seen each other in a while. But for a few glances that were just shy of openly frosty, they ignored Kittredge completely. He got the feeling that he was responsible for the morning's exertions.

The distinguished-looking gentleman addressed him in flawless English. "Señor Kittredge, we will all leave here together. You will pretend to be part of a security entourage escorting Maria and myself through the lobby of the bank."

He reached into his jacket pocket and produced an earpiece.

"Wear this," he said, handing it to Kittredge.

"Your job will be only to keep your rather large mouth shut and walk next to Alejandro." He nodded to the largest of his compatriots, who smiled perfunctorily.

"Where are we going?" Kittredge asked.

The distinguished gentleman let loose a small, annoyed chuckle. "Maria was right. You ask too many questions. We are moving because you have compromised this location. As Maria explained last night, communications from here are generally secure. But when you contact a communications node that is under surveillance, such as the intensive care unit of DC General Hospital, it is possible with time and resources to trace the origin of the call. Our adversaries have both time and resources."

"I'm sorry," Kittredge said. "I didn't realize. . ." His sentence faded away under the glare of the man's hard gaze.

"It was a risk we took. You are inexperienced and impulsive. We will control you more closely in the future."

He glanced at Kittredge's cocktail. "Finish your breakfast. It is time for us to go."

* * *

Kittredge took his place at the tail end of the entourage, walking in tandem with Alejandro, a mountain of a Venezuelan. He noticed that the other men wearing earpieces put their fingers to their ears, straining to hear instructions, but Kittredge's earpiece was completely silent. *For show only,* he realized. He was along for the ride, again.

It was an interesting and exciting environment, but he resented his role as tyro. He realized that he wanted to be an insider, someone in the know, someone important in a difficult and harsh world, someone leading an inexperienced newbie by the hand, inspiring awe with his nonchalant gravitas.

Gaining that sort of importance would take time, undoubtedly. But he felt a deep desire to become the kind of person he was now following, the distinguished man in the almost-tuxedo, surrounded by heavies, an international beauty adorning his arm.

Their foray through the Banco de Caracas lobby was brief and anticlimactic, though they drew stares from everyone. *Anonymity through ostentation*, Kittredge thought. *What an interesting phenomenon.*

The front two "security men" opened the doors for the rest of the entourage, and Kittredge saw three black Suburbans parked at the curb as he exited the bank building. Maria and the older guy – Rojo was his name, if Kittredge had overheard correctly during the group's pre-departure conversation – piled into the second Suburban in line.

Three security men climbed into the driver's seats of the three Suburbans.

Kittredge was momentarily confused about what to do, but he felt Alejandro's strong grip on his arm, leading him toward a white sedan at the tail end of the procession. Alejandro opened the rear passenger's side door for him, and Kittredge climbed in.

The front and rear seats of the sedan were separated by thick Plexiglass. As Kittredge fastened his seatbelt, he noticed that there were no door handles. He got a sinking feeling in the pit of his stomach. Apparently, Rojo wasn't bullshitting about controlling him more closely.

Was he now a prisoner?

It certainly had that vibe about it.

Chapter 43

El Jerga – The Shiv – was thankful that the Friday morning sun had finally climbed high enough in the sky to no longer be reflected into his eye by the rearview mirror as he headed west. He was near Pittsburgh, a name that he thought apropos, if his single job in Pittsburgh years ago had provided a representative sampling of the kind of life available in the rough post-industrial town.

Pittsburgh wasn't his destination for the day. He motored westward, being careful to drive neither too fast nor too slow. His papers were authentic-looking, but were merely expensive forgeries. He didn't stand a chance if anyone checked them against a database of real green cards, so he didn't crave the attention of a traffic cop or state patrolman. His organization had yet to fully adapt to the new realities of the digital age, but he knew that El Grande was working hard to rectify the potentially crippling shortfalls.

His watch alarm beeped. Time to check in. His careful route planning paid off, and he was within two exits of the rest stop.

He pulled off the highway and parked near the brick structure housing the restrooms, ensuring that the nose of his car pointed south.

He retrieved a laptop computer and a strange-looking antenna from his trunk, set both in the passenger's seat, and powered on the laptop. He set the antenna on the dashboard and raised it at an angle, pointing it in the general vicinity of the geosynchronous communications satellites he sought. He plugged the antenna into the USB port of the laptop computer, locked the car door, and availed himself of the restroom while the system initialized.

When he returned, a nondescript welcome screen encouraged him to enter his thirty-two-digit case-sensitive password. El Jerga complied, entering a collection of unrelated Spanish and English words. It wasn't perfectly secure, he knew, but it was a damn sight better than in the old days.

Twenty-two thousand miles above the equator, the telecommunications satellite mulled his logon request. *Surreal,* he thought.

After several seconds, the distant satellite granted him access to the network, and he opened a normal web browser window, into which he typed a twelve-digit IP address. It was the equivalent of a computer's mailing address, and the particular computer with which he desired to communicate, which was physically located somewhere in South America, was ready and waiting for him.

The communications portal looked like an old-school web chatroom, though that similarity was lost on El Jerga. He'd never been an online kind of guy, until forced by his increasingly tech-savvy employers.

The cursor flashed expectantly at him, but he strictly obeyed the communications protocol: no typing, except in response to a query from his handlers.

At precisely seven minutes after seven a.m. Eastern, a message appeared on the chat board: "Good morning. Please authenticate."

El Jerga typed a separate password, also thirty-two digits in length, and waited for his handler's response.

It came a little over a minute later. "Difficult news follows." A photograph slowly loaded, its encoded form traveling through open air and space for over forty-five thousand miles.

As the screen slowly filled, El Jerga was filled with a growing sense of dread. His fears were fully realized when the photograph's final pixels arrived. His throat constricted in the familiar place, and his hands shook with rage.

The photograph showed a face he hadn't seen in months, but one he'd known and loved since childhood, dressed in a tan jacket and red scarf, lying lifeless on a bed of grass and fallen autumn leaves.

"When?" El Jerga typed.

"Sunday."

"You waited this long to tell me?"

"I'm sorry," the typed message eventually said. "It took this long to confirm it was him. I will see to it that you avenge him."

Like you have any say in the matter, El Jerga seethed.

His uncle had raised him since he was a boy, after his father died in the oilfield uprising. He had followed his uncle into the clandestine services, which had led him to loyalties of both necessity and convenience in a difficult journey that had ultimately revealed, cultivated, and refined his unique talents and proclivities.

"Send the picture." El Jerga typed, hands still shaking.

"Your target is Agency," came El Grande's reply. "Proceed slowly and with caution. The stakes are high."

As if trivia ever warranted assassinations, El Jerga thought with a snort. El Grande fancied himself a warrior-leader, but El Jerga viewed him as little more than a middleman, an office worker with fanciful affectations but infinitesimal power. El Jerga tolerated him only in small doses under normal circumstances.

These were not normal circumstances.

Killing was always both business and pleasure for El Jerga, but suddenly, it was also about honor, family, and Hammurabi's code. He would repay his uncle's killers, eye for eye, tooth for tooth, and death for death.

The picture of his next victim appeared slowly, just as the picture of his uncle's death-distorted visage had appeared moments before.

His target was rail-thin, bald, and had a skinny face with hollow cheekbones. Not at all unlike his last victim, though this man seemed less strung-out. The photograph showed him wearing some sort of green utility uniform with zippers and bright patches.

El Grande's final instructions appeared moments later: "More to follow. Make this one memorable."

El Jerga felt his heart pound in his chest and adrenaline zing through his veins. It was an order he could follow without compunction.

Chapter 44

Sam drove the rented Rav4 with abandon through the streets of Alexandria, cursing impatiently with the growing gridlock as the Friday morning commuters became a maddening throng.

It took her several cycles of the light to get past the Highway 1 intersection, and she was fit to be tied by the time she turned south toward her house.

It was a horrible idea, she knew.

The voice in the back of her head, the one she'd learned to heed without question as a result of one painful lesson after another, was screaming at her to go *anyplace* but home.

She still strongly suspected that Homeland was no longer on Team Sam, and knew for a fact that the Metro DC police department certainly wasn't heading up the Sam Jameson fan club. One or both agencies would undoubtedly have her house on round-the-clock surveillance, Sam thought.

Going home might very well be the worst decision of her life.

But she had to see for herself. She couldn't *not* go home.

She now believed that, unlikely as it might seem, Brock might have been telling her the truth when he denied knowing Arturo Dibiaso. The cell phone evidence had seemed so unequivocally damning just half an hour before, until Sam connected the dots regarding the Pentagon slug line.

Suddenly, it seemed entirely plausible that Brock could have ridden in the same car with Arturo Dibiaso on two separate occasions without ever having any inkling who the man was, or what he was up to.

And, Sam realized, she had been looking for an excuse, *any* excuse, to give Brock the benefit of the doubt. He fit her perfectly, in every way she could think of and many more that she discovered all the time, and she realized that she desperately hoped that her original assessment – that Brock had lied to her and everyone else – was dead wrong.

She made several aggressive lane changes that ultimately netted no advantage in traffic, but satisfied her need to do something more proactive than simply sit motionless next to hundreds of other idling steel boxes.

She couldn't help but worry that while she sat on her ass in traffic, something dreadful may be happening to Brock.

Hope was now a curse, she realized as the light finally changed. She was now scared to death for Brock's safety. He had fallen off the grid, Dan had told her moments earlier, with no sign of him other than some blood on the floor of the house they shared together.

She'd thought a thousand times in the last several minutes of dialing Brock's cell, but Dan told her that DHS had found it in his car, parked in front of their house. That meant that DHS probably had Brock's cell in their possession, and she didn't want to highlight her position by calling.

She longed for her smart phone to check traffic, but she knew that it would only have added to her growing aggravation and anxiety. So she inched along with the sheeple on their morning commute, hands gripping her steering wheel with far more force than necessary, jaws clenched shut.

* * *

She'd made it to within half a mile of her residence and was accelerating to take advantage of a momentary traffic letup, when she realized that she badly needed to get control of her emotions.

If you're going to do something dumb, at least don't be stupid about it.

She needed to take her time, to approach patiently and methodically, to make sure that if someone was watching, she found them before they found her.

She turned a block early, following the gentle bend around the road as it climbed the steep hill. Two blocks later, she drove past the house that was directly uphill from hers, carefully checking parked cars for occupants and watching the street for passersby.

She saw nothing. If there was surveillance on this block, it wasn't overt.

Sam paused between houses to glimpse downhill into her backyard. Trees, fences, and vegetation prevented a clear view of the entire yard, but what she could see looked clear. It would have been a great time for a multi-spec photo, but she didn't have the specialized camera with her, and didn't have the time to wait while Dan analyzed the photos.

She didn't linger too long, fearing notice by unseen eyes hidden behind bedroom curtains, or by cameras hidden out of view. She continued, turning left down the hill toward her street.

Her heart rate was up, she noticed. She felt the Kimber .45 in its holster under her arm, grateful for its reassurance, but cursing herself for not taking a bulletproof vest with her during her hasty departure from home on Monday.

Stupid mistakes like that were how pros turned up just as dead as amateurs, Sam knew. But as a practical matter, it was often hard to transcend one's humanity, which had an uncanny tendency to bite one in the ass at the most inopportune moments.

She turned left and drove slowly past her house, large sunglasses over her face, white scarf draped over her flame-red hair, eyes darting quickly between places to catch anything out of order.

The construction crew was hard at work on the front of her house. They'd cleaned up the debris, and were now repairing the damage done by the explosion in the wee hours of Sunday morning.

If I was a bastard trying to screw with me, Sam thought, *I'd put a guy or two on that construction crew.* Undoubtedly, the thought had also occurred to her pursuers, so she formulated a plan to deal with the crew as she passed down the street, noticing nothing else out of the ordinary.

Sam turned the car around, parked at her curb behind a worker's truck, chambered a round in her pistol, and set the safety. Then she got out of her car.

Her legs felt rubbery and her heart pounded. She made her way up the drive, and several crew members stopped to watch her. "Morning ma'am," one of them said when she cleared her throat.

"Morning," she said, surprised at how steady her voice sounded given the turmoil going on in her chest. "Just got off the phone with the immigration guys. Apparently they're doing a random inspection of the job site. I have no idea why they picked my house for this, but they insisted. Anyway, they said 8:45-ish. If you guys want to take a powder, or if you have to drive somewhere or something, I understand."

The foreman stepped up to speak privately with her while mild mayhem broke out among the rank and file on the construction crew. "We carpooled, and not all the guys have their green cards on them," he said slowly, looking at her in a knowing kind of way.

"No problem," Sam said. "Do what you have to do. I think the immigration laws are messed up anyway."

"Thank you, ma'am. We'll make the time up at the end of the day, I promise. I know you want your house back."

It took only a few moments for the men to pile into the back of two pickup trucks. "I really appreciate the head's up," the foreman said to her as he drove off with a truck full of migrant workers. "We'll be back soon."

No rush, Sam thought to herself.

She felt her heart rate slow a bit, until her thoughts returned to what might be lurking inside her house. She took a deep breath, steeled herself, and ducked beneath the protective plastic that stood where her front door used to be.

Once she was out of view of the street, Sam drew her pistol. She made her way slowly through the entryway and went up the stairs, pausing to clear each closet along the way. She took her time clearing each of the upstairs rooms, finding nothing out of the ordinary.

She made a point to check for Brock's suitcase, which she found in its normal spot. She surveyed his clothes; while she didn't keep an inventory of his socks and underwear, it didn't look like his drawer was missing any items. If he was on the run, he hadn't taken the time to prepare, she thought.

Either that, or he had a hit-and-run kit stashed somewhere.

Of course he did, she realized. Right next to hers, in the panic room.

She shook her head at her own stupidity, then made her way slowly downstairs to the kitchen. She was only a couple of steps past the breakfast nook when she saw the dark crimson stain on the hardwood floor.

She felt her breath quicken. Blood wasn't a new sight for her, but *Brock's blood* was something else altogether. She wasn't prepared for the effect it would have on her, and she felt tears welling in her eyes.

Several deep breaths later, she continued on her slow search of her own home, taking her time and leaving all of the doors open as she searched them.

Sam noticed that the butcher's knife was missing from the Wusthof block on the marble countertop. Not a good sign. She forced herself to remain calm.

Minutes later, she had completed her sweep of the inside of her house, stopping to check the doors leading to the backyard. All were locked, and she didn't open them, though she glanced between the curtains to search the yard for signs of a struggle. *Or bastards hiding in the bushes,* she thought, tightening her grip on the pistol.

Finally, there was no place left to search but the basement vault. She had the grim task ahead of her of sifting through hours of video footage to see what had happened to Brock, hoping for a clue to his whereabouts.

She steeled herself, typed in the nine-digit access code, heard the latch retract, and slowly opened the door.

She'd only opened the door a foot when her blood froze and her heart leapt into her throat.

Protruding from the darkness of the panic room was the barrel of a large caliber handgun, pointed at her face.

Chapter 45

It's damned sweaty in this country, Quinn observed to himself.

It was late fall further up in the northern climes, but in Caracas, just seven hundred miles north of the equator, soggy and sultry was a year-round reality. Three thousand feet of elevation took the edge off of what would otherwise be a vicious tropical heat, but Quinn was still uncomfortable in the midday warmth.

He stood atop a building wearing overalls and a bright orange vest. He had an earpiece in his ear, with an integral microphone that picked up the vibrations of his skull when he spoke. A thin cord connected the apparatus to a radio transmitter on his belt.

He pretended to be working on a large air conditioning unit on the top of the building, but even the most lenient supervisor would be unimpressed with his work ethic. He kept taking breaks to peer over the edge of the roof.

His young apprentice was no better, one of the twenty-somethings from Fredericks' soiree earlier in the week. Operation Syphilis, Phase Two, was underway in earnest.

Quinn chuckled to himself. *Phase Two. Like a real VIP assassination. Only it's being run by Fredericks the Clown.*

"Check in," Quinn commanded, peering over the rooftop down to Urdaneta Avenue, which led to El Palacio de Miraflores, the daytime hangout of El Cucaracha.

Even the codename of the target was a Fredericks-ism.

Cucaracha, the Spanish word for cockroach, demanded the feminine definitive article, *La*. La Cucaracha, it should have been. But Fredericks had shoved the masculine definitive, *el*, in front of the word. Quinn hated shit like that. It was so annoyingly common.

"High Two," said a voice on the radio in response to Quinn's command. The voice had come from the twenty-something next to him on the roof, who was staring at the innards of the air conditioning unit like a pig studying a wristwatch.

"Stroller One and Two," said a female voice, still seductive despite the radio's static. Quinn searched until he found them fifteen stories below, walking along the Urdaneta Avenue sidewalk. He bristled to see the hot young thing whom he badly wanted to know in the biblical sense holding hands with another of the twenty-somethings. Quinn was certain Fredericks had arranged the assignments purely to thwart his libido.

"Copy, Strollers. Cruiser?" Quinn said, holding the earpiece in place instinctively but unnecessarily.

"Cruiser's up." The old man. Quinn saw him at the other end of Urdaneta, sporting a ridiculously long, white beard and a bowler hat, hunched over a walker and hustling along like an Arctic glacier.

"Needles has you loud and clear." Quinn couldn't see her. She was the frumpy middle-aged agent, seated at a bus stop bench on the near side of the avenue just beneath Quinn's building. She was knitting. Perfectly frumptacular.

"Moped loud and clear, too." The red Vespa was just visible, idling at the curb nearest the Palacio.

"Movement," someone said, and Quinn's eyes snapped to the

Miraflores Palace's gates. They were indeed in motion, retreating into the wall far more rapidly than might befit a stately entrance and exit. The no-nonsense gate's operation was no doubt engineered to cope with the violence of one of the world's most dangerous cities. Caracas had hovered near the top of the list of the world's best places to become a murder victim for the last seventeen millennia. Or something like that, Quinn thought.

"Steady and ready," Quinn said. It was a stupid thing to say, really. If he hadn't said it, would his agents have freaked out? Fallen asleep? Doubtful.

"Buggies," Moped said, as the first of the black limousines poured from behind the palace gates. "They don't screw around," he editorialized, impressed by how quickly the entourage charged into the intersection.

"Photos," Quinn said. Again, it was a silly thing to say. Photographing the security detail was the point of the day's op. Would the team have forgotten to properly position the cameras hidden in various spots on their disguises, had he said nothing to them? Probably not, but if they screwed it up, it wouldn't be because he failed to remind them.

The whole thing was over in a little over a minute. Eight limousines in all, splitting into four groups of two, each traveling a different route. It was an age-old technique designed to keep would-be assassins from knowing the precise position of the likely mark.

Quinn was also certain the photos would reveal no giveaways in the limousines themselves. They were all probably exactly alike, each of them an identical million-dollar armored Mercedes able to withstand a grievous roadside blast or multiple hits from any projectile smaller than an RPG.

"That's a wrap," he said as the last of the limousines disappeared into the city. "Don't get nabbed on the way to the debrief."

* * *

Quinn couldn't figure out why it was seventy-five degrees outside, but ninety degrees in the stuffy apartment. The problem was made worse by the bevy of video equipment now set up on the countertops.

Fredericks' body odor dominated the little kitchen, and, to a person, each of the operatives made a face of disgust upon entering the debriefing as they ran into a wall of middle-aged, overweight stench. "Couldn't you find a more uncomfortable safe house to hold us hostage in?" Quinn asked Fredericks, who ignored him.

"Thanks for making it back so quickly," Fredericks said as the last of the team assembled. "Countersurveillance reports that you're clean, except for an interesting episode with a white sedan that I'll tell you about in a little bit. First, let's have your assessments." He looked at Quinn expectantly.

Quinn cut to the chase. "A handshake and a hug at the front door, or nothing. I don't see a way in past all the security without a small army."

"Concur," said the older gentleman, his gratuitously long beard and bowler hat now removed and stored safely back in the wardrobe department. "Everything was armored and well-manned."

Moped spoke up next. "They have entry and exit procedures

wired like clockwork. There's no margin."

Fredericks looked at the attractive young female agent, who nodded her assent. "Plus the route surveillance team. We spotted at least three pseudo-pedestrians. Maybe four. Wired and packing." Meaning, the foot surveillance team was connected to the main security team via two-way radio, and they were carrying handguns.

Fredericks nodded. "That checks with my assessment as well. Mary, tell them what you told me a minute ago."

The frumpy-looking lady nodded, then spoke in a slow, matronly tone. "They were watching you two up on the roof, from a white sedan. The driver got out to snap a few photos of you. Strangest thing, though, the back seat looked like it was configured for hauling perps. It was sealed off by plexiglass like a cop car, and there was a guy inside who looked like he was along for the ride."

She handed over a smart phone displaying the photo she had taken, which Fredericks connected to the large video monitor using a converter cable.

"Thank Facebook for the facial recognition database," Fredericks said. "The Agency made them a strong offer."

The comment drew knowing smirks from the crowd at the table. They assumed, correctly, that the offer went something like this: we're the CIA, so give us your shit. It was surprisingly compelling despite its lack of subtlety.

The computer crunched piles of digital data that characterized the backseat passenger's facial features, then compared the data to Facebook's hundreds of millions of faces.

It took a little under a minute, which astounded the older

spooks in the crowd, but didn't faze the twenty-somethings in the least.

Quinn read the facial recognition report and shook his head. Peter Kittredge.

Fredericks whistled. "Our newest friend," he said, throwing a knowing glance at Quinn.

The hint wasn't lost on Quinn. Fredericks wanted Kittredge killed, and he wanted Quinn to arrange it.

Quinn had already spoken his mind in private to Fredericks, and he decided to make his position a bit more publicly known as well. "He's in perfect position. We couldn't have planned it better, and he happens to be an expert on the topic we're going to see Cucaracha about. Let's just use a little finesse."

It was an incongruous thing to hear from Quinn, a mountain of a man with feral, mismatched eyes and a steroid-enhanced physique. He looked like he was far more accustomed to pulling arms and legs free of their joints than finessing anything, but his strength and brutality always played second fiddle to his instincts and intellect, which were nearly flawless. If there was ever a born operative, it was Quinn, and despite their good-natured mutual disdain, Fredericks respected his opinion.

"Okay. But that little faggot makes me nervous."

"Let the record so reflect," Quinn said. "And you're not allowed to say faggot any more. Didn't you attend the sensitivity training?"

"Find him. I'll need some assurance from him," Fredericks said.

"Obviously. I didn't think you wanted to swap recipes."

Out of the corner of his eye, Quinn saw the attractive girl laugh. He thought for the second time in as many days that maybe he had a chance with her. He'd have to deal with the Kittredge thing as quickly as possible, and maybe he could schedule some time to go over case notes with the girl, to hear her thoughts. And then maybe he'd get to hear her moans. He smiled inwardly.

Fredericks' nasal voice brought him back. "So it's settled, then," the fat case officer was saying. "We ride in on the ambassador's coattails, spin a yarn, hand him the pen full of Ebola, and ride off into the sunset."

"Hepatitis," Quinn corrected.

"Right. What did I say?"

"Forget it."

"Surveillance schedule stays unchanged for the moment," Fredericks said. "I have to talk to the embassy fucktards and the Washington fucktards. Then I'll contact you guys. Stay available."

Recognizing that the meeting had ended, and eager to depart the lethal radius of Fredericks' hygiene problem, the Operation Syphilis team cleared the cramped kitchen.

"Take a shower, Bill," Quinn offered on the way out. "You smell like a dead goat."

Chapter 46

Kittredge didn't have a terrific feeling about the way the day was progressing. He'd started with an extremely pleasant liaison with Maria, a very heterosexual encounter that he'd thoroughly enjoyed, to his enduring surprise.

But then the phone had rung and the day had gone rapidly to shit.

He sat glumly in the back seat of the sedan and stared at the back of Alejandro's head through the plexiglass. He'd seen a similar view once before, when he was seventeen years old and caught behind the school with a joint. The policeman had hauled him away in a cruiser to make a point, then dropped him off at home without so much as a word to his parents.

Kittredge didn't have a great feeling that this particular trip in the back of a converted police cruiser would end quite so plummy.

Alejandro had made one stop so far, and Kittredge was having a difficult time wrapping his mind around its purpose. Alejandro had stopped the car at the curb on Urdaneta Avenue, gotten out, snapped a few dozen photos of the surrounding buildings, random passersby and a passing motorcade of limousines, then returned without so much as a word.

Kittredge had asked him politely about the stop, but hadn't received even a head nod to acknowledge his presence, much less an answer to his question.

It was clear from Maria and Rojo's comments that his current status as *persona non grata* was a direct result of his having called the hospital the night before to inquire about Charley's condition. He wasn't sure what else they expected him to do, though. It wasn't as if he had the ability to stop by Charley's room and see for himself, and he didn't trust the VSS to shoot straight with him.

Sure, Maria had engineered his escape from what he assumed was a CIA-orchestrated attack. For that, he was certainly grateful.

On the other hand, Maria had confirmed his suspicions that El Grande and his pack of heavies was behind Charley's rearranged cerebral cortex, and possibly responsible for ransacking his and Charley's Caracas apartment.

All in all, Kittredge figured, he could be forgiven for hedging his bets and searching for a neutral point of view on Charley's status.

Kittredge realized that he had run headlong into the fundamental question inherent to the clandestine world, the question of who the hell to trust, and when to trust them.

And, he thought, perhaps the more important questions related to how far one should trust them, and when to stop.

He was certain that he lacked the sophistication to make solid judgements of that nature, at least at the moment. More accurately, he figured, he just lacked the training to spot the signs that gave away a sudden change in rules and roles.

But that was certainly something that could be learned, he thought. How did humans become good at anything? Practice, patience, and persistence. He had felt extremely *alive* during a few of those crazy, breathless moments over the past week, and he wouldn't mind cultivating a little more of that kind of excitement in his life.

And the pay was actually pretty good, when people didn't steal it from him.

He just wasn't sure it was a forgiving enough field to accommodate on-the-job training. He was a lightweight in every sense of the word, and the only reason he was still alive was because, at various times, the Agency and the VSS *wanted* him alive.

Still, that was something. He was useful, maybe only by virtue of his various affiliations with the embassy, the Agency, and the ragtag Venezuelan guerrillas, but useful nonetheless.

For the moment.

He worried that he might have worn out his utility with the VSS. Alejandro was anything but friendly, and they had clearly segregated him from the rest of the entourage, stuffing him in the back of what amounted to a paddy wagon. He hadn't seen a black Suburban since they left the bank building, so he had no idea where Rojo, Maria, and the other security guards might have gone.

He might never have been inside El Grande and Maria's inner circle, but it was clear that his current trust trajectory was heading in the wrong direction.

A significant part of him hoped to reverse that trend. He wanted to fit in with El Grande's crowd, he realized. He wanted to spend more time with Maria, and he wasn't a huge fan of the Agency deviants he'd met. He would enjoy doing his part to make life difficult for the CIA, as long as he didn't get killed as a result.

That, he supposed, was the rub. How to have your cake and eat it too. *I don't ask for much,* he thought wryly.

And it was clear that in light of his current status as a man in need of a few good friends, any such thoughts were borderline delusional.

Kittredge's reverie was interrupted when Alejandro turned abruptly into an alley and gunned the engine. Kittredge checked his seatbelt, certain that a collision with a trash dumpster, bum, or building was imminent.

"What gives?" he asked.

"Your amigos," Alejandro said. He reached an intersection with another alley, and reefed the big sedan to the right, barely missing the brick facade of a dilapidated building as he did so. They were traveling parallel to the main road but now in the opposite direction, Kittredge realized.

Alejandro again stood on the accelerator, eliciting another protest from the backseat. "What good does it do to lose them if we wrap ourselves around a building?"

"They told me you were kind of a *puta,*" Alejandro said, smiling for the first time all day.

The sedan charged through two more blocks, bottoming out on each cross-alley drainage channel, before Alejandro jammed on the brakes and slid to a stop between two dumpsters. Kittredge heard the car trunk pop open, and Alejandro exited, stopping on his way to the trunk to open the rear driver's side door, closest to the building wall.

Kittredge climbed out, and had barely stood up when Alejandro threw clothes at him. "Quickly. Change your clothes. Put the mustache and glasses on first."

You've got to be kidding me, Kittredge thought. *A disguise? Are we twelve years old?*

"Faster," Alejandro said.

"This is ridiculous. Is this going to work?"

"Maria was right. You are nothing but questions and problems." Alejandro sported a ridiculous cowboy hat atop white slacks and a tan blazer. *Out of fashion in any decade,* Kittredge's inner fashionista observed.

Alejandro straightened a newly-affixed goatee and strode off.

"Wait," Kittredge said.

"Get shot if you want to, but I'm not in the mood for it," Alejandro said.

Kittredge hustled to catch up, now wearing a blue sport coat, blue slacks, giant sunglasses, and a large black mustache. If anyone had looked closely, they'd certainly have spotted the color difference between his sandy brown hair and his swarthy black mustache, and he felt a strange combination of self-consciousness and fear as he matched Alejandro's long strides.

They walked back to the main road, turned left, and disappeared down a subway stairwell a dozen paces from the corner.

Alejandro handed him some change for the ticket dispenser and guided Kittredge to the northbound platform of the Blue Line.

Several long, uncomfortable moments passed before the train arrived, which Kittredge filled by looking around nervously.

"Stop it," Alejandro told him through clenched teeth. "Relax and smile." Kittredge forced a tight-lipped grin, but was nowhere close to relaxing.

The train finally rumbled to a stop and disgorged its passengers.

"Get off at San Jose," Alejandro said, shoving Kittredge toward the open train door.

Kittredge turned to ask about their final destination in case they became separated, but Alejandro had melted into the crowd and disappeared.

* * *

The remainder of the trip had gone uneventfully, with the exception of a few panic-filled moments at the San Jose station, where Kittredge realized that he had no idea where to go or whom to look for.

Alejandro had reappeared as if by magic, no longer sporting the cowboy hat or goatee. Kittredge didn't recognize him until he spoke, something along the lines of, "Are you coming, jackass?"

Alejandro escorted him to a waiting car, this time a Dongfeng S30. It was a memorable name for a car, Kittredge thought, but it was a thoroughly forgettable ride. Kittredge realized that they'd taken the subway to the north side of the city, only to weave through town in a nausea-inducing dash reminiscent of a rally race in order to reach Caracas' posh east side. Apparently there was a lot of wasteful overhead involved in clandestine travel.

Then there was the garden shed. That's where Kittredge had sat for the better part of the afternoon, locked inside a sweltering hut full of garden tools and the smell of earth and cut vegetation, situated at the edge of a vast manicured pool and yard adorning a mansion in the hills above the eastern side of Caracas.

He wasn't chained up, and he thought he might be able to escape the shed if he put his mind to it, but where would he go after that?

Much of his time had been spent sweating through the rough phase of the hangover that had finally caught up with him. He had nearly retched several times, when the lawnmower fumes, fecund air, and crushing humidity had mixed together in just the right way.

He either wanted a tall, stiff drink, or never to have another drink again in his life, whichever occurred first.

It was a crazy situation, no matter how Kittredge sliced it. He had been out of touch with his Company handlers for a couple of days, which was a rash and colossally stupid thing to do, possibly evidenced by the shooting incident in Maria's apartment the previous evening.

And he now found himself locked up like a prisoner by his newest friends, the VSS, whose buxom agent he'd had the pleasure of balling both before and after she saved his bacon in spectacular fashion from his Agency friends.

That – sex with a femme fatale – had made him question his homosexuality, which was a reality he had established in his life at no small cost, so his thorough and repeated enjoyment of Maria's charms had become quite an existential puzzle for him.

It was a lot for a mind to take in. Especially a sober mind, which is why Kittredge did his best to escape the sobering situation using a few of the zen tricks he'd read about over the years, but had never gained any proficiency in using.

He tried meditation, which was mainly about getting your

mind to shut the hell up. It always sounded really simple to Kittredge, until he attempted it, and he inevitably ended up in a state of utter annoyance at the myriad voices all shouting to be heard inside his head, none of which would give him the courtesy of a moment's silence.

Think you're sane? Try meditating. He'd heard that somewhere, and he didn't disagree. Each of the Kittredges running around in his mind had clever things to say about the stench, heat, humidity, hangover, and probability of living through the next few days, none of which Kittredge appreciated hearing over and over again, even from himself. Or from his selves, as it were.

He was therefore far more relieved than he should have been when a familiar face entered the shed late in the afternoon. El Grande himself appeared, cigar in hand like an omnipresent cliché, gravitas and importance having replaced the friendlier personage Kittredge remembered from their time together in the jungle just a couple of days earlier.

His expression wasn't unfriendly, but Kittredge felt a distance that wasn't present in El Grande's personality earlier. It seemed a lot like. . .weight. Kittredge thought he might have an inkling of what that felt like, and he suspected that he might be personally responsible for some of El Grande's current travails.

Kittredge made room for El Grande on the garden shed's workbench.

"Maria, she is something, no?" El Grande asked.

It was a hell of an opener. Kittredge wasn't sure if a good response was possible.

"She sure is," he said, as neutrally as he could.

"She has a special place in my heart," he said.

Perfect. I slept with the boss' girlfriend, Kittredge thought.

This thought must have been displayed prominently on his face, Kittredge surmised, because El Grande laughed aloud.

"Don't worry, my friend," he said, to Kittredge's relief. "She is not property. She loves whom she chooses. But I was surprised at this choice."

"Me too, honestly," Kittredge said. "But maybe for different reasons," he added.

El Grande chuckled.

"I certainly meant no disrespect," Kittredge said awkwardly, "and I would never have—"

El Grande cut him off with the wave of his cigar. "Please, do not think of it any more. If a girl like her chooses to have you, you are chosen. It is best not to over-think things like this. I would have done the same in your shoes. I know this, because I did the same in your shoes," El Grande said with a chuckle and a wistful look in his eye. "But things change, no?"

"I guess they do," Kittredge agreed.

"And now, I'm afraid that there is another important change that we must make." El Grande's mien hardened a bit, and the distance returned to his eyes.

Kittredge felt his chest constrict. Discussing their mutual enjoyment of Maria's favors wasn't exactly lighthearted banter, but El Grande apparently had even less enjoyable topics on his mind.

"You have been absent from your friends in the CIA for a

couple of days now. It has been long enough for you to establish credibility that you know us, and have access to us, no?"

Kittredge was pretty sure he knew where El Grande was headed. Perhaps he even knew that it was inevitable. But he was still scared to death at the prospect. He kept his silence.

El Grande took a long, exaggerated pull from his cigar.

Straight to the lungs, Kittredge noticed. *Maybe this guy is a legitimate badass, in spite of all the posturing.*

"It is time for you to return to your apartment in Caracas," El Grande said, smoke punctuating each word.

Kittredge blinked involuntarily, and was certain that El Grande registered his fear.

"You must also initiate contact with your CIA handlers. It can be no other way."

Kittredge shook his head, recalling the more memorable moments spent chained to the basement floor in the Alexandria safe house, with Quinn blithely tossing salt onto his ablated back. He shuddered.

El Grande reached a hand out and put it on his shoulder. "Si, it is a risk. But it is one you must take. If you run, they will hunt you like an animal. If you stay with us, they will find you, and they will find us in the process."

"I think they'll kill me."

"As I said, it is a risk," El Grande said, returning to his cigar with a contemplative look on his face. "Maybe a thirty percent chance, I think."

More cigar smoke, which added to Kittredge's returning

nausea.

"But I think that now, more than ever, you have something they want," El Grande said. "You know what that is, no?"

Kittredge nodded.

"Si. Of course you know. Do you think you can keep it from them?" El Grande arched his eyebrows in query.

It was a loaded question. Kittredge knew how little time it would take Quinn to inflict otherworldly pain, and he doubted his ability to protect El Grande, his band of VSS men, or even Maria from the onslaught.

In the end, it wouldn't really matter if he held out for an hour or a week. Quinn would break him, and he would tell the Cocksuckers In Action everything he knew about the VSS.

El Grande had to know this, too, Kittredge realized. "No, I probably can't keep it from them," he said.

El Grande smiled, patted his shoulder, and nodded. "Of course not. It is not possible. So don't try. Never resist a stronger enemy's strength," he said.

Kittredge searched El Grande's eyes, and as he did so, the grave look gave way to a warm sparkle, which spread to a smile that covered the Venezuelan guerrilla's whole face. "We know this, too," he said. "So your visits have been carefully engineered."

He paused to inhale a lungful of unadulterated cigar smoke, then continued, "Which means that you can be as careless as you want when you go back to the gringos. How do they say? Sing like a bird." He laughed.

Kittredge was suddenly irate. "You manipulated me."

El Grande shook his head, still laughing. "This is, how you say, a *theme* with you, no? Manipulation. You said the same thing to Maria."

Kittredge was taken aback. *How the hell did he know that? Have these assholes been listening and watching, too? Just like Quinn and Fredericks?*

Or did Maria talk about the details of our private moments together with El Grande?

He decided he disliked any of those possibilities. He felt the familiar emotions of violation and victimization.

A discomforting thought struck. "At the apartment, when the shooting started, Maria threatened to kill me rather than let the CIA capture me again," Peter recalled. "Now you're throwing me back at them? What gives?"

El Grande smiled sympathetically. "Peter, listen to me," he said. "Many people depend on me. I take steps to protect them. Now, you depend on me a little bit too, no?"

Kittredge remained silent.

"Of course you do," El Grande went on. "Caracas is a dangerous town, and you have chosen a dangerous path."

El Grande shifted his weight and crossed his legs, then took another long drag from his cigar. His eyes got a faraway look. "Maria did what she had to do in a very tenuous time."

Kittredge mulled this over, still feeling played. He felt even less happy about his role as equal parts baggage and pawn.

El Grande noticed the continuing disquiet, and patted Kittredge's shoulder. "Besides, it would have been monstrous of me," he said, avuncular overtones heavy in his voice, "to put you in a position where you had to protect a secret for me, no? Because you cannot do it. They will pull it out of you. You have ten fingernails and ten toenails, and they will rip them out one at a time. That causes a lot of pain, enough to make you tell them everything you know."

Kittredge nodded. He had no doubt that Quinn, the feral-eyed monster, would enjoy doing exactly as El Grande had described. He shuddered again.

El Grande let the fingernail torture imagery marinate, then went on. "So I have done you a favor. I have only let you see what you needed to see, and no more. You have no knowledge that can hurt us."

Kittredge nodded slowly.

"But you *can* still hurt us, my friend," El Grande said. "By staying. They will find you, eventually, and they will find us as a result. So you must go."

He let it sink in.

"I hope that when you go," El Grande continued after a moment, "you will speak to them, and make it right with them, and tell them what they want to know."

Another lungful of smoke. "And we will continue to help each other after that, no? Like a business arrangement. And maybe more, if Maria still wishes for more. Si?"

Kittredge mulled silently, then shook his head sullenly. "There's no good exit strategy here, is there?"

El Grande clapped him on the shoulder. "Mi amigo, no strategy is necessary," he said, standing and making his way toward the garden shed door. "Because there is no exit."

Chapter 47

Adrenaline slammed through Sam's veins as she saw the gun pointed at her face from within the darkness of her basement safety room.

She sprang into action.

She ducked and sidestepped, moving her body closer to the intruder's arm while swinging her left forearm counterclockwise in a vicious arc. It connected with the gunman's forearm, which smashed against the edge of the door, still ajar from Sam's cautious opening a split second before.

She used her right elbow to smash the man's rib cage, tightening her grip on her own pistol to ensure it wasn't jarred loose by the impact.

Her elbow connected with a vengeance, and she heard a loud groan as the air escaped from the man's lungs.

There was something familiar about the groan.

It actually sounded like the man had tried to say something.

She ripped the gun from his hand, leapt back, and trained her weapon on the writhing shadow splayed on the floor inside the panic room.

"Don't shoot me, Sam!" wheezed a familiar voice.

"Brock?"

"I don't know what's going on, but–"

"Oh my God, Brock!" She launched herself at him, wrapping

her arms and legs around him, embracing him as tightly as she ever had, feeling herself start to choke up.

"Oh my God," she said. "I thought you were dead, I'm so sorry, so sorry for everything."

He returned her embrace with equal enthusiasm and even greater strength.

"I've never lied to you, Sam," he said when his breath returned. "Never."

"I know, and I'm so sorry for doubting you. It's just that Ekman–"

"I'll kill him," Brock said.

"No, it's okay, it's just that he showed me how your cell phone location overlapped Dibiaso's, and I freaked out, and–"

"I've never met that guy, Sam, I swear to you. You've got to believe me."

"I do, baby, that's what I'm saying. I figured it out, it was the slug line, right?"

Brock was confused. "Every day for the last three months. Why?"

"That's it. That's what happened. Dibiaso rode next to you, twice."

"Holy shit. Are you sure?"

"Trust me," Sam said. "I've been to hell and back with this one, and it sounds crazy, but I'm pretty sure."

"Do you know why another cop broke into our house?"

"When?"

"Yesterday afternoon. I think he came in through the back yard somehow. He drew a Taser on me, in my own damned home!"

"I'm sorry, baby, I don't know how you got dragged into this. . ."

"I don't either. He surprised me in the kitchen, and I threw the butcher knife at him. I was aiming for his balls, but I think I got his thigh. Bled like a stuck pig."

"So that explains the blood that the DHS guys found."

"Yeah, I watched them from the panic room while they searched the house. I've been holed up down there watching movies ever since the thing with the cop. I missed my appointment with Ekman and Jarvis. They finally agreed to talk to me. I was going to take a lie detector test, the whole nine. I was desperate to get them to talk some sense into you, but I thought I'd better not take any chances after that cop showed up and tried to zap my ass."

"Good move. But they thought you skipped town or something."

"I didn't want to talk to them about what happened, because I thought they might be part of the whole thing."

"That was smart. I'm still not sure myself," Sam said. "Brock, I'm so sorry I doubted you. It just looked so obviously like you lied to me about Dibiaso, and you know I have that thing with honesty. . ."

"I know, Sam. I've never met him, and I probably wouldn't recognize him if you showed him to me."

"That's the thing. Nobody knows who this guy is. But he visited the Pentagon twice that we know about, because he took his cell phone with him. I think he signed in as Martinson, and Charlie

Landers escorted him in both times."

"Landers is in on this? That prick. He still wants to give me paperwork because we're dating before my divorce is final."

"I see why no one likes him. He is a prick."

She pulled away. "Listen, Brock, we should probably stay holed up for a while while we figure out what to do next. I didn't see any Metro guys on my way in, but that could easily have changed by now." She rose and closed the door to the basement vault.

"I can't believe you're back," he said. "I thought I'd lost you. I drove Gable crazy. I probably called him fifty times over the past few days."

"He's good people. He understands. I'm going to call him." She smiled at Brock. "Just as soon as we have a chance to get properly reacquainted," she said.

* * *

"I think it's a new record for us," Sam said, still breathless.

"Fourgasm," Brock said. "Impressive!"

"I've missed you."

Brock smiled. "I've missed you right back. Where have you been, by the way?"

Sam filled him in on the past few days' events, starting with her hasty departure from Ekman's office on Monday morning after seeing the printouts of Brock's cell phone locations next to Dibiaso's, then her grisly discovery later that afternoon at Phil Quartermain's apartment, and her subsequent days spent on the run.

She told him about the music box connection that linked John Abrams, Everett Cooper, and Fatso's company, Executive Strategies, and she talked to him in detail about her late evening conversation in Fatso Minton's study in Dayton.

Brock was shocked about the unlikely connection, but got a kick out of her breaking into Fatso's house through the doggy door.

Jeff Jensen, the CSI who died of an overdose in the restroom stall of a DC restaurant on his lunch hour, struck Brock as a likely casualty of the same group of highly antisocial people.

"We're in this thing up to our eyeballs," he observed.

"It would be nice to have some idea of what it's all about," she said.

She wondered aloud about whether Ekman and Jarvis had an agenda, other than bureaucratic self-preservation and a concomitant drive to distance themselves from any situation that might smell mildly of trouble.

But she could certainly see why the cell phone information that seemed to link Dibiaso with Brock might have thrown them off track. Sam had herself interpreted the same information as unequivocal evidence of Brock's guilt, and the unlikelihood of not one but *two* slug line trips taken together was a strong indicator of intrigue from almost any angle one chose to view it.

Even though she had a very compelling reason to see the data from a different point of view, she had been unable to do so.

Thankfully, it *wasn't* really intrigue, and Sam felt more gratitude than she had words to express. Her time on the run and in hiding over the past few days had barely provided enough mental activity to keep her anguish over Brock's apparent betrayal down to a subterranean simmer.

Even so, it had boiled over at regular intervals, and she was certain that if she'd had more time to experience the loss, it would have proven emotionally devastating. She'd waited for Brock for a lifetime, and losing him would have been tantamount to losing part of herself.

A chilling thought followed: What if she, Ekman, and Jarvis weren't the only ones to mistakenly associate Brock with Dibiaso? What if Dibiaso was a real bastard, with really angry enemies? Wouldn't those same enemies view Brock as guilty by association?

Holy hell. Maybe I've been thinking about this the wrong way.

"Brock, what if this whole thing is about *you*, and not about me?"

"That thought occurred to me, about the time the Metro guy drew the Taser on me in the kitchen. I had no idea why at the time, but thinking about it now, it strikes me that those carpool rides with Dibiaso might have been enough to put some stink on me."

"So all roads lead to Dibiaso," Sam said. "Did you notice anything strange during your rides home on the 11th and 18th of last month?"

Brock laughed. "I could've sat next to SecDEF himself and not noticed. It's a freaky vibe in the slug line. Nobody says a word to anyone else, nobody makes eye contact, and I can count on one hand the number of smiles I've seen."

"That's really weird," Sam said. "But it's in keeping with the feeling I got walking around the inside of the Pentagon. I've never seen so many unhappy people in the same place at one time."

"It's really grim," Brock agreed.

His expression changed. "You said Landers had something to do with this?"

Sam described her interview with Brock's boss, the diminutive, unfriendly two-star general.

Brock wasn't surprised that she hadn't learned much, other than that Charlie Landers was an asshole. "I can't put my finger on it," he said, "but I think that guy is crooked. He rolls with a bunch of shifty-eyed CFR types, and they stop by the office all the time. He sends me to go fetch them from the Metro entrance and sign them in. They're usually industry people, think tank shills, or lobbyists. It's actually weird that Landers signed this guy in himself – he's big on enjoying the perks of rank."

"Yeah, it had me wondering, too. It would have been a great job for his secretary," Sam said.

"She's a peach, isn't she?"

Sam laughed. "Ice queen."

"I would be pissed off too, if I had to play fluffer for a petty tyrant like Landers."

Sam didn't know much about the Council on Foreign Relations, so Brock filled her in. He knew a bit about it from having to play escort on Landers' behalf. It was a large political organization with members from all walks of life, connected by their membership in what Brock termed an invitation-only ideology club.

It wasn't a completely homogeneous group, of course, but they all seemed to share a particularly powerful position in society. Sam and Brock knew that it was possible to make serious, reliable, low-risk money in the markets only by throwing enough weight around to actually *move* the markets. And collectively, even individually in some cases, the CFR crowd had the necessary financial and political capital to do just that.

"Oligarchs, then," Sam said.

"Yeah, I guess that's about right," Brock said. "With their own training program. I think Landers was a mid-level guy, but I got the sense he was very hungry to climb that ladder. He fell all over himself with those people. Almost embarrassing, really."

Sam wondered aloud whether Dibiaso – or Martinson, the name he had apparently used to sign in on the Pentagon visitor list – was a CFR player.

"They have their own military, you know," Brock said.

"The CFR? You sound like a conspiracy nut."

"I mean, a paramilitary more than anything else. They have high-ranking Pentagon folks on their membership roster, but I've heard whispers that they fund shill corporations for paramilitary contractors and what people call OGAs, or Other Governmental Agencies."

"CIA," Sam said.

"That's a good guess. I think NSA is tied in a sweaty love knot with them, too, and probably even the Defense Intelligence Agency."

"Sounds like a great crowd not to mess with."

"People don't mess with them for long, I don't think."

"And they probably have a very long list of pissed-off people who are waiting for an opportunity to take a swing at them."

"Like anyone with an address outside the Continental US, for example," Brock said with a chortle.

It reminded Sam of their many conversations on the US strategy vis-a-vis terrorism. Brock felt that terrorism was largely a problem of sentiment, not tactics, and that great counter-tactics often caused really shitty sentiment.

It wasn't a difficult argument to understand, he'd often said. It would only take a few bombs raining down on a few neighborhoods before the locals turned decidedly sour on whoever was dropping them.

They'd experienced that phenomenon recently; they had survived the attack, barely, but the episode was frightening, infuriating, and grossly inconvenient.

We make enemies faster than we can kill them, she recalled him saying on many occasions. It was a dumb approach if peace was the goal.

On the other hand, if expansion, unrest, and an ever-increasing military and intelligence budget were the goals, it was a brilliant strategy.

And the American defense industry wasn't complaining much, either.

"So, let's assume the worst," Sam said. "You and I are on the shit list of someone powerful and capable. It doesn't really matter if they're CFR, or Agency, or someone aligned against the Agency, as far as we're concerned. What matters is that they think we're somehow involved in their world."

"I think we're also on your bosses' shit list, Sam. Ekman and Jarvis were not helpful or cooperative. I don't know why they resisted talking to me until yesterday, but they wanted nothing to do with me."

"Maybe they were tightening up their case against you. They probably wanted to hit you with the maximum horsepower when they did finally bring you in for questioning."

"There's nothing to hit me with."

"Maybe they figured that out."

Sam thought for a second longer. "Or maybe they found something else that seemed like it might fit with the Dibiaso scenario."

"Great."

Silence stretched on as their minds churned, Sam running her fingers idly through his hair. Then Brock spoke up. "What's the DC Metro thing all about, then?"

Sam thought about it for a bit. "They seem like bit players to me. There's that Venezuelan thing, Bolero, Jarvis called it. And if the Agency linkage turns out to be real, Metro is definitely not a prime mover. It might just be that a few of the beat cops are hired footmen."

"Persistent bastards, whatever they are."

Sam agreed. She told him about her most recent run-in, which was several days ago on the highway en route to Quartermain's house.

"Strange they haven't turned up chasing after you since then," Brock said.

"Not really. I'm not your average government employee, after all. I can be slippery when I want to be."

Brock apologized for doubting her skills. "I was projecting my cluelessness onto you."

"That makes you male," she teased, following up with a solid bite where his neck met his shoulder. "Which I love dearly, by the way," she added.

He tightened his embrace around her midsection, and thoughts of further biological shenanigans entered their minds, causing southerly blood flow to areas already a bit sore from their recent exertions.

Then her burner phone buzzed on the nightstand near the bed in the panic room.

They groaned together. "Things being what they are," he said, "maybe you should get that."

It was Dan Gable. "Good, I'm glad you haven't changed phones again yet," he said when she picked up.

She brought Dan up to date.

"Never a dull moment with you, is there? Anyway, I have bad news and bad news. Which do you want first?"

She didn't encourage him with a response. Dan took the hint. "Ekman and Jarvis are getting serious about seeing you, Sam. It's Friday, and you haven't been by the office since Monday."

"I told Ekman an obvious lie on Monday, and I took his ignoring it as tacit approval to do what I had to do."

"I think that's probably worn off by now, so it's probably time for a more lasting peace," Dan said.

He had a point. Sam's mistrust of Ekman and Jarvis had caused her to cast them in the role of adversary, a role they may not otherwise have taken up. Now that the facts about Brock and Dibiaso had come out, Sam thought there might be room for a truce.

If she could convince them of Brock's innocence, that is.

Making peace with her bosses wasn't practical earlier, before she discovered Brock's innocence, because she didn't know what the Dibiaso problem might have portended. DHS may very well have connected her to something very unsavory, by virtue of Brock's apparent relationship with Dibiaso. She couldn't really blame them for keeping her at arms length and withholding information from her while they figured out if she was culpable in some way.

Except that they've jeopardized our lives in the process.

Angry as that made her, she simply had to remove some of the variables. It might be worth a try to get Jarvis and Ekman back on her team.

If it worked, there would still be security concerns, because neither of them were much more than office-bound information sieves. Even if they stopped mistrusting her and Brock, she would still have to closely manage their access to any information she turned up.

And she would have to take care of her own physical security, no matter how fervently they protested. A DHS safe house would be a great place to get butchered.

"You speak wisdom, Dan," Sam finally said. "As usual. I'll put you in for a raise."

"You keep saying that."

"I mean it this time."

"You keep saying that, too."

Sam hesitated before asking her next question of Dan, but

ultimately decided that he deserved a place in the Trust Tree. "I'm going to show you a little leg here, Dan, so be forewarned."

"This doesn't sound good, but go ahead."

"In your professional opinion, are Ekman and Jarvis in league with the Metro thugs?"

Dan chuckled at the thought of their two bosses orchestrating intrigue and double-deals. "In a parallel universe, where they might be smart enough to carry on a double-cross like that without giving themselves away, I'd still vote no."

"Are you sure you aren't underestimating them?"

"Maybe I am," Dan admitted. "But what would be the upside for them?"

"A fat wad of cash from whoever is throwing it around upstream of this op," Sam ventured.

"I don't think so. I think Ekman and Jarvis are true believers. I think they guzzled all the Kool-Aid and came back for more. I think you're under their thumb at the moment because they're scared to death about the Dibiaso connection. They'd rather you get killed than stir up trouble on their watch."

Sam mulled that over. She tended to agree with the last part, but maybe not the first. "I agree that they're not standup guys. But I'm not sure they're that dumb, especially Jarvis. Stupidity is a great hiding place for brilliance."

Dan laughed. "If there's any brilliance in Jarvis, it's hidden better than Anne Frank."

"Yeah, on second thought, I'm afraid I agree with you there. But it doesn't hurt to consider the possibilities."

"If you're thinking of coming in from the cold, I fully support the idea," Dan said. "You strike me as someone in need of fewer enemies right now."

Exactly.

Ekman and Jarvis might not swing around to her side, especially since it would require them to view the same data in a different light, but it was probably worth a try. Worst case, things would be just as they are, with Sam and her superiors in an uneasy and transient detente, both sides waiting for the other shoe to drop.

"Thanks, Dan. Strong points, and I'll have to chew on them."

"That's what you say when you're about to blow me off," Dan said with a laugh.

"Bullshit. I never blow you off, except when I'm ignoring you." She changed the subject: "Any news on the FAA homework that's now overdue?"

"You're such a taskmaster," Dan said. "But yes, that's the other bad news I was calling about. You asked me to find out about those three aircraft that were flying over your house last Saturday night at roughly the time of the explosion."

"Yes, and my curiosity hasn't diminished any, given yesterday's police visit," Sam said.

"Well, one of the planes was a redeye on its way into Reagan. Another one was way up at forty grand, blitzing west on its way to Denver. So I've tentatively ruled those two out, in favor of the third one."

"Do tell."

"A C-123, a two-engine turboprop with a retractable cargo

door for inflight air drops. Registered to Executive Strategies."

"Oh my God, Dan, are you sure?"

"It gets better. The plane was flown by Fatso Minton."

Chapter 48

Peter Kittredge watched the sun trace its high mid-afternoon arc from his bedroom window. The trip from the posh eastern suburb of Caracas back to his apartment had taken surprisingly little time. Alejandro had taken none of the prior precautions against being followed – they hadn't doubled back via blind alleyways, made sudden freeway exits, stopped at drive-throughs, or swapped cars in a crowded parking garage.

Instead, they had driven straight from the pickup point, which was a two-mile hike from the putrid, sweltering garden shed in which Kittredge had spent most of the day, directly to El Banco de Caracas, where Kittredge had retrieved his phone from the safety deposit box.

Then they'd driven unhurriedly to Kittredge's apartment in the embassy district.

It was almost as if El Grande wanted Company assets to watch the drop off. Maybe it was a not-so-subtle way of nudging him out of the VSS nest, Kittredge thought as he picked up yet another article of clothing from the mess strewn about his bedroom floor.

His day hadn't been exactly peachy before arriving back at home, but the sight of his wrecked apartment had brought back the seriousness of his situation like a slap in the face. These were extremely serious people, and it appeared that they had taken up semi-permanent residence in his life. At least, that's the slightly melodramatic metaphor he'd spoken aloud to himself as he'd set to work cleaning up the mess.

He'd been working his way through stacks of his and Charley's clothing, hoping to whip the ransacked bedroom into semi-livable shape by nightfall. He'd noticed nothing missing, though he knew it would take weeks to figure out whether anything had been stolen.

They hadn't been shy about roughing things up, though. He shook his head in wonder at the quantity of broken glass from picture frames, mirrors, and Charley's omnipresent knick-knacks. Kittredge picked thousands of glass shards from their clothing. It was tedious work, and he wasn't making the kind of progress he'd hoped.

His hand brushed against his pocket, and he felt the hard edge of his cell phone. He'd been avoiding turning it on, for fear of what the messages might hold, but his cleanup efforts had put him in a take-charge kind of mood. With a deep breath, he powered it on.

Five messages, all from Quinn. He listened to the first one, left sometime on Tuesday. It consisted mostly of an elaborate and questionably relevant joke about buggery being the only lasting Greek contribution to humanity, followed by a presumptuous demand for a meeting. "Be downstairs at five, sharp, and I'll pick you up at the curb," Quinn's deep voice intoned.

Oops. Sorry I missed your meeting, asshole, Kittredge thought.

The remaining messages were increasingly less friendly and patient, and Kittredge deleted the last two without listening to them.

Time to figure a couple of things out, he decided.

He found the number to Charley's room in the DC hospital. It rang only three or four times before a female voice picked up. "Mr. Arlinghaus' room, Nurse Williamson speaking." Kittredge went through the routine with the phone password again, then listened intently as the nurse described Charley's condition.

Charley was beginning to make rapid, involuntary limb movements, which the nurse said was a sign of either healing in the motor cortex, or what she called coupled dreaming, where Charley's thoughts were inciting his body to move in response, like a dog chasing rabbits in its sleep.

Either way, it was a positive sign. While she wouldn't hazard a guess about when Charley might wake up and become lucid again, or even whether that was on the horizon, she did say that the doctors were far less concerned about his prognosis than a couple of days earlier.

Kittredge thanked her and signed off. He felt a mixture of difficult emotions as the week's events clashed together in his mind.

Seven days earlier, he had been on the prowl for a one-night stand with a pretty male waiter at his favorite DC haunt. Then he had been Quinn's guest, chained to the cement floor in the basement of an Alexandria safe house while Quinn did medieval things to him. Then came the revelation about the surveillance cameras in his DC crash pad, followed by Charley's attack, and Quinn shoving him out of the car at the airport for a flight to Caracas.

And then it had really gotten crazy.

A man could use a drink right about now. Kittredge made for the liquor cabinet, dismayed to find its contents a sticky mess of desiccated spirits and broken glass.

That was more than inconvenient, and he felt his face flush with anger all over again as he grabbed his wallet to make for the liquor store around the corner. He'd spent plenty of time sober today, he thought, and he was certainly deserving of an evening constitutional to add a more pleasant veneer to the grim work of putting his apartment back together.

There was also the difficult business of orchestrating his reintroduction to his Company cohorts, which was also best faced with liquid fortification.

He had just turned toward the front door when his phone rang. Quinn. Adrenaline crashed in his stomach and his heart rate doubled.

You've got to do this sometime, he reasoned. *Might as well get it over with.*

"Hi Quinn. Torture anyone lately?"

He heard Quinn's harsh laugh on the other end of the connection. "Not yet, but I was hoping you were free later."

Funny. Kittredge kept quiet, forcing Quinn to make the next move. It felt like a powerful thing to do, even if it was only symbolic.

"That's an interesting shirt, by the way," Quinn said. "Very festive. Looks good on you, though."

Kittredge shuddered, still not used to the idea of being watched.

He recovered quickly. "Thanks Quinn. Describe it to me." Kittredge thought he'd test to see whether Quinn was bluffing.

"Okay, Secret Agent Man. The eggplant sets off your eyes,

and I like the lemon pinstripes. Unusual, but very stylish."

Not bluffing. "Where's the camera, Quinn? I want to look at you while I'm talking to you."

"Look at you, growing up so quickly. Just a few days ago, you got an extreme case of vaginitis over this kind of thing."

"Well, it was a long week. Lots of growth opportunities."

"Why don't you tell me about it, Peter." It wasn't a question.

Kittredge told him. It made him weak in the knees, and he had to work hard to control his breathing, but he told Quinn about his new VSS contacts, their safe houses, and their agenda.

He lied about the tunnel, saying he didn't know which two buildings it connected – he wanted to keep Company paws from defiling the extraordinary apartment in which he'd made love to Maria, an episode he now held with some degree of preciousness – but he was otherwise completely truthful and forthcoming.

And he didn't pull any punches with regard to the markedly better treatment he had received at the hands of the VSS. "One might be forgiven for being confused about who the bad guys are in this whole thing," he said.

Quinn laughed. "Maybe so. But it's probably healthier for you to suspend your disbelief and stay on the home team."

"I'm talking to you, aren't I?"

"A smart choice. I'm really impressed, Kittredge. You're really showing some backbone here. That's a good thing. Maybe there's hope for you yet. But the cynic in me says that you didn't have any other real options."

Quite true, Kittredge thought glumly, feeling pangs of guilt and remorse at having spoken of the confidences he'd shared with the VSS, even though El Grande had encouraged him to do just that.

Quinn went on to say that he had a bunch of questions, and he'd drop by in a few moments to take Kittredge out for a beer.

"No, thanks," Kittredge said. "I have to get my apartment put back together. But if you'd like some quality time together, feel free to stop by and help."

Quinn laughed. "I'd rather watch. In fact, maybe you should think of me as your personal bodyguard. This is a tough town, you know. Did you hear, there was a shooting not too far from here last night? Crazy shit. A fella really has to watch out." He laughed that cold, harsh laugh again, and it somehow reached into Kittredge's bones and shook them.

These are truly terrible people, he thought for the hundredth time. If he'd had any doubt before about whether the Agency was behind the harrowing episode, he had none now.

"Thanks, Quinn. Swell of you. I'll be sure to leave the bathroom door open so you can watch me take a crap."

"I'd like that, thanks."

Kittredge hung up.

He didn't want to venture out, but he wasn't about to endure the remainder of the evening sober. He grabbed some cash and his apartment key and made for the liquor store.

* * *

It took less than half an hour to retrieve a fresh bottle of vodka from the store nearby. He chose the big bottle, which he knew was a sign either of a man planning a party or a man with a problem.

Nothing new for the store clerk either way. The clerk checked him out with only the briefest of perfunctories.

He walked slowly back toward the apartment, stealing glances out of the corners of his eyes at passersby, wondering whether any of them were part of a surveillance team.

He even ducked into a recessed doorway and watched the sparse foot traffic carefully for a minute or so, looking for anything strange. Then, realizing that he really had no idea what he was looking for, and that he probably looked very foolish to any *real* surveillance team that might be watching, he walked back to his apartment without further attempts at spy craft.

He sat on his sofa and enjoyed the view while his first drink hit his bloodstream. It was a beautiful sensation, the first few sips of pure vodka burning his esophagus in that familiar pleasurable pain, which was a reward in itself, but was inevitably followed by the even greater bliss of a burgeoning buzz. The world took on a far more tolerable tinge.

Maybe it was the booze, but Kittredge rapidly shed his guilt at having told Quinn about El Grande and the VSS. The Venezuelans, after all, had approached *him*, not the other way around.

And they had approached him with full knowledge of his situation with the Agency. Whatever he was to them, whatever role they hoped he would play in their greater drama, he wasn't going to feel badly about it.

In fact, he thought, *that's probably what they wanted in the first place. Someone to shuttle between camps, stir the pot a bit.*

Maybe they had something violent in mind, and needed

Kittredge to help them smoke out the Agency players. Or maybe they had sized up their Agency opponents and concluded, probably correctly, that they were well beyond their depth. Maybe Kittredge's role was to help them start a little backchannel detente.

Or maybe the VSS was really out for blood, using him to probe the Caracas contingent of Cocksuckers In Action for weaknesses, watching how they surveilled him, observing how they responded to various scenarios.

Who the hell knows?

Kittredge decided he'd play his part, whatever it might be, and may the best bastards win. Maybe in the process, a few of them would get what they deserved. One could only hope.

Except Maria.

She was different, he decided.

Chapter 49

Fredericks' phone buzzed and jangled.

Quinn shot him a dirty look. "You've been a desk ape for too long," he chided. "Ringing telephones are for dead men."

Fredericks ignored him and answered the phone.

Curmudgeon's dulcet tones greeted him with the first half of an authentication: "The first panacea of a mismanaged nation. . ."

"Is inflation of the currency," Fredericks responded.

"The second is war," Curmudgeon finished.

"The last part was totally unnecessary, except to prove how smart you are," Fredericks said to his handler.

Curmudgeon's easy laugh sounded in Fredericks' ear. "Hemingway is my favorite suicide victim."

"I thought as a priest, you weren't allowed to condone suicide."

"I don't. But that doesn't stop me from picking a favorite."

"I'd go with Marilyn Monroe myself," Fredericks said.

"She didn't commit suicide."

"She's still my favorite. What do you want?"

"I heard something through the grapevine that might interest you," Curmudgeon said. "Bravo has confirmed that Alpha has accepted the invitation to your party, and wishes you Godspeed and good luck."

Bravo was the Intermediary.

And Alpha was the goddamned Facilitator.

If he wasn't the most powerful human on the planet, Fredericks had no idea who might hold that title. Not even the President toyed with the Facilitator.

Holy shit, Fredericks thought. *We're really going to do this.* He realized that a part of him never thought they'd get green-lighted, but there it was, straight from the top, and delivered by Curmudgeon.

"Start the party at your discretion," the priest-spy said. "But be advised that we have backchannel confirmation of the necessary precursors, so don't cut any corners. I don't need to remind you of the stakes."

"Right. Thanks," Fredericks said.

"Good luck." With that, Curmudgeon hung up.

Fredericks turned to Quinn, seated next to him at the kitchen table in the cramped apartment that had served as the Operation Syphilis headquarters over the past few days. "We're a go."

"I'll round up the usual suspects," Quinn said.

* * *

Kittredge had just put the finishing touches on Vodka Number Four, which was going to be a masterpiece of a drink, containing nothing but near-freezing vodka and a twist of lime, when his phone rang. It had been just a bit under seven full days since his Agency friends had revealed their presence in his life, but he was already thoroughly sick of them. "Hello, Fredericks."

"Are you soused again?"

"Insufficiently. What do you want?"

"Get dressed."

"I am dressed."

"Stay that way. Quinn is coming by."

"I'd rather drink alone, thanks."

"He's going to pick you up. You're going to the tailor shop."

Kittredge was confused. He'd never made an information drop at the tailor shop during his short and unremarkable career as a spy for Exel Oil, so he wasn't sure what the Agency could possibly want to do with him there.

"I'm confused," he said.

"I thought you gay guys were all in to fashion and whatnot. I thought some clothes shopping would be a nice gesture."

"I think you have me confused with a TV show. Thanks anyway, but I'll stay here."

"Actually," Fredericks said in his don't-screw-with-me tone, "this is the part where you earn your paycheck."

"You don't pay me," Kittredge observed.

"Consider your lack of incarceration, and every dollar you will make in your remaining lifetime as a free citizen, to be the amount that I am paying you to do whatever the hell I tell you to do."

Compelling, Kittredge thought.

But bottomless and infinite.

He sighed, feeling owned. "When?"

"He'll be there in ten minutes. You really are going to the tailor to fit some clothes. Gotta look nice for Hugo."

"Who's Hugo?"

"You'll see soon enough." Fredericks hung up.

Kittredge downed his drink with imprudent quickness, and was halfway through another by the time Quinn arrived at his door.

Chapter 50

El Jerga's blood was up, more so than usual. His target may not have personally killed his uncle, but for El Jerga, mere association was guilt enough.

He would do his job, as he always did, but he would make it last.

It would be payback, and maybe even healing. He would savor its sweet depravity, relish the all-too-brief foray to the edge of his own humanity, enjoy the thrilling view into the abyss of his own soul as he killed again.

What would he ever do without a suitable conflict to feed his growing addiction? El Jerga knew he needn't worry much about that at the moment. This particular conflict was just beginning.

His approach was completely unnoticed, byproduct of his obvious ethnicity and the mop and bucket he pushed over the hard tile floors. He whistled a Venezuelan tune, an old favorite of his, one that his uncle used to sing to him when he was an anguished boy trying to recover from the loss of his father.

He was still an anguished soul, he knew, but unlike the first time someone he loved was taken from him, El Jerga now had the power to retaliate. He held that power in his hands, to be sure, but its true source was the blackness of his soul and the hardness of his heart.

This is the one, he thought as he read the name stenciled on the door.

He knocked twice, announced "Housekeeping," and opened the door.

That's him, El Jerga thought as he spied the man behind the desk.

All skin and bones. He was disappointed that the pictures were so accurate. There wasn't much flesh for him to flay.

But he would make do.

* * *

The man hadn't lasted nearly as long as El Jerga had wished, expiring more to end the pain than due to any particular wound.

It was a powerful thing, El Jerga thought, watching the precise moment when a man decided he would rather die than endure any further pain.

It was something of a cliché, of course, the kind of thing that people wrote songs or television shows about, but it was an immensely intense experience in the flesh. Making the decision to trade all of one's tomorrows for the immediate end to an unbearable pain – *that* was truly a sublime moment to watch, to be a part of.

To cause.

El Jerga wiped the fishing knife clean for the fifth time. If killing was a barely-controlled compulsion, then cleaning up afterwards was an absolute obsession. He'd already burned the clothes and scattered their ashes in the Ohio River, where he now sent the fishing knife to what he hoped would be its final, frigid resting place.

El Jerga had left the tattered remains of the skinny man, with his gaunt skin detached from the muscle in some places and sliced in grotesque, macabre patterns in others, as a monument to the war that was just beginning.

For Venezuela.

For Uncle.

He got back into the fake cleaning company's van, stopped off at the warehouse to change vehicles, and drove to a cluster of chain hotels just off of I-70, noticing the pleasant way the setting sun cast the high overcast in bright pink hues.

He picked the most crowded hotel, parked his car, and waited in line to check in.

"Staying long?" the jowly clerk asked. The words sounded like they were formed somewhere in her sinus cavity, then came out her nose. El Jerga mused that the Midwest was home to perhaps the least pleasing incarnation of the gringo's tongue he'd yet encountered. New Yorkers were bad, but at least they didn't draw out the agony by speaking so slowly.

"Two nights," El Jerga lied, noticing the clerk's eyes travel immediately to his throat upon hearing his wrecked voice. Her gaze snapped self-consciously back up to his eyes. He'd long ago accepted the inevitable reaction as a lingering effect of his injury.

He handed her his driver's license and credit card. They both said Juan Capistrano. "Like the saints and the swallows?" the clerk said. *Swallows* sounded flat and nasal, as if she were attempting to make the word as ugly as it could be.

El Jerga nodded without smiling, received the key card from her chubby hand, and rolled his empty suitcase past the elevators to the computer room.

It was empty, so he took a seat at the terminal furthest from the door.

He typed a long URL into the browser window. It was a nonsensical collection of four words, followed by the .biz top-level domain identifier. The page that loaded contained nothing but a text entry field, with no instructions.

El Jerga entered another long string of unrelated words, yet another password he'd had to memorize for this job. He hoped he'd remembered it correctly.

The website accepted his password, and a single page loaded.

At the top of the page was a single sentence: "I should have given them to you in the first place." El Jerga scrolled down and discovered a picture, obviously a formal portrait of someone in a blue military uniform with a bunch of shiny objects and ribbons on his breast, lapels, and epaulets, taken in front of a black background and an American flag.

It gets serious, El Jerga thought. *Already, we provoke the gringo military.*

But El Jerga was just as much a soldier as his target, accustomed to following orders and getting paid handsomely for his trouble.

And he wasn't about to question an order that would allow him to unleash his demons. He relished another ecstatic orgy of murderous depravity, irrespective of the purpose behind it.

His mind had begun formulating a plan of attack, engineering a situation where his target wouldn't have an opportunity to use his military training, when he noticed a second photograph beneath the first.

He felt growing elation as he scrolled down the page, revealing a tall, poised, stunning redhead photographed while crossing a street in yoga pants, sports bra, and dark sunglasses. He felt vague recollection, but he couldn't place the context. He didn't know her, but he had seen her somewhere before.

He looked with growing glee at her flaming red hair, full breasts, tight belly, fair skin and strong, athletic legs.

El Jerga longed to savor her tastes and smells, and he wondered how her voice would sound, begging for mercy, screaming in agony, moaning in defeat and abject resignation to the fate that he would visit upon her in a slow and measured way.

She was meant to be relished, her quality and uniqueness thoroughly enjoyed, her every curve explored and defiled.

He would take his time with her.

Chapter 51

When in doubt, stop doubting, Sam reminded herself.

She and Brock had thoroughly discussed their next move, and despite their many misgivings, they had ultimately agreed that this was their only real option.

They strode into the Homeland Security headquarters building as if they owned the place. Heads turned, and Sam noticed the whispers and sideways glances as they made their way toward the executive offices. The gossip had clearly made its rounds.

"Hi, Patty," Sam said as she strode past Ekman's secretary. Patty opened her mouth as if to protest, but didn't.

Sam strode past her, Brock in tow.

She opened the closed door to Ekman's office. "Hi, Frank," she said lightly. "Brock and I thought we'd chat with Jarvis now. You're invited, too." It was an outrageous presumption, employed for its shock value, and Sam didn't wait for a reply before turning on her heel and leaving.

Ekman followed, a heartfelt protest about scheduling Jarvis' time in advance failing to slow Sam's pace.

Feeling a little awkward on Ekman's behalf, Brock said hello and shook his hand, still walking quickly to keep up with Sam as she crossed the short distance to Jarvis' corner office.

Jarvis' secretary was also unable to forestall the arrival of Hurricane Sam, and Jarvis' eyes opened wide as she walked into his office.

"Hi Tom," Sam said. "Brock and I thought it was probably time for us to have a conversation."

Sam sat in one of the two chairs arranged in front of Jarvis' desk, and Brock followed her lead, feeling both amused and awkward watching Sam run roughshod over her bosses.

Tom Jarvis found his voice. "I take it you've been well, Sam?" His face settled into a frown. "Mere mortals typically inform their supervisors of their whereabouts when they take a couple of days off. You're obviously in a different category. At least in your own mind."

"My apologies, Tom. It was probably tough for you to keep the crosshairs on me. It must have been frustrating."

Jarvis took off his reading glasses and set them on his desk, a look of disapproval crossing his face. "So you've been off on your own, making up your own rules, running your own private investigation?"

"Someone had to."

Jarvis snorted. "You think you're above all of this, and all of us, but you're not. You're a person of interest in an open investigation. I've given you a hell of a lot more leeway than you deserve, and I don't appreciate your lack of respect."

Sam chuckled. "Tom, don't ever confuse deference and respect."

Her gaze turned hard, vicious even. "If I'd rolled over for you, stayed home darning my socks while you and the rest of your professional clock watchers took turns bungling this investigation,

Brock and I would be dead. No doubt about it. Just like Jensen, Quartermain, Cooper, and Abrams. *Four stiffs*, Tom!" Her voice echoed off the paneled walls.

Jarvis' face reddened and his jaw clenched. Ekman sighed heavily behind her.

"If you had any idea what to do about this case," Sam said, "you'd have already done it."

"That's it, Sam," Jarvis spat. "You just don't know when to stop pushing, do you? As of right now, I'm placing you on administrative leave."

Sam laughed. "Whatever helps you feel better, Tom. But first, you should get out a tape recorder and a pad of paper. Brock and I have a few things to go over with you, and you'll want to take careful notes."

Sam's patronizing tone did nothing to reduce Jarvis' agitation. "You will have nothing to do with this case, and you will remain in protective custody until it's solved."

"Sure thing, Tom. Anything else?"

"I'm also going to convene a retention review panel. I'm not convinced your continued service as the chief of the counterintelligence branch is warranted, in light of your erratic behavior."

Sam smiled. "Let it all out. Don't bottle up those emotions."

Jarvis reddened more, and a vein in his neck throbbed noticeably.

Brock put his hand on Sam's thigh as if to restrain her before she did any more damage, but she simply grabbed his hand and held it as if they were at the movies.

Sam smiled at Jarvis. Her face held no sign of remorse, submission, or even acknowledgement of the severity of the administrative blows Jarvis had just inflicted on her.

Time to play the trump card, she thought.

"What's rule number one?" she asked.

Jarvis pounded his fist on the top of his desk. "Don't fuck with me, Sam!"

"I wouldn't dream of it, Tom. I'm just curious – when did they change rule number one? I must have missed the memo."

"You know full well that an agent in the field is always authorized to take the actions necessary to preserve life and limb," Jarvis said, seething. "That has never changed, but if you think–"

"It's the sacred covenant," she said, cutting Jarvis off. "And it's interesting that you recited it just now, because I thought I heard you say something very different just a minute ago, Tom," Sam said quietly.

She waited a moment before going on. "What you said a minute ago was that following your *desires* for this case was more important than taking the actions necessary to preserve *our* lives and *our* limbs. Brock's and mine. Because it isn't a question of whether someone has a bead on us. It's a question of when they will catch up to us."

"You could have had Homeland protection, Sam," Jarvis said angrily. "You *would* have had protection, if you hadn't gone rogue for a week."

Sam shook her head. "You're not getting it, Tom. These guys

aren't ragheads waving AK's around in the desert, or self-radicalizing teenagers in a DC slum somewhere. They're on the government payroll, doing terrible things to other Americans, on American soil. They're cops, or Agency goons, or mercenaries, or Homeland people, or all of the above, and they're killing other officers who are also on the job, Tom."

Sam let it sink in.

"Think about that," she said. "Who can you trust if the system is after you?"

Another long pause. Ekman squirmed. Jarvis clenched his jaw. Brock gripped her hand way too tightly.

Sam pressed her attack. "So while you were thinking about how to spin all of this during the next staff meeting, we were out in the real world trying to keep from getting our damned throats slit. *By the good guys,* Tom."

Sam's eyes bored through Jarvis.

He met her gaze, took a deep breath, and finally nodded. "I see your point."

Brock loosened his crushing grip on her hand. It had tightened painfully as the tension in the room had reached a peak. The blood returned to Sam's fingers, and she gave his hand a grateful squeeze.

"So what's changed?" Jarvis asked, his face returning to its normal sallow hues. "Why come in now?"

"Because everything I've learned so far says that the finger points back at the government. I'm here to force the issue with you. If you're involved somehow, or Ekman," she'd almost forgotten about him, but now shot him a glance over her shoulder, "I'm here to smoke you out. And if you're on the good guy roster, I'm here to tell you it's time to stop pussyfooting around, because this thing is already miles beyond ugly."

Jarvis nodded slowly. "Ballsy move," he finally said.

"Practical, really," Sam said. "It's a lot of work hiding from everyone."

"Except for Dan Gable," Ekman said. "I know he's been talking to you behind my back."

Sam laughed. "Are you jealous, Frank?"

Then she got serious again. "I just never really got the trustworthy vibe from either of you, even after I took the polygraph."

Ekman looked at her, incredulous. "You can't be serious, Sam. What about the Dibiaso connection? I mean, holy shit, what would you have done?"

Sam shook her head. "I would have gone to bat for my agent, Frank. But you treated me like a suspect and left me completely exposed. You very nearly had blood on your hands."

Ekman was silent.

Jarvis spoke up. "Frank and I were looking forward to hearing Brock's explanation about his connection with Dibiaso, before he disappeared yesterday."

"Sorry about that," Brock said. "I was attacked in my kitchen by a cop."

"Is the blood yours?" Ekman asked.

Brock shook his head. "Nope. I caught him in the leg with a butcher knife."

"I doubt the attacker went to a hospital, but we need to run a check anyway," Sam said.

Jarvis shook his head. "This is beyond anything I've ever seen, or even heard of. Are you sure the guy was a cop?"

"All I know is that he wore a Metro uniform and pulled a Taser on me," Brock said.

"And you believe this?" Jarvis looked skeptically at Sam.

"I don't have to. I watched the security camera footage."

"I'll want a copy, of course."

Jarvis' brow furrowed, and he rubbed his chin, a troubled, thoughtful look on his face. "The attack is certainly important," he said, "but let's get to the Dibiaso thing. I need you to clarify your relationship with him, Brock."

"Easy," Brock said. "There's no relationship." He and Sam spent the next few minutes bringing Jarvis and Ekman up to speed on the unfortunate slug line coincidence that had erroneously linked Brock with Dibiaso.

"This doesn't prove anything, Sam," Jarvis said. "The fact remains that Brock and Dibiaso rode together, twice within a couple of weeks."

"Right. That is undisputed fact," Sam said. "But there is no relationship there. No phone calls, no texts, no other meetings, not so much as a word exchanged between them. It's freaky and unnatural to ride silently in cars with strangers, but that's the Pentagon for you."

"She's right," Ekman said. "I've looked through the phone records several times already. There's nothing else connecting them."

"That doesn't mean they're not working together," Jarvis said.

"You're right," Sam said. "But it sounds like you're asking us to prove a negative. You know that's impossible, Tom."

Jarvis contemplated. He leaned back in his chair and crossed his legs, then spoke again. "Minton. I want to know how you know Minton."

"Trust me, I have plenty to say about Minton," Sam said. "But first, I'd like you guys to run a name for me."

She looked closely at Jarvis' face. "The name is Avery Martinson," she said.

Jarvis' pupils dilated, and his face held a wooden expression for a fraction of a second.

You know him, you bastard, Sam thought.

"That's the name that Dibiaso used to sign in to the Pentagon visitor log," she said.

"Dibiaso visited the Pentagon?" Ekman asked.

"You know he did, unless you didn't bother to plot the cell phone locations on a map. You did that, didn't you?"

Ekman stayed silent again.

"My God, Francis," Sam said. "And you guys wonder why I don't trust you. You're both completely useless."

"That's enough," Jarvis said, tired of Sam's insubordination. "Stop browbeating us, and let's figure this out."

"I'd like that, Tom. Let's start by talking about how well you know Martinson."

"I didn't say I knew Martinson," Jarvis protested.

Sam smiled. "You may not have said it," she said. "But you

definitely told me."

"You're mistaken." Jarvis said, but his flushed face and fluctuating pupils told her otherwise.

Confirmed, she thought. *I'll have to circle back to that one. Feels significant.*

She decided to take advantage of Jarvis' mental backpedaling. "I'll give you a pass on Martinson for the moment, Tom. But it's a rock you know I'll have to turn over eventually. For now, though, what stops you from crossing us off your list of persons of interest?"

Jarvis' eyes narrowed slightly. Sam wondered whether her play was perhaps a bit too aggressive, but she quickly dismissed the thought. She didn't have time to waste.

Jarvis thought about it for a while. "If I buy your carpool theory," he finally said, "and I'm not saying I do, but for the sake of argument, let's pretend I do. If I buy that theory, I'm still really troubled by your relationship with Edward Minton."

"Easy," Sam said. She and Brock explained their relationship with Fatso, and went into detail about the frequency and content of their correspondence over the years. Sam filled them in on her trip to Dayton to question Minton, and explained Executive Strategies' mercenary contracting niche.

"I would say that Executive Strategies is a lead we'll have to pursue carefully," Sam concluded, "because of the turf problems we'll run into."

She looked closely at Jarvis and said, "Fatso's company obviously works for the Agency."

She noticed the strange, wooden expression on Jarvis' face

again.

Maybe the rumors are true, and Jarvis is an Agency mole, she thought. It would certainly explain a few things.

And possibly make this conversation the biggest mistake of my life.

But it occurred to her that she was well beyond the point of no return. There was nothing to do now but move forward.

"There's another tiny detail worth mentioning," she said. "Fatso was flying the airplane that likely bombed our house."

Jarvis raised his eyebrows. "Are you sure?"

"Dan confirmed it."

Time for the haymaker.

"And Frank knew that already," Sam said. She looked at Ekman icily. "Didn't you, Frank?"

Ekman put on a surprised expression.

Sam didn't buy it. "Spare me the theatrics. You stopped by the FAA on Monday."

Ekman flushed and glanced at Jarvis, who shook his head just slightly.

"I wasn't fishing just now," Sam said. "I know it's a fact. I went to the FAA myself."

Sam saw sweat pool on Ekman's upper lip. *Such an amateur.*

He nodded reluctantly. "I did."

"But you didn't think I needed to know what you learned?"

Ekman glanced again at Jarvis, who took the cue. "Frank didn't have authorization to tell you."

Sam nodded slowly, a fire in her eyes. "So it wasn't just a bad feeling, after all," she said. "You two really were hanging me out to dry."

"Of course not, Sam!" Jarvis sounded artificially upset.

He spoke quickly, his eyes avoiding Sam, and she was certain he was conjuring his explanation. "The FAA information was inconclusive, and there was still reasonable doubt about your involvement–"

"Bullshit," Sam cut him off. "You had a warrant. It took you fifteen minutes to figure out the connection with Minton. Even if you didn't know for certain whether Minton dropped that bomb on us, you knew it was a strong possibility."

Jarvis reddened.

"And no matter what you thought might have been going on with Brock and Dibiaso, you had an obligation to warn me. But you two were too busy covering your own asses, you nutless bags of manure."

"Wait a minute here, Sam," Jarvis said. "There are national security concerns–"

"I'm sure the Inspector General will be very interested in hearing them," Sam said. "You can forget your fucking promotions, both of you."

She got up to leave.

Brock followed, visibly angry. "I know a betrayal when I see one," he said. "I will hunt you bastards down and kill you with my bare hands if anything happens to her. That's a promise, not a threat."

He gave Jarvis and Ekman a hard look before turning to follow

Sam.

They had taken two steps toward the door when Jarvis spoke. "Wait," he said.

Sam kept moving, and Brock followed behind her.

"Sam, wait," Jarvis said again. "Let's please talk about this. I'm sure we can find a way forward."

Sam stopped. A small smile crossed her lips. She recognized the bureaucratic language of surrender.

You're mine, you pussies, she thought as she turned around. She spoke slowly and calmly. "I'll tell you how this is going to go down. One whimper from either of you, and I will kick up a shit storm like you've never seen."

Ekman and Jarvis looked at her, resignation in their eyes.

"First, Brock and I are going to return to Dayton for another friendly chat with Fatso." Sam's voice was low and even.

Jarvis blinked, and opened his mouth as if to protest, but Sam silenced him with a raised finger. "I will do that with your full support and resources, Tom," she said. "No questions asked. And Frank will accompany us."

She looked at Ekman. "You are now my human shield. We'll be attached at the hip. If they want to get to me, they'll have to take you down in the process."

Ekman and Jarvis exchanged uneasy glances. She could tell they were looking for an out. "It's not a request, gentlemen," she reminded them. "You're both guilty of dereliction of duty, and I will destroy both of you without batting an eye."

The silence clanged around for several long moments. Sam

looked at Jarvis, her gaze unrelenting.

Finally, Jarvis nodded, beaten.

He had just opened his mouth to speak when the office door opened and Dan Gable walked in, all five-eight and two hundred stocky pounds of him, carrying a manila folder.

"Sorry to barge in," Gable said. He saw the glum look on Jarvis' face. "Looks like a fun party," he deadpanned. "Unfortunately, I've got something you all need to see."

He pulled photos out of the folder. "I'll warn everybody that these are a bit gruesome."

It was a ridiculous understatement. Brock looked away after a brief glimpse of the blood and exposed sinew and innards.

Sam's stomach turned, but she forced herself to study the macabre, inhuman scene.

The victim's skin was flayed in strips, some of which hung loosely from the muscle beneath, like torn jeans. The man had been partially disemboweled. His lips had been removed, sliced clean off, leaving his face locked in a permanent, satanic death howl.

Sam recognized his hollow cheek bones, the shape of his face, and his bald head.

And his eyes.

"Jesus," she said.

"That's Fatso Minton."

What's next?

Get the #1 Bestselling Book Two in the Incident Trilogy:

The Incident: Reckoning

What readers say:

"The best writing in decades. Move over, Lee Child."

"Some of the best action and spy thriller fiction you will ever read."

"Right up there with Patterson, Baldacci, Forsyth, and DeMille."

"The best thriller I've ever read."

"LOVE LOVE LOVE this series!"

Get insider deals on upcoming releases

Be sure to join #1 Bestselling Author Lars Emmerich's readers' group. You'll receive insider deals on upcoming releases, and you'll be treated to subscriber-only giveaways and sales.

Just visit www.larsemmerichbooks.com/landingpage/launch-team/.

Books by Amazon #1 Bestselling Author Lars Emmerich

The Incident: Inferno Rising

The Incident: Reckoning

Fallout

Descent

Devolution

Meltdown

Mindscrew

Blowback

Excerpt from #1 Bestseller

THE INCIDENT: RECKONING

Chapter 1

Six corpses and a bomb.

It had been a shitty week. And though it was Friday, there was no end in sight.

Special Agent Sam Jameson emerged from Homeland Security Deputy Director Tom Jarvis' office and walked quickly down the hallway toward the elevators. She was on her way to her office in the bowels of the country's third largest bureaucracy.

Brock followed in Sam's wake. She was still overcome with relief at her discovery of the coincidence that had falsely associated her lover with a brood of very bad people, who Sam suspected were responsible for as many as five of those corpses.

Maybe the bomb, too. It was hard to say.

It was good to have Brock back in her life. Now, they could try to stay alive together, instead of trying to stay alive apart.

She wasn't quite sure why the cops had it in for her, and she hadn't gotten much help from her two bosses at Homeland.

Tom Jarvis was a douchebag bureaucrat, and Francis Ekman was a milquetoast sycophant, and she was still uncertain why they'd withheld a key piece of information: the name of the guy who had probably dropped the bomb in the front yard of their very expensive Alexandria brownstone.

If Fatso Minton had indeed dropped that bomb, karma had already delivered its comeuppance. Sam was certain that the gruesome imagery of Fatso's mutilated body would add itself to the regular rotation of macabre horrors in her dreams.

Sam and Brock moved like a phalanx through the sea of Homeland clerks milling about in the hallways. Dan Gable hustled to keep pace.

Frank Ekman, Sam's newly-appointed human shield, brought up the rear. There was a strong chance that Homeland was compromised, and a strong chance that Ekman and Jarvis were themselves the problem, but Sam and Brock had been forced to bring this particular enemy close. It was necessary to reduce the number of variables in their world. It was tough to run from both the good guys and the bad guys at the same time.

"Wait here, Frank," Sam said as they passed Ekman's office. Sam's boss did as she told him. Sam had him over a barrel.

Ekman peeled off, nodded at his secretary, and shut the door to his office.

"Will you please call me right away if he goes anywhere?" Sam whispered to the secretary, who gave her a puzzled look in response. "We have plans," Sam explained. The secretary nodded.

The pencil pushers averted their eyes as Sam, Brock and Dan approached the elevator lobby. The kind of people who were content to sit in dark cubicles writing memos harbored a natural aversion to alphas, the kind of people who caught spies and flew fighter jets. The clerks cleared away.

They also whispered amongst themselves. There had been rumors that Sam was somehow tainted by involvement in unsavory activities, rumors likely started and perpetuated by the bureaucrat whose office Hurricane Sam had just left.

She had left Tom Jarvis red-faced and with his mouth agape. It hadn't mattered much that he sat two rungs above her on the organizational chart, and just two rungs below The Man Himself. What mattered was that Jarvis was no match for Sam, and his decades of office work hadn't stacked up well against her years in the real world.

She pushed the button and waited for the elevator. She smiled at a few of the staring cubicle dwellers, who immediately looked away. Dan and Brock watched with amusement.

They held their conversation until they were alone in the elevator, when Dan spoke up. "I'm glad you're here in person. A few things have come up that I'm glad we don't have to talk about by phone."

"I imagine," Sam said. "It's been a hell of a week for you, too. I appreciate all of your help. You've been a godsend."

"No sweat. How's the remodeling going?" he asked with a twinkle in his eye.

"Great. We saved a ton of money on the demolition," Sam quipped.

The elevator dinged, and they made their way to Sam's office, with its million-dollar view of Capitol Hill in one direction and the Washington Monument in the other.

Sam sat behind her desk, drew a long breath, rubbed her eyes, and blew the air out slowly. "What a grisly scene," she said, referring to the pictures Dan had brought into Jarvis' office minutes earlier.

In addition to the human tragedy, Fatso's death was wildly inconvenient. Sam had planned to return to Fatso's home in Dayton to ask him a few more pointed questions.

One pointed question, really: why did you drop a goddamned bomb on my goddamned house?

"So we're back at square one?" she asked Dan.

"Fortunately, no. That's what I wanted to talk to you about." He sat in a chair adjacent to the couch in Sam's office. "Who's the one guy you'd love to have a conversation with?" he asked.

"Dibiaso," Sam said without hesitation. "Jarvis apparently knows him as Martinson."

"Exactly. His burner phone was active for roughly two weeks, and he made several dozen calls."

Brock shook his head. "What are the odds that he and I rode together twice in the same damned carpool?"

"Stranger than fiction," Sam said.

"Here's the deal," Dan said. "I have no idea how Ekman and Jarvis learned Dibiaso was using that particular burner phone. I haven't found anything confirming it, and neither of those clowns are talking."

Sam shook her head. "That's a problem."

"It *sounds* like a problem," Dan said, "But it may not really *be* a problem. Here's why. The phone's user – maybe Dibiaso, maybe someone else – spoke with roughly a dozen people. I accessed those phone records via the trapdoor—"

"You got a warrant?" Sam interjected.

Dan laughed. "You're joking, right? Who needs a warrant in

the digital age?"

Sam shook her head. "I didn't hear that."

"As I was saying," Dan went on, "I looked at those records. All of them were burners, little prepaid phones that weren't in use for much more than a few weeks."

"Not helpful," Sam said.

"Right," Dan said. "Definitely not ideal for our purposes. They're easy to track geographically, but it's really tough to associate those accounts with any particular person. You have to have some other information, like the phone's location data overlapping with a person's known address, or credit card information used to purchase the phone."

"Do you have that?" Brock asked.

"No. We have nothing at all, on anyone who used any of the phones that Dibiaso – or whatever his name is – spoke with using the burner number that Ekman gave us. Those phones were all bought with cash and used in public places."

"Doesn't sound like good news," Brock said, looking glum.

"No, but it's very telling," Sam said. "These dudes were more than investment bankers cheating on their wives."

"It does have a pro vibe about it," Dan said. "But there's one thing that jumped out at me."

Sam nodded, hoping to accelerate Dan's dramatic pause.

"One of the phones subsequently popped up in a foreign country. Any guesses?"

"California?"

Dan frowned. "Venezuela."

Sam nodded thoughtfully. "So that improves our confidence that whoever used this phone – who I think signed the Pentagon visitor log as Avery Martinson, and Ekman and Jarvis refer to as Arturo Dibiaso – is somehow relevant to the Bolero investigation."

"That sounds interesting, but inconclusive," Brock said.

"And not very helpful, really," Sam said.

"Right, but the thing is, we got lucky twice," Dan said. "Whoever ventured down to Venezuela with that phone was a bit sloppy. They turned the phone off twice in front of one particular address, and turned it on a couple of times in the same spot."

Sam sat up. "Almost like they turned it off while they were home, and turned it on again when they left."

"Exactly," Dan said. "Didn't want to give away where they were staying. Except they weren't smart about it."

"So you got the address, then?"

Dan handed her a slip of paper.

Sam looked at Brock. "Ever been to Caracas?"

"I'll brush up on my French."

"Spanish."

"Guten Tag, Fräulein."

"You're a natural."

Chapter 2

Peter Kittredge picked dirty underwear off the floor of his Caracas apartment.

He found himself in a rough spot.

While the Agency-inflicted wounds on his back were healing, Kittredge wasn't certain whether he would ever fully recover from the wounds his participation in a CIA assassination had inflicted on his conscience.

And he had nothing to wear. Someone had ransacked his apartment, and he wasn't finished picking the broken glass out of his carefully tailored ensembles. Plus, he hadn't done laundry in almost two weeks.

It was funny how the small things got to a person. Putting on a pair of unwashed underwear was symbolic of the mayhem that had taken over his entire life.

He selected a reasonably clean white tee from the pile of dirty clothes still strewn about the bedroom floor and pulled it free of the mess.

As he draped it over his head, he heard something clatter on the hardwood. It had a hard, plastic sound.

Several seconds of searching ended the mystery: an old-school cell phone. Nothing smart about it. It had a tiny display, actual buttons, and a stubby antenna sticking up from the top.

Kittredge had never seen it before.

Charley. You cheating bastard.

Theirs was an open relationship. They could have sex with whomever they wanted, whenever they wanted. The only caveats were not to play coy about it, and not to get emotionally attached.

Burner phones were a far more dangerous sign in an open relationship than in an exclusive one. In the latter, there was the chance that it was just casual sex. In the former, it was the kiss of death. It meant emotional attachment.

Or a parallel life. In Charley's case, that seemed extremely likely. That parallel life may have included another serious relationship, or maybe not. Kittredge wasn't sure whether he cared to know.

He was certain that he should have felt something, but he didn't. He was numb. His VSS acquaintances had intimated that there was much more to Charley Arlinghaus than he knew. And Kittredge certainly had misgivings of his own regarding his boyfriend.

Ex-boyfriend, maybe. He wasn't sure.

Charley had sort of nudged Kittredge into spying for Exel Oil. It had happened so slowly that Kittredge almost hadn't noticed until he was already a long way in, probably too far in to get out.

And El Grande, the VSS guerrilla-looking guy who'd taken Kittredge under his wing, had claimed that Exel Oil and the CIA were really the same thing, working by various means to muscle in on the vast crude reserves under Venezuela's lush jungles. The Venezuelan government had long ago thrown out the gringo oil vultures, as El Grande occasionally referred to them, but America's otherworldly oil lust was nobody's secret.

Sonuvabitch, Kittredge thought. *A fine mess I dove into.*

But it was better than dying of boredom in his modest embassy office, grinding through hopelessly uninteresting economic reports, he thought.

There was a reckless, wild, adventurous soul hidden beneath the sterile mountain of buttoned-down behavior and even more buttoned-down economic data that, before his exciting but ill-fated adventure spying for Exel Oil, had been the extent of his daily reality.

I'm well and truly screwed, Kittredge thought with absolute certainty, *and this will definitely end poorly.*

But I probably still wouldn't change much if I had it to do over again.

He craved the rush, the ride. Even the abject fear was delicious in its vibrancy.

Sometimes.

Other times, it was just abject fear.

Kittredge turned on the burner phone. It took forever to time in. It wasn't password-protected. Its call history was empty, and there were no voice or text messages.

He sighed. It would have been great to learn something about what Charley had been up to, but it occurred to Kittredge that at the moment, he probably already had all the excitement and intrigue he could handle.

As if on cue, his own phone buzzed.

Quinn. "Wear something nice, that shows off your broad

shoulders." Delivered with a fake lisp.

"Go to hell, Quinn."

"Peter, my boy, life's nothing without a sense of humor."

Kittredge didn't respond.

"Anyway, good chat," Quinn said. "Hurry down. I'm illegally parked at your curb." Quinn hung up.

Kittredge finished dressing in dirty clothes and left his apartment.

* * *

"Super-Agent Kittredge, how the hell's it hanging?" Fredericks clapped him on the back.

Kittredge winced, his scabbed-over skin howling in protest.

"Still a little tender back there?" Fredericks leaned in conspiratorially. "Quinn goes overboard sometimes. He's afraid to admit that he likes torturing people."

"Well, it does make him a certifiable psychopath," Kittredge said, taking a seat in the US embassy's first-floor conference room next to an embassy coworker.

Kittredge had been surprised to learn from Quinn during the short drive from his apartment to the embassy that the morning's festivities would be attended by none other than Ambassador Wolfe himself.

"Does he know?" Kittredge had asked.

Quinn had played dumb. "Does who know what?"

"You know what I mean. Does the ambassador know what you're doing?"

"We." Quinn had corrected. "What *we* are doing. Partners

forever, remember? Says so on the paper you signed."

"I'm serious, Quinn. Is he in on this?"

"No questions, little buddy. Those are unhealthy. Just play your part, speak your lines, and everything will come up roses."

The ambassador arrived late, as was customary, hurriedly breezing in after everyone else had settled into their seats. It was an old trick used to solidify the pecking order. Everyone else in the room stood up at his arrival, as if he was a military general. It grated on Kittredge, just like it always did.

Maybe that was one of those little things that had driven Kittredge over the edge.

Fredericks spoke. "Mr. Ambassador, thank you for your time. I'm Jeff Santos, from the State Department Economic Policy Directorate."

Kittredge was taken aback by the outright lie.

His face must have betrayed his shock, because Quinn was looking daggers at him. It felt like Quinn's crazy, mismatched wolf eyes were boring through him. Kittredge shuddered. *Pure evil in there,* he thought, working hard to restore passivity to his own expression.

Fredericks' nasal voice droned on. "We're thankful that Mr. Kittredge has volunteered to brief the economic data during our meeting this afternoon."

What the hell? Kittredge hadn't volunteered to brief anything to anyone.

All eyes in the room turned to him, and he felt his face flush. He managed a wan smile and a small, nervous wave.

"He's one of our best," Ambassador Wolfe said, a mostly-genuine smile on his face. "Pete, let's go over the data afterwards."

It's Peter, you ass. You've only known me for three years.
"Sounds great, Mr. Ambassador."

Fredericks continued. "Really, the point of the whole thing is to show the economic benefits of the scale our companies can bring to the oil extraction operation here in Venezuela. We think the Venezuelans will ultimately be receptive, once they see how much they stand to gain through increased efficiency. And the infrastructure benefits go without saying."

Kittredge would never have guessed that Fredericks could have conjured or even memorized such a statement. Perhaps the hard-boiled gumshoe routine and the gruff exterior were just an act, meant to disguise a much sharper intellect than Fredericks had revealed during any of their earlier interactions.

Impressive.

Spooky.

Just like Quinn. The giant of an agent could change in a flash between his bumpkin and philosopher affectations, and the vacillations between his normal-guy and murderous psychopath personas were lightning fast.

The meeting at the embassy concluded uneventfully, though Kittredge suddenly found himself obligated to attend a mid-afternoon appointment with the ambassador to cover the materials for the briefing with the Venezuelan Economic Development Consortium. The consortium met at four thirty. *Nothing like off-the-cuff diplomacy. Maybe that's why it always seems to end up in violence.*

Kittredge was none too pleased at the prospect of preparing and delivering a briefing, as there wasn't much emotional or intellectual space in his life at the moment to accommodate such a large responsibility on such short notice, but he reasoned that he eventually had to dive back into his life as an economic advisor to the ambassador. *Might as well be now,* he thought as the meeting broke up.

Quinn shook his hand on the way out. "Pleasure to meet you this morning, Mr. Kittredge," he said loudly.

Kittredge looked askance at the feral-eyed assassin. In truth, Kittredge had met Quinn just shy of a week earlier, when the giant sociopath had taken a belt sander and a bag of salt to his lower back to extort what amounted to an oath of lifetime fealty to the Agency. Before Kittredge could voice the biting sarcasm that popped to mind, Quinn's grip tightened like a vice around his hand.

Kittredge took the hint. "Pleasure to meet you. And *Mister Santos,* too," he said with an edge to his voice.

Quinn winked and joined the flow of embassy functionaries and CIA operatives moving out the conference room door.

* * *

Kittredge had a solid afternoon of work ahead of him preparing for the briefing he was apparently on the hook to deliver. He still had no idea who his audience might be, other than it comprised a vague collective the embassy people referred to as the Venezuelan Economic Development Consortium.

There was something else on his mind, too.

I've got to warn El Grande.

He knew that the CIA wanted to kill someone in the VEDC, a person they called El Cucaracha. Kittredge had no idea who that might be, although during a recent conversation, Fredericks had thrown out a first name: Hugo.

There were probably half a million Venezuelans named Hugo, so that wasn't a terribly specific clue. And as far as Kittredge could tell, membership on the VEDC was a revolving door kind of thing on the Venezuelan side, with random local luminaries making haphazard cameo appearances at various events.

None of that information had helped him narrow down who Fredericks' target might be.

To make matters worse, Quinn and Fredericks had revealed absolutely nothing about the method of assassination, other than to say that there wouldn't be any violence. Puzzling. Not to mention contradictory by definition, Kittredge thought.

This was all of more than passing interest to Kittredge, beholden as he was to each of the involved parties.

No drama there, he thought wryly.

He made his way through embassy security, and wound out onto Calle los Estanques, toward the unfortunately-named Cafe Ole. It was a long walk for lunch, particularly given the mediocre cafe fare, but lunch was only a peripheral purpose. He would have preferred to summon a taxi, but doing so would have signaled a different thing entirely.

He ordered patacones, or fried green plantains, and a creamy lasagna known as pasticho Venezolano. Far too rich for an afternoon of intellectually involved work, Kittredge realized with a sigh, but El Grande's contact instructions had been very clear. La Tizanda, a sickeningly sweet fruit smoothie, rounded out the order.

As he took the order, the waiter spoke the magic words: "I hope you enjoy this meal very much, Señor."

Kittredge delivered his scripted reply. "I have no doubt that I will."

The waiter nodded, then disappeared into the kitchen.

He returned moments later with Kittredge's order. Tucked beneath the small plate of patacones was a small slip of paper. It contained an address, which Kittredge guessed would take five minutes to reach on foot.

He ate quickly, feeling the rich, starchy foods expand in his belly. He'd have to talk to El Grande about a healthier order next time. He paid cash and left, walking as quickly as the gut bomb would allow.

Kittredge reached the specified apartment building, and took the stairs to find the right apartment number. He knocked four times.

He heard footsteps within, then a frail female voice: "Are you the television repairman?"

It was the question he expected to hear. "No, but I passed him on the way up," he said.

The door opened to reveal an old Venezuelan lady, hunched at the waist and again just below the neck. She waved him in with a bony hand, tottered over to a radio, and turned the music on to cover their conversation.

Kittredge cringed. He had always thought that Latin music was a caricature of itself, and being constantly subjected to omnipresent, droning beats beneath melodramatic wailing was one of the few things he truly hated about living in Venezuela.

The old woman motioned him toward a chair. He sat. She pulled a second chair close to his and settled slowly next to him, leaning her ear toward him. He spoke slowly and clearly into her ear, suppressing his revulsion at the stale, senescent air that surrounded the ancient woman. "For El Grande: Agency planning unknown action against codename El Cucaracha, first name Hugo, during VDEC meeting today," he said.

She repeated his message three times, perfectly each time. He had no idea who the woman was, but her mind was in far better shape than her gnarled body.

It was all very simple. Treason usually was. Uncomplicated, but definitely not easy. While the Central Intelligence Agency had encouraged Kittredge to maintain an ongoing relationship with the Venezuelan Special Services, Fredericks and Quinn had warned him in no uncertain terms about divulging operational details. Routine check-in, he would tell Quinn. It would have looked suspicious if he hadn't gone. Something along those lines.

"El Grande thanks you," the old woman spoke into his ear.

He nodded. "Give my regards to Maria."

The woman gave him a knowing smile. "Of course."

Chapter 3

"Caracas, then," Brock said. "Any chance we can pack a few things first?"

"Better to buy what we need than risk a trip back home," Sam said. "Now that we've put our cards on the table with Jarvis, we have to watch our backs even more closely. Either we've cleared the air or doubled our exposure, depending on how big a bastard he is."

Dan grunted his assent, and Brock nodded.

"I'll get us booked," Sam said.

Dan protested. "Not a good idea to leave transportation trails back to you, boss."

"I agree," she said. "That's why this particular trail will lead back to our new human shield."

Dan nodded with a knowing smile.

Sam sent Dan back to his office with a task: hack into Jeff Jensen's computer account. She wanted to know what Jensen may have discovered before his untimely death a few days earlier.

Then she got to work. She inserted her government ID card into her desktop computer's Common Access Card receptacle. She typed in her personal identification number and watched the blue whirly disk spin on the screen while the ancient Dell paperweight shuffled electrons around inside at glacial speed.

No fewer than seven warning panes popped open, ranging from threats of dire consequences for attaching portable storage media to the government system, notices that use of the computer system implied consent to search, notices of an overdue flu shot, and even a high-wind warning from Wednesday.

Sam shook her head. She had no idea why a windowless building full of clerks needed real-time warning of gusty winds. Each inane announcement required her acknowledgement, after which the spinning blue asshole, as she called it, returned again to mock her impatience.

I hate this freaking place, she thought for the thousandth time.

She stayed at Homeland because it was on a very short list of places where she could pursue her calling without getting thrown in jail. She loved hunting down the world's bastards. It was okay when justice involved a jail sentence for them. It was also okay when it involved a more permanent solution.

Sam clicked around until she found what she was looking for: Francis Ekman's government travel credit card information.

In what was universally regarded as a sweetheart deal struck between the bankers running the credit card companies and the ex-bankers running the federal treasury, all government travel expenditures were to be accomplished using a commercial credit card. Individuals were personally liable for all expenses until the government got good and ready to reimburse them, and may the gods help you if you didn't fill out your forms properly.

It was a huge hassle, and Sam didn't blame Ekman for sloughing the task off on her for several of his recent trips. She had resented playing travel agent on his behalf, and had given him an earful, but she had exacted instant revenge by storing all of his information for a rainy day.

Like today.

She booked three one-way trips to Caracas on his card. One was for a man and a woman pulled from the inactive alias list in the Homeland database. The unused legends had the names Thomas Brownstein and Tricia Leavens. Thomas was to fly to Caracas via Charlotte, while Tricia's reservations were for a direct flight from DC.

She booked Francis Ekman's ticket as well, using his own name and following the same itinerary as Tricia's. She placed Ekman in the seat directly in front of hers. Better to keep an eye on him.

She didn't book him under an alias for a simple reason. She wanted to advertise his presence, either as deterrent or invitation to any bastards lurking within Homeland's ranks. Sometimes you had to stir things up in order to get them to settle down.

It took well over half an hour to book the flights, the unfortunate consequence of a bespoke multimillion dollar travel system commissioned by Homeland. The system had half the functionality of the online tools already available to consumers, and it worked at a tectonic pace, when it wasn't down for weekly maintenance. It was one more reason Sam disliked the lumbering, incompetent, insipid government she served.

By the time she had finished, Brock was snoring on the couch in her office. She printed the tickets, then nudged him awake.

She picked up her phone and punched the hot key for Ekman's office. "Hi, Patty. Just wanted to let Frank know that we're leaving in an hour."

Brock heard Patty fuss in the background.

"Sorry, can't say where we're going. Security and all."

More fussing.

"Sorry, Patty, I also can't say whether he'll need an overnight bag." Sam made some sympathetic noises, then hung up.

She led Brock back to the elevators. They went down to the building's dank basement, and wound their way through the warren of dark cement hallways to what Homeland agents euphemistically referred to as the Travel Agency.

Its formal name was the Field Documents Branch, and it was one of the few government offices that knowingly employed convicted criminals. Forgers, to be exact. They'd all served their sentences and subsequently chosen to use their powers for good rather than evil. Or, as they often joked, they wanted to work where they could do some serious damage to humanity.

"Hey, Ron," Sam said as she recognized a familiar face. "Got a few minutes?"

"Anything for you, Sam," he said.

"It's not Sam today. Meet Tricia Leavens," she said. Then she looked at Brock and said, "This handsome fellow is Thomas Brownstein. We just need you to work your magic for us. And I'll apologize in advance that we're in a bit of a hurry."

"Everyone is," Ron said. He cross-checked the aliases in the database of unassigned legends, then checked Brock's military identification card.

"Pretty unusual for a military guy to get a Homeland alias,"

Ron observed. "Usually some extra paperwork involved."

Sam smiled. "Usually," she said with a wink. "But there's not always time for that."

"Right," Ron said. "Sometimes you gotta get out there and crack skulls, and catch up on the trivia later."

Sam loved her occasional interactions with people like Ron, people who understood the bigger picture. Without them, nothing at the Department of Homeland Security would ever get done.

Ron motioned Sam and Brock toward the camera, and they took turns posing for their ID photos. Twenty minutes later, they each had a driver's license, passport, library card, credit and ATM cards, miscellaneous receipts to stuff in their wallets for authenticity, and a fact sheet detailing their fake lives.

All of the items looked worn and used, an extremely important touch often overlooked by amateurs.

The fact sheets were made out of a strange paper that felt thin and brittle.

"The usual routine," Ron said. "Study the legends until you can recite them in your sleep. Then you can either burn the paper or eat it. But probably not both."

Sam chuckled. "Thanks, Ron."

"And I'm required to harass you with the usual warning that you'll have to account for all of your expenditures at the end of the op, blah blah blah."

Sam smiled. Ron's healthy perspective on the bullshit was not unexpected, given his background.

"You're also supposed to turn in your personal credentials to me," he said.

"Yeah, silly us. We must have left them in our other pants," she said.

Ron winked. "I know how that goes. Never know when you'll find yourself with a strong need to be someone else. If there's an audit this afternoon, I'm sure I'll think of something."

Sam gave Ron a hug and thanked him, and she and Brock left the field documents office.

"I love this spy shit," Brock said. "Where do we get our ninja stars and exploding pens?"

"Sorry," Sam said. "We spend all our money hiring people to write emails to each other."

They rode the elevator back up to her floor, and made their way to Dan's office. They found him hunched over his computer keyboard, glancing quickly between his two large screens at windows full of what looked to Sam like machine language.

"Can you see the Matrix?" Brock quipped.

"I like the blonde," Dan said. Esoteric movie quotes were apparently a universal guy thing, Sam thought.

"Hate to interrupt the fraternity boy handshake," she said, "but have you made any progress working on the Jensen thing?"

"Sure have. It was actually pretty easy. I was able to convince the network administrator that I had a legitimate need to see Jeff's files."

"Unheard of," Sam said.

"Well, I also bribed her. She's a big chocolate lover. Emphasis on *big*."

"Good work. Learn anything?"

Dan described how Jeff's coworkers had slowly taken over his crime scene investigation case work since his death, and how one of them had commented on a set of partial fingerprints. The other CSI had received the results, but was unable to decipher the origin of the partial prints.

"Gotta be the partials from the music box at Phil's," Sam said. Dan nodded. Sam had illegally lifted the music box from Phil Quartermain's apartment moments after discovering that the DC Metro investigator's throat had been slit. Homeland CSI Jeff Jensen had agreed, after Sam applied the right leverage, to run forensic tests on the music box outside of normal channels.

Jensen's examination had produced a set of partial prints that couldn't be immediately matched, but Jensen had apparently entered the partials into the database for further analysis. The mainframe did in a matter of days what it would have taken several million man-hours to do manually: overlay the fingerprint fragments in hundreds of different locations and orientations on top of every individual fingerprint in the database, until it found a match within a reasonable confidence. It was a grueling process that took enormous computing power, and it didn't always result in a match.

In this case, Dan explained, the computer had found a match. "Unfortunately," he said, "the record is sealed."

"Balls," Sam said.

"That was my reaction, too."

"So we're dead in the water? I mean, opening sealed records requires months of haggling with lawyers and other bottom feeders."

Dan looked offended. "I thought you held me in higher regard than that," he said with mock indignation. "You seem to have forgotten that I did juvie time in high school for hacking. Let me see what I can do."

"Thanks, Dan. I'm glad you're on my team."

"Can you fix my parking tickets?" Brock asked.

"For a small fee."

A pensive look crossed Dan's face. "Listen," he said, "something has been bugging me."

"I apologize for whatever I've done," Sam said.

"Not that. It's been bothering me how quickly Jensen was killed after you enlisted his help with the music box evidence."

Sam nodded. "It would make sense if they had been tracking me. They could've easily figured out that we spent time together, which might have been the kiss of death for him. But I haven't seen hide or hair of anyone, DC Metro guys included, since right after Quartermain's murder on Monday."

Dan looked pensive. He scrunched his face and scratched what would have been his neck, if he had a neck. Instead, he had one giant set of shoulders with a head stuck on top of them. He was built like a bodybuilder, which seemed an unlikely frame to house the mind of an investigative computer genius with the temperament to sit in front of a computer monitor for weeks at a time in order to solve difficult cases. He complemented Sam's tenacious fieldwork perfectly, with equally tenacious network ops. It was increasingly a cyber world, and Dan was among the very best.

"You found a CD ROM in the music box, didn't you?" he

finally asked.

Sam nodded. "It had the financial data linking Abrams and Cooper to Executive Strategies and JIE Associates."

"And you used Jensen's computer to access the data?"

"I did."

Dan asked for the CD ROM, which Sam happened to have tucked into her pocket.

"You're setting a bad example, walking around with crime scene evidence up your sleeve," he chided as he took the computer disk from her and dropped it into a waiting tray on his own computer.

He opened several more windows full of what looked like alphabet soup. It had an old-school computer aesthetic, nothing but a black background behind undecipherable code made up of ugly green font. But it seemed to make sense to Dan.

He scratched his chin, typed, mumbled, nodded his head, and typed some more.

"Care to let me in on the secret?" Sam asked.

"Here's the deal," Dan said. "Ever heard of an outfit called Hack Team?"

Sam shook her head, but Brock piped up. "Spyware guys? I saw a documentary a while ago."

"That's right," Dan said. "They produce some of the world's best spyware and sell it exclusively to governments, mostly the kind who can't afford to write their own."

"Seemed like they did business with some shady people," Brock said. "Though you can't always believe what you see in a documentary."

"In this case, it's pretty accurate. Don't tell anyone I told you this," Dan said with a conspiratorial air, "but the federal government is actually ten times shadier. It's just that we're much quieter about it."

Brock nodded. "Figures."

"But Hack Team sells their stuff all over the world," Dan went on. "They even have a slick little video sales pitch. Their software is supposed to be untraceable, but they're too vain not to bury a signature line or two inside the code. It's plain as day, if you know what you're looking for."

"What does it do?" Sam asked.

"Nothing much. Just records your position, your keystrokes, any ambient audio in the room, and even takes video, if your laptop has a built-in camera, all without alerting the user that anything funny is going on. They can also hack any passwords to bank accounts, social media sites, you name it."

"Jesus," Sam said. "That's dastardly."

"And then some," Dan agreed. "It's the dictator's perfect tool."

Brock nodded. "Actually," he said, "I think using something like that pretty much turns *any* government into a de facto dictatorship."

"It's a brave new world," Dan agreed. "Anyway, politics aside, it's pretty easy for whoever put the Hack Team software on this disk to set up an alert. As soon as the user accesses the data, they'll have instant access to everything on that laptop, and instant access to everyone who uses it."

Sam shuddered. "So they watched me look through the data."

Dan nodded grimly. "I'm surprised they didn't find you, Sam." He looked concerned. "You don't still have the laptop, do you?"

She shook her head. "I dropped it off back at Jeff's," she said slowly.

Her face darkened and her eyes moistened. "I got him killed. He had rounded the corner. He was beating his drug habit, getting his life back together, and I got him killed."

"Bullshit, baby," Brock said, draping an arm around her shoulders. "You're not responsible for someone else's crime."

"I should have been smarter than that."

Dan shook his head. "It's not like you had many other options."

Brock's watch alarm beeped, interrupting Sam's self-flagellation. "If we're going to Caracas today, we need to roll," he said.

"Can you find me a list of countries we suspect of using Hack Team software?" Sam asked on the way out of Dan's office.

"Sure thing," Dan said. "It won't be one hundred percent accurate, because that kind of stuff is hard to track, but our guys keep a pretty close watch on it. It'll be a long list though."

"I have a specific country in mind," Sam said.

Chapter 4

El Jerga turned down the volume on his rented sedan's radio. He was approaching the city from the west, and he needed the mental bandwidth to navigate while dodging traffic.

His highly enjoyable and lucrative trip to the Midwest was a pleasant, glowing memory. His target hadn't survived as long as El Jerga had hoped, but it had been long enough for the demons inside him to run amok. The skinny man's otherworldly howls of agony fueled their frenzy.

If he was a deviant, El Jerga rationalized, his environment certainly shouldered some portion of the culpability. Venezuela's overly politicized society demanded muscle of all sorts, and a man of his particular brand of eager proclivity was almost infinitely useful to innumerable would-be masters.

El Jerga had picked and chosen his affiliations carefully, always aligned with the interests of his beloved uncle, may El Señor have mercy on his soul, and always furthering the cause of the little guy. His father had died in one of the thousands of oil field uprisings, fighting for livable pay and less deadly conditions, and those values had taken on a talisman's import for El Jerga as he came of age under his uncle's tutelage.

Because his enemies were still strong, El Jerga had an ideologue's zeal. An untested philosophy is always easy to support, because its shortcomings aren't yet as painfully obvious as those of a sitting government. Governing a society is a messy, involved, and invariably ugly process, and El Jerga's self-evident truths were thus far unsullied by the welter of pragmatic politics.

That made his ideology a convenient justification for the ungodly atrocities El Jerga loved to commit against his fellow man. When he was at work on someone, he relished the way the power of life and death flowed through him. It excited him on a visceral, wordless, precognitive level. It was progeny of some atavistic remnant of the predators from which humans evolved, but from which El Jerga had somehow descended without evolving.

He was more animal than human, and he knew it. He used it shamelessly, not because it was okay in and of itself, but because it was okay in light of his cause. He would still have given himself over to his wanton hunger without the cause, of course, but it was wonderful to have found a community that cultivated and cherished his unique talents.

Match made in heaven.

El Jerga took the exit for Dulles International Airport, automatically thinking of the airport's namesakes, the Dulles family. He had studied their history. They swung the hammer of the gods. They thought they were gods. And godly. They believed that their religion, some apocalyptic good versus evil dogma, should guide their statecraft. So they had decimated the godless. What qualified a race or nationality as godless in the minds of the Dulles brothers wasn't entirely clear, but they certainly had blood on their hands, El Jerga had concluded.

The horrendous hypocrisy in his thinking was hidden from El

Jerga by his need not to see it.

He parked the large sedan in the short-term parking lot at Dulles, shuffled in his slow way into the ticketing area of the large, light-filled airport atrium, and took a seat.

He listened.

He heard many uncomfortably loud announcements, about smoking and unattended baggage and suspicious persons and parking violations and flight delays.

Then he heard what he was listening for. "Mister Palms, Mister Harold Palms, please pick up a white courtesy phone."

He picked up the courtesy phone. "Stand by for your party," the operator announced.

A gruff gringo voice came on the line. "Seven," he said.

"Nueve," El Jerga answered. The code sum was sixteen.

"Hurry," the gringo said. "Thirty minutes. Take the subway to the office. Cleaning crew will meet you. When you're done, use the L'Enfant station for your egress. It'll be sanitized by friends."

"Acknowledged," El Jerga croaked.

He hung up the phone, hustled back to his car, exited the airport after paying the parking fee, and drove more quickly than was wise toward the Tysons Corner park-and-ride complex.

Cutting it close, he thought. Wasn't his fault. He was on time. Wasn't his problem if they didn't have their act together.

Still, he was anxious. And disappointed. A daylight hit at the office would afford him none of the pleasures that he had allowed himself to lust for. He wanted to take his time, to savor his victims. Especially the girl. But he would be forced to work quickly and silently.

Pity.

He looked at his watch again.

He would be lucky either way, he decided. Lucky if he made it to the gringo government building in time to do his duty, because it would mean another impressively large paycheck. His hookers weren't cheap, and he had grown accustomed to the eager favors his wallet garnered.

But he would be equally lucky if he missed them. It would keep his hopes alive for a long, fulfilling engagement. He longed to hear her screams, taste her flesh, draw her blood, revel in his release over her gorgeous, powerless form.

All in the name of the cause, of course.

Get the #1 Bestselling Book Two of **the Incident Trilogy**:

The Incident: Reckoning

What readers say:

"The best writing in decades. Move over, Lee Child."

"Some of the best thriller fiction you will ever read."

"Right up there with Patterson, Baldacci, Forsyth, and DeMille."

"The best thriller I've ever read."

"LOVE LOVE LOVE this series!"